THE CLAY SANSKRIT LIBRARY
FOUNDED BY JOHN & JENNIFER CLAY

GENERAL EDITOR

SHELDON POLLOCK

EDITED BY

ISABELLE ONIANS

WWW.CLAYSANSKRITLIBRARY.ORG
WWW.NYUPRESS.ORG

Artwork by Robert Beer.
Typeset in Adobe Garamond at 10.25 : 12.3 pt.
Editorial input from Dániel Balogh, Ridi Faruque,
Chris Gibbons, Tomoyuki Kono,
Andrew Skilton & Eszter Somogyi.
Printed and Bound in Great Britain by
TJ International, Cornwall on acid free paper

GARLAND OF THE BUDDHA'S PAST LIVES

VOLUME ONE

by ĀRYAŚŪRA

TRANSLATED BY

Justin Meiland

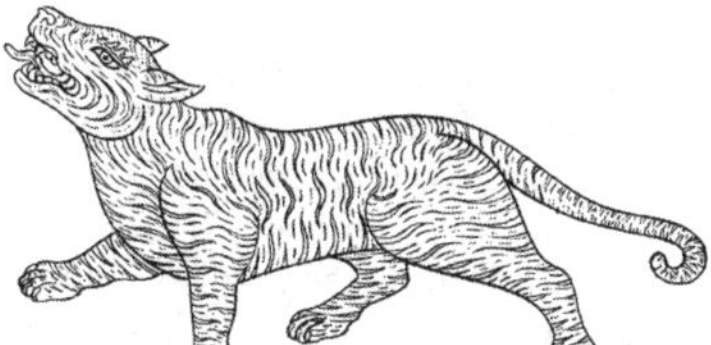

NEW YORK UNIVERSITY PRESS

JJC FOUNDATION

2009

First Edition 2009

The Clay Sanskrit Library is co-published by
New York University Press
and the JJC Foundation.

Further information about this volume
and the rest of the Clay Sanskrit Library
is available at the end of this book and
on the following websites:
www.claysanskritlibrary.org
www.nyupress.org

ISBN 978-0-8147-9581-1

Library of Congress Cataloging-in-Publication Data
Āryaśūra.
[Jātakamālā. English & Sanskrit]
Garland of the Buddha's past lives / by Ārya Śūra ;
translated by Justin Meiland. -- 1st ed.
p. cm.
Miracle stories of the Buddha's past lives.
In English and Sanskrit (romanized) on facing pages;
includes translation from Sanskrit.
Includes bibliographical references and index.
ISBN 978-0-8147-9581-1
1. Buddhist stories, Sanskrit--Translations into English.
2. Aryasura--Translations into English.
I. Meiland, Justin, 1937- II. Title.
BQ1462.E5M47 2009
294.3'82325--dc22
2008046726

CONTENTS

CSL CONVENTIONS

Sanskrit Alphabetical Order

Vowels:	*a ā i ī u ū ṛ ṝ ḷ ḹ e ai o au ṃ ḥ*
Gutturals:	*k kh g gh ṅ*
Palatals:	*c ch j jh ñ*
Retroflex:	*ṭ ṭh ḍ ḍh ṇ*
Dentals:	*t th d dh n*
Labials:	*p ph b bh m*
Semivowels:	*y r l v*
Spirants:	*ś ṣ s h*

Guide to Sanskrit Pronunciation

a	b*u*t
ā, â	f*a*ther
i	s*i*t
ī, î	f*ee*
u	p*u*t
ū, û	b*oo*
ṛ	vocalic *r*, American p*ur*dy or English p*re*tty
ṝ	lengthened *ṛ*
ḷ	vocalic *l*, ab*le*
e, ê, ē	m*a*de, esp. in Welsh pronunciation
ai	b*i*te
o, ô, ō	r*o*pe, esp. Welsh pronunciation; Italian s*o*lo
au	s*ou*nd
ṃ	*anusvāra* nasalizes the preceding vowel
ḥ	*visarga*, a voiceless aspiration (resembling the English *h*), or like Scottish lo*ch*, or an aspiration with a faint echoing of the last element of the preceding vowel so that *taiḥ* is pronounced *taih^i^*
k	lu*ck*
kh	blo*ckh*ead
g	*g*o
gh	bi*gh*ead
ṅ	a*n*ger
c	*ch*ill
ch	mat*chh*ead
j	*j*og
jh	aspirated *j*, he*dgeh*og
ñ	ca*ny*on
ṭ	retroflex *t*, *t*ry (with the tip of tongue turned up to touch the hard palate)
ṭh	same as the preceding but aspirated
ḍ	retroflex *d* (with the tip

	of tongue turned up to touch the hard palate)
ḍh	same as the preceding but aspirated
ṇ	retroflex *n* (with the tip of tongue turned up to touch the hard palate)
t	French *t*out
th	ten*t h*ook
d	*d*inner
dh	guil*dh*all
n	*n*ow
p	*p*ill
ph	u*ph*eaval
b	*b*efore
bh	a*bh*orrent
m	*m*ind
y	*y*es
r	trilled, resembling the Italian pronunciation of *r*
l	*l*inger
v	*w*ord
ś	*sh*ore
ṣ	retroflex *sh* (with the tip of the tongue turned up to touch the hard palate)
s	hi*ss*
h	*h*ood

CSL Punctuation of English

The acute accent on Sanskrit words when they occur outside of the Sanskrit text itself, marks stress, e.g., Ramáyana. It is not part of traditional Sanskrit orthography, transliteration, or transcription, but we supply it here to guide readers in the pronunciation of these unfamiliar words. Since no Sanskrit word is accented on the last syllable it is not necessary to accent disyllables, e.g., Rama.

The second CSL innovation designed to assist the reader in the pronunciation of lengthy unfamiliar words is to insert an unobtrusive middle dot between semantic word breaks in compound names (provided the word break does not fall on a vowel resulting from the fusion of two vowels), e.g., Maha·bhárata, but Ramáyana (not Rama·áyana). Our dot echoes the punctuating middle dot (·) found in the oldest surviving samples of written Indic, the Ashokan inscriptions of the third century BCE.

The deep layering of Sanskrit narrative has also dictated that we use quotation marks only to announce the beginning and end of every direct speech, and not at the beginning of every paragraph.

CSL Punctuation of Sanskrit

The Sanskrit text is also punctuated, in accordance with the punctuation of the English translation. In mid-verse, the punctuation will not alter the sandhi or the scansion. Proper names are capitalized. Most Sanskrit meters have four "feet" (*pāda*); where possible we print the common *śloka* meter on two lines. In the Sanskrit text, we use French *Guillemets* (e.g., *«kva saṃcicīrṣuḥ?»*) instead of English quotation marks (e.g., "Where are you off to?") to avoid confusion with the apostrophes used for vowel elision in sandhi.

SANDHI

Sanskrit presents the learner with a challenge: *sandhi* (euphonic combination). Sandhi means that when two words are joined in connected speech or writing (which in Sanskrit reflects speech), the last letter (or even letters) of the first word often changes; compare the way we pronounce "the" in "the beginning" and "the end."

In Sanskrit the first letter of the second word may also change; and if both the last letter of the first word and the first letter of the second are vowels, they may fuse. This has a parallel in English: a nasal consonant is inserted between two vowels that would otherwise coalesce: "a pear" and "an apple." Sanskrit vowel fusion may produce ambiguity.

The charts on the following pages give the full sandhi system.

Fortunately it is not necessary to know these changes in order to start reading Sanskrit. All that is important to know is the form of the second word without sandhi (pre-sandhi), so that it can be recognized or looked up in a dictionary. Therefore we are printing Sanskrit with a system of punctuation that will indicate, unambiguously, the original form of the second word, i.e., the form without sandhi. Such sandhi mostly concerns the fusion of two vowels.

In Sanskrit, vowels may be short or long and are written differently accordingly. We follow the general convention that a vowel with no mark above it is short. Other books mark a long vowel either with a bar called a macron (*ā*) or with a circumflex (*â*). Our system uses the

VOWEL SANDHI

Final vowels:

a	ā	i	ī	u	ū	ṛ	e	ai	o	au	*Initial vowels:*
' â	" â	y a	y a	v a	v a	r a	e '	ā a	o '	āv a	a
' ā	" ā	y ā	y ā	v ā	v ā	r ā	a ā	ā ā	a ā	āv ā	ā
' ê	" ê	' î	" î	v i	v i	r i	a i	ā i	a i	āv i	i
' ē	" ē	' ī	" ī	v ī	v ī	r ī	a ī	ā ī	a ī	āv ī	ī
' ô	" ô	y u	y u	' û	" û	r u	a u	ā u	a u	āv u	u
' ō	" ō	y ū	y ū	' ū	" ū	r ū	a ū	ā ū	a ū	āv ū	ū
a' r	a" r	y ṛ	y ṛ	v ṛ	v ṛ	' ṝ	a ṛ	ā ṛ	a ṛ	āv ṛ	ṛ
' âi	" âi	y e	y e	v e	v e	r e	a e	ā e	a e	āv e	e
' āi	" āi	y ai	y ai	v ai	v ai	r ai	a ai	ā ai	a ai	āv ai	ai
' âu	" âu	y o	y o	v o	v o	r o	a o	ā o	a o	āv o	o
' āu	" āu	y au	y au	v au	v au	r au	a au	ā au	a au	āv au	au

CONSONANT SANDHI

Permitted finals: k	ṭ	t	p	ṅ	n	m	*(Except āḥ/aḥ)* ḥ/r	āḥ	aḥ	*Initial letters:*
k	ṭ	t	p	ṅ	n	ṃ	ḥ	āḥ	aḥ	k/kh
g	ḍ	d	b	ṅ	n	ṃ	r	ā	o	g/gh
k	ṭ	c	p	ṅ	ṃś	ṃ	ś	āś	aś	c/ch
g	ḍ	j	b	ṅ	ñ	ṃ	r	ā	o	j/jh
k	ṭ	ṭ	p	ṅ	ṃṣ	ṃ	ṣ	āṣ	aṣ	ṭ/ṭh
g	ḍ	ḍ	b	ṅ	ṇ	ṃ	r	ā	o	ḍ/ḍh
k	ṭ	t	p	ṅ	ṃs	ṃ	s	ās	as	t/th
g	ḍ	d	b	ṅ	n	ṃ	r	ā	o	d/dh
k	ṭ	t	p	ṅ	n	ṃ	ḥ	āḥ	aḥ	p/ph
g	ḍ	d	b	ṅ	n	ṃ	r	ā	o	b/bh
ṅ	ṇ	n	m	ṅ	n	ṃ	r	ā	o	*nasals* (n/m)
g	ḍ	d	b	ṅ	n	ṃ	r	ā	o	y/v
g	ḍ	d	b	ṅ	n	ṃ	*zero*[1]	ā	o	r
g	ḍ	l	b	ṅ	l̃[2]	ṃ	r	ā	o	l
k	ṭ	c ch	p	ṅ	ñ ś/ch	ṃ	ḥ	āḥ	aḥ	ś
k	ṭ	t	p	ṅ	n	ṃ	ḥ	āḥ	aḥ	ṣ/s
gg h	ḍḍ h	dd h	bb h	ṅ	n	ṃ	r	ā	o	h
g	ḍ	d	b	ṅ/ṅṅ[3]	n/nn[3]	m	r	ā	a[4]	*vowels*
k	ṭ	t	p	ṅ	n	m	ḥ	āḥ	aḥ	*zero*

[1]ḥ or r disappears, and if a/i/u precedes, this lengthens to ā/ī/ū. [2]e.g. tān+lokān=tā̃l lokān.
[3]The doubling occurs if the preceding vowel is short. [4]Except: aḥ+a=o '.

macron, except that for initial vowels in sandhi we use a circumflex to indicate that originally the vowel was short, or the shorter of two possibilities (*e* rather than *ai*, *o* rather than *au*).

When we print initial *â*, before sandhi that vowel was *a*

î or *ê*,	*i*
û or *ô*,	*u*
âi,	*e*
âu,	*o*
ā,	*ā*
ī,	*ī*
ū,	*ū*
ē,	*ī*
ō,	*ū*
ai,	*ai*
āu,	*au*

’, before sandhi there was a vowel *a*

When a final short vowel (*a*, *i*, or *u*) has merged into a following vowel, we print ’ at the end of the word, and when a final long vowel (*ā*, *ī*, or *ū*) has merged into a following vowel we print ” at the end of the word. The vast majority of these cases will concern a final *a* or *ā*. See, for instance, the following examples:

What before sandhi was *atra asti* is represented as *atr’ âsti*

atra āste	*atr’ āste*
kanyā asti	*kany” âsti*
kanyā āste	*kany” āste*
atra iti	*atr’ êti*
kanyā iti	*kany” êti*
kanyā īpsitā	*kany” ēpsitā*

Finally, three other points concerning the initial letter of the second word:

(1) A word that before sandhi begins with *ṛ* (vowel), after sandhi begins with *r* followed by a consonant: *yatha” rtu* represents pre-sandhi *yathā ṛtu*.

(2) When before sandhi the previous word ends in *t* and the following word begins with *ś*, after sandhi the last letter of the previous word is *c*

and the following word begins with *ch*: *syāc chāstravit* represents pre-sandhi *syāt śāstravit*.

(3) Where a word begins with *h* and the previous word ends with a double consonant, this is our simplified spelling to show the pre-sandhi form: *tad hasati* is commonly written as *tad dhasati*, but we write *tadd hasati* so that the original initial letter is obvious.

COMPOUNDS

We also punctuate the division of compounds (*samāsa*), simply by inserting a thin vertical line between words. There are words where the decision whether to regard them as compounds is arbitrary. Our principle has been to try to guide readers to the correct dictionary entries.

Exemplar of CSL Style

Where the Devanagari script reads:

कुम्भस्थली रक्षतु वो विकीर्णसिन्धूररेणुर्द्विरदाननस्य ।
प्रशान्तये विघ्नतमश्छटानां निष्ठ्यूतबालातपपल्लवेव ॥

Others would print:

kumbhasthalī rakṣatu vo vikīrṇasindūrareṇur dviradānanasya /
praśāntaye vighnatamaśchaṭānāṃ niṣṭhyūtabālātapapallaveva //

We print:

kumbha|sthalī rakṣatu vo vikīrṇa|sindūra|reṇur dvirad'|ānanasya
praśāntaye vighna|tamaś|chaṭānāṃ niṣṭhyūta|bāl'|ātapa|pallav" êva.

And in English:

May Ganésha's domed forehead protect you! Streaked with vermilion dust, it seems to be emitting the spreading rays of the rising sun to pacify the teeming darkness of obstructions.

("Nava·sáhasanka and the Serpent Princess" 1.3)

INTRODUCTION

The *Jātaka* Genre

TRADITION HOLDS THAT when the Buddha became enlightened he acquired the ability to see his own past lives as well as those of others. This belief in the possibility of knowing previous rebirths opened the door to a whole genre of literature called *jātaka* (literally "birth-story"), which was dedicated to depicting the past lives of the Buddha when he was still aspiring for enlightenment. It is in these vibrant portrayals of deeds performed by the future Buddha in a variety of different rebirths, including as animals, deities, ascetics, kings, brahmins, and others, that Buddhist narrative often becomes its most captivating. The "Garland of the Buddha's Past Lives" (*Jātakamālā*) by Arya·shura (Āryaśūra), translated here in two Clay Sanskrit Library volumes, is one of the most famous examples of this hugely popular genre.

The importance of *jātaka* stories in traditional Buddhist culture cannot be overestimated. Not only in India but throughout Asia, *jātaka*s have played a prominent role in Buddhist art, literature, ritual, and pedagogy and are still popular today in many Buddhist societies.[1] Whether scattered throughout exegetical texts or gathered together in separate collections, *jātaka*s pervade Buddhist literature in various manifestations, where they are frequently found in large numbers. Five hundred and forty seven *jātaka*s make up a text called the *Jātakaṭṭhavaṇṇanā*, just one of several collections in the Pali tradition, with some stories containing hundreds of verses, while Arya·shura's "Garland of the

Buddha's Past Lives" consists of thirty-four tales, widely acclaimed for their sophisticated style. In the visual arts, a significant number of *jātaka* sculptures are found at the *stūpa* monuments of Bharhut and Sanchi in Central India, thereby laying claim to being some of the earliest extant Buddhist art (approximately first century BCE).[2] Similarly, Arya·shura's "Garland of the Buddha's Past Lives," which has enjoyed a celebrated reputation in both India and Tibet, seems to have played an important role at Ajanta in Maharashtra, where verse inscriptions from the text are found alongside mural paintings of the *Kṣāntivādijātaka* and "The birth-story of Maitri·bala" (*Maitrībalajātaka* 8.1, approximately fifth century CE) (LÜDERS 1902). In sum, one could justly assert that, in terms of their pervasiveness and the sheer frequency of their representation, *jātaka*s enjoy a position in Buddhist culture that rivals even the life-story of the Buddha himself.

The Bodhi·sattva and the Perfections

When considering the doctrinal background of the *jātaka* genre, it is important to understand that in mainstream Indian Buddhist thought there are three qualitatively different types of enlightenment or, to use a more correct translation, "awakening" (*bodhi*), a state that brings an end to suffering and rebirth through a direct insight into the impermanent nature of the world. They are: the awakening of an *arhat*, the awakening of a *pratyeka/buddha*, and the awakening of a perfectly-awakened Buddha (*samyak/saṃbuddha*). An *arhat* becomes awakened by hearing and following a Buddha's teaching (hence the term *śrā-*

vaka, "hearer"), whereas a *pratyeka/buddha* becomes awakened by himself without hearing the teaching of a Buddha. A perfectly-awakened Buddha also realizes nirvana by himself. However, his level of wisdom and morality is greater than that of an *arhat* or *pratyeka/buddha*. Not only does he cultivate, to a supreme level and over countless eons, a group of virtues called the "perfections" (*pāramitā*), he also establishes a teaching (*śāsana*) and a monastic following (*saṃgha*) in his determination to save the world from the suffering of continuous rebirth. All Indian Buddhist traditions agree in judging the path to perfect Buddhahood as the highest. Mahayana Buddhism differs only in that it demands an exclusive adherence to this most difficult of spiritual paths.

A person who vows to become a perfectly awakened Buddha is called a Bodhi·sattva ("Awakening Being").[3] It is therefore a prerequisite of any *jātaka* story to identify one of its characters as the Bodhi·sattva figure, who is usually, but not always, the protagonist. In the "Garland of the Buddha's Past Lives," the Bodhi·sattva is always born as a male and often in an eminent form of rebirth, with well-developed mental and physical qualities. A cursory survey reveals that in thirteen of the thirty-four stories in the "Garland of the Buddha's Past Lives" the Bodhi·sattva is born as royalty; in five stories he is born as a brahmin; in three stories he is born as a god; in nine stories he is, or becomes, an ascetic; and in eleven stories he is born as an animal.[4]

According to the exegetical literature, every *jātaka* story is supposed to reflect the Bodhi·sattva's cultivation of a particular perfection (with the total number of perfections varying depending on the tradition). In reality, however, such doctrinal niceties are often not reflected in the stories themselves or otherwise form the background of attention. While *jātaka* stories do often assume a didactic tone, to see them merely as decorative illustrations of doctrinal tenets, made palatable for popular consumption, would be a gross simplification. On the contrary, it is often here in the polysemous context of narrative expression, with its complex imagery and potent allusions, that tensions within Buddhist thought are most sensitively probed and Buddhist values most ambiguously negotiated.

Historical Background to Arya·shura's "Garland of the Buddha's Past Lives"

The general rule that we know little about the historical context of classical Indian authors is unfortunately no less applicable to Arya·shura.[5] A small amount of information is provided by a Sanskrit commentary called the *Jātakamālāṭīkā*, which states that Arya·shura was a prince in the Deccan who became a Buddhist monk (KHOROCHE 1989: xi). But this probably owes more to hagiography than historical fact and, given the late date of the text, conjecturally dated by PETER KHOROCHE (1989: xi) to the fourteenth century CE, one cannot be certain that it is solidly based.[6]

Most scholarship agrees in dating Arya·shura to approximately the fourth century CE, a conjecture based largely on stylistic considerations.[7] More concrete evidence for this date has, however, been provided by MICHAEL HAHN

(1981), who has shown that passages composed by the Indian poet Hari·bhatta (Haribhaṭṭa) are quoted in a Chinese text called "The Sutra of the Wise Man and the Fool" (*Hsien-yü-ching*), which dates to 445 CE, thereby providing a lower limit for the author. Since Hari·bhatta openly refers to Arya·shura as his paradigm (HAHN 2007: 4), we can assume that Arya·shura lived earlier than Hari·bhatta (as is also suggested by their literary styles), although how much earlier is unclear.

The title *Jātakamālā* can be translated literally as "a garland of birth-stories."[8] It is a term that appears to have been treated as a sub-genre within the *jātaka* tradition, since it is also used of later works composed by authors such as Hari·bhatta (fifth century CE) and Gopa·datta (eleventh century CE).[9] The *Jātakamālā* is not the only work said to have been composed by Arya·shura. The Tibetan Tanjur lists five other texts: the *Bodhisattvajātakadharmagaṇḍī*, the *Subhāṣitaratnakaraṇḍakakathā*, the *Supathadeśanāparikathā*, the *Prātimokṣasūtrapaddhati*, and the *Pāramitāsamāsa* (MEADOWS 1986: 3ff.). Of these, only two, the *Subhāṣitaratnakaraṇḍakakathā* and the *Pāramitāsamāsa*, still exist in Sanskrit, while the others are available in Tibetan translation. It is uncertain, however, whether to take these attributions at face-value. Buddhist traditions commonly seek to invest a text with authority by associating it with a famous figure and there seems to have been considerable confusion over the identity of Shura (Śūra), who is linked with names such as Matri·cheta (Mātṛceṭa) and Ashva·ghosha (Aśvaghoṣa) (MEADOWS 1986: 6f.). CAROL MEADOWS (1986: 8ff.) also argues that doctrinal divergences between the *Jātakamālā* and the *Pāramitāsamāsa* suggest different authorship.

If we limit our investigation to the *Jātakamālā*, Arya·shura's doctrinal affiliations are also unclear. On the whole, the text seems to express mainstream Buddhist values without subscribing to the philosophy of any particular school. One sole verse mentions the term "supreme vehicle" (*yāna/vara*), which may tempt the interpretation of a Mahayana affiliation (1.41 [28]). This, however, is debatable. Not only would one expect a more clear expression of Mahayana partisanship than this single indirect allusion, but also the term "supreme vehicle" seems merely to refer to the Bodhi·sattva path to perfect Buddhahood (sometimes described as *buddha/yāna*), which, as explained above, is a spiritual career accepted by all Buddhist traditions, not only by the Mahayana. That *yāna/vara* need not have Mahayana connotations is further illustrated by the *Mahāvastu* (2.46), a non-Mahayana text, which uses the synonymous term *yāna/śreṣṭha* to refer to the path to Buddhahood (SENART 1882–97). Indeed, contrary to common impressions, the use of the word *yāna* to refer to a path to awakening is not restricted to the Mahayana but is found in non-Mahayana texts such as the **Mahāvibhāṣā*, which on more than one ocassion refers to the notion of three *yāna*s.[10]

The fact that the first thirty stories of the *Jātakamālā* seem to be structured around the three perfections of giving, virtue, and forbearance also need not imply a Mahayana affiliation. While it is true that these moral qualities correspond to the first three of six perfections listed in some Mahayana texts, the Sarvásti·vadins, an influential non-Mahayana tradition, also posit the same list of perfections.[11]

The Structure and Style of the "Garland of the Buddha's Past Lives"

In his "History of Buddhism in India" (1608 CE), Tara·natha states that Arya·shura intended to compose one hundred stories but died before he could complete the task (KHOROCHE 1989: xi). Although the figure of one hundred seems arbitrary, Tara·natha's statement (based on unknown Indian sources) that the "Garland of the Buddha's Past Lives" is incomplete can be supported by the fact that the text concludes, in an apparently abrupt manner, with the noticeably minor story of the woodpecker, an ending for which there seems no particular doctrinal or thematic significance.[12]

It has often been pointed out that the perfections provide a framework for the "Garland of the Buddha's Past Lives." But here too there appears to be disruption in the text. Although the first thirty stories are formatted on the first three perfections, of giving (*dāna*), virtue (*śīla*), and forbearance (*kṣānti*), the structure breaks down with the last four stories, which cannot be said to reflect the fourth perfection of "vigor" (*vīrya*). The Tibetan commentator Yeshe Gyeltsen (*ye shes rgyal mtshan*) attempts to solve the problem by arguing that story 31 represents the perfection of vigor (*vīrya*), story 32 the perfection of meditation (*dhyāna*), and stories 33 and 34 the perfection of wisdom (*prajñā*), thereby conveniently completing the six perfections (MEADOWS 1986: 18). But this seems to stretch the content of the stories too far. As Meadows has pointed out (1986: 18f.), stories 33 and 34 instead clearly reflect the virtue of forbearance (*kṣānti*), while story 31 focuses largely on giving (*dāna*) and truth (an aspect of virtue), and story 32 on renunciation (also an aspect of virtue). Meadows argues that the last four stories should instead be seen as recapitulations of the first thirty and suggests that it was in fact never Arya·shura's intention to tackle the last three perfections. On the contrary, since the first three perfections are suited to householders, and particularly kings, whereas the last three perfections are more suited to monks, the absence of the last three perfections is not a flaw but reflects the text's focus on instructing the laity.

Turning away from the issue of perfections, there are also other ways in which the stories are bound together.[13] Numerous themes, images, and metaphors are repeated, echoed, and developed across various narratives, forming a web of allusions and cross-references; for example, the motif that the Bodhi·sattva acts like a relative toward strangers, or the numerous idyllic portrayals of the forest, or the frequent reactions of devotion expressed by witnesses to the Bodhi·sattva's deeds. Furthermore, while the general format of the work is unstable, the structure of the individual stories is largely predictable and fixed, creating a sense of expectation as the reader embarks on a new tale.

Every tale starts with a maxim. For example, story 30 begins: "If it results in the welfare of others, even pain is esteemed by the virtuous as a gain." There then follows the phrase *tad/yath" ânuśrūyate* ("it has been transmitted as follows"). After this a description of the Bodhi·sattva's background leads to the commencement of the plot. Usually, but not always, the story concludes by restating the opening maxim. Finally, most of the stories have an epilogue that instructs monks as to the proper occasion for reciting the tales. While scholars may be tempted to see these epilogues as interpolations, they are found in all extant manuscripts. Moreover, since they offer an important glimpse of how the stories might have been used pedagogically by monks, I have decided to keep them in the translation.

The "Garland of the Buddha's Past Lives" is composed in an elegant mixture of verse and prose known as *campū*. Although Arya·shura's text is not the earliest example we have of this genre (fragments survive of a text from the second century CE called the *Kalpanāmaṇḍitikā Dṛṣṭāntapaṅkti* by Kumára·lata), it is the first time that *campū* reaches such a high level of refinement, leading to its praise by Indian aesthetic theorists (KHOROCHE 1989: xvi). While the Sanskrit is simple and clear, and the ornamentation light compared to later authors, the "Garland of the Buddha's Past Lives" is conspicuous for the variety of its poetic meters, the wealth of its vocabulary, and the sophistication of its literary devices in both verse and prose. It is beyond the scope of this introduction to cover the range of techniques employed by Arya·shura,[14] including a deft treatment of metaphor, but as an example of his artistry, one might cite his use of *śikhā*, a particular variety of *yamaka* (repetition or echo), whereby the second half of each quarter verse repeats the same syllables:

*upayujya yan mada/**balād a/balā***
*vinibandhayed a**pi tarau pitarau**,*
*gaṇayec ca sā dhana/**patiṃ na patiṃ**,*
*tad idaṃ ghaṭe **vinihitaṃ nihitam**!*

When a woman is weak from intoxication,
she can even tie her parents to a tree
and ignore her husband, though he were Kubéra himself.
Such is the treasure stored in this pot! (17.28 [17])

Although Arya·shura's individual literary skill cannot be doubted, he was, of course, also working within a tradition, a fact he is keen to emphasize when he states that he contradicts neither sacred tradition nor the Buddha's words (1.4 [3]). Many of his stories derive material from the *jātaka* tradition that preceded him. He especially makes use of canonical *jātaka* verses, equivalent or similar to the stanzas preserved in the Pali *Jātakaṭṭhavaṇṇanā*,[15] and indeed thirty of the thirty-four stories in the "Garland of the Buddha's Past Lives" have parallels in the *Jātakaṭṭhavaṇṇanā*.[16] That said, Arya·shura was not afraid of innovation. In "The Birth-Story of the Hare" (6), for example, the Bodhi·sattva dies by sacrificing himself into a fire for a brahmin, a conspicuous departure from earlier versions, as preserved in the *Jātakaṭṭhavaṇṇanā* (no. 316) and *Cariyāpiṭaka* (1.10), in which the hare survives the fire unscathed (Ohnuma 2007: 29). Arya·shura thus constantly seeks to strike a balance between the need for traditional authority on the one hand and the aspiration to develop the *jātaka* genre through fresh literary expression on the other.

Central Themes in the "Garland of the Buddha's Past Lives"[17]

In his introductory verses, Arya·shura spells out some central motives behind composing the "Garland of the Buddha's Past Lives." While presented as an act of compassion performed "out of concern for the good of the world" (1.4 [3]), the text is primarily portrayed as an expression of devotion and reverence for the Buddha and his past deeds (vv. 1.2 [1], 1.5 [4]):

With this handful of flowers of poetry,
I devoutly honor his miraculous feats [...]
With bowed head, I revere this matchless being.

Although the didactic value of the stories is stressed—"These commendable acts offer clear signposts revealing the path to Buddhahood" (1.3 [2])—Arya·shura appears unsatisfied by the mere articulation of doctrine. On the contrary, he intends his stories to have an emotional and aesthetic effect, aimed at inspiring devotion in his audience:

May even the hard-hearted
become softened!
And may religious teachings
hereby increase with charm! (1.3 [2])

The devotional impact Arya·shura intends his narratives to achieve is reflected by the characters in the text when they witness the Bodhi·sattva's miraculous deeds.[18] Repeatedly we are told of how demons, gods, kings, ascetics, and householders are astonished by the Bodhi·sattva's feats and become filled with devotion and joy:

Gods gathered with troops of nymphs,
their eyes blooming with wonder.
A delightful breeze began to blow.
Joy expanded in the hearts of every being. (2.78 [40])

The natural surroundings are also influenced by the Bodhi·sattva's virtue, resulting in earthquakes, flowers falling from the sky, and oceans breaking over their shores (2.76 [38]).

This emphasis on devotion is tied up with the Bodhi·sattva's role as a savior. Often described with images such as father, relative, protector, guide, teacher, or doctor,[19] the Bodhi·sattva repeatedly acts out of compassion for beings in distress or provides refuge for the wicked he converts. The response of his disciple Ájita in "The Birth-Story on the Tigress" is typical (1.54): "I pay homage in every manner to this illustrious being, a refuge for all living creatures, a source of immense compassion and boundless goodness, a true Bodhi·sattva." The Bodhi·sattva's tactics as savior and instructor vary, depending on the situation. In some stories he seeks to instill fear, whether by admonishing a king who is addicted to liquor with an aggressive sermon as in "The Birth-Story on the Jar" (17) or by enforcing virtue through a police state as in "The Birth-Story on the Sacrifice" (10). In other stories the Bodhi·sattva's techniques take on a more directly physical, and corporeal, form of salvation, as he sacrifices his body to be eaten by a hungry tigress (story 1) or allows demons to drink his blood (story 8).

The importance of the Bodhi·sattva's role as savior is linked to his frequent portrayal as a virtuous king who protects society. As Meadows has noted (1986: 9), numerous stories express "a preoccupation with proper political rule," whereby *nīti*, politics based on personal gain (*artha*), is to be replaced by virtue (*dharma*). This is, for example, expressed in "The Birth-Story of Vishvan·tara," in which the prince gives gifts, "unswayed by the falsehood of politics" (9.22 [10]). The ideal king should experience the pains and pleasures of his people as if they were his own (8.4 [1]) and should carefully guard his moral conduct since his behavior is imitated by his subjects (13.87 [38], 17.10 [4]). MEADOWS suggests that this preoccupation with advising kings "reflects a courtly milieu" (ibid.) for the "Garland of the Buddha's Past Lives." Whether or not one accepts this argument, it is certainly the case that the notion of an ideal king who sacrifices everything for virtue is a prominent theme. In particular, this virtue is an absolute form of morality based on renunciant values of non-anger and non-desire, the direct opposite of the stereotyped behavior of the kshatriya class.

While kings are to incorporate renunciant values within their role as social paradigms, other stories express an antagonism between renunciation and society through the figure of the ascetic. This is particularly expressed in stories 18–20 which criticize the desire-based life of the householder in favor of asceticism. In "The Birth-Story of the Childless Ascetic," for example, the Bodhi·sattva states:

The household life is a great discomfort,
for both the wealthy and the poor.
The wealthy suffer the toil of guarding money,
the poor suffer the toil of acquiring it.
As there is no happiness in such a life,

both for the wealthy and the poor,
to delight in it is a delusion.
Evil in fact is its source. (18.22 [11]–23 [12])

According to Arya·shura's framework, ascetic renunciation is seen as an aspect of virtue (*śīla*), the second perfection. The other seven stories treated within the perfection of virtue are structured around the five precepts, a set of restraints central to Buddhist morality. "The Birth-Story of Shakra" (11) thus portrays the precept against killing; "The Birth-Story of the Brahmin" the precept against stealing; "The Birth-Story of Unmadayánti" (13) the precept against immoral sexual conduct; "The Birth-Story of Supáraga" (14), "The Birth-Story of the Fish" (15), and "The Birth-Story of the Quail Chick" (16) the precept against lying; and "The Birth-Story on the Jar" (17) the precept against alcohol. The key feat performed by the Bodhi·sattva in stories 14–16 is an "affirmation of truth" (*saty'|âdhiṣṭhāna*), whereby a statement of truth produces a magical effect on the outside world.

If we turn to the first ten stories of the "Garland of the Buddha's Past Lives," the importance of renunciant values, combined with the Bodhi·sattva's role as a savior, becomes accentuated through the perfection of giving.[20] The practice of giving is fundamental to the Buddhist path. Not only is it essential for the survival of the Buddhist monastic community, it is also the basis for cultivating morality and developing a renunciant attitude of non-attachment. This renunciant significance is highlighted by "The Birth-Story of Agástya" (7), in which the Bodhi·sattva's main practice as an ascetic renouncer is, in fact, to give gifts.

Different types of gift are given by the Bodhi·sattva, including wealth and even his own body. Due to its transient nature, wealth is depicted negatively as a source of greed and attachment, which ascetics discard "as though it were chaff" (7.8). But while wealth is considered worthless, the act of giving is sometimes described as extracting the "essence" or "worth" (*sāra*) out of wealth:[21]

Wealth itself is essenceless and trifling.
Its essence lies in being given by benefactors of the world.
When given, it becomes a treasure.
When ungiven, it ends only in loss. (2.91 [50])

This "essence" or "treasure" is merit, often portrayed as a purified, more permanent form of wealth, which, unlike material riches, can be taken to the next life:

Wealth must one day be left behind
and then it is of no use.
By giving up one's wealth correctly,
one produces a kind of asset. (3.32 [20])

You should give to the virtuous,
gracing your gift with reverence.
For wealth deposited this way
cannot be lost and follows you after death. (9.70 [29])

Reiko Ohnuma (2007: 205ff.) has observed a similar theme when the body is given away. In such stories, the Bodhi·sattva is often said to make use of an otherwise useless and impure body by giving it away and thereby extracting its "essence" (8.71 [33]).

There are also different motivations behind the Bodhi·sattva's gifts. Some stories (3 and 4) depict an alms offering,[22] whereby a layperson offers food to a monk out of devotion and respect. In the majority of stories, however, the Bodhi·sattva gives either out of compassion or out of pure renunciation, as suits his role as a renunciant protector who is famed for his non-attachment and compassionate deeds. When the Bodhi·sattva gives out of pure renunciation, the dynamics of the gift differ radically from the devotional gift of an alms offering. In the latter case, the moral standing of the recipient is crucial; in the former case, the nature of the recipient is often irrelevant, the emphasis being on giving for giving's sake. "Gifts should be given: that alone is why I give," states the Bodhi·sattva in "The Birth-Story of Vishvan·tara" (9.61 [26]).

A striking example of a compassionate gift is provided by "The Birth-Story on the Tigress," in which the Bodhi·sattva offers his body to a hungry tigress with the following motivation:

It is neither ambition, nor desire for fame,
nor the attainment of heaven, nor kingship,
nor my own perpetual happiness that motivates me.
My sole concern is to benefit others. (1.44 [30])

Likewise, in "The Birth-Story of Maitri·bala," the Bodhi·sattva joyfully gives his body to a group of demons, stating:

When I look at the helpless creatures
incessantly suffering bitter toils and woes,
my mind cannot be satisfied
merely by dispelling my own sorrows. (8.106 [54])

In both stories, however, the Bodhi·sattva's concern is not limited solely to helping the recipients of his gift. The gift is instead viewed as part of a greater design aimed at attaining Buddhahood, or "omniscience," and the benefit this brings the world. Immediately after the above verse, the Bodhi·sattva therefore states:

Through this pure deed, may I attain Omniscience.
By conquering the vices that are my enemies,
may I raise the world out of the ocean of existence
with its huge surging waves of old age, sickness,
and death. (8.107 [55])

The potential conflict between the needs of the recipient and the Bodhi·sattva's focus on awakening is probed by "The Birth-Story of the Hare." Here the Bodhi·sattva's desire to fulfill his spiritual path contradicts the wishes of his recipient, who in fact requests the Bodhi·sattva not to sacrifice his body for him. The Bodhi·sattva responds thus:

Giving is a duty and my heart wishes to give.
And it is apt when I have a guest such as you.
An opportunity like this cannot easily be gained.
I rely on you to ensure my gift is not in vain. (6.55 [32])

Far from fulfilling the needs of the recipient, the emphasis is on the Bodhi·sattva's pure renunciant attitude and the miraculous extent to which he is willing to give.[23] In stories such as this the Bodhi·sattva performs an absolute form of giving that bears little or no relational significance to the context at hand. Nor is the text reluctant to explore the ramifications of this absolute type of giving. On the contrary, as OHNUMA has observed (2007: 91ff.), such stories often seek to emphasize the transcendent, and at times transgressive, nature of the Bodhi·sattva's gifts by portraying them as unconventional actions that lead to conflicts with kings, ministers, and other representatives of society's norms.[24]

Perhaps the most striking instance of this is expressed in "The Birth-Story of Vishvan·tara" (9), in which the Bodhi·sattva gives away his wife and children to a brahmin as slaves. As STEVEN COLLINS has emphasized (1998: 497ff.), this is an act of renunciation that fundamentally jars with social values and the text portrays with sensitive detail the suffering caused by this absolute form of giving, including stirring scenes in which the Bodhi·sattva's children tearfully try to dissuade their father from his gift and in which his wife becomes hysterical with distress. Nor is the Bodhi·sattva himself unaffected by the pain involved in his dedication to renunciant values:[25]

> *The Bodhi·sattva's mind was shaken by the children's pitiable lament. Although he told himself that one should feel no regret after giving a gift, his heart burned with an incurable fire of sorrow. His mind seized up, like someone fainting from a powerful poison, and he collapsed there and then.* (9.143)

Although it is significant that the Bodhi·sattva's wife ultimately gives her approval (*anumodana*) to her husband's gift of their children, thereby bringing resolution to the story and in fact enabling the Bodhi·sattva to complete his gift when she too is given away, the ambiguities raised by the text mean that one cannot take the story simply as a glorification of the Bodhi·sattva's practice of giving.

While the "Garland of the Buddha's Past Lives" is fervent in its devotion for the Bodhi·sattva's deeds, it also thus invites its audience to explore some of the difficulties involved in a soteriological path that transcends conventional values, as exemplified by the Bodhi·sattva's extreme and miraculous feats. Far from diluting the devotional tone of the text, however, this transcendent aspect serves to heighten it further. For it is precisely the fact that the Bodhi·sattva's deeds are extraordinary and "unable to be imitated" (1.5 [4]) that they are so astounding and awe-inspiring, filling the audience with devotion for their heroic savior and his renunciant path.

The Sanskrit Text

It has been my good fortune to benefit from the excellent critical edition of the *Jātakamālā* by ALBRECHT HANISCH, who consults not only the extant Sanskrit manuscripts but also Tibetan translations of the *Jātakamālā*, as well as the Sanskrit and Tibetan *ṭīkā* commentaries. For a detailed analysis of variants and other textual issues, I refer the reader to this extremely useful work. Unfortunately, HANISCH's edition is not yet complete and presently ends at story 15. For stories 16–34, I have used HEINRICH KERN's edition, which I have frequently emended by referring to manuscript readings listed in KHOROCHE's "Towards a New Edition of Ārya-Śūra's Jātakamālā" (1987), taking particular advantage of the older and more reliable readings provided by manuscripts N and T. All such departures from KERN's edition are listed at the end of this volume. HAHN's text-critical comments (2001) on stories 33 and 34 have also been invaluable. Finally, the *Jātakamālā* translations by J.S. SPEYER (1895) and KHOROCHE (1989), both of them pioneering works in their own time, have been constant sources of help and inspiration.

Notes

1 The present Thai king, His Majesty King Bhumibol Adulyadej, recently produced an adapted translation of the *Mahājanaka Jātaka*, a scene from which is depicted on cinema screens throughout Thailand during the royal anthem.

2 LÜDERS (1941: 139) discusses an inscription of a verse from the *Aṇḍabhūtajātaka* at Bharhut. This is one of the earliest surviving written citations of a canonical text.

3 K.R. NORMAN (1997: 104f.) argues that the Sanskrit word *bodhi/sattva* is a back formation from the Prakrit *bodhi/satta*, the Sanskrit equivalent of which is either *bodhi/ṣakta* or *bodhi/śakta*. These two compounds can be translated as "aspiring for awakening" (literally "attached to awakening") and "capable of awakening" respectively. The compound *bodhi/sattva* has the significantly different meaning of "awakening being," or to use MONIER-WILLIAMS' translation: "one whose essence is perfect knowledge" (see MONIER-WILLIAMS s.v.).

4 **Royalty**: stories 2, 3, 8, 9, 10, 11 (Shakra, king of the gods), 13, 15 (fish king), 17 (Shakra), 22 (goose king), 27 (monkey king), 32, 33. **Brahmin**: stories 1, 7, 12, 19, 21. **God**: stories 11, 17, 29. **Ascetic**: stories 1, 7, 18, 19, 20, 21, 23, 28, 32. **Animal**: stories 6, 15, 16, 22, 24, 25, 26, 27, 30, 33, 34.

5 The word *ārya* is a term of respect. Śūra is also called Ācārya Śūra and Bhadanta Śūra. See KHOROCHE (1985: 63).

6 Khoroche (1985: 63) notes that the date of the text is unknown, but that it cannot be earlier than 700 CE since it refers to Dandin.

7 See Meadows (1986: 4) and Khoroche (1989: xii–xiii) for a summary.

8 A second title is also used: *Bodhisattvāvadānamālā*, "a garland of the Bodhi·sattva's exploits."

9 See Hahn (1992), (2007) and Meadows (1986: 5). See also verses 7–8 in Soméndra's preface to Ksheméndra's *Bodhisattvāvadānakalpalatā*, cited in Hahn (1992: 13), in which we are told that there exist many *Jātakamālās* that have been composed by "Gopa·datta and other teachers."

10 Bhikkhu Dhammajoti (1998: 71ff.). I am also grateful to Bhikkhu Dhammajoti for a reference to the **Saṃyuktābhidharmahṛdaya* (116), in which the *tri/yāna* ("three vehicles") are mentioned. For a translation of this text, see Dessein (1999). I am grateful to Peter Skilling for his comments on this matter.

11 Lamotte (1988: 626). The six perfections are: giving (*dāna*), virtue (*śīla*), forbearance (*kṣānti*), vigor (*vīrya*), meditation (*dhyāna*), and wisdom (*prajñā*).

12 It is debatable whether the expectation for a climactic conclusion is justified when dealing with this type of literature, especially when it is a collection. A counter-example, however, is provided by the *Jātakaṭṭhavaṇṇanā*, in which the *Vessantarajātaka* (547) does appear to produce something of a dramatic finale.

13 There is a danger of overestimating the importance of the perfections. Indeed, it is noteworthy that the word *pāramitā* is never mentioned in the entire *Jātakamālā*. Moreover, the story (particularly the maxim) often needs to be interpreted first, sometimes heavily, before the relevant perfection is gleaned. The *Jātakaṭṭhavaṇṇanā* again provides an interesting comparison. There the issue of perfections is often irrelevant, or at best ambiguous, being instead the concern of the meta-interpretations of commentarial exegesis.

14 See Basu (1988) for a literary analysis of the *Jātakamālā*. See also Hahn (2007), who lists examples of Hari·bhatta's style. See Gerow (1971) for a summary of literary devices in Indian literature.

15 Dating the *Jātakaṭṭhavaṇṇanā* is problematic since it developed within an oral culture. The verses are traditionally considered canonical and can be given a lower limit of the first century BCE (although many must be earlier), whereas the prose is commentarial and has a lower limit of approximately the fifth century CE (although again much must date back far earlier).

There are major differences between the *Jātakaṭṭhavaṇṇanā* and *Jātakamālā*. The *Jātakamālā*'s stories are not spoken by the Buddha and consequently do not have a frame-story set in the present, linking the Buddha's life with the *jātaka*. Arya·shura's text usually identifies only the Buddha's past life character, whereas the *Jātakaṭṭhavaṇṇanā* often identifies the past life characters of others contemporary to the Buddha, including his chief monks and nuns, as well as his wife and child. Both texts agree in not portraying a chronological sequence of past lives. But whereas the *Jātakaṭṭhavaṇṇanā* orders its stories according to their number of verses, the *Jātakamālā* is ordered on thematic concerns.

It could be argued that the *Jātakaṭṭhavaṇṇanā*'s mixture of verse and prose, often described as *ākhyāna*, provides a precedent for *campū*. In contrast to the *Jātakamālā*, however, verses in *ākhyāna* literature often rely on the prose for their meaning to be understood. *Campū* literature is also more refined in literary expression and has no strict hierarchy of verse and prose.

16 Khoroche (1989: 257ff.) provides a useful list of correspondences with the *Jātakaṭṭhavaṇṇanā* and other texts at the beginning of his notes to each story.

17 The comments in this section focus largely on stories 1–20 translated in the present volume. For comments on stories 21–34, please see the introduction to Volume Two.

18 In "The Birth-Story on the Tigress" (1.26–28), the Bodhi·sattva predicts the emotional reactions that his feat will produce in others, including faith, astonishment, incitement, and joy.

19 For example, 34.2+: "Protected this way by the Great Being, the creatures in that forest area prospered happily, just as if they had a teacher, kinsman, a doctor, or a king."

20 See Ohnuma (2007), especially 140ff. for an analysis of giving in Buddhism. See Meadows (1986: 15) for an analysis of story 10, which appears to straddle both giving and virtue.

21 "Giving, they say, extracts the essence out of wealth" (3.35 [23]).

22 The mental attitude of joy is, however, central to all forms of giving. See 8.44–8.46 for a group of verses in which joy is emphasized.

23 A common motif is that Shakra, the king of the gods, tests the Bodhi·sattva's resolve, thereby revealing the extent of his virtue. See Ohnuma (2007: 67ff.) for an interesting analysis of Shakra's role.

24 See especially stories 2, 8, and 9. A similar conflict is expressed in stories 18 and 20, in which the Bodhi·sattva's renunciation of society as an ascetic meets strong opposition.

25 For this more fallible and "human" side to the Bodhi·sattva, see also "The Birth-Story of Unmadayánti" (13), in which the Bodhi·sattva is a king who struggles with his lust for a minister's wife.

Select Bibliography

Basu, R. 1989. *Eine literatur-kritische Studie zu Āryaśūras Jātakamālā zusammen mit einer kritischen Edition der anonymen Jātakamālāṭīkā und einer kritischen Edition der Jātakamālāpañjikā des Vīryasiṃha*. PhD dissertation, Bonn.

Collins, S. 1998. *Nirvana and other Buddhist felicities: Utopias of the Pali Imaginaire*. Cambridge: Cambridge University Press.

Dessein, B. 1999. *Saṃyuktābhidharmahṛdaya: Heart of Scholasticism, with Miscellaneous Additions.* 2 parts. Delhi: Motilal Banarsidass.

Dhammajoti, Bhikkhu K. 1998. "The Defects in the Arhat's Enlightenment: His *Akliṣṭa-ajñāna* and *Vāsanā*." *Buddhist Studies (Bukkyō Kenkyū)* 27. 65–98.

Edgerton, F. 1953. *Buddhist Hybrid Sanskrit Grammar and Dictionary.* 2 Vols. New Haven: Yale University Press.

Gerow, E. 1971. *A Glossary of Indian Figures of Speech.* The Hague: Mouton & Co.

Hahn, M. 1981. "Das Datum des Haribhaṭṭa." In: K. Bruhn and A. Wetzler (eds.). *Studien zum Jainismus und Buddhismus: Gedenkschrift für Ludwig Alsdorf*. Wiesbaden: Franz Steiner. 107–120.

———. 1986–1992. *Variant Readings on Āryaśūra's Jātakamālā as found in the Jātakamālāṭīkā. Journal of Oriental Research, Madras* 56–62 (1986–1992). 233–253.

——— (ed.). 1992. *Haribhaṭṭa and Gopadatta: Two Authors in the Succession of Āryaśūra. On the Rediscovery of Parts of their Jātakamālās.* Tokyo: The International Institute for Buddhist Studies.

———. 2001. "Text-critical Remarks on Āryaśūra's *Mahiṣa-* and *Śatapattrajātaka*." In: Raffaele Torella (ed.). *Le Parole e i Marmi: Studi in onore di Raniero Gnoli nel suo 70 compleanno.* Roma: Istituto Italiano per l'Africa e l'Oriente. Serie Orientale Roma XCII. 377–397.

——— (ed.). 2007. *Haribhaṭṭa in Nepal: Ten Legends from his Jātakamālā and the Anonymous Śākyasiṃhajātaka.* Tokyo: The International Institute for Buddhist Studies.

Hanisch, A. (ed.). 2005. *Āryaśūras Jātakamālā: Philologische Unterschungen zu den Legenden 1 bis 15.* 2 vols. Marburg: Indica et Tibetica Verlag.

Kern, H. (ed.). 1891. *The Jātaka-mālā: Stories of Buddha's Former Incarnations, Otherwise Entitled Bodhi-sattva-avadāna-mālā, by Ārya-çūra.* Cambridge: Harvard University Press (repr. 1914, 1943).

Khoroche, P. 1985. "Jātakamālāṭīkā." *South Asian Studies* 1. 63–66.

———. 1987. *Towards a New Edition of Ārya-Śūra's Jātakamālā*. Bonn: Indica et Tibetica Verlag.

——— (trans.). 1989. *Once the Buddha Was a Monkey: Ārya Śūra's Jātakamālā*. Chicago and London: The University of Chicago Press.

Lamotte, É. 1988. *History of Buddhism: From the Origins to the Śaka Era*. Trans. Sara Webb-Boin. Louvain-La-Neuve: Institut Orientaliste.

Lüders, H. 1902. "Ārya-Śūra's Jātakamālā und die Fresken von Ajaṇṭā." *Nachrichten von der Königlichen Gesellschaft der Wissenschaften zu Göttingen* 5. 758–762.

———. 1941. *Bhārhut und die buddhistische Literatur*. Leipzig: Kommissionsverlag F.A. Brockhaus.

Meadows, C. (ed. and trans.). 1986. *Ārya-Śūra's Compendium of the Perfections: Text, Translation and Analysis of the Pāramitāsamāsa*. Bonn: Indica et Tibetica Verlag.

Monier-Williams, M. 1899. *A Sanskrit-English Dictionary*. Oxford: Oxford University Press.

Norman, K.R. 1997. *A Philological Approach to Buddhism: The Bukkyō Dendō Kyōkai Lectures 1994*. London: Routledge.

Ohnuma, R. 2007. *Head, Eyes, Flesh, and Blood: Giving Away the Body in Indian Buddhist Literature*. New York: Columbia University Press.

Olivelle, P. 1993. *The Āśrama System: History and Hermeneutics of a Religious Institution*. New York: Oxford University Press.

Senart, É. (ed.). 1882–1897. *Le Mahāvastu*. 3 vols. Paris: Imprimerie Nationale.

Speyer, J.S. (trans.). 1895. *The Jātakamālā, or Garland of Birth-Stories of Āryaśūra*. London: Henry Frowde.

Weller, F. (ed.) 1955. *Die Fragmente der Jātakamālā in der Turfansammlung der Berliner Akademie.* Deutsche Akademie der Wissenschaften, Institut für Orientforschung, Veröffentlichung Nr. 24, Berlin.

All references to Pali texts are to Pali Text Society editions.

GARLAND OF THE BUDDHA'S PAST LIVES
VOLUME I

śrīmanti sad|guṇa|pari-
graha|maṅgalāni
kīrty|āspadāny an|avagī-
ta|mano|harāṇi
pūrveṣu janmasu muneś
carit'|âdbhutāni
bhaktyā sva|kāvya|kusum'|âñ-
jalin" ârcayiṣye. [1]

ślāghyair amībhir abhilak-
ṣita|cihna|bhūtair
ādeśito bhavati yat
Sugatatva|mārgaḥ,
syād eva rūkṣa|manasām
api ca prasādo!
dharmyāḥ kathāś ca ramaṇī-
yataratvam īyuḥ! [2]

lok'|ârtham ity abhisamī-
kṣya kariṣyate 'yaṃ
śruty|ārṣa|yukty|a|viguṇe-
na pathā prayatnaḥ
lok'|ôttamasya carit'|â-
tiśaya|pradeśaiḥ
svaṃ prātibhaṃ gamayituṃ
śruti|vallabhatvam. [3]

Homage to the Buddha

1.1

Glorious are the deeds
of the Sage in his past births.
Fame resides in them,
fine virtues filling them with auspice.
Impossible to censure,
they captivate the mind.
With this handful of flowers of poetry,
I devoutly honor his wondrous feats.

These commendable acts
offer clear signposts
revealing the path
to Buddhahood.*
May even the hard-hearted
become softened!
And may religious teachings
hereby increase with charm!

Never contradicting sacred tradition,
the Buddha's words, or reason,*
and out of concern for
the good of the world,
I will strive to make my muse
pleasing to its audience
by relating the exceptional deeds
of the world's supreme being.

1.5 sv'|ârth'|ôdyatair api par'|âr-
tha|carasya yasya
n' âiv' ânvagamyata guṇa|
pratipatti|śobhā
«Sarvajña» ity a|vitath'|â-
kṣara|dīpta|kīrtiṃ
mūrdhnā name tam a|samaṃ
saha|Dharma|Saṃgham. [4]

In acting for others, 1.5
he displayed a radiant virtue
unable to be imitated
even by those intent on their own cause.
His glory blazes truthfully
in the name "Omniscient One."
With bowed head, I revere this matchless being,
the Teaching, and the Community.*

STORY 1

THE BIRTH-STORY ON THE TIGRESS

SARVA | SATTVEṢV A | KĀRAṆA | parama | vatsala | svabhāvaḥ sarva | bhūt' | ātma | bhūtaḥ pūrva | janmasv api sa Bhagavān iti. Buddhe Bhagavati paraḥ prasādaḥ kāryaḥ.

tad | yath" ânuśrūyate, ratna | traya | gurubhiḥ pratipatti | guṇ' | âbhirādhita | gurubhir guṇa | pracaya | gurubhir asmad | gurubhiḥ parikīrtyamānam idaṃ Bhagavataḥ pūrva | janm' | âvadānam.

Bodhisattvaḥ kila pratijñ" | âtiśaya | sadṛśair dāna | priya | vacan' | ârtha | caryā | prabhṛtibhiḥ prajñā | parigraha | nir | a | vadyaiḥ kāruṇya | nisyandair lokam anugṛhṇan,

sva | dharm' | âbhiraty | upanata | śuci | vṛttiny udit' | ôdite mahati brāhmaṇa | kule janma | parigrahaṃ cakāra. sa kṛta | saṃskāra | kramo jāta | karm' | ādibhir abhivardhamānaḥ prakṛti | medhāvitvāt sānāthya | viśeṣāj jñāna | kautūhalād a | kausīdyāc ca na | cireṇ' âiv' âṣṭā | daśasu vidyā | sthāneṣu sva | kula | kram' | â | viruddhāsu ca sakalāsu kalāsv ācāryakaṃ param avāpa.

I.10 sa Brahmavad Brahma | vidāṃ babhūva,
rāj" êva rājñāṃ bahu | māna | pātram,
s' | âkṣāt Sahasrākṣa iva prajānāṃ,
jñān' | ârthinām artha | caraḥ pit" êva. [5]

EVEN IN HIS PREVIOUS births, the Lord* naturally felt a spontaneous and immense affection for all creatures, identifying himself with every living being. One should therefore show the highest devotion toward the Lord Buddha.

Tradition has handed down the following story regarding a deed performed by the Lord in a past life. It is a tale that used to be proclaimed by my teacher, who was devoted to the Three Jewels* and profound in his examination of virtues, and who pleased his own teacher with his moral behavior and goodness.*

The Bodhi·sattva,* tradition tells us, used to favor the world with outpourings of compassion. Suited to the extraordinary vow he had made,* they included gifts, kind words, and acts of welfare, his grasp of wisdom making them beyond reproach.

He is said to have once taken his birth in a great and eminent brahmin family. Pure in conduct, the family delighted in following the duties prescribed by its class. As he grew up, the Bodhi·sattva underwent the normal series of rites, passing through the birth ceremony and other rituals. And due to his innate intelligence, his specialized tutoring, his curiosity for knowledge, and his lack of indolence, he quickly mastered the eighteen sciences and the arts*, none of which conflicted with the customs of his clan.

For Brahman-knowing brahmins he was like Brahman.* 1.10
Among kings he was respected like a king.
For the people he was like thousand-eyed Shakra* in person.

tasya bhāgya|guṇ'|âtiśaya|samāvarjito mahā|lābha|sat|kāra|yaśo|viśeṣaḥ prādur|abhūt. dharm'|âbhyāsa|bhāvita|matiḥ kṛta|pravrajyā|paricayas tu Bodhisattvo na ten' âbhireme.

sa pūrva|caryā|pariśuddha|buddhiḥ
kāmeṣu dṛṣṭvā bahu|doṣa|jātam
gārhasthyam a|svāsthyam iv' âvadhūya
kaṃ cid vana|prastham alaṃ|cakāra. [6]

sa tatra niḥ|saṅgatayā tayā ca
prajñ"|âvadātena śamena c' âiva
pratyādideś' êva ku|kārya|saṅgād
viśliṣṭa|śiṣṭ'|ôpaśamaṃ nṛ|lokam. [7]

maitrī|mayeṇa praśamena tasya
visyandin" êv' ânuparīta|cittāḥ
paras|para|droha|nivṛtta|bhāvās
tapasvivad vyāḍa|mṛgā viceruḥ. [8]

1.15 ācāra|śuddhyā nibhṛt'|êndriyatvāt
saṃtoṣa|yogāt karuṇā|guṇāc ca
a|saṃstutasy' âpi janasya loke
so 'bhūt priyas tasya yath" âiva lokaḥ. [9]

alp'|êccha|bhāvāt kuhan"|ân|abhijñas
tyakta|spṛho lābha|yaśaḥ|sukhebhyaḥ
sa devatānām api mānasāni
prasāda|bhakti|pravaṇāni cakre. [10]

To seekers of knowledge he gave support
like a father.*

His good fortune and superior qualities meant he acquired great wealth, esteem, and fame. But the Bodhi·sattva took no pleasure in such things. His mind was occupied with practicing virtue and he was intimate with the renunciant life.

With a mind purified by past deeds,
he could see the many faults in desires.
Discarding the householder life like an illness,
he went to adorn a forest area.

The detachment he displayed there,
and tranquility, cleansed by wisdom,
seemed to accuse the world of men, their addiction
to evil dividing them from the calm of the wise.

Vicious wild beasts wandered like ascetics,
abstaining from harming each other,
their minds pervaded by the serene loving kindness
seeming to pour from the Bodhi·sattva.

His pure conduct and control over his senses, 1.15
his contentment and compassion,
made him dear even to strangers in the world,
just as the world was dear to him.

His needs were few. He knew nothing of envy.
Discarding all desire for gain, glory, or pleasure,
he made even the minds of the gods
incline to him with faith and devotion.

śrutv" âtha taṃ pravrajitaṃ manuṣyā
guṇais tadīyair avabaddha|cittāḥ
vihāya bandhūṃś ca parigrahāṃś ca
tac|chiṣyatāṃ siddhim iv' ôpajagmuḥ. [11]

śīle śucāv indriya|bhāvanāyāṃ
smṛty|a|pramoṣe praviviktatāyām
maitry|ādike c' âiva manaḥ|samādhau
yathā|balaṃ so 'nuśaśāsa śiṣyān. [12]

atha kadā cit sa Mah"|ātmā pariniṣpanna|bhūyiṣṭhe pṛthū|bhūte śiṣya|gaṇe pratiṣṭhāpite 'smin kalyāṇe vartmany avatārite naiṣkramya|sat|pathaṃ loke saṃvṛteṣv iv' âpāya|dvāreṣu rāja|mārgī|kṛteṣv iva su|gati|mārgeṣu dṛṣṭa|dharma|sukha|vihār'|ârthaṃ tat|kāla|śiṣyeṇ' Âjiten' ânugamyamāno yog'|ânukūlān parvata|darī|nikuñjān anuvicacāra.

1.20 ath' âtra vyāghra|vanitāṃ dadarśa giri|gahvare
prasūti|kleśa|doṣeṇa gatāṃ vispanda|mandatām, [13]

parikṣām'|ēkṣaṇa|yugāṃ kṣudhā chātatar'|ôdarīm
āhāram iva paśyantīṃ bālān sva|tanayān api, [14]

stanya|tarṣād upasṛtān mātṛ|viśrambha|nir|vyathān
rorūyita|ravaiḥ krūrair bhartsayantīṃ parān iva. [15]

Captivated by his virtues,
men abandoned relatives and possessions
at the news he had become a renouncer,
entering his instruction as if it were perfection itself.

He taught his disciples as best as he could
in virtue, integrity, purification of the senses,
maintenance of awareness, detachment,
loving kindness and other mental concentrations.

His throng of disciples became huge and most of them attained perfection. By laying down the beautiful path and establishing the world on the virtuous road of renunciation, it was as if the gates to hell had been closed and the paths to heaven had become as broad as royal highways. One day the Great One* happened to be wandering around mountain caves and thickets that were conducive to meditation, enjoying his surroundings in the company of Ájita, a disciple of his at the time.

There, in a mountain cave, 1.20
he saw a young tigress
undergoing birth pains,
hardly able to move.

Her eyes sunken,
her belly emaciated by hunger,
she looked at her cubs, her own offspring,
as if they were food.

Trusting their mother, the cubs fearlessly
sidled up to her, craving her teats,
only to be terrified by her fierce, roaring howls,
menacing them as though they were foes.

Bodhisattvas tu tāṃ dṛṣṭvā
dhīro 'pi karuṇā|vaśāt
cakampe para|duḥkhena
mahī|kampād iv' âdri|rāṭ. [16]

mahatsv api sva|duḥkheṣu
vyakta|dhairyāḥ kṛp"|ātmakāḥ
mṛdun" âpy anya|duḥkhena
kampante yat tad adbhutam. [17]

1.25 atha Bodhisattvaḥ sa|saṃbhram'|āmreḍita|padaṃ svabhāv'|âtiśaya|vyañjakaṃ karuṇā|bala|samāhit'|âkṣaraṃ śiṣyam uvāca:

«vatsa! vatsa!

paśya saṃsāra|nairguṇyaṃ!
mṛgy eṣā sva|sutān api
laṅghita|sneha|maryādā
bhoktum anvicchati kṣudhā. [18]

aho bat' âtikaṣṭ" êyam ātma|snehasya raudratā
yena māt" âpi tanayān āhārayitum icchati! [19]

ātma|sneha|mayaṃ śatruṃ ko vardhayitum arhati
yena kuryāt pada|nyāsam īdṛśeṣv api karmasu? [20]

1.30 tac chīghram anviṣyatāṃ tāvat kutaś cid asyāḥ kṣud|duḥkha|pratīkāra|hetur yāvan na tanayān ātmānaṃ c' ôpahanti. aham api c' âināṃ prayatiṣye sāhasād asmād vārayitum.»

sa tath" êty asmai pratiśrutya tad|āhār'|ânveṣaṇa|paro babhūva. atha Bodhisattvas taṃ śiṣyaṃ sa|vyapadeśam ativāhya cintām āpede:

The sight of the tigress made
the Bodhi·sattva, though self-composed,
shake with compassion at another's suffering,
just as the king of mountains shakes in an earthquake.

It is miraculous how the compassionate,
notably steadfast in their own sufferings,
however great, tremble at the suffering of others,
however small.

The force of his compassion then moved the Bodhi·sattva 1.25
to address his disciple with words that revealed his superior nature:

"My dear friend! My dear friend!" he repeated emotionally.

"Observe the worthless nature of samsara!*
This wild animal is so hungry,
she is ready even to eat her own young,
violating the boundaries of affection.

How cruel is the brutality of self-love,
when even a mother will eat her offspring!

Who would foster the enemy that is self-love
if it produces actions such as this?

Go quickly and find a way to relieve her hunger so that 1.30
she does not kill her young and destroy herself. I too will endeavor to restrain her from this violent act."

Ájita consented and busied himself with seeking food for the tigress. But after dismissing his disciple on this pretext, the Bodhi·sattva had the following thought:

«saṃvidyamāne sakale śarīre
kasmāt parasmān mṛgayāmi māṃsam?
yādṛcchikī tasya hi lābha|saṃpat
kāry'|âtyayaḥ syāc ca tathā mam' âyam. [21]

api ca,

nir|ātmake bhedini sāra|hīne
duḥkhe kṛta|ghne satat'|â|śucau ca
dehe parasmāy upayujyamāne
na prītimān yo na vicakṣaṇaḥ saḥ. [22]

1.35 sva|saukhya|saṅgena parasya duḥkham
upekṣyate śakti|parikṣayād vā.
na c' ânya|duḥkhe sati me 'sti saukhyaṃ.
satyāṃ ca śaktau kim upekṣakaḥ syām? [23]

satyāṃ ca śaktau mama yady upekṣā
syād ātatāyiny api duḥkha|magne
kṛtv" êva pāpaṃ mama tena cittaṃ
dahyeta kakṣaṃ mahat" âgnin" êva. [24]

tasmāt kariṣyāmi śarīrakeṇa
taṭa|prapāt'|ôdgata|jīvitena
saṃrakṣaṇaṃ putra|vadhāc ca mṛgyā
mṛgyāḥ sakāśāc ca tad|ātmajānām. [25]

"Why should I hunt for meat from elsewhere
when my entire body is available before me?
It rests on chance whether Ájita finds food.
And if he does, it will impede my duty.

Besides,

This body has no self. It breaks up and has no worth.
A source of pain, it is ungrateful and ever unclean.
What wise man would not feel joy
at making their body useful to another being?

People overlook the suffering of another 1.35
when powerless to help or attached to their happiness.
But I cannot be happy while another suffers.
How can I be indifferent if I am able to help?

If a person—even a murderer*—drowns in suffering
and I remain indifferent, though I can help,
my mind would burn like brushwood ignited
by a huge fire, as if I had committed a crime.

By falling off this precipice,
I will use my lifeless body
to protect the tigress from killing her young
and save the young from their mother.

kiṃ ca bhūyaḥ,

saṃdarśanaṃ loka|hit'|ôtsukānām
uttejanaṃ manda|parākramāṇām
saṃharṣaṇaṃ tyāga|viśāradānām
ākarṣaṇaṃ saj|jana|mānasānām. [26]

1.40 viṣādanaṃ Māra|mahā|camūnāṃ
prasādanaṃ Buddha|guṇa|priyāṇām
vrīḍ"|ôdayaṃ sv'|ârtha|parāyaṇānāṃ
mātsarya|lobh'|ôpahat'|ātmanāṃ ca. [27]

śraddhāpanaṃ yāna|var'|āśritānāṃ
vismāpanaṃ tyāga|kṛta|smayānām
viśodhanaṃ svarga|mahā|pathasya
tyāga|priyāṇām anumodi|nṝṇām. [28]

kadā nu gātrair api nāma kuryāṃ
hitaṃ pareṣām iti yaś ca me 'bhūt
mano|rathas taṃ saphalī|kriyāsaṃ
saṃbodhim agryām api c' â|vidūre. [29]

api ca,

na spardhayā n' âiva yaśo|'bhilāṣān
na svarga|lābhān na ca rājya|hetoḥ
n' âtyantike 'py ātma|sukhe yath" âyaṃ
mam' ādaro 'nyatra par'|ârtha|siddheḥ. [30]

1.45 tathā mam' ânena samāna|kālaṃ
lokasya duḥkhaṃ ca sukh'|ôdayaṃ ca
hartuṃ ca kartuṃ ca sad" âstu śaktis
tamaḥ prakāśaṃ ca yath" âiva bhānoḥ. [31]

What is more,

This will be an example to those eager to benefit
the world,
an incitement to those of little courage,
a delight to those accomplished in charity,
a lure to the minds of the virtuous.

Disheartening the great armies of Mara,* 1.40
it will gladden those fond of the Buddha's qualities,
and arouse shame in those intent on self-profit,
their natures afflicted by envy and greed.

Inspiring faith in followers of the supreme vehicle,*
it will astound those who sneer at renunciation
and clear the highway to heaven
for approving men who cherish charity.

By offering up my very own limbs,
I can also fulfill my wish
of benefiting other beings
and come nearer to attaining the highest awakening.

Furthermore,

It is neither ambition nor desire for fame,
nor the attainment of heaven nor kingship,
nor my own perpetual happiness that motivates me.
My sole concern is to benefit others.

May I thus have the power 1.45
to destroy the suffering of the world
and also produce its happiness,
just as the sun dispels darkness and creates light.

dṛṣṭaḥ śruto 'nusmṛtim āgato vā
spṛṣṭaḥ kathā|yogam upāgato vā
sarva|prakāraṃ jagato hitāni
kuryām a|jasraṃ sukha|saṃhitāni.» [32]

evaṃ sa niścitya par'|ârtha|siddhyai
prāṇ'|âtyaye 'py āpatita|pramodaḥ
manāṃsi dhīrāṇy api devatānāṃ
vismāpayan svāṃ tanum utsasarja. [33]

atha sā vyāghrī tena Bodhisattvasya śarīra|nipāta|śabdena samutthāpita|kautūhal'|âmarṣā viramya sva|tanaya|vaiśas'|ôdyamāt tato nayane vicikṣepa. dṛṣṭv" âiva ca tad Bodhisattva|śarīram udgata|prāṇaṃ sahas" âbhisṛtya bhakṣayitum upacakrame.

atha sa tasya śiṣyo māṃsam an|āsādy' âiva pratinivṛttaḥ, «kutr' ôpādhyāya?» iti vilokayaṃs tad Bodhisattva|śarīram udgata|prāṇaṃ tayā vyāghra|yuvatyā bhakṣyamāṇaṃ dadarśa. sa tat|karm'|âtiśaya|vismayāt prativyūḍha|śoka|duḥkh'|āvegas tad|guṇ'|āśraya|bahu|mānam iv' ôdgirann idam ātma|gataṃ bruvāṇaḥ śobheta:

1.50 «aho day" âsya vyasan'|āture jane!
sva|saukhya|naiḥsaṅgyam aho Mah"|ātmanaḥ!
aho prakarṣaṃ gamitā sthitiḥ satām!
aho pareṣāṃ mṛditā yaśaḥ|śriyaḥ! [34]

Whether I am seen, heard, or remembered,
or become the stuff of stories from being encountered,
may I benefit the world in every way
and perpetually bring it happiness."

Making this resolution, he felt joy
at ending his life to benefit others
and hurled down his body,
astounding even the composed minds of the gods.

The thud made by the fall of the Bodhi·sattva's body aroused the curiosity and anger of the tigress. Delaying her impulse to butcher her young, she cast her eyes around her and when she caught sight of the Bodhi·sattva's lifeless body, she rushed forward suddenly and began to eat it.

The Bodhi·sattva's disciple then returned, having failed to obtain any meat. As he searched around for his teacher, he spotted the Bodhi·sattva's lifeless body being devoured by the tigress. The astonishment Ájita felt at his teacher's remarkable deed countered any shock of grief or sorrow. On the contrary, he seemed to gleam as he spoke the following words to himself, admiring the Bodhi·sattva's commitment to virtue:

"What compassion he has for those suffering misfortune! 1.50
How unattached the Great One is to his own happiness!
Through him the conduct of the good has reached its peak!
The fame and glory of his enemies have been crushed!

aho parākrāntam apeta|sādhvasaṃ
guṇ'|āśrayaṃ prema paraṃ vidarśitam!
aho namas|kāra|viśeṣa|pātratāṃ
prasahya nītā sva|guṇ'|â|tanus tanuḥ. [35]

nisarga|saumyasya vasuṃdharā|dhṛter
aho pareṣāṃ vyasaneṣv a|marṣitā!
aho madīyā gamitā prakāśatāṃ
khaṭuṅkatā vikrama|saṃpad" ânayā. [36]

anena nāthena sa|nāthatāṃ gataṃ
na śocitavyaṃ khalu sāṃprataṃ jagat
parājay'|āśaṅkita|jāta|saṃbhramo
dhruvaṃ viniśvāsa|paro 'dya Manmathaḥ. [37]

sarvathā namo 'stv asmai mahā|bhāgāya sarva|bhūta|śaraṇyāy' âti|vipula|kāruṇyāy' â|prameya|sattvāya bhūt'|ârtha|Bodhisattvāy' êti.»

1.55 atha sa tam arthaṃ sa|brahma|cāribhyo nivedayām āsa.

tat|karma|vismita|mukhair atha tasya śiṣyair
gandharva|yakṣa|bhujagais tri|daś'|âdhipaiś ca
māly'|âmbar'|ābharaṇa|candana|cūrṇa|varṣaiś
channā tad|asthi|vasu|dhā vasudhā babhūva. [38]

What supreme love he has shown,
brave, fearless, and founded on goodness!
His body, by no means slender in virtue,*
has instantly become a vessel of supreme veneration!

Gentle in generosity and sturdy as the earth,
how intolerant he is of the sorrows of others!
His accomplishment in bravery
reveals my own harsh qualities!

The world should never be commiserated
for gaining a protector such as him.
Desire surely sighs deeply on this day,
quivering with fear of defeat!

I pay homage in every manner to this illustrious being, a refuge for all living creatures, a source of immense compassion and boundless goodness, a true Bodhi·sattva."

Ájita then informed his fellow ascetics of what had 1.55
happened.

The pupils were astonished
by the Bodhi·sattva's deeds,
and with *gandhárvas*, *yakshas*,*
snakes and chief deities,
they strewed the earth
bearing the treasure of his bones
with showers of garlands, clothes,
ornaments and sandal powder.*

tad evaṃ, sarva|sattveṣv a|kāraṇa|parama|vatsala|svabhāvaḥ sarva|bhūt'|ātma|bhūtaḥ pūrva|janmasv api sa Bhagavān iti. Buddhe Bhagavati paraḥ prasādaḥ kāryaḥ.

«jāta|prasādaiś ca Buddhe Bhagavati prītir utpādayitavyā. evam āyatana|gato naḥ prasāda» ity evam apy upaneyam. tathā sat|kṛtya Dharmaḥ śrotavyaḥ. evaṃ duṣ|kara|śata|samudānītatvāt karuṇā|varṇe 'pi vācyam: «evaṃ svabhāv'|âtiśaya|niṣpādikā par'|ânugraha|pravṛtti|hetuḥ karuṇ"» êti.

So it is that, even in his previous births, the Lord naturally felt a spontaneous and immense affection for all creatures, identifying himself with every living being. One should therefore show the highest devotion toward the Lord Buddha.

One should also draw the following conclusion: "Alongside feelings of faith, one should generate joy in the Lord Buddha. For this will give foundation to our devotion." Similarly one should listen to the Teaching* with respect. For it is has been delivered to us through hundreds of such difficult deeds. And one should also narrate this story when praising compassion, saying: "Compassion thus produces an outstanding nature. For it motivates a person to favor others."

STORY 2

THE BIRTH-STORY OF SHIBI

2.1 Duṣ|kara|śata|samudānīto 'yam asmad|arthaṃ tena Bhagavatā Sad|Dharma, iti sat|kṛtya śrotavyaḥ.

tad|yath" ânuśrūyate.

Bodhisattva|bhūtaḥ kil' âyaṃ Bhagavān a|parimita|kāl'|âbhyāsāt sātmī|bhūt'|ôpacita|puṇya|karmā kadā cic Chibīnāṃ rājā babhūva.

sa bālyāt prabhṛty eva vṛddh'|ôpāsana|ratir vinay'|ânurakto 'nurakta|prakṛtiḥ prakṛti|medhāvitvād an|eka|vidy"|âdhigama|vimalatara|matir utsāha|mantra|prabhāva|śakti|daiva|saṃpannaḥ svā iva prajāḥ prajāḥ pālayati sma.

2.5 tasmiṃs tri|varg'|ânuguṇā guṇ'|âughāḥ
saṃharṣa|yogād iva saṃniviṣṭāḥ
samasta|rūpā vibabhur na c' āsur
virodha|saṃkṣobha|vipanna|śobhāḥ. [1]

viḍamban" êv' â|vinay'|ôddhatānāṃ
dur|medhasām āpad iv' âtikaṣṭā
alp'|ātmanāṃ yā madir" êva lakṣmīr
babhūva sā tatra yath"|ârtha|nāmā. [2]

udāra|bhāvāt karuṇā|guṇāc ca
vitt'|âdhipatyāc ca sa rāja|varyaḥ
reme 'rthinām īpsita|siddhi|harṣād
a|kliṣṭa|śobhāni mukhāni paśyan. [3]

THE LORD ACQUIRED the Good Teaching for us through hundreds of difficult feats. One should therefore listen to it reverently. 2.1

Tradition has handed down the following story.

When he was a Bodhi·sattva, the Lord once lived as king of the Shibis.* He acquired this position through an accumulation of pure deeds that had become ingrained in his nature by repeated practice over a limitless period of time.

From as early as his childhood, he delighted in serving his elders and took pleasure in self-discipline. Loved by his people, he applied his natural intelligence to purify his mind by studying various branches of knowledge. Blessed by fortune, he was endowed with energy, prudence, strength, and power, and protected his people as if they were his offspring.

Hordes of virtues suited to the three pursuits* 2.5
seemed to have joyfully set up camp in him,
glittering radiantly as a group,
their splendor unimpaired by clash or conflict.

Like a façade for those inflated with arrogance,
a terrible calamity for fools,
and a drug for the small-minded,
success was in him exactly what the word states.

His exalted nature, compassion, and wealth
made him an exemplary king
who delighted at seeing beggars' faces
gleam brightly with joy on receiving their desire.

atha sa rājā dāna|priyatvāt samantato nagarasya sarv'|ôpakaraṇa|dhana|dhānya|samṛddhā dāna|śālāḥ kārayitvā sva|māhātmy'|ânurūpaṃ yath"|âbhiprāya|saṃpāditaṃ s'|ôpacāra|manoharam an|atikrānta|kāla|su|bhagaṃ dāna|varṣaṃ Kṛta|yuga|megha iva vavarṣa. annam ann'|ârthibhyaḥ, pānaṃ pān'|ârthibhyaḥ, śayan'|āsana|vasana|bhojana|gandha|mālya|suvarṇa|rajat'|ādi† tat|tad|arthibhyaḥ.

atha tasya rājñaḥ pradān'|āudārya|śravaṇād vismita|pramudita|hṛdayā nānā|dig|abhilakṣita|deśa|nivāsinaḥ puruṣās taṃ deśam abhijagmuḥ.

2.10 parītya kṛtsnaṃ manasā nṛ|lokam
anyeṣv a|labdha|praṇay'|âvakāśāḥ
tam arthinaḥ prīti|mukhāḥ samīyur
mahā|hradaṃ vanya|gajā yath" âiva. [4]

atha sa rājā samantataḥ samāpatato lābh'|āśā|pramudita|manasaḥ pathika|nepathya|pracchādita|śobhasya vanīpaka|janasya,

viproṣitasy' êva suhṛj|janasya
saṃdarśanāt prīti|vijṛmbhit'|âkṣaḥ
yācñāṃ priy'|ākhyānam iv' âbhyanandad
dattvā ca tuṣṭy" ârthi|janaṃ jigāya. [5]

In his love of giving, the king had alms halls built throughout the city, abounding with wealth, grain, and every type of provision. In keeping with his magnanimous nature, he would rain down showers of gifts, as if he were a cloud in the Krita Era.* Given promptly and with charming deference, the generous gifts satisfied everyone's desire. Food was given to those who asked for food, water to those who asked for water, and beds, seats, lodgings, meals, perfumes, garlands, gold, silver, and other objects to whoever requested them.

Men from various regions and well-known countries came to the king's realm, the news of his liberal nature filling their hearts with astonishment and joy.

Even surveying the entire world with their minds, 2.10
they could find no others to give scope to
    their requests.
So the petitioners approached the king with
    joyful faces,
like forest elephants approaching a large lake.

Joyful at the prospect of gain, a crowd of beggars swarmed around the king on all sides, their traveling clothes concealing their fineries.

Seeing them made the king's eyes widen with joy,
as if a band of friends had returned from abroad.
Their requests delighted him like welcome messages.
His gifts made him happier than the beggars
    themselves.

dān'|ôdbhavaḥ kīrti|mayaḥ sa gandhas
tasy' ârthināṃ vāg|anila|prakīrṇaḥ
madaṃ jahār' ânya|nar'|âdhipānāṃ
gandha|dvipasy' êva para|dvipānām. [6]

atha kadā cit sa rājā dāna|śālāḥ samanuvicaraṃs tṛptatvād arthi|janasya praviralaṃ yācanaka|jana|saṃpātam abhisamīkṣya dāna|dharmasy' ân|utsarpaṇān na tuṣṭim upajagāma.

2.15 tarṣaṃ vininye 'rthi|janas tam etya,
na tv arthinaḥ prāpya sa dāna|śauṇḍaḥ.
na hy asya dāna|vyavasāyam arthī
yācñā|pramāṇena śaśāka jetum. [7]

tasya buddhir abhavat: «ati|sabhāgyās te sat|puruṣa|viśeṣā ye viśrambha|niryantraṇa|praṇayam arthibhiḥ sva|gātrāṇy api yācyante. mama punaḥ pratyākhyāna|rūkṣ'|âkṣara|vacana|saṃtarjita iv' ârthi|jano dhana|mātrake 'py a|pragalbha|praṇayaḥ saṃvṛtta» iti.

atha kṣit'|īśasya tam atyudāraṃ
gātreṣv api sveṣu nivṛtta|saṅgam
vijñāya dān'|āśrayiṇaṃ vitarkaṃ
pati|priyā str" îva mahī cakampe. [8]

atha Śakro dev'|êndraḥ kṣiti|tala|calanād ākampite vividha|ratna|prabh"|ôdbhāsini Sumerau parvata|rāje «kim idam» iti samutpatita|vitarkas tasya rājña imaṃ vitark'|

*His reputation for generosity was a fragrance
wafted about by the wind of the beggars' voices,
destroying the pride of other kings,
like a tusker's scent dispels the ichor of other elephants.

One day, while he was surveying his alms halls, the king noticed that the crowd of petitioners had greatly diminished because their needs had been satisfied and he felt disappointed that his virtuous practice of giving had been obstructed.

Though the petitioners were sated on reaching him, 2.15
he was not on receiving them, so intoxicated was he
with giving.
No beggar could quell the king's determination
to give,
whatever the size of their request.

The king then had this thought: "Great is the fortune of those eminently virtuous men who are entreated by beggars with confident and unrestrained requests for their very limbs! But to me petitioners only make meek requests for mere wealth, as if scared by harsh words of refusal."

Observing Shibi's lofty thought,
so dedicated to giving and unattached to his body,
the earth, herself under the king's rule,
trembled like a woman who loves her husband.

When the earth quaked, so Mount Suméru,* that king of mountains, also shook, glistening with the radiance of various gems. Stirred by the event, Shakra, the king of the gods, investigated its cause and when he realized the earthquake was produced by the king's extraordinary thought,

âtiśayaṃ dharaṇi|tala|calana|nimittam avetya vismay'|āvarjita|hṛdayaś cintām āpede:

«dān'|âtiharṣ'|ôddhata|mānasena
vitarkitaṃ kiṃ svid idaṃ nṛ|peṇa
ābadhya dāna|vyavasāya|kakṣyāṃ
sva|gātra|dāna|sthira|niścayena? [9]

2.20 tan mīmāṃsiṣye tāvad enam iti!»

atha tasya rājñaḥ pariṣadi niṣaṇṇasy' amātya|gaṇa|parivṛtasya samucitāyāṃ kṛtāyām arthi|janasya «kaḥ kim icchat'» îty āhvāna|ghoṣaṇāyām samudghāṭyamāneṣu koś'|âdhyakṣ'|âdhiṣṭhiteṣu maṇi|kanaka|rajata|dhana|nicayeṣu viśliṣyamāṇa|puṭāsu vividha|vasana|paripūrṇa|garbhāsu vastra|peḍāsu samupavartyamāneṣu vinīta|vividha|vāhana|skandha|pratiṣṭhita|yugeṣu vicitreṣu yāna|viśeṣeṣu,

pravṛtte 'rthi|jana|saṃpāte Śakro devānām indro vṛddham andhaṃ brāhmaṇa|rūpam abhinirmāya rājñaś cakṣuḥ|pathe prādur|abhavat. atha sa rājñā kāruṇya|maitrī|paribhāvitayā dhīra|prasanna|saumyayā pratyudgata iva pariṣvakta iva ca dṛṣṭyā «ken' ârtha» ity upanimantryamāṇaḥ kṣitip'|ânucarair nṛpati|samīpam upetya jay'|āśīr|vacana|puraḥsaraṃ rājānam ity uvāca:

«dūrād a|paśyan sthaviro 'bhyupetas
tvac|cakṣuṣo 'rthī, kṣitipa|pradhāna.
ek'|ēkṣaṇen' âpi hi, paṅkaj'|âkṣa,
gamyeta, lok'|âdhipa, loka|yātrā.» [10]

he pondered the matter the following way, his heart filled with wonder:

"What is this thought conceived by the king,
his mind elated by excessive joy in giving?
He has set the limit of his will to give
with the firm resolve to offer his limbs!

I will test him!" 2.20

At that time the king was seated in the assembly hall, surrounded by a troop of ministers. The customary announcement was made, inviting people to receive what they wanted. Under the supervision of the treasurer, heaps of jewels, gold, silver, and wealth were revealed. Baskets filled with various clothes were untied, while fine and colorful carriages were dragged forward, yoked to the necks of various trained animals.

There, among the assembled beggars, Shakra, the king of the gods, took on the form of an old blind brahmin, manifesting himself right before the king's eyes. The king looked at the brahmin with a gaze that seemed to advance forward and embrace him, so calm, tranquil, and gentle were his eyes and so suffused with compassion and friendliness. When the king's attendants asked him what he desired, the brahmin approached the king, greeted him with benedictions of victory, and said the following:

"I, an old man who cannot see, have come
from afar to beg for your eye, greatest of kings.
Lotus-eyed ruler of the people, one eye
suffices to conduct the affairs of the world."

atha Bodhisattvaḥ samabhilaṣita|mano|ratha|prasiddhyā paraṃ prīty|utsavam anubhavan, «kiṃ svid idaṃ satyam ev' ôktaṃ brāhmaṇena syād, uta vikalp'|âbhyāsān may" âivam upadhāritam?» iti jāta|pratyavamarśaś cakṣur|yācñā|priya|vacana|śravaṇa|tṛṣita|matis taṃ cakṣur|yācanakam uvāca:

2.25 «ken' ânuśiṣṭas tvam ih' âbhyupeto
māṃ yācituṃ, brāhmaṇa|mukhya, cakṣuḥ?
‹su|dus|tyajaṃ cakṣur› iti pravāda|
saṃbhāvanā kasya mayi vyatītā?» [11]

atha sa brāhmaṇa|veṣa|dhārī Śakras tasya rājña āśayaṃ viditv" ôvāca:

«Śakrasya, Śakra|pratim', ânuśiṣṭyā
tvāṃ yācituṃ cakṣur ih' āgato 'smi.
saṃbhāvanāṃ tasya mam' âpi c' āśāṃ
cakṣuḥ|pradānāt saphalī|kuruṣva.» [12]

atha sa rājā Śakra|saṃkīrtanān, «nūnam asya brāhmaṇasya bhavitrī devat"|ânubhāvād anena vidhinā cakṣuḥ|sampad» iti matvā pramoda|viśad'|âkṣaram enam uvāca:

«yen' âbhyupeto 'si manorathena,
tam eṣa te, brāhmaṇa, pūrayāmi.
ākāṅkṣamāṇāya mad ekam akṣi
dadāmi cakṣur|dvayam apy ahaṃ te! [13]

2.30 sa tvaṃ vibuddha|nayan'|ôtpala|śobhit'|āsyaḥ
saṃpaśyato vraja yath"|âbhimataṃ janasya
‹syāt kiṃ nu so 'yam uta n'› êti vicāra|dolā|
lolasya, ‹so 'yam› iti c' ôtthita|vismayasya.» [14]

The Bodhi·sattva felt the greatest joy at achieving his heart's desire. But he was unsure whether the brahmin's words were really true or whether he had imagined them because of habitually harboring them in his mind. Thirsting to hear this delightful request for his eye, he said to the petitioner:

"Who has ordered you to come here 2.25
to request my eye, eminent brahmin?
An eye is very difficult to give up.
Who assumes this axiom does not apply to me?"

Understanding the king's intent, Shakra made the following reply in his guise as a brahmin:

"Shakra told me to come here
to request your eye, Shakra-like king.
Give me your eye and fulfill
Shakra's high regard and my hopes."

At the mention of Shakra, the king thought: "It is surely through divine power that this brahmin will gain an eye," and addressed him with words that sparkled with joy:

"I will fulfill the desire
for which you visit me, brahmin.
Though you wish for one eye,
I will give you both!

Leave as you please, watched by the people, 2.30
open lotus-eyes adorning your face.
The people will sway with doubt as to whether it's you,
but feel wonder when they realize it is."

atha tasya rājño 'mātyāś cakṣuḥ|pradāna|vyavasāyam avetya sa|saṃbhram'|āvega|viṣāda|vyathita|manaso rājānam ūcuḥ:

«dān'|âti|harṣād a|nayam
a|samīkṣy' â|hit'|ôdayam
prasīda, deva, mā m" âivaṃ.
na cakṣur dātum arhasi. [15]

ekasy' ârthe dvi|jasy' âsya
mā naḥ sarvān parākṛthāḥ!
alaṃ śok'|âgninā dagdhuṃ
sukha|saṃvardhitāḥ prajāḥ. [16]

dhanāni lakṣmī|pratibodhanāni
śrīmanti ratnāni payasvinīr gāḥ
rathān vinīt'|âśva|yujaḥ prayaccha
mad'|ōrjita|śrī|lalitān dvi|pāṃś ca. [17]

2.35 samuccaran|nūpura|nisvanāni
śarat|payod'|âbhyadhika|dyutīni
gṛhāṇi sarva'|rtu|sukhāni dehi.
mā dāḥ sva|cakṣur, jagad|eka|cakṣuḥ. [18]

vimṛśyatām api ca tāvan, mahā|rāja:

anyadīyaṃ kathaṃ nāma
cakṣur anyatra yojyate?
atha daiva|prabhāvo 'yaṃ,
tvac|cakṣuḥ kim apekṣate? [19]

The royal ministers were worried, shocked, and distressed when they learned of the king's intention to give away his eyes and said to him:

"Your extreme joy in giving makes you
unable to see it is wrong and damaging.*
Please, Your Majesty, don't do this.
You should not give away your sight.

Do not cast all of us aside
for the sake of one brahmin!
Do not raise your people to be happy,
only to let them burn with sorrow's fire.

Offer fortune-bringing wealth,
glorious jewels, milk-giving cows,
chariots yoked with trained horses,
or fine, graceful elephants, proud in rut.

Give houses pleasant in every season, 2.35
echoing with the sound of tinkling anklets,
brighter than autumn clouds.
But don't give away your sight, you the world's
sole eye.

Your Majesty should also consider this:

How can one person's eye
be used by another?
If through divine intervention,
why is your eye needed?

api ca, deva,

cakṣuṣā kiṃ daridrasya par'|âbhyudaya|sākṣiṇā?
dhanam eva yato dehi, deva, mā sāhasaṃ kṛthāḥ.» [20]

2.40 atha sa rājā tān amātyān s'|ânunaya|madhur'|âkṣaram ity uvāca:

«a|dāne kurute buddhiṃ
‹dāsyām'› îty abhidhāya yaḥv
sa lobha|pāśaṃ prabhraṣṭam
ātmani pratimuñcati. [21]

‹dāsyām'› îti pratijñāya yo 'nyathā kurute manaḥ,
kārpaṇy'|â|niścita|mateḥ kaḥ syāt pāpataras tataḥ? [22]

sthirī|kṛty' ârthinām āśāṃ ‹dāsyām'› îti pratijñayā
visaṃvādana|rūkṣasya vacaso n' âsti niṣkrayaḥ. [23]

yad api c' ôktaṃ, ‹devat"|ânubhāvād eva cakṣur asya kiṃ na saṃbhavat'› îty atr' âpi śrūyatām:

2.45 n'|âika|kāraṇa|sādhyatvaṃ kāryāṇāṃ nanu dṛśyate.
kāraṇ'|ântara|sāpekṣaḥ syād daivo 'pi vidhir yataḥ. [24]

Besides, Your Majesty:

Why does this poor beggar need an eye?
To see the prosperity of others?
Just give him some money, Your Majesty,
and stop acting recklessly."

Addressing his ministers with courteous and gentle words, the king then replied: 2.40

"Those who decide not to give
when they have said they'll give,
place their neck in the noose of greed
after releasing themselves from it.

Who could be more wicked
than those who promise to give
but change their mind,
their resolve unsteadied by stinginess?

There is no acquittal for a person
who strengthens the hopes of beggars
by promising they'll give
and then cruelly breaks their word.

And as for your question as to why divine power alone cannot produce his eye, listen:

Endeavors are clearly accomplished 2.45
by a variety of factors.
Likewise even fate, though divine,
must rely on different means.

tan me dān'|âtiśaya|vighnāya vyāyantum n' arhanti bhavanta iti.»

amātyā ūcuḥ: «‹dhana|dhānya|ratn'|ādi devo dātum arhati, na sva|cakṣur› iti vijñāpitam asmābhiḥ. tan na devaṃ vayam a|tīrthe pratārayāmaḥ....»

rāj" ôvāca:

«yad eva yācyeta, tad eva dadyān.
n' ân|īpsitaṃ prīṇayat' îha dattam.
kim uhyamānasya jalena toyair?
dāsyāmy ataḥ prārthitam artham asmai.» [25]

2.50 atha tasya rājño rūḍhatara|viśrambha|praṇayaḥ sneh'|āvegād an|apekṣit'|ôpacāro 'mātya|mukhyas taṃ rājānam ity uvāca:

«mā tāvad bhoḥ!

yā n' âlpena tapaḥ|samādhi|vidhinā
saṃprāpyate kena cid,
yām āsādya ca bhūribhir makha|śataiḥ
kīrtiṃ divaṃ c' āpnuyāt,
saṃprāptām atipatya tāṃ nṛpatitāṃ
Śakra'|rddhi|vispardhinīṃ
kiṃ dṛṣṭvā nayane praditsati bhavān?
ko 'yaṃ kutastyo vidhiḥ? [26]

labdh'|âvakāśas tri|daśeṣu yajñaiḥ,
kīrtyā samantād avabhāsamānaḥ,
nar'|êndra|cūḍā|dyuti|rañjit'|âṅghriḥ
kiṃ lipsamāno nu dadāsi cakṣuḥ?» [27]

Do not therefore try to obstruct my exceptional gift."

The ministers replied: "We have only advised Your Majesty to give wealth, grain, jewels, and other such offerings rather than your own eyes. We are not trying to lure Your Majesty into vice."

The king answered:

"One should give what is requested.
An undesired gift brings no joy.
What use is water to one swept away by a river?
I shall therefore give this man his desire."

The chief minister, who was very close to the king and intimate with him, then disregarded courtesy in a rush of affection and said to the monarch: 2.50

"Stop, sir!

Kingship is acquired
through no small toil and dedication.
Taking hundreds of sacrifices to achieve,
it is the means for attaining fame and heaven.
Yet you discard it, though it lies in your grasp,
an asset vying with Shakra's power.
What insight impels you to give away your eyes?
What is this behavior? Where does it originate?

Gleaming with fame in every direction,
you have attained a place among gods through
sacrifice.
Your feet are tinged with the radiance of kings' crowns.
What will you gain by giving your eye?"

atha sa rājā tam amātyaṃ s'|ânunayam ity uvāca:

2.55 «n' âyaṃ yatnaḥ sārvabhaumatvam āptuṃ
n' âiva svargaṃ n' âpavargaṃ na kīrtim.
trātuṃ lokān ity ayaṃ tv ādaro me
yācñā|kleśo mā ca bhūd asya moghaḥ.» [28]

atha sa rājā nīl'|ôtpala|dala|rucira|kānti nayanam ekaṃ vaidya|paridṛṣṭena vidhinā śanakair a|kṣatam utpāṭya parayā prītyā cakṣur|yācanakāya prāyacchat. atha Śakro dev'|êndras tādṛśam ṛddhy|abhisaṃskāraṃ cakre yathā dadarśa sa rājā sa|parijanas tat tasya cakṣuś cakṣuḥ|sthāne pratiṣṭhitam. ath' ônmiṣit'|âika|cakṣuṣaṃ cakṣur|yācanakam abhisamīkṣya sa rājā parameṇa harṣeṇ' āpūryamāṇa|hṛdayo dvitīyam apy asmai nayanaṃ prāyacchat.

tataḥ sa rājā nayane pradāya
vipadma|padm'|ākara|tulya|vaktraḥ
paurair a|sādhāraṇa|tuṣṭir āsīt,
samagra|cakṣur dadṛśe dvi|jaś ca. [29]

antaḥ|pure 'tha manuj'|âdhipateḥ pure ca
śok'|âśrubhir vasumatī siṣice samantāt.
Śakras tu vismayam avāpa parāṃ ca tuṣṭiṃ
saṃbodhaye nṛ|pam a|kampya|matiṃ samīkṣya. [30]

atha Śakrasya vismay'|āvarjita|hṛdayasy' âitad ity abhavat:

The king politely replied to the minister:

"I do not strive to own the entire world, 2.55
nor to acquire heaven, liberation, or fame.
My sole concern is to save the world
and not nullify the trouble he takes for his request."

The king then ordered one of his eyes to be carefully removed, using proper medical procedure so that it remained undamaged. With immense joy he offered the beggar the eye, which gleamed with the beauty of a blue lotus petal. Shakra, the king of the gods, then performed an act of magic so that the king and his retinue perceived the eye to be fixed in the brahmin's socket. When he saw the beggar bearing this single open eye, the king's heart became filled with the greatest joy and he gave him the second eye too.

At the gift of his eyes, the king's face
resembled a lotus-pond empty of lotuses,
bearing a look of joy, unshared by his citizens.
The brahmin, however, was seen with eyes intact.

Throughout the palace and royal city,
the ground was sprinkled with tears of grief.
But Shakra felt astonishment and great joy
at seeing the king's unshakeable aspiration for
awakening.

His heart filled with wonder, Shakra then had this thought:

2.60 «aho dhṛtir! aho sattvam! aho sattva|hit'|âiṣitā!
pratyakṣam api karm' êdaṃ karot' îva vicāraṇām! [31]

tan n' âyam āścarya|sattvaś ciram imaṃ parikleśam anubhavitum arhati yataḥ prayatiṣye cakṣur asy' ôpāya|pradarśanād utpādayitum.»

atha tasya rājñaḥ kramāt saṃrūḍha|nayana|vraṇasy' âvagīta|pratanū|bhūt'|ântaḥpura|paura|jānapada|śokasya praviveka|kāmatvād udyāna|puṣkariṇyās tīre kusuma|bhār'|ānata|taru|vara|nicite mṛdu|surabhi|śiśira|sukha|pavane madhu|kara|gaṇ'|ôpakūjite paryaṅkeṇa niṣaṇṇasya Śakro dev'|êndraḥ purastāt prādur|abhavat. ka eṣa iti ca rājñā paryanuyukto 'bravīt:

«Śakro 'ham asmi dev'|êndras
tvat|samīpam upāgataḥ.» [32ab]

«svāgatam! ājñāpyatāṃ ken' ârtha!» iti sa upacāra|puraḥsaram ukto rājānaṃ punar uvāca:

2.65 «varaṃ vṛṇīṣva, rāja'|ṛṣe.
yad icchasi tad ucyatām.» [32cd]

atha sa rājā pradāna|samucitatvād an|abhyasta|yācñā|kārpaṇya|mārgo dhṛty" â|vismaya|śauṭīryam enam uvāca:

"What strength! What courage! 2.60
What desire to benefit living beings!
Though I see this feat with my own eyes,
I almost doubt it has occurred!

It is not right for a man of such astounding courage* to suffer this way for long. I will therefore strive to show him a way of restoring his eyesight."

The king's wounded eyes healed up in due course and the grief of the people in the palace, city, and countryside gradually lessened, becoming the topic of hackneyed songs. One day, in his fondness for solitude, the king was sitting cross-legged on the bank of a lotus-pond in a park. Fine trees bowed under the weight of blossoms; a gentle breeze blew, cool, fragrant, and soothing; and the area hummed with swarms of honey-making bees. While he sat there, Shakra, the king of the gods, appeared before the king. When asked who he was, the god replied:

"I am Shakra, king of the gods.
I have come to visit you."

"Welcome! Please tell me your need!" Addressed with such polite words, Shakra replied to the king:

"Choose a boon, royal seer. 2.65
Tell me whatever you desire."

The king was accustomed to giving and it was not his habit to tread the path of petitions and poverty. With composure, modesty, and humility, he replied with the following words:

«prabhūtaṃ me dhanaṃ, Śakra,
śaktimac ca mahad balam.
andha|bhāvāt tv idānīṃ me
mṛtyur ev' âbhirocate. [33]

kṛtv" âpi paryāpta|manorathānāṃ
prīti|prasād'|âdhika|locanāni
mukhāni paśyāmi na yācakānāṃ
yat, tena mṛtyur dayito mam', Êndra.» [34]

Śakra uvāca, «alam anena te vyavasāyena! sat|puruṣā ev' ēdṛśāny anuprāpnuvanti. api ca pṛcchāmi tāvad bhavantam:

2.70 imām avasthāṃ gamitasya yācakaiḥ
kathaṃ nu te saṃprati teṣu mānasam?
pracakṣva tat tāvad, alaṃ nigūhituṃ,
vrajec ca saṃpratyayanīyatāṃ yathā.» [35]

rāj" ôvāca, «ko 'yam asmān vikatthayitum atra|bhavato nirbandhaḥ? api ca, dev'|êndra, śrūyatām:

tad" âiva c' âitarhi ca yācakānāṃ
vacāṃsi yācñā|niyat'|âkṣarāṇi
āśīr|mayāṇ' îva mama priyāṇi
yathā, tath" ôdetu mam' âikam akṣi!» [36]

atha tasya rājñaḥ saty'|âdhiṣṭhāna|balāt puṇy'|ôpacaya|viśeṣāc ca vacana|samanantaram ev' êndra|nīla|śakal'|ākrānta|madhyam iva nīl'|ôtpala|dala|sadṛśam ekaṃ cakṣuḥ prādur|abhavat. prādur|bhūte ca tasmin nayan'|āścarye pramudita|manāḥ sa rājā punar api Śakram uvāca:

"My wealth is abundant,
my army powerful and great.
But blindness makes only death
attractive to me now.

Unable to see the faces of petitioners
gleam brightly with joyful serenity
at having their wishes fulfilled,
I have come to cherish death, Indra."

"Enough of such thoughts!" Shakra answered. "Only good men achieve what you have attained. Let me ask you this instead:

How can your mind still dwell on beggars 2.70
when they've brought you to this plight?
And then tell me, hiding nothing,
what conclusion your mind has reached."

"Why do you insist on making me boast?" the king asked. "Nevertheless, lord of the gods, listen to these words:

If both in the past and present,
the petitioning voices of beggars
have been as dear to me as blessings,
may one of my eyes arise!"

Because of the power of the king's affirmation of truth and because of his exceptional accumulation of merit, an eye appeared as soon as he uttered these words. It resembled the petal of a blue lotus and a piece of sapphire seemed to lie in its center. The king was filled with joy at the appearance of this miraculous eye and addressed Shakra once more:

«yaś c' âpi māṃ cakṣur ayācat' âikaṃ,
tasmai mudā dve nayane pradāya
prīty|utsav'|âik'|âgra|matir yath" āsaṃ,
dvitīyam apy akṣi tathā mam' âstu!» [37]

2.75 ath' âbhivyāhāra|samanantaram eva tasya rājño vispardhamānam iva tena nayanena dvitīyaṃ cakṣuḥ prādur|abhūt.

tataś cakampe sa|dharādharā dharā.
vyatītya velāṃ prasasāra sāgaraḥ.
prasakta|gambhīra|manojña|nisvanāḥ
prasasvanur dundubhayo div'|âukasām. [38]

prasāda|ramyaṃ dadṛśe vapur diśāṃ.
rarāja śuddhyā śarad' îva bhāskaraḥ.
paribhramac candana|cūrṇa|rañjitaṃ
papāta citraṃ kusumaṃ nabhas|talāt. [39]

samāyayur vismaya|phulla|locanā
div'|âukasas tatra sah'|âpsaro|gaṇāḥ.
vavau manojñ'|ātma|guṇaḥ samīraṇo.
manaḥsu harṣo jagatāṃ vyajṛmbhata. [40]

udīritā harṣa|parīta|mānasair
maha"|rddhibhir bhūta|gaṇaiḥ sa|vismayaiḥ
nṛ|pasya karm'|âtiśaya|stav'|āśrayāḥ
samantataḥ śuśruvire giraḥ śubhāḥ: [41]

2.80 «aho bat' audāryam! aho kṛpālutā!
viśuddhatā paśya yath" âsya cetasaḥ!
aho sva|saukhyeṣu nir|utsukā matir!
namo 'stu te 'tyadbhuta|dhairya|vikrama. [42]

"If, despite being asked for one eye,
I joyfully gave the brahmin two,
and if I solely felt delight and jubilation,
may I also receive a second eye!"

As soon as he said this, a second eye appeared to him, as if rivaling the first. 2.75

The earth and her mountains shook.
The ocean surged forward, breaking its shore.
Heavenly drums sounded,
continuous, deep, and charming.

In every direction the sky displayed a delightful clarity.
The sun shined with the purity of an autumn glow.
Flowers of various hues fell from the firmament,
floating around, tinged with sandal powder.

Gods gathered with troops of nymphs,
their eyes blooming with wonder.
A delightful breeze began to blow.
Joy expanded in the hearts of every being.

Filled with wonder and joy,
powerful spirits made auspicious utterances,
praising the king's superior deeds,
heard in every direction:

"What nobility! What compassion! 2.80
See the purity of his heart!
How indifferent his mind is to his happiness!
We pay homage to you, miracle of bravery and
courage!

sa|nāthatāṃ sādhu jagad gataṃ tvayā!
punar vibuddh'|ēkṣaṇa|paṅkaja|śriyā!
a|mogha|rūpā bata puṇya|saṃcayāś;
cirasya dharmeṇa khal' ūrjitaṃ jitam.» [43]

atha Śakraḥ «sādhu! sādhv!» ity enam abhisaṃrādhya punar uvāca:

«na no na vidito, rājaṃs, tava śuddh'|āśay'|āśayaḥ.
evaṃ tu pratidatte te may" ême nayane, nṛ|pa. [44]

samantād yojana|śataṃ śailair api tiras|kṛtam
draṣṭum a|vyāhatā śaktir bhaviṣyaty anayoś ca te.» [45]

2.85 ity uktvā Śakras tath" âiva c' ântardadhe.

atha Bodhisattvo vismaya|praharṣ'|āpūrṇa|manobhir manda|manda|nimeṣa|pravikasita|nayanair amātyair anuyātaiḥ pauraiś c' âbhivīkṣyamāṇo jay'|āśīr|vacana|puraḥsaraiś ca brāhmaṇair abhinandyamānaḥ pura|varam ucchrita|dhvaja|vicitra|patākaṃ pravitanyamān'|âbhyudaya|śobham abhigamya parṣadi niṣaṇṇaḥ sabhājan'|ârtham abhigatasy' âmātya|pramukhyasya† brāhmaṇa|vṛddha|paura|janasy' âivam ātm'|ôpanāyikaṃ dharmaṃ deśayām āsa:

How splendid the world has you as its protector!
Your glorious lotus-eyes have opened once more!
Stores of merit are not in vain.
For virtue in time wins through mightily."

Praising him with cries of "Excellent! Excellent!," Shakra addressed the king once more, saying:

"The purity of your mind
was not unknown to me, Your Majesty.
That is why, king,
I have given you back your eyes.

With these eyes
you will have unimpeded sight
for a hundred leagues on every side,
even when obstructed by rocks."

Saying this, Shakra disappeared at that very spot. 2.85

The Bodhi·sattva then proceeded to the palace, which was draped with raised banners and colorful flags, exhibiting a festive radiance. Hailed by brahmins with benedictions of victory, he was stared at by the townspeople and by the ministers who followed him, their eyes wide open and hardly blinking, their hearts filled with wonder and joy. Seated in the assembly hall, the king then delivered a teaching on the Truth, drawn from his own experiences, to a crowd of brahmins, elders, and citizens, headed by ministers who had gathered to do him honor:

«ko nāma loke śithil'|ādaraḥ syāt
kartuṃ dhanair arthi|jana|priyāṇi
divya|prabhāve nayane mam' ême
pradāna|puṇy'|ôpanate samīkṣya? [46]

an|eka|śail'|ântaritaṃ yojanānāṃ śatād api
a|dūra|sthita|vispaṣṭaṃ dṛśyaṃ paśyāmi sarvataḥ. [47]

par'|ânukampā|vinay'|âbhijātād
dānāt paraḥ ko 'bhyuday'|âbhyupāyaḥ,
yan mānuṣaṃ cakṣur ih' âiva dattvā
prāptaṃ may" â|mānuṣa|divya|cakṣuḥ. [48]

2.90 etad viditvā, Śibayaḥ, pradānair
bhogena c' ârthān saphalī|kurudhvam.
loke parasminn iha c' âiṣa panthāḥ
kīrti|pradhānasya sukh'|ôdayasya. [49]

dhanasya niḥ|sāra|laghoḥ sa sāro
yad dīyate loka|hit'|ônmukhena.
nidhānatāṃ yāti hi dīyamānam.
a|dīyamānaṃ nidhan'|âika|niṣṭham.» [50]

tad evaṃ, duṣ|kara|śata|samudānīto 'yam asmad|arthaṃ tena Bhagavatā Sad|Dharma, iti sat|kṛtya śrotavyaḥ.

"Who in this world would be lax
in favoring a beggar with wealth
when they see my eyes of divine power,
produced by the merit of giving?

I can see an object in any direction
as clearly as if it were near,
even when concealed by mountains
and a hundred leagues afar.

Giving arises from humility and compassion
for others.
What way of gaining prosperity is greater than this?
In this very life, after giving a human eye,
I have received a non-human, divine eye.

Knowing this, Shibis, make your wealth bear fruit 2.90
by giving gifts and enjoying the reward.
This is the path to fame and increased happiness
in both this world and the next.

Wealth itself is essenceless and trifling.
Its essence lies in being given by benefactors
of the world.
When given, it becomes a treasure.
When ungiven, it ends only in loss."

So it is that the Lord acquired the Good Teaching for us through hundreds of difficult feats. One should therefore listen to it reverently.

Tathāgata|māhātmye pūrvavac ca karuṇā|varṇe 'pi vācyam ih' âiva puṇya|phala|pradarśane c': «âivaṃ sat|kṛty' ôpacitāni puṇyān' îh' âiva puṣpa|mātram ātma|prabhāvasya kīrti|saṃtati|mano|haraṃ pradarśayant'» îti.

One should also narrate this story when discussing the Tatha·gata's magnanimity,* or when praising compassion as in the previous story, or when illustrating the rewards that arise in this life from pure deeds, saying: "In this way, the merit accumulated through good actions reveals, in this very life, the mere bud of its power through the captivating reward of uninterrupted fame."

STORY 3

THE BIRTH-STORY ON THE LUMP OF GRUEL

3.1 CITTA|PRASĀD’|ÔDGATAṂ pātr’|âtiśaya|pratipāditaṃ ca n’ âlpakaṃ nāma dānam asti vipāka|mahattvāt.

tad|yath” ânuśrūyate.

Bodhisattva|bhūtaḥ kil’ âyaṃ Bhagavān Kośal’|âdhi|patir babhūva. tasy’ ôtsāha|mantra|prabhāva|śakti|saṃpat|prabhṛtīnāṃ prakarṣiṇām api rāja|guṇānāṃ vibhūtim atiśiśye daiva|saṃpad|guṇa|śobhā.

guṇās tasy’ âdhikaṃ rejur daiva|saṃpad|vibhūṣaṇāḥ,
kiraṇā iva candrasya śarad|unmīlita|śriyaḥ. [1]

3.5 tatyāja dṛptān api tasya śatrūn
rakt” êva reme tad|apāśriteṣu
ity āsa tasy’ ânya|nar’|âdhipeṣu
kopa|prasād’|ânuvidhāyinī Śrīḥ. [2]

dharm’|ātmakatvān na ca nāma tasya
par’|ôpatāp’|â|śivam āsa cetaḥ.
bhṛty’|ânurāgas tu tathā jajṛmbhe
dviṣatsu Lakṣmīr na yath” âsya reme. [3]

so ’n|antar’|âtītāṃ svāṃ jātim anusasmāra. tad|anusmaraṇāc ca samupajāta|saṃvego viśeṣavattaraṃ śramaṇa|brāhmaṇa|kṛpaṇa|vanīpakebhyaḥ sukha|hetu|nidānaṃ dānam adāt. śīla|saṃvaram c’ ân|avaraṃ poṣadha|niyamaṃ ca parva|divaseṣu samādade. abhīkṣṇaṃ ca rāja|parṣadi svasmiṃś c’ ântaḥ|pure puṇya|prabhāv’|ôdbhāvanāl lokaṃ

Due to the greatness of the reward, no gift is small when offered to a superior recipient with a faithful mind. 3.1

Tradition has handed down the following story.

When he was a Bodhi·sattva, our Lord is said to have ruled over Kóshala. The splendor of his godlike perfection surpassed even his abundant royal qualities, distinguished though they were, including accomplishments in vigor, guidance, strength, and power.

Adorned by godlike perfection,
his virtues radiated even more,
just as autumn enhances
the splendor of moonbeams.

Fortune belonged to him but to other kings 3.5
she dispensed both anger and favor.
Abandoning his enemies, proud though they were,
she was like an affectionate lover to his subjects.

As virtue was inherent in his nature,
he had no cruel thoughts at the torment of his foes.
But so expansive was the devotion of his subjects
that Prosperity displayed no love for his enemies.

One day the king recalled his preceding birth. When he remembered it, he became alarmed* and offered up even more exceptional gifts, gratifying ascetics, brahmins, paupers, and beggars. In addition to practicing the noble moral restraints, he undertook the *póshadha* discipline on the days marking the junctures of the moon.* And in his desire to impel the world toward goodness by demonstrating the

śreyasi niyoktu|kāmaḥ pratīta|hṛdayo gāthā|dvayam iti niyat'|ârthaṃ babhāṣe:

«na Sugata|paricaryā
vidyate sv|alpik" âpi
pratanu|phala|vibhūtir....
yac chrutaṃ kevalaṃ prāk
tad idam a|lavaṇāyāḥ
śuṣka|rūkṣ'|âruṇāyāḥ
phala|vibhava|mahattvaṃ
paśya kulmāṣa|piṇḍyāḥ! [4]

ratha|turaga|vicitraṃ
matta|nāg'|êndra|līlaṃ
balam a|kṛśam idaṃ me,
medinī kevalā ca,
bahu dhanam, anuraktā
śrīr, udārāś ca dārāḥ,
phala|samudaya|śobhāṃ
paśya kulmāṣa|piṇḍyāḥ!» [5]

3.10 tam amātyā brāhmaṇa|vṛddhāḥ paura|mukhyāś ca kautūhal'|āpūrṇa|manaso 'pi na prasahante sma paryanuyoktuṃ kim abhisamīkṣya mahā|rājo gāthā|dvayam idam abhīkṣṇaṃ bhāṣata iti. atha tasya rājño vāllabhyād a|vyāhatatara|viśrambha|praṇaya|prasādā devī samutpanna|kautūhalā saṃkathā|prastāv'|āgataṃ parṣadi paryapṛcchad enam:

«niyatam iti, nar'|êndra, bhāṣase
hṛdaya|gatāṃ mudam udgirann iva.
bhavati mama kutūhal'|ākulaṃ
hṛdayam idaṃ kathitena tena te. [6]

power of pure action, he would repeatedly and earnestly utter two verses, with a devout heart, in both the royal assembly and palace:

"Even minute service to a Buddha brings great fruit.
See what previously has only been heard!
Here is the great and abundant reward
of a lump of unsalted, dry, coarse, and brown gruel!

My mighty army, gleaming with chariots and horses,
swaying with lordly elephants in rut; the entire earth;
my great wealth; Fortune's devotion; and a noble wife.
See the splendid fruits arising from a lump of gruel!"

Though their minds were filled with curiosity, neither 3.10
the ministers, nor the brahmin elders, nor the chief citizens ventured to ask what insight had led the great king to utter these two verses repeatedly. But the queen, being the king's favorite, was graced by an intimacy and affection that was less constrained. And so, her curiosity aroused, she questioned the king in the assembly when a favorable opportunity for conversation arose:

"You constantly recite these verses,
as if expressing a heartfelt joy, lord of men.
I am filled with curiosity
at the words you speak.

tad arhati śrotum ayaṃ jano yadi,
pracakṣva tat kiṃ nv iti bhāṣase, nṛ|pa.
rahasyam evaṃ ca na kīrtyate kva cit
prakāśam asmāc ca may" âpi pṛcchyate.» [7]

atha sa rājā prīty|ati|snigdhayā† dṛṣṭyā samavekṣya devīṃ smita|pravikasita|vadana uvāca:

«a|vibhāvya|nimitt'|ârthaṃ
śrutv" ôdgāram imaṃ mama
na kevalaṃ tav' âiv' âtra
kautūhala|calaṃ manaḥ. [8]

3.15 samagram apy etad amātya|maṇḍalaṃ
kutūhal'|āghūrṇita|lola|mānasam,
puraṃ ca s'|ântaḥ|puram atra; tena me
niśamyatāṃ yena may" âivam ucyate. [9]

svapna|prabuddha iva jātim anusmarāmi
yasyām ih' âiva nagare bhṛtako 'ham āsam.
śīl'|ânvito 'pi dhana|mātra|samucchritebhyaḥ
karm'|âbhirādhana|samārjita|dīna|vṛttiḥ. [10]

so 'haṃ bhṛtiṃ paribhava|śrama|dainya|śālāṃ
trāṇ'|āśayā svayam a|vṛtti|bhayād vivikṣuḥ
bhikṣ"|ârthinaś ca caturaḥ śramaṇān apaśyam
vaśy'|êndriyān anugatān iva bhikṣu|lakṣmyā. [11]

If I am worthy of hearing it,
explain, king, why you utter these words.
A secret is not proclaimed everywhere like this.
That is why I ask you so openly."

Looking at his queen with immense loving affection, the king's face spread open with a smile as he said:

"Yours is not the only mind
to stir with curiosity
at hearing me utter
these unclarified words.

This entire circle of ministers 3.15
rocks and sways with curiosity,
as does the city and palace.
Learn then the reason for my words.

As if waking from a dream, I recall a past life
when I worked as a hired laborer in this same city.
Though a decent man, I earned a paltry living,
working for people elevated merely by wealth.

Desperate for an escape, afraid of poverty,
I was to start a job, that home of disgrace, toil,
and woe,
when I saw four ascetics begging alms, senses
controlled,
trailed, it seemed, by the glory of monkhood.

tebhyaḥ prasāda|mṛdunā manasā praṇamya
kulmāṣa|mātrakam adāṃ prayataḥ sva|gehe.
tasy' âṅkur'|ôdaya iv' âiṣa yad anya|rāja|
cūḍā|prabhāś caraṇa|reṇuṣu me niṣiktāḥ. [12]

tad etad abhisaṃdhāya may" âivaṃ, devi, kathyate
puṇyair na ca labhe tṛptim arhatāṃ darśanena ca. [13]

3.20 atha devī praharṣa|vismaya|viśālatar'|âkṣī sa|bahu|mānam udīkṣamāṇā rājānam uvāca:

«upapanna|rūpaḥ puṇyānām ayam evaṃ|vidho vipāk'|âbhyudaya|viśeṣaḥ. puṇya|phala|pratyakṣiṇaś ca mahā|rājasya yad ayaṃ puṇyeṣv ādaraḥ. tad evam eva pāpa|pravṛtti|vimukhaḥ pit" êva prajānāṃ samyak|paripālana|su|mukhaḥ puṇya|guṇ'|ârjan'|âbhimukhaḥ.

yaśaḥ|śriyā dāna|samṛddhayā jvalan
pratiṣṭhit'|ājñaḥ pratirāja|mūrdhasu
samīraṇ'|ākuñcita|sāgar'|âmbarāṃ
ciraṃ mahīṃ dharma|nayena pālaya!» [14]

rāj" ôvāca, «kiṃ hy etad, devi, na syāt?

so 'haṃ tam eva punar āśrayituṃ yatiṣye
śreyaḥ|pathaṃ samabhilakṣita|ramya|cihnam.
lokaḥ praditsati hi dāna|phalaṃ niśamya.
dāsyāmy ahaṃ kim iti n' ātma|gataṃ niśāmya?» [15]

My mind softened by faith, I bowed,
devoutly giving them a mere lump of gruel
in my house.
That seed has sprouted and rival kings now spread
the glow of their crowns on the dust of my feet.

This, my queen, is the reason
I recite these verses
and am never sated by pure deeds
or by seeing *arhat*s."*

The queen's eyes widened with joy and amazement. Looking at the king reverently, she said: 3.20

"This exceptional reward is in keeping with your pure actions. Your Majesty's regard for merit surely derives from witnessing the fruit of your own good deeds. That is why you turn your back on wicked conduct and focus instead on acquiring merit and virtue, earnestly protecting your people, just as a father protects his children.

Blazing with a fame and glory enriched by giving,
may you firmly rule over the heads of rival kings!
Through just policies may you long protect the earth,
its ocean a blanket wrinkled by the wind!"

"Why should it not be so, my queen?" the king replied.

"I will strive again to tread the path to felicity,
its delightful signposts conspicuously marked.
The world will give when it sees the fruit of giving.
How can I not give when I see it in myself?"

3.25 atha sa rājā devīṃ devīm iva śriyā jvalantīm ati|snigdham avekṣya śrī|saṃpatti|hetu|kutūhala|hṛdayaḥ punar uvāca:

«candra|lekh" êva tārāṇāṃ
strīṇāṃ madhye virājase.
akṛthāḥ kiṃ nu, kalyāṇi,
karm' âti|madhur'|ôdayam?» [16]

devy uvāca, «asti, deva, kiṃ cid. aham api pūrva|janma| vṛttaṃ anusmarām'» îti. «kathaya! kathay' êdānīm!» iti ca s'|ādaraṃ rājñā paryanuyukt" ôvāca:

«bālye 'nubhūtam iva tat samanusmarāmi.
dāsī satī yad aham uddhṛta|bhaktam ekam
kṣīṇ'|āsravāya munaye vinayena dattvā
supt" êva tatra samavāpam iha prabodham. [17]

etat smarāmi kuśalaṃ, nara|deva, yena
tvan|nāthatām upagat" âsmi samaṃ pṛthivyā.
‹kṣīṇ'|āsraveṣu na kṛtaṃ tanu nāma kiṃ cid›
ity uktavān asi yath" âiva munis tath" âiva.» [18]

3.30 atha sa rājā puṇya|phala|pradarśanāt puṇyeṣu samutpādita|bahu|mānām abhiprasanna|manasaṃ pariṣadaṃ vismay'| âik'|âgrām avetya niyatam īdṛśaṃ kiṃ cit samanuśaśāsa:

As he gazed at his queen with immense affection, the king noticed that she was blazing with a god-like splendor. Curious as to the cause of her glorious beauty, he addressed her once more, saying: 3.25

"You gleam brightly among women,
like the crescent moon among stars.
What have you done, lovely queen,
to produce this sweet reward?"

"There is a reason, Your Majesty," the queen answered. "I too remember an event in a previous birth." "Tell me! Tell me now!" the king earnestly requested her. To which she replied:

"I remember it as if it were a childhood experience.
A slave-girl, I respectfully gave a ladle of food
to a sage who had destroyed his corruptions.*
It's as if I were sleeping there and have woken here.

I also recall, god among men, that this good deed
led to acquiring you as my lord to share with the earth.
That sage said the same thing as you: 'No deed done
for a person without corruptions can be called small.'"

Noticing how the assembly had become filled with devotion and utter astonishment, and how his illustration of the fruits of merit had aroused their respect for pure action, the king firmly addressed them with words somewhat as follows: 3.30

«alpasy' âpi śubhasya vistaram imaṃ
  dṛṣṭvā vipāka|śriyaḥ
syāt ko nāma na dāna|śīla|vidhinā
  puṇya|kriyā|tat|paraḥ?
n' âivaṃ draṣṭum api kṣamaḥ sa puruṣaḥ
  paryāpta|vitto 'pi san
yaḥ kārpaṇya|tamisray" āvṛta|matir
  n' āpnoti dānair yaśaḥ. [19]

tyaktavyaṃ vivaśena yan na ca tathā
  kasmai cid arthāya yat
tan nyāyena dhanaṃ tyajan yadi guṇaṃ
  kaṃ cit samudbhāvayet.
ko 'sau tatra bhajeta matsara|pathaṃ
  jānan guṇānāṃ rasaṃ?
prīty|ādyā vividhāś ca kīrty|anusṛtā
  dāna|pratiṣṭhā guṇāḥ. [20]

dānaṃ nāma mahā|nidhānam anugaṃ
  caur'|ādy|a|sādhāraṇaṃ.
dānaṃ matsara|lobha|doṣa|rajasaḥ
  prakṣālanaṃ cetasaḥ.
saṃsār'|âdhva|pariśram'|âpanayanaṃ
  dānaṃ sukhaṃ vāhanaṃ.
dānaṃ n'|âika|sukh'|ôpadhāna|su|mukhaṃ
  san|mitram ātyantikam. [21]

vibhava|samudayaṃ vā dīptam ājñā|guṇaṃ vā
  tri|daśa|pura|nivāsaṃ rūpa|śobhā|guṇaṃ vā
yad abhilaṣati sarvaṃ tat samāpnoti dānād.
  iti parigaṇit'|ârthaḥ ko na dānāni dadyāt? [22]

"Who would not be devoted to pure action
through the moral practice of giving,
if they see the extent of the glorious reward
of even a small good deed?
It is not worth even glancing
at those who, though wealthy,
fail to gain a reputation for giving,
enveloped by the darkness of stinginess.

Wealth must one day be left behind
and then it is of no use.
By giving up one's wealth correctly,
one produces a kind of asset.
Who would walk the path of selfishness
if they knew how virtues taste?
For joy and many other virtues are
based on giving and followed by fame.

Giving is a companion and mighty treasure,
unshared by villains such as thieves.
Giving cleanses the mind of the dust
caused by the evils of selfishness and greed.
Giving is a comfortable vehicle,
dispelling the toils of journeying through samsara.
Giving is a good and constant friend,
dedicated to providing various felicities.

Through giving one attains every desire:
a mass of wealth, a blazing position of command,
residence in the city of gods, or splendid beauty.
Who would not offer gifts if they contemplate this?

3.35 sār'|ādānaṃ dānam āhur dhanānām.
aiśvaryāṇāṃ dānam āhur nidānam.
dānaṃ śrīmat sajjanatv'|âvadānaṃ.
n'|âlpa|prajñaiḥ pāṃsu|dānaṃ su|dānam.» [23]

atha sā parṣat tasya rājñas tad|grāhakaṃ vacanaṃ sa|bahumānam abhinandya pradān'|ādi|pratipatty|abhimukhī babhūva.

tad evaṃ, citta|prasād'|ôdgataṃ pātr'|âtiśaya|pratipāditaṃ ca n' âlpakaṃ nāma dānam asti vipāka|mahattvād.

iti prasanna|citten' ân|uttare puṇya|kṣetra Ārya|Saṅghe dānaṃ dadatā parā prītir utpādyā: «a|dūre mam' âpy evaṃ|vidhā ato viśiṣṭatarāś ca sampattaya» iti.

Giving, they say, extracts the essence out of wealth. 3.35
Giving, they say, is the basis of sovereignty.
Giving is the glorious conduct of the virtuous.
Even a gift of dust is good when offered by the wise."

Filled with joy and reverence at the king's persuasive words, the assembly became intent on practicing giving and other virtues.

So it is that, due to the greatness of the reward, no gift is small when offered to a superior recipient with a faithful mind.

Those with devout hearts should thus feel the greatest joy at giving a gift to the Community of Nobles,* that unrivalled field of merit, thinking: "I will soon receive rewards such as these and even greater ones too."

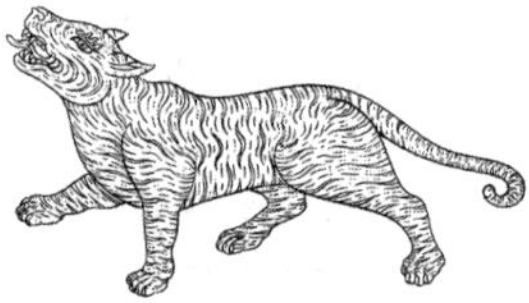

STORY 4

THE BIRTH-STORY OF THE MERCHANT

4.1 ATYAYAM APY A|VIGAṆAYYA ditsanti sat|puruṣāḥ. kena nāma svasthena na dātavyaṃ syāt? tad|yath" ânuśrūyate.

Bodhisattva|bhūtaḥ kil' âyaṃ Bhagavān bhāgy'|âtiśaya|guṇād utthāna|saṃpadā c' âdhigata|vipula|dhana|samṛddhir a|viṣama|vyavahāra|śīlatvāl loka|bahu|māna|niketa|bhūta udār'|âbhijanavān an|eka|vidyā|kalā|vikalp'|âdhigama|vimalatara|matir guṇa|māhātmyād rājñā samupahṛta|saṃmānaḥ pradāna|śīlatvāl loka|sādhāraṇa|vibhavaḥ śreṣṭhī babhūva.

arthibhiḥ prīta|hṛdayaiḥ kīrtyamānam itas tataḥ
tyāga|śaury'|ônnataṃ nāma tasya vyāpa diśo daśa. [1]

4.5 «dadyān, na dadyād» iti tatra n' āsīd
vicāra|dolā|cala|mānaso 'rthī.
khyāt'|âvadāne hi babhūva tasmin
viśrambha|dhṛṣṭa|praṇayo 'rthi|vargaḥ. [2]

n' âsau jugop' ātma|sukh'|ârtham arthaṃ,
na spardhayā lobha|parābhavād vā.
sa tv arthi|duḥkhaṃ na śaśāka soḍhuṃ
«n' âst'» îti vaktuṃ ca tato jugopa. [3]

atha kadā cit tasya Mahā|sattvasya bhojana|kāle snāt'|ânuliptasya kuśala|sūd'|ôpakalpite samupasthite varṇa|gandha|rasa|sparś'|ādi|guṇa|samudite vicitre bhakṣya|bhojy'|

GOOD MEN DISREGARD even peril so as to give. Who then would not give if they are in a situation that is safe? 4.1

Tradition has handed down the following story.

When he was a Bodhi·sattva, the Lord is said to have been a merchant. Due to his exceptional good fortune and dynamic nature, he had acquired an abundance of wealth and riches. Respected by people for the integrity of his fair business practices, he descended from an eminent family and his mind was greatly purified by studying a diverse range of sciences and arts. His virtuous magnanimity earned him the respect of his king and he shared his wealth with the world through his moral practice of giving.

Elevated by his heroic giving,
his name pervaded the ten directions,
proclaimed here and there
by petitioners with joyful hearts.

No beggar swayed with doubt 4.5
as to whether he would give.
A crowd of petitioners made confident requests,
trusting that man of renowned deeds.

He never guarded wealth for his own pleasure,
nor to rival others, nor because overcome by greed.
Unable to endure the hardships of beggars,
he guarded only against making refusals.

One day, when it was meal time and the Great Being* had washed and oiled himself, various hard and soft foods were placed before him. Prepared by an expert cook, the meal boasted fine colors, fragrances, tastes, and textures. A

ādi | vidhau tat | puṇya | saṃbhāra | vivṛddhi | kāmo jñān' | âgni | nirdagdha | sarva | kleś' | êndhanaḥ pratyeka | buddhas tad | gṛham abhijagāma bhikṣ" | ârthī. samupetya ca dvāra | koṣṭhake vyatiṣṭhata.

a|śaṅkit'|â|cañcala|dhīra|saumyam
 avekṣamāṇo yuga|mātram urvyāḥ
tatr' âvatasthe praśam'|âbhijātaḥ
 sa pātra|saṃsakta|kar'|âgra|padmaḥ. [4]

atha Māraḥ pāpīyān Bodhisattvasya tāṃ dāna|saṃpadam a | mṛṣyamāṇas tad | vighn' | ârtham antarā ca taṃ bhadantam antarā ca dvāra | dehalīṃ jvālā | karāl' | ôdaram an | eka | pauruṣam ati|gambhīraṃ bhayānaka|darśanaṃ pratibhaya| nirghoṣaṃ narakam abhinirmame visphuradbhir an | ekair jana|śatair ācitam.

4.10 atha Bodhisattvaḥ pratyeka | buddhaṃ bhikṣ" | ârthinam abhigatam ālokya patnīm uvāca: «bhadre, svayam āryāya piṇḍapātaṃ deh'» îti. sā «tath"» êty asmai pratiśrutya praṇītaṃ bhakṣya|bhojyam ādāya prasthitā. narakam ālokya dvāra | samīpād bhaya | viṣāda | cañcal' | âkṣī sahasā nyavartata. «kim etad?» iti ca bhartrā paryanuyuktā samāpatita|sādhvas'| āpihita|kaṇṭhī tat kathaṃ cid asya kathayām āsa.

atha Bodhisattvaḥ «katham ayam āryo mad | gṛhād an | avāpta|bhikṣa eva pratiyāsyat'» îti sa|saṃbhramas tat tasyāḥ kathitam an|ādṛtya svayam eva praṇītaṃ bhakṣya|bhojyam ādāya tasya mah" | ātmanaḥ piṇḍa | pātaṃ pratipādayitu |

*pratyéka·buddha** then approached the Bodhi·sattva's house, seeking alms. The fire of his knowledge had burned away the fuel of all his defilements* and he stood at the merchant's door, eager to increase the Bodhi·sattva's store of merit.

Calm and unagitated, steady and mild,
looking ahead the distance of a yoke,
he stood there, noble with tranquility,
his lotus-fingers clutching a bowl.

But wicked Mara could not tolerate the Bodhi·sattva's success in giving. Aiming to obstruct him, he magically made a hell appear between the venerable monk and the threshold of the door. Extremely deep, the hell measured several men in breadth. Horrifying to look at and emitting terrible sounds, its belly gaped with flames and several hundred quivering people were piled up inside it.

When he spotted the *pratyéka·buddha* arriving to seek alms, the Bodhi·sattva told his wife to give almsfood to the noble monk. Obeying her husband, she took the selection of different fine foods and headed off. But on seeing the hell near the door, she immediately turned back, her eyes rolling with fear and despair. When her husband asked her what had happened, she could hardly tell him as her throat was choked with fear. 4.10

The Bodhi·sattva, however, was worried that the noble monk might leave his house without receiving alms. Paying no attention to what his wife had to tell him, he picked up the different fine foods himself and approached the doorway, eager to give the illustrious monk an alms-offering.

kāmo dvāra|koṣṭhaka|samīpam abhigatas tam ati|bhīṣaṇam antarā narakaṃ dadarśa. tasya «kiṃ svid idam?» iti samutpanna|vitarkasya Māraḥ pāpīyān bhavana|bhitter niṣpatya saṃdṛśyamāna|divy'|âdbhuta|vapur antarikṣe† sthitvā hita|kāma iva nām' âbravīt:

«gṛha|pate, Mahārauravo nām' âyaṃ mahā|narakaḥ.

arthi|praśaṃsā|vacana|pralubdhā
  hiṃsanti dāna|vyasanena ye 'rthān
śarat|sahasrāṇi bahūni teṣām
  asmin nivāso '|su|labha|pravāsaḥ. [5]

arthas tri|vargasya viśeṣa|hetus.
  tasmin hate kena hato na dharmaḥ?
dharmaṃ ca hatv" ârtha|nibarhaṇena
  kathaṃ nu na syān naraka|pratiṣṭhaḥ? [6]

4.15 dāna|prasaṅgena ca dharma|mūlaṃ
  ghnatā tvay" ârthaṃ yad akāri pāpam,
tvām attum abhyudgatam etad asmāj
  jvāl"|ôgra|jihvaṃ narak'|Ântak'|āsyam. [7]

tat sādhu dānād viniyaccha buddhim.
  evaṃ hi sadyaḥ patanaṃ na te syāt.
viceṣṭamānaiḥ karuṇaṃ rudadbhir
  mā dātṛbhir gāḥ samatām amībhiḥ. [8]

pratigrahītā tu jano 'bhyupaiti
  nivṛtta|dān'|âpanayaḥ suratvam.
tat svarga|mārg'|āvaraṇād viramya
  dān'|ôdyamāt saṃyamam āśrayasva.» [9]

There he saw the terrifying hell and while he was wondering what this phenomenon could be, wicked Mara flew out of the house-wall and stood in the air, displaying a divine and miraculous form. Feigning a desire to benefit the Bodhi·sattva, Mara then said:

"This great hell is called Maha·ráurava, householder.*

Here live those who, seduced by the flattery of beggars,
destroy their wealth through the evil of giving.
They stay here for thousands of autumns.
It is not easy for them to escape.

Wealth is the principal basis of the three pursuits.
When that is destroyed, how can morality survive?
If one destroys morality by crushing wealth,
how can one not take up a place in hell?

Your attachment to giving has destroyed 4.15
the root of morality, making you sin.
That's why this hell arises to devour you,
its face like Death, its tongue vicious with flames.

Please then restrain your mind from giving.
If you do, you will not now fall into hell.
Do not join these almsgivers,
who writhe with pitiful laments.

By abstaining from the vice of giving,
it is the receivers of gifts that attain divinity.
Practice restraint and cease this zeal for giving,
which obstructs the path to heaven."

atha Bodhisattvo «nūnam asy' âitad dur|ātmano mad|dāna|vighnāya viceṣṭitam» ity avagamya sva|sattv'|âvaṣṭambha|dhīra|vinaya|madhur'|âkṣar'|â|vicchedaṃ* niyatam ity avocad enam:

«asmadd|hit'|âvekṣaṇa|dakṣiṇena
vidarśito 'yaṃ bhavat" ārya|mārgaḥ.
yuktā viśeṣeṇa ca daivateṣu
par'|ânukampā|nipuṇā pravṛttiḥ. [10]

4.20 doṣ'|ôdayāt pūrvam an|antaraṃ vā
yuktaṃ tu tac|chānti|pathena gantum.
gate prayāmaṃ hy apacāra|doṣair
vyādhau cikitsā|praṇayo vighātaḥ. [11]

idaṃ ca dāna|vyasanaṃ madīyaṃ
śaṅke cikitsā|viṣaya|vyatītam.
tathā hy an|ādṛtya hit'|âiṣitāṃ te
na me manaḥ saṃkucati pradānāt. [12]

dānād a|dharmaṃ ca yad ūcivāṃs tvam
arthaṃ ca dharmasya viśeṣa|hetum,
tan mānuṣī n' êyam avaiti buddhir
dānād ṛte dharma|patho yath" ârthaḥ. [13]

nidhīyamānaḥ sa tu dharma|hetuś,
cauraiḥ prasahy' âtha vilupyamānaḥ,
ogh'|ôdar'|ântar|vinimagna|mūrtir,
hut'|âśanasy' âśanatāṃ gato vā? [14]

The Bodhi·sattva understood that the Evil One was clearly trying to obstruct his act of giving. He therefore firmly addressed Mara with words that were forceful with courage and resolve, but that never lost their modesty or charm:

"In your sincere concern for my welfare,
you have revealed the path of noble men.
It is especially apt that the gods are so skilled
in their compassion for others.

But an illness should be quelled 4.20
before it arises, or as soon as it appears.
If malpractice allows a disease to advance,
medicine is bound to have no effect.

I fear my present vice of giving
is beyond the scope of medicine.
Regardless of your desire for my welfare,
my heart cannot shrink from giving.

You say evil springs from giving
and profit is the principal cause of virtue.
But my human mind cannot understand
how wealth can be the path of virtue without giving.

Does wealth produce virtue when hoarded,
or when violently plundered by thieves,
or when it sinks into the belly of the ocean,
or when it becomes food for oblation-eating fire?

yac c' ârtha|dātā narakaṃ prayāti
pratigrahītā tu sur'|êndra|lokam,
vivardhitas tena ca me tvay" âyaṃ
dān'|ôdyamaḥ saṃyamayiṣyat" âpi. [15]

4.25 an|anyathā c' âstu vacas tav' êdaṃ
svargaṃ ca me yācanakā vrajantu!
dānaṃ hi me loka|hit'|ârtham iṣṭaṃ
n' êdaṃ sva|saukhy'|ôdaya|sādhanāya!» [16]

atha Māraḥ punar api Bodhisattvaṃ hit'|âiṣ" îva dhīra|hasten' ôvāca:

«hit'|ôktim etāṃ mama cāpalaṃ vā
samīkṣya yen' êcchasi tena gaccha.
sukh'|ânvito vā bahu|māna|pūrvaṃ
smart" âsi māṃ vipratisāravān vā.» [17]

Bodhisattva uvāca, «mārṣa, marṣayatu bhavān.

kāmaṃ patāmi narakaṃ sphurad|ugra|vahniṃ
jvāl"|âvalīḍha|śithil'|âvanatena mūrdhnā,
na tv arthināṃ praṇaya|darśita|sauhṛdānāṃ
saṃmāna|kālam avamānanayā hariṣye.» [18]

4.30 ity uktvā Bodhisattvaḥ sva|bhāgya|bal'|âvaṣṭabdho jānānaś ca nir|atyayatāṃ dānasya nivāraṇ'|âika|rasam avadhūya sva|jana|parijanaṃ sādhvas'|ân|abhibhūta|matir abhivṛddha|dān'|âbhilāṣo naraka|madhyena prāyāt.

You say donors go to hell
and recipients go to heaven.
But this only increases my zeal to give,
despite your wish to restrain me.

May your words prove true 4.25
and may my petitioners go to heaven!
For it is to benefit the world that I wish to give
and not to achieve my own happiness!"

Mara then once again firmly addressed the Bodhi·sattva, feigning concern for his well-being:

"Judge whether my words are beneficial
or unreliable. And then go as you please.
Whether happy or remorseful,
you will remember me with esteem."

"Don't take it badly, good sir," the Bodhi·sattva answered.

"I would gladly fall into a hell of violent blazing fire,
my flopped and hanging head licked by flames,
than incur contempt when honoring petitioners
who express their friendship through requests."

Saying these words, the Bodhi·sattva remained sure that 4.30
his giving was not wrong and, with a mind unafflicted by fear and his desire for giving increased still further, he brushed aside his family and retinue, who were intent on restraining him, and proceeded into the middle of the hell, secure in the strength of his good fortune.

puṇy'|ânubhāvād atha tasya tasminn
a|paṅka|jaṃ paṅkajam udbabhūva,
avajñay" êv' âvajahāsa Māraṃ
yac chuklayā kesara|danta|paṅktyā. [19]

atha Bodhisattvaḥ padma|saṃkrameṇa sva|puṇy'|âtiśaya| nirjāten' âbhigamya pratyeka|buddhaṃ prasāda|saṃharṣ'| āpūrṇa|hṛdayaḥ piṇḍa|pātam asmai prāyacchat.

manaḥ|prasāda|pratibodhan'|ârthaṃ
tasy' âtha bhikṣur viyad utpapāta.
varṣañ jvalaṃś c' âiva sa tatra reje
sa|vidyud|uddyota|payoda|lakṣmyā. [20]

avamṛdita|manorathas tu Māro
dyuti|parimoṣam avāpya vaimanasyāt
tam abhimukham udīkṣituṃ na sehe,
saha narakeṇa tatas tiro|babhūva. [21]

4.35 tat kim idam upanītam? evam:

«atyayam apy a|vigaṇayya ditsanti sat|puruṣāḥ. kena nāma svasthena na dātavyaṃ syād?» iti.

«na sattvavantaḥ śakyante bhayād apy a|gatiṃ gamayitum» ity evam apy upaneyam.

The power of his merit made a lotus appear
before him, unique in not rising from mud,
seeming to grin contemptuously at Mara
with its row of white teeth-like stamens.

Stepping onto that lotus, which sprang from the Bodhi·sattva's exceptional store of merit, he approached the *praty·éka·buddha* and offered him almsfood, his heart filled with devotion and joy.

To display his delight,
the monk flew into the air,
pouring down rain and blazing brightly,
glorious as a cloud gleaming with lightning.

Mara, however, was robbed of his splendor.
Despondent, his plans crushed,
unable to look the Bodhi·sattva in the face,
he disappeared along with the hell.

What then has this story shown? Namely: 4.35

Good men disregard even peril so as to give. Who then would not give if they are in a situation that is safe?

It also shows that virtuous people cannot be led to follow the wrong path, even when faced with danger.

STORY 5
THE BIRTH-STORY OF THE MERCHANT AVISHÁHYA

5.1 NA VIBHAVA|KṢAY'|ĀŚAṄKAYĀ samṛddhy|āśayā vā pradāna|vaidhuryam upayānti sat|puruṣāḥ. tad|yath" ânuśrūyate.

Bodhisattvaḥ kila tyāga|śīla|kula|vinaya|śruta|jñān'|â|vismay'|ādi|guṇa|samudito Dhanadāyamāno vibhava|saṃpadā sarv'|âtithitvād an|uparata|dāna|sattro loka|hit'|ârtha|pravṛtto dāyaka|śreṣṭhaḥ śreṣṭhī babhūva. mātsary'|ādi|doṣ'|â|viṣahyo «'viṣahya» iti prakāśa|nāmā.

iṣṭ'|ârtha|saṃpatti|vimarśa|nāśāt
  prīti|prabodhasya viśeṣa|hetuḥ
yath" ârthināṃ darśanam āsa tasya
  tath" ârthināṃ darśanam āsa tasya. [1]

5.5 «deh'» îti yācñā|niyat'|ârtham ukto
  «n' âst'» îti n' âsau gadituṃ śaśāka.
hṛt'|âvakāśā hi babhūva citte
  tasy' ârtha|saktiḥ kṛpayā mahatyā. [2]

tasy' ârthibhir nirhriyamāṇa|sāre
  gṛhe babhūv' âbhyadhikaḥ praharṣaḥ
viveda sa hy ugra|ghanān an|arthān
  a|kāraṇa|kṣipra|vināśino† 'rthān. [3]

bhavanti lokasya hi bhūyas" ârthā
  lobh'|āśrayā dur|gati|mārga|sārthāḥ
par'|ātmanor abhyuday'|āvahatvād
  arthās tadīyās tu babhur yath"|ârthāḥ. [4]

GOOD MEN DO NOT stop giving out of concern for depleted wealth, nor out of desire for riches. 5.1

Tradition has handed down the following story.

The Bodhi·sattva is said to have once been a merchant. Endowed with virtues such as generosity, morality, noble birth, discipline, learning, knowledge, and humility, he resembled wealth-giving Kubéra* in his affluent riches. Since he treated every person as a guest, his donations and sacrifices never ceased. A supreme donor, intent on benefiting the world, he was unable to be conquered by faults such as miserliness. For this he was widely known as Avisháhya, "The Unconquerable."

The certainty of attaining what they desired
awakened joy in both him and the beggars.
Seeing the beggars affected him the same way
as seeing him affected the beggars.

When constantly asked to give, 5.5
he was unable to say he had nothing.
For great compassion had rid his heart
of attachment to possessions.

Instead he felt immense joy
when beggars stripped his house of its goods.
For "goods," he knew, were vicious, crude evils,
quickly able to disappear without reason.*

Goods, based on greed, are for most people
like caravans on the road to bad rebirths.*
But for him they were goods in the true sense,
in bringing prosperity to both others and himself.

atha tasya Mahā|sattvasya yath"|âbhilaṣitair a|kliṣṭaiḥ śiṣṭ'|ôpacāra|vibhūṣaṇair vipulair artha|visargair yācanaka|janaṃ samantataḥ saṃtarpayataḥ,

pradān'|āudārya|śravaṇād vismay'|āvarjita|manāḥ Śakro dev'|êndraḥ pradāna|sthira|niścayatām asya jijñāsamānaḥ pratyahaṃ dhana|dhānya|ratna|paricchada|jātaṃ tat tad antar|dhāpayām āsa. «api nām' âyaṃ vibhava|parikṣay'|āśaṅkayā mātsaryāya pratāryet'» êti.

5.10 pradān'|âdhimuktasya tu punar Mahā|sattvasya

yathā yathā tasya vineśur arthāḥ
  sūry'|âbhisṛṣṭā iva toya|leśāḥ,
tathā tath" âitān vipulaiḥ pradānair
  gṛhāt pradīptād iva nirjahāra. [5]

atha Śakro dev'|êndras tyāga|parāyaṇam eva taṃ Mahā|sattvam avetya prakṣīyamāṇa|vibhava|sāram api vismitatara|matis tasy' âika|rātreṇa sarvaṃ vibhava|sāram antar|dhāpayām ās', ânyatra rajju|kuṇḍalakād dātrāc c' âikasmāt.

atha Bodhisattvaḥ prabhātāyāṃ rajanyāṃ yath"|ôcitaṃ prativibuddhaḥ paśyati sma dhana|dhānya|paricchada|pari-jana'|rddhi|śūnyaṃ niṣkūja|dīnaṃ sva|bhavanaṃ rākṣasair iv' ôdvāsitam an|abhirāma|darśanaṃ, «kim idam?» iti ca samutthita|vitarkaḥ samanuvicaraṃs tad rajju|kuṇḍalakaṃ dātraṃ ca kevalam atra dadarśa. tasya cintā prādur|abhavat:

The Great Being's unwearied and abundant gifts of wealth satisfied petitioners in every direction. Meeting every individual desire, they possessed the added ornament of being given with elegant courtesy.

Shakra, the king of the gods, was filled with astonishment when he heard about Avisháhya's magnanimous generosity and he desired to test Avisháhya's firm resolve to give. Day after day he made Avisháhya's money, grain, gems, and clothing disappear, thinking that concern over his dwindling wealth might lure Avisháhya into becoming miserly.

The Great Being, however, remained intent on giving. 5.10

Whenever his goods diminished,
like specks of water struck by the sun,
he made huge offerings by taking more
out of his house, as if it were on fire.

Shakra, the king of the gods, felt even greater astonishment when he saw the Great Being still devoted to charity, despite the fact that his wealth continued to decrease. He therefore made Avisháhya's entire fortune disappear in a single night, leaving only a small piece of rope and a solitary sickle.

On waking up as usual at dawn, the Bodhi·sattva saw that his house was stripped of all its goods, including his money, grain, clothes, and servants. Dreary and filled with a melancholy silence, the house appeared to have been plundered by demons. "What's happened here?" he pondered. Looking around, he saw the sole remaining sickle and piece of rope and thought:

«yadi tāvat kena cid yācitum an|ucita|vacasā sva|vikram'|ôpajīvinā mad|gṛhe praṇaya evaṃ darśitaḥ, s'|ûpayuktā eva me arthāḥ. atha tv idānīṃ mad|bhāgya|doṣād ucchrayam a|sahamānena† kena cid an|upayuktā eva vidrutās, tat kaṣṭam....

5.15 calaṃ sauhṛdam arthānāṃ viditaṃ pūrvam eva me.
arthinām eva pīḍā tu dahaty atra mano mama. [6]

pradāna|satkāra|sukh'|ôcitāś ciraṃ
viviktam arthair abhigamya mad|gṛham
kathaṃ bhaviṣyanti nu te mam' ârthinaḥ
pipāsitāḥ śuṣkam iv' āgatā hradam?» [7]

atha Bodhisattvaḥ sva|dhairy'|âvaṣṭambhād an|āsvādita|viṣāda|dainyas tasyām apy avasthāyām an|abhyasta|yācñā|kramatvāt parān yācituṃ paricitān api na prasehe. «evaṃ duṣ|karaṃ yācitum» iti tasya bhūyasī yācanaka|janeṣv anukampā babhūva. atha sa Mah"|ātmā yācanaka|jana|sv|āgat'|ādi|kriy"|âvekṣayā svayam eva tad rajju|kuṇḍalakaṃ dātraṃ ca parigṛhya pratyahaṃ tṛṇa|vikray'|ôpalabdhayā vibhava|mātray" ârthi|jana|praṇaya|saṃmānanāṃ cakāra.

atha Śakro dev'|êndras tasy' êmām a|viṣāditāṃ parame 'pi dāridrye pradān'|âbhimukhatāṃ c' âvekṣya sa|vismaya|

"Perhaps someone unused to begging, who earns a living from brute strength, came to show favor to my house. In that case my possessions have been put to good use! But it would be terrible if someone has squandered my possessions and not put them to good use, simply because they could not tolerate the elevated position I hold—for which my good fortune is to blame.

I knew before that 5.15
wealth is an erratic friend.
But it torments me that
beggars should suffer for this.

Long used to the joy of being honored by gifts,
how will my petitioners fare when they arrive
at my home stripped of its goods,
like thirsty men arriving at a parched lake?"

But the Bodhi·sattva remained firm in his resolve and indulged neither in despair nor in sadness. Despite his plight, he did not ask anything from others, however close they were to him, unaccustomed as he was to begging. Instead he felt even greater compassion for the crowds of petitioners, as he reflected over how difficult it was to beg. Concerned that he should still be able to offer some welcome to the throng of petitioners, the Great One took up the sickle and piece of rope and used the paltry wealth he gained from selling grass to honor the beggars' requests daily.

Shakra, the king of the gods, was filled with wonder and respect when he saw how unaffected Avisháhya was by despair and how determined he was to give, despite his extreme poverty. Revealing his divine and wondrous form, he

bahu|mānaḥ saṃdṛśyamāna|divy'|âdbhuta|vapur antarikṣe sthitvā dānād vicchandayaṃs taṃ Mahā|sattvam uvāca: «gṛha|pate!

5.20 suhṛn|manas|tāpa|karīm avasthām
imām upetas tvam ati|pradānaiḥ
na dasyubhir n' âiva jal'|ânalābhyāṃ
na rājabhiḥ saṃhriyamāṇa|vittaḥ. [8]

tat tvā hit'|âvekṣitayā bravīmi:
niyaccha dāna|vyasan'|ânurāgam!
itthaṃ|gataḥ sann api cen na dadyā,
yāyāḥ punaḥ pūrva|samṛddhi|śobhām. [9]

śaśvat kṛśen' âpi parivyayeṇa
kālena dṛṣṭvā kṣayam añjanānām
cayena valmīka|samucchrayāṃś ca
vṛddhy|arthinaḥ saṃyama eva panthāḥ.» [10]

atha Bodhisattvaḥ pradān'|âbhyāsa|māhātmyaṃ vidarśa-yañ Chakram uvāca:

«an|āryam āryeṇa, sahasra|netra,
su|duṣ|karaṃ suṣṭhv api dur|gatena.
mā c' âiva tad bhūn mama, Śakra, vittaṃ
yat|prāpti|hetoḥ kṛpaṇ'|āśayaḥ syām! [11]

5.25 icchanti yācñā|maraṇena gantuṃ
duḥkhasya yasya pratikāra|mārgam,
ten' āturān kaḥ kula|putra|mānī
‹n' âst'› îti śuṣk'|âśanin" âbhihanyāt? [12]

stood in the air and tried to destroy the Great Being's desire to give with the following words:

"Householder!

Your excessive gifts have led you to this plight, 5.20
bringing torment to your friends.
Neither thieves, floods, fires, nor kings
have taken this wealth from you.

I address you out of concern for your welfare:
restrain your disastrous passion for giving!
For despite your present plight, if you give no more,
you may return to the former splendor of your riches.

Constant spending, however slight,
depletes earnings in time.
Anthills, too, build up through accumulation.
Those seeking profit thus practice restraint."

In response, the Bodhi·sattva addressed Shakra with words that revealed the magnanimity of his habit of giving:

"Thousand-eyed god, it is very hard for a noble man
to commit an ignoble deed, however bad his plight.
May I never own wealth, Shakra,
if to attain it I must be a niggard!

When people seek to alleviate their suffering 5.25
by turning to the death-like practice of begging,
who, with any pride in a noble birth, would slay
such victims with the thunderbolt of a refusal?

tan mad|vidhaḥ kiṃ svid upādadīta
ratnaṃ dhanaṃ vā divi v" âpi rājyam,
yācñ"|âbhitāpena vivarṇitāni
prasādayen n' ârthi|mukhāni yena? [13]

mātsarya|doṣ'|ôpacayāya yaḥ syān
na tyāga|cittaṃ paribṛṃhayed vā,
sa tyāgam ev' ârhati mad|vidhebhyaḥ
parigraha|cchadma|mayo vighātaḥ. [14]

vidyul|latā|nṛtta|cale dhane ca
sādhāraṇe n'|âika|vighāta|hetau
dāne nidāne ca sukh'|ôdayānāṃ
mātsaryam āryaḥ ka iv' āśrayeta? [15]

tad darśitā, Śakra, mayi svat" êyaṃ;
hit'|âbhidhānād anukampito 'smi.
sv|abhyasta|harṣaṃ tu manaḥ pradānais
tad|utpathe kena dhṛtiṃ labheta? [16]

5.30 na c' âtra manyor anuvṛtti|mārge
cittaṃ bhavān arhati saṃniyoktum.
na hi sva|bhāvasya vipakṣa|durgam
ārodhum alpena balena śakyam!» [17]

Śakra uvāca, «gṛha|pate! paryāpta|vibhavasya paripūrṇa|kośa|koṣṭh'|âgārasya samyak|pravṛtta|vividha|vipula|karm'|ântasya virūḍh'|āyater loke vaśī|kṛt'|āiśvaryasy' âyaṃ kramo, n' êmāṃ daśām abhiprapannasya. paśya:

How can a man such as I accept
jewels, wealth, or even kingship in heaven
and not use them to brighten the faces of petitioners,
pale from the torment of begging?

Men such as I should reject possessions.
They foster the sin of selfishness
and decrease one's desire to give.
They are a ruin disguised as an asset.

Wealth is fickle, like the dance of a flicker of lightning.
Open to all, it produces numerous evils.
Giving, on the other hand, increases happiness.
How can a noble person practice selfishness?

You have revealed your true form to me
and favored me with kind words, Shakra.
But the joy of giving is ingrained in my heart.
How can I remain content if I stray from that path?

Do not let your mind 5.30
become angry at this.
For a hostile fortress guards my character;
it would take more than a small army to assail it!"

"Householder!" Shakra replied. "You act as if you were wealthy, as if your treasury and stores were full, as if you had various large and thriving businesses, as if your future were prosperous, or as if you had secured lordship over the world! But your behavior does not match your situation. Look here:

sva|buddhi|vispanda|samāhitena vā
yaśo|'nukūlena kul'|ôcitena vā
samṛddhim ākṛṣya śubhena karmaṇā,
sapatna|tejāṃsy abhibhūya bhānuvat, [18]

jane prasaṅgena vitatya saṃnatiṃ,
prabodhya harṣaṃ sa|suhṛtsu bandhuṣu,
avāpta|saṃmāna|vidhir nṛ|pād api
Śriyā pariṣvakta iv' âbhikāmyayā. [19]

atha pradāne pravijṛmbhita|kramaḥ
sukheṣu vā n' âiti janasya vācyatām.
a|jāta|pakṣaḥ kham iv' āurukṣayā
vighāta|bhāk kevalayā tu ditsayā. [20]

5.35 yato dhanaṃ saṃyama|naibhṛt'|āśrayād
upārjyatāṃ tāvad. alaṃ praditsayā!
an|āryat" âpy atra ca nāma kā bhaven
na yat pradadyād vibhaveṣv a|bhāviṣu?» [21]

Bodhisattva uvāca, «alam ati|nirbandhen' âtra|bhavataḥ.

ātm'|ârthaḥ syād yasya garīyān para|kāryāt
ten' âpi syād deyam an|ādṛtya samṛddhim.
n' âiti prītiṃ tāṃ hi mahaty" âpi vibhūtyā
dānais tuṣṭiṃ lobha|jayād yām upabhuṅkte. [22]

Earn riches by practicing an ethical trade,
either one that suits your dynamic intelligence
or one in keeping with your family and reputation.
And, like the sun, exceed the splendor of your rivals.

Spread your help earnestly among people.
Awaken joy in your friends and kinsmen
And receive honor from the king himself,
as if Fortune embraced you with love!

If your actions extend toward giving or pleasure,
no-one will comment on the matter.
But those who only wish to give will suffer ruin,
like an unfledged bird eager to fly into the sky.

Acquire riches by being calm and restrained. 5.35
Cease your desire to give!
How can it be ignoble not to give gifts
if you do not have any wealth?"

"Do not press me too greatly, honorable lord," the Bodhisattva replied.

"Even if a person's self-concern is greater than
their altruism,
they should still give gifts and disregard riches.
For the joy received from wealth, however opulent,
is less than the satisfaction of conquering greed
through giving.

n' âiti svargaṃ kevalayā yac ca samṛddhyā,
dānen' âiva khyātim avāpnoti ca puṇyām.
mātsary'|ādīn n' âbhibhavaty eva ca doṣāṃs,
tasyā hetor dānam ataḥ ko na bhajeta? [23]

trātuṃ lokān yas tu jarā|mṛtyu|parītān
apy ātmānaṃ ditsati kāruṇya|vaśena,
yo n' āsvādaṃ vetti sukhānāṃ para|duḥkhaiḥ,
kas tasy' ârthas tvad|gatayā syād api lakṣmyā? [24]

5.40 api ca, dev'|êndra,

saṃpattir iva vittānām a|dhruvā sthitir āyuṣaḥ.
iti yācanakaṃ labdhvā na samṛddhir avekṣyate. [25]

eko rathaś ca bhuvi yad vidadhāti vartma,
ten' âparo vrajati dhṛṣṭataraṃ tath" ânyaḥ.
kalyāṇam ādyam imam ity avadhūya mārgaṃ
n' â|sat|patha|praṇayane ramate mano me. [26]

arthaś ca vistaram upaiṣyati cet punar me,
hartā manāṃsi niyamena sa yācakānām.
evaṃ|gate 'pi ca yathā|vibhavaṃ pradāsye.
mā c' âiva dāna|niyame pramadiṣma, Śakra!» [27]

One does not reach heaven through riches alone.
But one acquires a pure reputation by giving.
Wealth hinders the conquest of selfishness and
other sins.
Who then would not practice giving?

If compassion makes a person willing to give up
their very self
to save the universe as it suffers from old age
and death,
and if the pain of others makes them ignorant of
the taste of pleasures,
why would they need glory, even such as yours?

Furthermore, king of the gods, 5.40

The fortune that derives from riches
is as unstable as the condition of life.
Wealth then is of no concern
to a man who has acquired petitioners.

When one carriage has formed a path on the ground,
a second carriage proceeds more surely, and so
with others.
My mind has no desire to tread a wicked path
and reject this beautiful, supreme road.

If my wealth becomes abundant once more,
that would certainly gladden the hearts
of my petitioners.
But, despite my plight, I will give as much
as my means allow.
May I never neglect my vow to give, Shakra!"

ity ukte Śakro dev'|êndraḥ samabhiprasādita|manāḥ «sādhu! sādhv!» ity enam abhisaṃrādhya sa|bahu|māna| snigdham avekṣamāṇa uvāca:

5.45 «yaśaḥ|sapatnair api karmabhir janaḥ
samṛddhim anvicchati nīca|dāruṇaiḥ
sva|saukhya|saṅgād an|apekṣit'|âtyayaḥ
pratāryamāṇaś capalena cetasā. [28]

a|cintayitvā tu dhana|kṣayaṃ tvayā
sva|saukhya|hāniṃ mama ca pratāraṇām
par'|ârtha|saṃpādana|dhīra|cetasā
mahattvam udbhāvitam ātma|saṃpadaḥ. [29]

aho bat' audārya|viśeṣa|bhāsvataḥ
pramṛṣṭa|mātsarya|tamisratā hṛdaḥ,
pradāna|saṃkoca|virūpatāṃ gataṃ
dhane pranaṣṭe 'pi na yat tad|āśayā. [30]

na c' âtra citraṃ para|duḥkha|duḥkhinaḥ
kṛpā|vaśāl loka|hit'|âiṣiṇas tava
him'|âvadātaḥ śikhar" îva vāyunā
na yat pradānād asi kampito mayā. [31]

yaśaḥ samudbhāvayituṃ parīkṣayā
dhanaṃ tav' êdaṃ tu nigūḍhavān aham.
maṇir hi śobh"|ânugato 'py ato 'nyathā
na saṃspṛśed ratna|yaśo|mah"|ârghatām. [32]

Shakra, the king of the gods, was gratified by these words and praised the Bodhi·sattva, saying, "Excellent! Excellent!" Gazing at him with respect and affection, he then said:

"In their pursuit of wealth, people take up jobs 5.45
that are base, cruel, and even threaten their reputation.
Attached to their own pleasures,
they disregard danger, misled by fickle minds.

You, however, pay no heed to your loss of wealth,
decrease in pleasures, or my seductions.
Firmly focused on the welfare of others,
you reveal the greatness of your accomplishments.

How brightly your heart shines with eminent nobility!
From it you have wiped the darkness of selfishness.
Despite your loss of wealth, no desire for riches
has changed your heart and made you limit your gifts.

You suffer at the sufferings of others
and compassionately seek the welfare of the world.
No wonder I cannot shake you from giving,
just as the wind cannot shake a snow-white mountain.

It is to test you and generate your fame
that I have hidden your wealth.
For only when examined can a jewel, however radiant,
acquire the great value of a renowned gem.

5.50 ataḥ pradānair abhivarṣa yācakān
hradān mahā|megha iv' âbhipūrayan.
dhana|kṣayaṃ n' āpsyasi mat|parigrahād.
idaṃ kṣamethāś ca viceṣṭitaṃ mama.» [33]

ity enam abhisaṃrādhya Śakras tac c' âsya vibhava|sāram upasaṃhṛtya kṣamayitvā ca tatr' âiv' ântar|dadhe.

tad evaṃ, na vibhava|kṣay'|âpekṣayā samṛddhy|āśayā vā pradāna|vaidhuryam upayānti sat|puruṣā iti.

So rain down gifts on your supplicants, 5.50
just as a great cloud fills up lakes.
Through my favor your wealth will never be exhausted.
Please also tolerate the way I have behaved."

Praising Avisháhya with these words, Shakra returned his wealth to him, asked for his pardon, and disappeared at that very spot.

So it is that good men do not stop giving out of concern for depleted wealth, nor out of desire for riches.

STORY 6

THE BIRTH-STORY OF THE HARE

6.1 TIRYAG|GATĀNĀM API Mahā|sattvānāṃ† śakty|anurūpā dāna|pravṛttir dṛṣṭā. kena nāma manuṣya|bhūtena na dātavyaṃ syāt?

tad|yath" ânuśrūyate.

kasmiṃś cid araṇya|pradeśe manojña|vīrut|tṛṇa|taru|nicite puṣpa|phalavati vaiḍūrya|nīla|śuci|salila|vāhinyā saritā vibhūṣita|paryante mṛdu|śādval'|āstaraṇa|sukha|saṃsparśa|darśanīya|dharaṇi|tale tapasvi|jana|vicarite Bodhisattvaḥ śaśo babhūva.

sa sattva|yogād vapuṣaś ca saṃpadā
  bala|prakarṣād vipulena c' âujasā
a|tarkitaḥ kṣudra|mṛgair a|śaṅkitaś
  cacāra tasmin mṛga|rāja|līlayā. [1]

6.5 sva|carm'|âjina|saṃvītaḥ sva|tanū|ruha|valkalaḥ
munivat tatra śuśubhe tuṣṭa|cittas tṛṇ'|âṅkuraiḥ. [2]

tasya maitry|avadātena mano|vāk|kāya|karmaṇā
āsur jihmita|daurātmyāḥ prāyaḥ śiṣya|sukhā mṛgāḥ. [3]

tasya guṇ'|âtiśaya|saṃbhṛtena sneha|gauraveṇa viśeṣavat-taram avabaddha|hṛdayās trayaḥ sahāyā babhūvur: udraḥ śṛgālo vānaraś ca. te paras|para|saṃbandha|nibaddha|snehā iva bāndhavā anyonya|praṇaya|saṃmānana|virūḍha|sauhṛdā iva ca suhṛdaḥ saṃmodamānās tatra viharanti sma.

Even as animals, Great Beings have displayed generosity to the best of their ability. Who then that is human would not give gifts? 6.1

Tradition has handed down the following story.

The Bodhi·sattva once lived as a hare in a forest area frequented by crowds of ascetics. Full of flowers and fruits, the region abounded with delightful plants, grasses, and trees. A river adorned its borders, flowing with pure water that was as blue as lapis lazuli, and the ground was covered with soft grass, pleasant both to touch and see.

His goodness, perfect beauty,
eminent strength, and abundant energy
meant cruel animals gave him no thought
as he roamed fearlessly with the grace of a king
of beasts.

Using his skin as a deer hide, 6.5
and his fur as a bark garment,
he looked as glorious as an ascetic,
content with blades of grass.

His actions in mind, speech, and body
were so cleansed by kindness
that animals normally crooked and evil
became mild as disciples.

The Bodhi·sattva had three friends who felt a special bond of affection and respect for him because of his outstanding virtue. They were: an otter, a jackal, and a monkey. These four lived happily together, like relatives bound by mutual ties of affection, or like companions who have developed a friendship based on respect for each other's

tiryak|svabhāva|vimukhāś ca prāṇiṣu day"|ânuvṛttyā laulya|praśamād vismṛta|steya|pravṛttyā ca dharm'|ânurodhinyā ca vṛttyā paṭu|vijñānatvād vinaya|niyama|dhīrayā ca ceṣṭayā devatānām api vismayanīyā babhūvuḥ.

sukh'|ânulome guṇa|bādhini krame
gun'|ânukūle ca sukh'|ôparodhini
naro 'pi tāvad guṇa|pakṣa|saṃśrayād
virājate kim bata tiryag|ākṛtiḥ? [4]

abhūt sa teṣāṃ tu śaś'|ākṛtiḥ kṛtī
par'|ânukampā|pratipad|gurur guruḥ
svabhāva|saṃpac ca guṇa|kram'|ânugā
yaśo yad eṣāṃ sura|lokam apy agāt. [5]

6.10 atha kadā cit sa Mah"|ātmā sāy'|âhna|samaye dharma|śravaṇ'|ârtham abhigataiḥ sa|bahu|mānam upāsyamānas taiḥ sahāyaiḥ paripūrṇa|prāya|maṇḍalam āditya|viprakarṣād vyavadāyamāna|śobhaṃ rūpya|darpaṇam iva tsaru|virahitam īṣat|pārśv'|âpavṛtta|bimbaṃ śukla|pakṣa|catur|daśī|candramasam uditam abhivīkṣya sahāyān uvāca:

asāv āpūrṇa|śobhena maṇḍalena hasann iva
nivedayati sādhūnāṃ candramāḥ poṣadh'|ôtsavam. [6]

wishes. Turning their backs on animal behavior, they were compassionate toward living creatures and had so quelled their greed that they had no thought for theft. Their moral conduct, keen acumen, and firm practice of disciplines and restraints filled the very gods with astonishment.

If the path of pleasure involves obstructing virtue
but the path of virtue involves obstructing pleasure,
to opt for the side of virtue would bring
even a man glory, how much more an animal?

The one with the form of a hare was their teacher.
Accomplished, profound in his compassion for others,
his excellent nature was attended by a series of virtues,
making their fame reach even the realm of heroes.

One day, at evening time, the friends came to hear the 6.10
Great One deliver a teaching and were sitting respectfully at his feet. The risen moon was almost full, with a section of its disc remaining slightly hidden, and due to its distance from the sun, it shone brightly like a silver mirror without a handle. When he realized that this was the moon of the fourteenth day of the bright half of the month, the hare addressed his friends, saying:

'Look! As if smiling with
its disc of brimming splendor,
the moon heralds
the *póshadha* festival to good men!

tad vyaktaṃ śvaḥ pañca|daśī yato bhavadbhiḥ poṣadha| niyamam abhisaṃpādayadbhir nyāy'|ôpalabdhen' āhāra| viśeṣeṇa kāl'|ôpanatam atithi|janaṃ pratipūjya prāṇa|saṃdhāraṇam anuṣṭheyam. paśyantu bhavantaḥ:

yat saṃprayogā virah'|âvasānāḥ,
samucchrayāḥ pāta|virūpa|niṣṭhāḥ,
vidyul|latā|bhaṅgura|lolam āyus,
ten' âiva kāryo dṛḍham a|pramādaḥ. [7]

dānena śīl'|ābharaṇena tasmāt
puṇyāni saṃvardhayituṃ yatadhvam.
vivartamānasya hi janma|dur|ge
lokasya puṇyāni parā pratiṣṭhā. [8]

6.15 tārā|gaṇānām abhibhūya lakṣmīṃ
vibhāti yat kānti|guṇena somaḥ
jyotīṃṣi c' ākramya sahasra|raśmir
yad dīpyate, puṇya|guṇ'|ôcchrayaḥ saḥ. [9]

dṛpta|svabhāvāḥ sacivā nṛ|pāś ca
puṇya|prabhāvāt pṛthiv"|īśvarāṇām
sad|aśva|vṛttyā hata|sarva|garvāḥ
prītā iv' ājñā|dhuram udvahanti. [10]

puṇyair vihīnān anuyāty a|lakṣmīr
vispandamānān api nīti|mārge.
puṇy'|âdhikaiḥ sā hy avabhartsyamānā
paryety a|marṣād iva tad|vipakṣān. [11]

Tomorrow must be the fifteenth. Practice the restraint of the *póshadha* vow and only nourish yourselves after a guest has happened to arrive and you have honored them with special food acquired in a moral way. Consider this:

Every union ends in separation.
Every rise concludes with an ugly fall.
Life is as transient and fickle as a flash of lightning.
You should therefore act resiliently and with diligence.

Strive to increase your merit
through giving, the ornament of virtue.
For merit is the best support for creatures
who wander the perils of rebirth.

It is because of their superior pure qualities 6.15
that the lovely splendor of the moon
surpasses the beauty of the stars
and the thousand-rayed sun outshines the gleaming
planets.

The power of the merit owned by kings
makes haughty ministers and monarchs
almost joyfully bear the yoke of the kings' commands,
their pride entirely quelled, like dutiful horses.

Misfortune trails those who lack merit,
however much they wriggle in politics.
As if enraged at being reviled by men of great purity,
she chases after opponents of merit.

duḥkha|pratiṣṭhād a|yaśo|'nubandhād
a|puṇya|mārgād uparamya tasmāt
śrīmatsu saukhy'|ôdaya|sādhaneṣu
puṇya|prasaṅgeṣu matiṃ kurudhvam. [12]

te tath" êty asy' ânuśāsanīṃ pratigṛhy' âbhivādya pradakṣiṇī|kṛtya c' âinaṃ svaṃ svam ālayam abhijagmuḥ. a|cira|gateṣu ca teṣu sahāyeṣu sa Mahātmā cintām āpede:

6.20 «atither abhyupetasya saṃmānaṃ yena tena vā
vidhātuṃ śaktir asty eṣām. atra śocyo 'ham eva tu. [13]

asmad|dant'|âgra|vicchinnāḥ paritiktās tṛṇ'|âṅkurāḥ
śakyā n' âtithaye dātuṃ! sarvathā dhig a|śaktitām! [14]

ity a|sāmarthya|dīnena ko nv artho jīvitena me
ānandaḥ śokatāṃ yāyād yasy' âivam atithir mama? [15]

tat kutr' êdānīm idam atithi|paricaryā|vaiguṇyān niḥ|sāraṃ śarīrakam utsṛjyamānaṃ kasya cid upakārāya syād iti?»

vimṛśan sa mah"|ātmā smṛtiṃ pratilebhe:

6.25 «aye!

Avoid then the path of impurity,
which is based on suffering and attended by disgrace.
Set your heart on opportunities for purity:
for they are a glorious way to produce happiness."

Obediently accepting his instruction, they saluted the hare and circled him reverently before returning to their respective homes. Then, not long after his friends had left, the Great One had this thought:

"The others can honor 6.20
any guest that arrives
with this or that offering.
But my situation is pitiful.

I cannot give a guest
blades of bitter grass,
chewed off by the tips of my teeth!
How utterly powerless I am!

Why live a life
of miserable impotence,
when my guests, who should bring joy,
cause only sorrow?

Where can I offer up this body so that it is of use to someone, a body which is after all worthless in providing no service to a guest?"

Reflecting this way, the heroic hare then gathered his wits and thought:

"Aha! 6.25

sv'|âdhīna|su|labham etan
nir|a|vadyaṃ vidyate mam' âiva khalu
atithi|jana|pratipūjana|
samartha|rūpaṃ śarīra|dhanam. [16]

tat kim ahaṃ viṣīdāmi?

samadhigatam idaṃ may" ātitheyaṃ,
hṛdaya, vimuñca yato viṣāda|dainyam!
samupanatam anena sat|kariṣyāmy
aham atithi|praṇayaṃ śarīrakeṇa.» [17]

iti viniścitya sa Mahā|sattvaḥ param iva lābham adhigamya parama|prīta|manās tatr' âvatasthe.

6.30 vitark'|âtiśayas tasya
hṛdi saṃpravijṛmbhitaḥ
āviś|cakre prabhāvaṃ ca
prasādaṃ ca div'|âukasām. [18]

tataḥ praharṣād iva s'|âcalā calā
mahī babhūv' â|nibhṛt'|ârṇav'|âṃśukā.
vitastaruḥ khe sura|dundubhi|svanā.
diśaḥ prasād'|ābharaṇāś cakāśire. [19]

prasakta|mandra|stanita|prahāsinas
taḍit|pinaddhāś ca ghanāḥ samantataḥ
paras|par'|āśleṣa|vikīrṇa|reṇubhiḥ
prasaktam enaṃ kusumair avākiran. [20]

I have something that belongs to myself
and that is readily available.
Inoffensive, it can be used to honor a guest.
That possession is my body.

So why should I be despondent?

I have found an offering to give a guest.
Cease your misery and despair, my heart!
With this measly body I will honor
the requests made by my guests."

After making this resolution, the Great Being felt the greatest joy, as if he had acquired a supreme attainment, and stayed where he was.

The exceptional idea 6.30
that bloomed in his heart
revealed his strength
and purity to the gods.

The earth and her mountains shook, as if with joy.
The ocean cloaking the earth became restless.
The sound of divine drums spread through the air.
The directions gleamed, adorned by brightness.

Clouds draped with lightning
chuckled with continuous deep rumblings,
repeatedly covering him with flowers
scattering pollen as they collided.

samudvahan dhīra|gatiḥ samīraṇaḥ
su|gandhi nānā|druma|puṣpa|jaṃ rajaḥ
mudā pravṛddhair a|vibhakta|bhaktibhis
tam arcayām āsa kṛś'|âṃśukair iva. [21]

tad upalabhya pramudita|vismita|manobhir devatābhiḥ samantataḥ parikīrtyamānaṃ tasya vitark'|âdbhutaṃ samāpūryamāṇa|vismaya|kautūhalena manasā tasya Mahā|sattvasya bhāva|jijñāsayā dvitīye 'hani gagana|tala|madhyam abhilaṅghamāne paṭutara|kiraṇa|prabhāve savitari, prasphurita|marīci|jāla|vasanāsu bhāsvar'|ātapa|visar'|âvaguṇṭhitāsv an|ālokana|kṣamāsu dikṣu, saṃkṣipyamāṇa|cchāyeṣv abhivṛddha|cīrī|virāv'|ônnāditeṣu van'|ântareṣu, vicchidyamāna|pakṣi|saṃpāteṣu, gharma|klam'|āpīt'|ôtsāheṣv adhvageṣu Śakro devānām adhipatir brāhmaṇa|rūpī bhūtvā mārga|praṇaṣṭa iv' âdhva|gaḥ kṣut|tarṣa|śrama|viṣāda|dīna|kaṇṭhaḥ sa|svaraṃ prarudann a|vidūre teṣāṃ vicukrośa:

6.35 «ekaṃ sārthāt paribhraṣṭaṃ
bhramantaṃ gahane vane
kṣuc|chrama|klānta|dehaṃ māṃ
trātum arhanti sādhavaḥ! [22]

mārg'|â|mārga|jñāna|niścetanaṃ māṃ
dik|saṃmohāt kv' âpi gacchantam ekam
kāntāre 'smin gharma|tarṣa|klam'|ārtaṃ
mā|bhaiḥ|śabdaiḥ ko 'tra māṃ hlādayeta?» [23]

A fragrant, steady breeze lifted pollen
from the flowers of various trees,
as if joyfully honoring him with fine cloths,
their designs losing shape as they billowed.

On all sides the gods praised the wondrous thought of the hare and their hearts filled with joy and amazement. When Shakra, the lord of the gods, heard of it, his mind brimmed with astonishment and curiosity and he desired to test the Great Being's character. So the next day, at the time when the sun hangs in the middle of the sky and its rays are at their most fierce, when the directions do not tolerate themselves to be seen, swathed by a mesh of pulsating rays and covered by waves of radiant heat, when shadows in the forests contract and the interiors of woods resound with the swelling noise of cicadas, when birds break off their flight and travelers feel their vigor drained by exhaustion from the heat, Shakra took on the form of a brahmin. Pretending to be a traveler who had lost his way, he loudly began to weep and wail not far from where the animals stayed, his voice pitiful from hunger, thirst, fatigue, and despair:

"My caravan is lost! 6.35
I wander alone in this dense forest,
weary from hunger and fatigue.
May the good save me!

I have no idea which way is right or wrong.
My directions muddled, I wander in this forest
aimlessly and alone, sick with heat, thirst, and fatigue.
Who here will cheer me with comforting words?"

atha te mahā|sattvās tena tasy' âtikaruṇen' ākrandita|śabdena samākampita|hṛdayāḥ sa|saṃbhrama|drutatara|gatayas taṃ deśam abhijagmuḥ. mārga|pranaṣṭ'|âdhva|ga|dīna|darśanaṃ c' âinam abhisamīkṣya samabhigamy' ôpacāra|puraḥsaraṃ samāśvāsayanta ūcuḥ:

«kāntāre vipranaṣṭo 'ham ity alaṃ saṃbhrameṇa te.
svasya śiṣya|gaṇasy' êva samīpe vartase hi naḥ. [24]

tad adya tāvad asmākaṃ
paricaryā|pratigrahāt
vidhāy' ânugrahaṃ, saumya,
śvo gant" âsi yath"|ēpsitam.» [25]

6.40 ath' ôdras tasya tūṣṇīṃ|bhāvād anumatam upanimantraṇam avetya harṣa|saṃbhrama|tvarita|gatiḥ sapta rohita|matsyān samupanīy' âvocad enam:

«mīn'|âribhir vismaraṇ'|ôjjhitā vā
trās'|ôtplutā vā sthalam abhyupetāḥ
kheda|prasuptā iva sapta matsyā
labdhā may"; âitān nivas' êha bhuktvā.» [26]

atha śṛgālo 'py enaṃ yath"|ôpalabdham anna|jātam upahṛtya praṇāma|puraḥsaraṃ s'|ādaram uvāca:

The hearts of the virtuous heroes* trembled when they heard the man's pitiful lament and they hastened swiftly toward the origin of the noise. There they saw the brahmin, who bore the wretched appearance of a lost traveler. Approaching him, they exchanged polite introductions, whereupon they consoled him, saying:

"You need not worry
about being lost in the forest.
  With us you will feel
as if you were with disciples.

Grant us today, good sir,
the favor of accepting our care.
And tomorrow you can
leave as you desire."

Understanding from the brahmin's silence that his invitation had been accepted, the otter hurried off, his pace hastened by joyful zeal, and returned with seven carp, which he offered with the following words: 6.40

"I found these seven fish as if asleep from tiredness.
Some forgetful fishermen left them behind,
or perhaps they leapt onto the land in fright.
Please eat them and spend the night here."

The jackal then also gathered whatever food was available to him. Bowing before the brahmin, he respectfully said these words:

«ekāṃ ca godhāṃ dadhi|bhājanaṃ ca
ken' âpi saṃtyaktam ih' âdhyagaccham.
tan me hit'|âvekṣitay" ôpayujya
vane 'stu te 'smin, guṇa|vāsa, vāsaḥ.» [27]

ity uktvā prīta|manās tad asmai samupajahāra.

6.45 atha vānaraḥ paripāka|guṇāt samupajāta|mārdavāni manaḥ|śilā|cūrṇa|rañjitān' îv' âtipiñjarāṇy ati|rakta|bandhana|mūlāni piṇḍī|kṛtāny āmra|phalāny ādāya s'|âñjali|pragraham enam uvāca:

«āmrāṇi pakvāny udakaṃ mano|jñaṃ
chāyāś ca sat|saṃgama|saukhya|śītāḥ:
ity asti me, Brahma|vidāṃ variṣṭha.
bhuktv" âitad atr' âiva tav' âstu vāsaḥ.» [28]

atha śaśo 'bhisṛty' âinam upacāra|kriy"|ân|antaraṃ sa|bahu|mānam udīkṣamāṇaḥ svena śarīreṇ' ôpanimantrayām āsa:

«na santi mudgā na tilā na taṇḍulā
vane 'bhivṛddhasya śaśasya ke cana.
śarīram etat tv anal'|âbhisaṃskṛtaṃ
mam' ôpayujy' âdya tapo|vane vasa. [29]

yad asti yasy' ēpsita|sādhanaṃ dhanaṃ
sa tan niyuṅkte 'rthi|jan'|āgam'|ôtsave.
na c' âsti dehād adhikaṃ ca me dhanaṃ.
pratīccha sarva|svam idaṃ yato mama.» [30]

"Here is a lizard and bowl of milk I found,
left behind by some person.
Have concern for my welfare and enjoy this food.
Reside in this forest, you seat of virtues!"

Saying this, the jackal joyfully offered him the food.

The monkey then took hold of some round mangoes that were soft with ripeness. Bright orange, as if dyed with orpiment powder, they were deep red at the base of their stalks. Cupping his hands in respect, he said to the brahmin: 6.45

'Ripe mangoes, refreshing water,
and cool shade as soothing as good company:
this is what I offer, supreme Brahman-knower.
Enjoy this food and reside here in the forest."

The hare then approached the brahmin. After addressing him courteously, he looked up at him with respect, whereupon he invited him to accept his body as a gift:

"A hare raised in the forest
has no beans, sesame seeds, or grains of rice.
But here is my body to cook on a fire.
Enjoy it today and reside in this ascetic forest.

At the joyous occasion of a beggar's arrival,
one gives a possession to cater to their needs.
I have no possessions other than my body.
Please accept it. It is everything I own."

6.50 Śakra uvāca:

«anyasy' âpi vadhaṃ tāvat
kuryād asmad|vidhaḥ katham,
iti darśita|sauhārde
kathā k" âiva bhavad|vidhe?» [31]

śaśa uvāca, «upapanna|rūpam idam āsann'|ânukrośe brāhmaṇye. tad ih' âiva tāvad bhavān āstām asmad|anugrah'|âpekṣayā yāvat kutaś cid ātm'|ânugrah'|ôpāyam āsādayām'» îti.

atha Śakro devānām indras tasya bhāvam avetya tapta|tapanīya|varṇaṃ sphurat|pratanu|jvālaṃ vikīryamāṇa|visphuliṅga|prakaraṃ nir|dhūmam aṅgāra|rāśim abhinirmame. atha śaśaḥ samantato vilokayaṃs tam agni|skandhaṃ dadarśa. dṛṣṭvā ca prīta|manāḥ Śakram uvāca:

«samadhigato 'yaṃ may" ātm'|ânugrah'|ôpāyaḥ.... tad asmac|charīr'|ôpabhogāt sa|phalām anugrah'|āśāṃ me kartum arhasi. paśya, mahā|brāhmaṇa:

6.55 deyaṃ ca ditsā|pravaṇaṃ ca cittaṃ
bhavad|vidhen' âtithinā ca yogaḥ.
n' âvāptum etadd hi sukhena śakyaṃ.
tat syād a|moghaṃ bhavad|āśrayān me.» [32]

ity anunīya saṃmānan'|ādar'|âtithi|priyatayā c' âinam abhivādya

tataḥ sa taṃ vahnim abhijvalantaṃ
nidhiṃ dhan'|ârthī sahas" êva dṛṣṭvā
pareṇa harṣeṇa samāruroha
toyaṃ hasat|padmam iv' âika|haṃsaḥ. [33]

Shakra then replied: 6.50

"How can someone such as I
cause the death of another being,
especially one like you,
who shows me such friendship?"

The hare answered: "Being a brahmin entails compassion; and so your words are in keeping with your status. But at least grant me the favor of remaining here while I find a way to favor myself as well."

Understanding his intent, Shakra, the king of the gods, created a heap of burning coals, the color of molten gold. Flickering with thin flames, the pile of coals was smokeless and scattered numerous sparks. The hare, meanwhile, was searching in every direction. When he spotted the blazing mass, he became filled with joy and addressed Shakra, saying:

"I have found a way to favor myself. Please fulfill my desire to perform this favor by enjoying my body. Look, great brahmin:

Giving is a duty and my heart wishes to give. 6.55
And it is apt when I have a guest such as you.
An opportunity like this cannot easily be gained.
I rely on you to ensure my gift is not in vain."

Entreating him this way, the hare saluted him with honor, respect, and hospitality, and

looking at the blazing fire,
just as a pauper gazes at treasure,
he suddenly leapt onto it with utter joy,
like a goose landing on a lake of smiling lotuses.

tad* dṛṣṭvā parama|vismay'|āvarjita|matir devānām adhipatiḥ svam eva vapur āsthāya divya|kusuma|varṣa|puraḥsarībhir manaḥ|śruti|sukhābhir vāgbhir abhipūjya taṃ Mahā|sattvaṃ kamala|palāśa|lakṣmī|samṛddhābhyāṃ bhāsur'|âṅguli|vibhūṣaṇ'|âlaṃkṛtābhyāṃ pāṇibhyāṃ svayam eva c' âinaṃ parigṛhya tri|daśebhyaḥ saṃdarśayām āsa:

«paśyantv atra|bhavantas tri|daś'|ālaya|nivāsino devāḥ, samanumodantāṃ c' êdam ati|vismayanīyaṃ karm'|âvadānam asya Mahā|sattvasya!

6.60 tyaktaṃ bat' ânena yathā śarīraṃ
niḥ|saṅgam ady' âtithi|vatsalena.
nir|mālyam apy evam a|kampamānā
n' âlaṃ parityaktum a|dhīra|sattvāḥ. [34]

jātiḥ kv' êyaṃ tad|virodhi kva c' êdaṃ
tyāg'|āudāryaṃ cetasaḥ pāṭavaṃ ca!
vispaṣṭo 'yaṃ puṇya|mand'|ādarāṇāṃ
pratyādeśo devatānāṃ nṛṇāṃ ca. [35]

aho bata guṇ'|âbhyāsa|
vāsit" âsya yathā matiḥ!
aho sad|vṛtta|vātsalyaṃ
kriy"|audāryeṇa darśitam!» [36]

atha Śakras tat|karm'|âtiśaya|vikhyāpan'|ârthaṃ loka|hit'|âvekṣī śaśa|bimba|lakṣaṇena Vaijayantasya prāsāda|varasya Sudharmāyāś ca deva|sabhāyāḥ kūṭ'|âgāra|karṇike candra|maṇḍalaṃ c' âbhyalaṃcakāra.

When he saw this, the lord of the gods became filled with great wonder. Assuming his true form, he honored the Great Being with words that were pleasing to the mind and ears and attended by showers of divine flowers. He then picked up the hare with his hands, which were adorned with glistening rings and which bore the lustrous beauty of lotus petals. Displaying the hare to the gods, he exclaimed:

"Look, you gods who dwell in heaven! And rejoice* in the astonishing feat of this Great Being!

See how, in his love of guests, 6.60
this creature gave up his body without attachment,
while those of unsturdy nature cannot discard
even a used garland without quivering!

His noble generosity and sharp mind
seem so contradictory to his animal birth!
His deed is a clear rebuke to both gods and men
who have weak regard for merit.

How infused his mind is
with the practice of virtue!
How devoted to morality
his noble act shows him to be!"

To proclaim the Great Being's exceptional deed, and eager to benefit the world, Shakra then adorned an image of a hare on the gables of Vaijayánta, his magnificent palace, and Sudhárma, the assembly hall of the gods, as well as on the disc of the moon.

sampūrṇe 'dy' âpi tad idaṃ śaśa|bimbaṃ niśā|kare
chāyā|mayam iv' ādarśe rājate 'bhivirājate. [37]

6.65 tataḥ prabhṛti lokena kumud'|ākara|hāsanaḥ
kṣaṇadā|tilakaś candraḥ śaś'|âṅka iti kīrtyate. [38]

tad evaṃ, tiryag|gatānām api Mahā|sattvānaṃ śakty|anurūpā dāna|pravṛttir dṛṣṭā. kena nāma manuṣya|bhūtena na dātavyaṃ syāt?

«tathā tiryag|gatā api guṇa|vātsalyāt saṃpūjyante sadbhir, iti guṇeṣv ādaraḥ kārya» ity evam apy upaneyam.

Even today a hare's image
shines on the full moon,
like a reflection
on a silver mirror.

From then on, the moon, 6.65
also called Opener of Night Lotuses
and Ornament on the Forehead of the Night,
became known in the world as Hare-Marked.*

So it is that, even as animals, Great Beings have displayed generosity to the best of their ability. Who then that is human would not give gifts?

And one should also conclude the following: "In their love of virtue, the good honor even animals. One should therefore have a regard for virtues."

STORY 7
THE BIRTH-STORY OF AGÁSTYA

7.1 TAPO|VANA|STHĀNĀM apy alaṃ|kāras tyāga|śauryaṃ, prāg eva gṛha|sthānām.

tad|yath" ânuśrūyate.

Bodhisattva|bhūtaḥ kil' âyaṃ Bhagavāl̄ loka|hit'|ârthaṃ saṃsār'|âdhvani vartamānaś cāritra|guṇa|viśuddhy|abhilakṣitaṃ kṣiti|tala|tilaka|bhūtam anyatamaṃ mahad brāhmaṇa|kulaṃ gagana|talam iva śarad|amala|paripūrṇa|maṇḍalaś candramāḥ samudyann ev' âbhyalaṃcakāra.

sa yathā|kramaṃ śruti|smṛti|vihitān avāpya jāta|karm'|ādīn saṃskārān adhītya s'|âṅgān Vedān kṛtsnaṃ vyāpya vidvad|yaśasā manuṣya|lokaṃ guṇa|priyair dātṛbhir abhyarthya pratigrāhyamāṇa|vibhavatvāt parāṃ dhana|samṛddhim adhijagāma.

7.5 sa bandhu|mitr'|āśrita|dīna|vargaṃ
sammānanīyān atithīn gurūṃś ca
prahlādayām āsa tayā samṛddhyā
deśān mahā|megha iv' âbhivarṣan. [1]

vidvattayā tasya yaśaḥ prakāśaṃ
tat tyāga|śauryād adhikaṃ cakāśe
niśā|karasy' êva śarad|viśuddhaṃ
samagra|bhāvād adhikānti bimbam. [2]

atha sa Mah"|ātmā ku|kārya|vyāsaṅga|doṣa|saṃbādhaṃ pramād'|āspada|bhūtaṃ dhan'|ârjana|rakṣaṇa|prasaṅga|vyākulam upaśama|virodhi vyasana|śara|śata|lakṣya|bhūtam a|paryanta|karm'|ânt'|ânuṣṭhāna|pariśramam a|tṛpti|

HEROIC GENEROSITY is an ornament even in forest ascetics, let alone in householders. 7.1

Tradition has handed down the following story.

When he was a Bodhi·sattva, traveling on the road of samsara for the benefit of the world, the Lord is said to have adorned an eminent brahmin family, just as the spotless sphere of the rising full-moon adorns the sky in autumn. Distinguished by their purity in conduct and virtue, the family was like an ornament on the forehead of the earth.

After attaining, in proper sequence, the birth-ritual and other sacraments that were prescribed by revelation and tradition, the Bodhi·sattva fully mastered the Vedas, and their auxiliary subjects the Vedángas, and pervaded the human world with his reputation for wisdom.* Endowed with these qualities, he acquired great riches by soliciting donors who were fond of virtue.

Like a mighty cloud pouring rain over lands, 7.5
he used his wealth to gladden relatives,
friends, dependents, and people in distress,
as well as venerable guests and teachers.

His fame gleamed from his wisdom.
but it shone even more due to his heroic giving,
just as the moon, cleansed by autumn,
is even more beautiful when full.

The Great One, however, came to perceive the householder life as unsatisfying and unsavory. Full of wicked attachments to vice, life as a householder was based on recklessness and involved an unruly addiction to acquiring and conserving wealth. A hindrance to tranquility, it was the

janakaṃ kṛś'|āsvādaṃ gārhasthyam avetya, tad|doṣa|vivikta| sukhāṃ ca dharma|pratipatty|anukūlāṃ mokṣa|dharm'| ārambh'|âdhiṣṭhāna|bhūtāṃ pravrajyām anupaśyan;

mahatīm api tāṃ dhana|samṛddhim a|parikleś'|âdhigatāṃ loka|saṃnati|mano|harāṃ tṛṇavad apāsya tāpasa|pravrajyā|vinaya|niyama|paro babhūva.

pravrajitam api taṃ Mahā|sattvaṃ yaśaḥ|prakāśatvāt pūrva|saṃstav'|ânusmaraṇāt saṃbhāvita|guṇatvāt praśam'| âbhilakṣitatvāc ca śreyo|'rthī janas tad|guṇa|gaṇ'|āvarjita| matis tath" âiv' âbhijagāma.

7.10 sa taṃ gṛhi|jana|saṃsargaṃ praviveka|sukha|pramāthinaṃ vyāsaṅga|vikṣep'|ântarāya|karam a|bahu|manyamānaḥ pravivek'|âbhirāmatayā dakṣiṇa|samudra|madhy'|âvagāḍham indra|nīla|bhed'|âbhinīla|varṇair anila|bal'|ākalitair ūrmi|mālā|vilāsair ācchurita|paryantaṃ sita|sikat'|āstīrṇa| bhūmi|bhāgaṃ puṣpa|phala|pallav'|âlaṃkṛta|viṭapair nānā| tarubhir upaśobhitaṃ vimala|salil'|āśaya|pratīraṃ Kārā|dvīpam adhyāsanād āśrama|pada|śriyā saṃyojayām āsa.

target of hundreds of arrows of woe, while the endless tasks one had to perform made it exhausting. Renunciation, on the other hand, offered a happiness that was free from such faults. Conducive toward the practice of morality, it formed the basis for undertaking the teaching of liberation.

Despite the magnitude of his riches, he therefore discarded, as though it were chaff, the wealth that he had acquired without trouble and that had the attractive quality of humbling the world, and instead became intent on the disciplines and restraints of ascetic renunciation.

Inspired by his hordes of virtues, people still however visited the Great Being, even though he had renounced society. In their search for spiritual felicity, they came partly because of his celebrated reputation, partly from recalling their previous intimacy with him, partly because of his esteemed virtue, and partly because of his remarkable serenity.

But the Great Being did not appreciate these crowds of 7.10
laypeople who destroyed the bliss of his solitude and obstructed his rejection of attachments. So he settled on the island of Kara, furnishing it with the glory of his hermitage. The island of Kara lies in the middle of the Southern Ocean, where its shores are draped by playful garlands of sapphire-blue waves driven along by powerful winds. The ground is strewn with white sand and various trees adorn the island, their boughs decorated with flowers, fruits, and buds. By the shore there lies a lake of immaculate water.

su|tanus tapasā tatra sa reje tapas" â|tanuḥ
navaś candra iva vyomni kāntatven' â|kṛśaḥ kṛśaḥ. [3]

praśama|nibhṛta|ceṣṭit'|êndriyo
  vrata|niyam'|âika|raso vane vasan
munir iti tanu|buddhi|śaktibhir
  mṛga|vihagair api so 'nvagamyata. [4]

atha sa Mah"|ātmā pradān'|ôcitatvāt tapo|vane 'pi nivasan kāl'|ôpanatam atithi|janaṃ yathā|saṃnihitena mūla|phalena śucinā salilena hṛdyābhiś ca svāgat'|āśīrvāda|peśalābhis tapasvi|jana|yogyābhir vāgbhiḥ saṃpūjayati sma. atithi|jan'|ôpayukta|śeṣeṇa ca yātrā|mātr'|ârtham abhyavahṛtena tena vanyen' āhāreṇa vartayām āsa.

tasya tapaḥ|prakarṣāt pravisṛtena yaśasā samāvarjita|hṛdayaḥ Śakro devānāṃ indraḥ sthairya|jijñāsayā tasya Mahā|sattvasya tasminn araṇy'|āyatane tāpasa|jan'|ôpabhoga|yogyaṃ mūla|phalam anupūrveṇa sarvam antardhāpayām āsa. Bodhisattvo 'pi dhyāna|prasṛta|mānasatayā saṃtoṣa|paricayād an|adhimūrcchitatvād āhāre śarīre c' ân|abhiṣvaṅgān na tad|antar|dhāna|hetuṃ manasi cakāra. sa taruṇāni taru|pallavāny adhiśrāya tair āhāra|prayojanam abhiniṣpādy'

Although greatly emaciated by austerities,
his asceticism made him far from thin in splendor,
just as the crescent moon in the sky,
though slender, is far from lean in beauty.

His actions and senses calmed by tranquility,
he lived in the forest, focusing solely on disciplines
and vows.
Even the animals and birds realized he was a sage,
despite their weak mental powers.

Although he lived in a hermitage, the Great One was so used to being generous that he would honor any guests who came along, offering them pure water and whatever roots and fruits were at hand and receiving them with charming words of welcome and benediction that were customary for an ascetic and that brought joy to the heart. He himself lived off the forest food left over from what he gave to guests, eating only as much as was necessary for his sustenance.

Shakra, the king of the gods, was enthralled by the widespread fame the Bodhi·sattva had earned for his exceptional asceticism and wished to test his resilience. He therefore gradually removed from the forest area inhabited by the Great Being any roots and fruits that would normally provide food for ascetics. The Bodhi·sattva's mind, however, was focused on meditation and contentment had become ingrained in him. Indifferent to food and unattached to his body, he did not even consider why this food had disappeared. Instead he managed to acquire food by cooking some fresh leaves. Feeling no cravings, nor any desire for

â|paritṛṣyamāṇa āhāra|viśeṣ'|ân|utsukaḥ sva|stha|matis tath" âiva vijahāra.

7.15 na kva cid dur|labhā vṛttiḥ saṃtoṣa|niyat'|ātmanām.
kutra nāma na vidyante tṛṇa|parṇa|jal'|āśayāḥ? [5]

vismitatara|manās tu Śakro dev'|êndras tasya ten' âvasthānena sthiratara|guṇa|saṃbhāvanas tat|parīkṣā|nimittaṃ tasminn araṇya|vana|pradeśe nidāgha|kāl'|ânila iva samagraṃ vīrut|tṛṇa|taru|gaṇaṃ parṇa|samṛddhyā viyojayām āsa. atha Bodhisattvaḥ pratyārdratarāṇi śīrṇa|parṇāni samāhṛtya tair udaka|svinnair an|utkaṇṭhita|matir vartayamāno dhyāna|sukha|prīṇita|manās tatr' âmṛta|tṛpta iva vijahāra.

a|vismayaḥ śrutavatāṃ
samṛddhānām a|matsaraḥ
saṃtoṣaś ca vana|sthānāṃ
guṇa|śobhā|vidhiḥ paraḥ. [6]

atha Śakras tena tasy' âdbhuta|rūpeṇa saṃtoṣa|sthairyeṇa samabhivṛddha|vismayaḥ s'|â|marṣa iva tasya Mahā|sattvasya vrata|kāle hut'|âgni|hotrasya parisamāpta|japyasy' âtithi|jana|didṛkṣayā diśo vyavalokayato brāhmaṇa|rūpam āsthāy' âtithir iva nāma bhūtvā purastāt prādur|abhūt. prīta|manāḥ samabhigamya c' âinaṃ Bodhisattvaḥ svāgat'|ādi|priya|vacana|puraḥsareṇ' āhāra|kāla|nivedanen' ôpanimantrayām

finer food, he dwelled with a self-composed mind in the same manner as he had done before.

Those trained to be content easily 7.15
find sustenance wherever they are.
Where can one not find
grass, leaves, or water?

The Bodhi·sattva's resilience filled Shakra, the king of the gods, with even greater amazement and made his admiration for the ascetic's virtue even more strong. But to test him still further, he stripped all the plants, grasses and trees of their leaves in that area of the forest, just as the wind does in summer. The Bodhi·sattva, however, gathered the fresher of the dry leaves and by boiling them he lived off them without anxiety. Delighting in the bliss of meditation, he dwelled there as though sated by ambrosia.

Modesty in the learned,
absence of greed in the rich,
and contentment in forest ascetics:
these are the highest form of virtue in each.

Shakra grew even more astonished at the miraculous tenacity of the Bodhi·sattva's contentment. Driven almost by anger, he took on the form of a brahmin and appeared before the Great Being, pretending to be a guest. It was the time of day when the Great Being performed his vows. He had just poured a sacrificial libation and completed his recitations and was now looking in every direction, eager to see a guest. Filled with delight, the Bodhi·sattva went up to the brahmin and, after addressing him with friendly words of welcome, he invited him by announcing it was time to

āsa. tūṣṇīṃ|bhāvāt tu tasy' âbhimatam upanimantraṇam avetya sa Mah"|ātmā

ditsā|prakarṣa|vikasan|nayan'|āsya|śobhaḥ
snigdhair manaḥ|śruti|harair abhinandya vākyaiḥ
kṛcchr'|ôpalabdham api tac chrapaṇaṃ samastaṃ
tasmai dadau svayam abhūc ca mud" âiva tṛptaḥ. [7]

7.20 sa tath" âiva praviśya dhyān'|âgāraṃ ten' âiva prīti|prāmodyena tad aho|rātram atināmayām āsa.

atha Śakras tasya dvitīye tṛtīye c' âhani tath" âiva vrata|kāle purataḥ prādur|abhūt. so 'pi c' âinaṃ pramuditatara|manās tath" âiva pratipūjayām āsa.

dān'|âbhilāṣaḥ sādhūnāṃ
kṛp"|âbhyāsa|vivardhitaḥ.
n' âiti saṃkoca|dīnatvaṃ
duḥkhaiḥ prāṇ'|ântikair api. [8]

atha Śakraḥ parama|vismay'|āviṣṭa|hṛdayas tapaḥ|prakarṣād asya prārthanā|mātr'|âpekṣaṃ tri|daśa|pati|lakṣmī|saṃparkam avagamya samutpatita|bhay'|āśaṅkaḥ svam eva vapur divy'|âdbhuta|śobham abhiprapadya tapaḥ|prayojanam enaṃ paryapṛcchat:

eat. Understanding from the brahmin's silence that his invitation had been accepted, the Great One's

face glistened and eyes bloomed
with immense desire to give.
Gladdening him with friendly words,
a delight to the heart and ears,
he gave the brahmin all the food
he had laboriously cooked,
while he remained satisfied
by joy alone.

He then entered his meditation hut in his usual manner 7.20
and passed the day and night in delight and joy.

On the second and third day, Shakra appeared before the Bodhi·sattva while he was performing his vows in the same way as before. And the Bodhi·sattva, for his part, worshipped Shakra in the same manner with even greater joy.

Compassion only increases
the desire the virtuous have for giving.
Though faced with life-threatening perils,
their gifts never pitifully shrink.

Shakra was utterly astounded. Realizing that the Bodhi·sattva could, because of his exceptional asceticism, acquire the glory of ruling over heaven if he just asked for it, he felt a surge of fear and anxiety. Assuming his true form, which glistened with divine and miraculous beauty, he then asked the Bodhi·sattva his reasons for practicing asceticism:

«bandhūn priyān aśru|mukhān vihāya
parigrahān saukhya|parigrahāṃś ca
āś"|âṅkuśaṃ nu vyavasṛjya kutra
tapaḥ|parikleśam imaṃ śrito 'si? [9]

7.25 sukh'|ôpapannān paribhūya bhogāñ
chok'|āturaṃ bandhu|janaṃ ca kṛtvā
na hetun" âlpena hi yānti dhīrāḥ
sukh'|ôparodhīni tapo|vanāni. [10]

vaktavyam etan mayi manyase cet,
kautūhalaṃ no 'rhasi tad vinetum.
kiṃ nāma tad yasya guṇa|śravena
vaśī|kṛt" âivaṃ bhavato 'pi buddhiḥ?» [11]

Bodhisattva uvāca, «śrūyatāṃ, mārṣa, yan|nimitto 'yaṃ mama prayatnaḥ.

punaḥ|punar|jātir atīva duḥkhaṃ,
jarā vipad vyādhi|virūpatā ca.
martavyam ity ākulatā ca buddher.
lokān atas trātum iha sthito 'smi.» [12]

atha Śakro «n' âyam asmad|gatāṃ śriyaṃ kāmayata» iti samāśvāsita|hṛdayaḥ su|bhāṣitena tena c' âbhiprasādita|matir «yuktam» ity abhipūjya tad asya vacanaṃ vara|pradānena Bodhisattvam upanimantrayām āsa:

7.30 «atra te tāpasa|jana|
pratirūpe su|bhāṣite.
dadāmi, Kāśyapa, varaṃ...
tad vṛṇīṣva yad icchasi.» [13]

"Abandoning your dear weeping relatives
and your possessions, those furnishings of joy,
on what do you pin your hopes
by resorting to this ascetic hardship?

The wise would not, for petty reasons, 7.25
dismiss easily acquired pleasures
and leave for unpleasant ascetic groves,
forcing their relatives to suffer in grief.

If you think it suitable to tell me,
please tame my curiosity.
What have you heard to be so virtuous
that it overpowers even your mind?"

"Listen, sir," the Bodhi·sattva replied, "to the reasons for my endeavor.

Repeated rebirth is a great anguish,
as is old age, misfortune, and the various diseases.
My mind is disturbed by the necessity of death.
That is why I stay in the forest to save the worlds."

Shakra was relieved that the Bodhi·sattva showed no desire to usurp his glory and was pleased by his wise words. Expressing his approval, he praised the Bodhi·sattva's speech and offered him the gift of a boon.

"Your wise words 7.30
befit an ascetic.
Let me give you a boon, Káshyapa.*
Choose what you like."

atha Bodhisattvo bhava|sukheṣv an|āsthaḥ prārthanām eva duḥkham avagacchan s'|ātmī|bhūta|saṃtoṣaḥ Śakram uvāca:

«dātum icchasi cen mahyam
anugraha|karaṃ varam,
vṛṇe tasmād aham imaṃ
devānāṃ pravaraṃ varam. [14]

dārān mano|'bhilaṣitāṃs tanayān prabhutvam
arthān abhīpsita|viśālatarāṃś ca labdhvā
yen' âbhitapta|matir eti na jātu tṛptiṃ,
lobh'|ânalaḥ sa hṛdayaṃ mama n' âbhyupeyāt.» [15]

atha Śakras tasya tayā saṃtoṣa|pravaṇa|mānasatayā su|bhāṣit'|âbhivyañjitayā bhūyasyā mātrayā saṃprasādita|matiḥ punar Bodhisattvaṃ «sādhu! sādhv!†»* iti praśasya vareṇ' ôpacchandayām āsa.

7.35 «atr' âpi te muni|jana|
pratirūpe su|bhāṣite
pratiprābhṛtavat prītyā
prayacchāmy aparaṃ varam.» [16]

atha Bodhisattvaḥ kleśa|viyogasy' âiva dur|labhatām asya pradarśayan vara|yācñ"|âpadeśena punar apy asmai Dharmaṃ deśayām āsa.

«dadāsi me yadi varaṃ
sad|guṇ'|āvāsa, Vāsava,
vṛṇe ten' êdam aparaṃ,
dev'|êndr', ân|avaraṃ varam. [17]

The Bodhi·sattva had no interest in the pleasures of ordinary existence. He even considered it a menace to make a request, so content was he by nature. So he addressed Shakra thus:

"If you would like
to favor me with a boon,
then from the gods
I request this fine boon.

May the fire of greed never enter my heart.
Greed makes the burning mind never sated
even by a delightful wife, children, or power,
or riches greater than one's desire."

Shakra felt even more gratified by the Bodhisattva's fondness for contentment that was illustrated by these fine words. Praising him with cries of "Excellent! Excellent!" he urged him to accept a further boon.

"Your wise words 7.35
are suited to a sage.
Let me joyfully offer you
another boon as a gift in return."

Under the pretext of requesting a boon, the Bodhi·sattva then once again instructed Shakra on the Teaching, expounding to him the difficulty of detaching oneself from defilements.

"Vásava, seat of virtues,*
king of the gods,
if you give me another boon,
I request one that is far from lowly.

arthād api bhraṃśam avāpnuvanti
varṇa|prasādād yaśasaḥ sukhāc ca
yen' âbhibhūtā dviṣat" êva sattvāḥ,
sa dveṣa|vahnir mama dūrataḥ syāt.» [18]

tac chrutvā Śakro devānām adhipatir vismaya | vaśāt «sādhv!» ity enam sa | bahu | mānaṃ abhipraśasya punar uvāca:

7.40 «sthāne pravrajitān kīrtir anurakt" êva sevate!
tad varaṃ pratigṛhṇīṣva mad atr' âpi su|bhāṣite.» [19]

atha Bodhisattvaḥ kleśa | prātikūlyāt kliṣṭa | sattva | saṃparka | vigarhāṃ vara | saṃpratigrah' | âpadeśena kurvann ity uvāca:

«śṛṇuyām api n' âiva jātu bālaṃ
na ca vīkṣeya na c' âinam ālapeyam
na ca tena nivāsa|kheda|duḥkhaṃ
samupeyāṃ. varam ity ahaṃ vṛṇe tvām.» [20]

Śakra uvāca:

«anukampyo viśeṣeṇa
satām āpad|gato nanu.
āpadāṃ mūla|bhūtatvād
bālyaṃ c' âdhamam iṣyate. [21]

7.45 karuṇ"|āśraya|bhūtasya bālasy' âsya viśeṣataḥ
kṛpālur api san kasmān na darśanam ap' îcchasi?» [22]

May the fire of hatred remain far from me.
Like an enemy, it destroys people,
making them lose wealth,
the purity of caste, and the joy of fame."

When he heard these words, Shakra, the king of the gods was so amazed that he praised the Bodhi·sattva reverently with shouts of "Excellent!" and then addressed him once more:

"How right that Fame 7.40
attends to ascetics like a lover!
Accept another boon from me
for your wise words."

Under the pretext of accepting the boon and in his aversion to defilements, the Bodhi·sattva then spoke words that censured contact with impure people:

"May I never so much as hear a fool,
nor see one nor speak to one.
May I never suffer the pain of living with one.
This is the boon I ask of you."

Shakra answered:

"Surely the virtuous should feel
particular pity for those in distress.
Stupidity is viewed as the vilest condition.
For it is the root of misfortune.

Why, despite your compassion, 7.45
do you not wish to see a fool,
though he in particular
is a source of pity?"

Bodhisattva uvāca, «a|gatyā, mārṣa. paśyatv atra|bhavān:

kathaṃ cid api śakyeta
yadi bālaś cikitsitum
tadd|hit'|ôdyoga|nir|yatnaḥ
kathaṃ syād iti mad|vidhaḥ? [23]

itthaṃ c' âiṣa cikitsā|prayogasy' â|pātram iti gṛhyatām.

su|naya|vad a|nayaṃ nayaty ayaṃ
param api c' âtra niyoktum icchati
an|ucita|vinay'|ārjava|kramo
hitam api c' âbhihitaḥ prakupyati. [24]

7.50 iti paṇḍita|māna|moha|dagdhe
hita|vādiṣv api roṣa|rūkṣa|bhāve
rabhase vinay'|âbhiyoga|māndyād.
vada kas tatra hit'|ârpaṇ'|âbhyupāyaḥ! [25]

ity a|gatyā, sura|śreṣṭha, karuṇā|pravaṇair api
bālyād a|dravya|bhūtasya na darśanam ap' îṣyate.» [26]

tac chrutvā Śakraḥ «sādhu! sādhv!» ity enam abhinandya su|bhāṣita|paritoṣita|matiḥ punar uvāca:

«na su|bhāṣita|ratnānām arghaḥ kaś cana vidyate.
kusum'|âñjalivat prītyā dadāmy atra tu te varam.» [27]

"Because, sir," the Bodhi·sattva replied, "he is beyond help. Consider this, good sir:

If it were somehow
possible to cure a fool,
how could a man such as I
not strive for his good?

You must grasp that it is useless to apply medicine in such a case.

He follows the wrong path as if it were right
and wishes to subject others to the same route.
Unfamiliar with propriety and rectitude,
he becomes angry, though advised for his own good.

Burning with the delusion of intellectual pride, 7.50
he is abrasively angry even toward those
counseling good.
And his weak self-control makes him violent.
Tell me the way to aid such a person!

That is why, best of gods, even those
with a propensity for compassion
refuse to set eyes on a man so worthless.
For he is beyond help and foolish."

Hearing this, Shakra applauded the Bodhi·sattva with cries of "Excellent! Excellent!" Gratified by his wise words, he again addressed the Bodhi·sattva, saying:

"Wise words are jewels
that have no price.
Let me joyfully give you a boon for them,
as if offering you a handful of flowers."

atha Bodhisattvaḥ sarv'|âvastha|sukhatāṃ saj|janasya pradarśayañ Chakram uvāca:

7.55 vīkṣeya dhīraṃ śṛṇuyāṃ ca dhīraṃ.
syān me nivāsaḥ saha tena, Śakra.
saṃbhāṣaṇaṃ tena sah' âiva bhūyād.
etad varaṃ, deva|vara, prayaccha. [28]

Śakra uvāca, «atipakṣapāta iva khalu te dhīraṃ prati. tad ucyatāṃ:

«kiṃ nu dhīras tav' âkārṣīd? vada, Kāśyapa, kāraṇam
a|dhīra iva yen' âsi dhīra|darśana|lālasaḥ.» [29]

atha Bodhisattvaḥ saj|jana|māhātmyam asya pradarśayann uvāca:

«śrūyatāṃ, mārṣa, yena me dhīra|darśanam ev' âbhilaṣati matiḥ.

7.60 vrajati guṇa|pathena ca svayaṃ,
nayati parān api tena vartmanā.
vacanam api na rūkṣam a|kṣamāṃ
janayati tasya hit'|ôpasaṃhitam. [30]

a|śaṭha|vinaya|bhūṣaṇaḥ sadā
hitam iti lambhayituṃ sa śakyate.
iti mama guṇa|pakṣa|pātinī
namati matir guṇa|pakṣa|pātini.» [31]

ath' âinaṃ Śakraḥ «sādh' ûpapanna|rūpam idam!» iti c' âbhinandya samabhivṛddha|prasādaḥ punar vareṇ' ôpanimantrayām āsa:

To demonstrate how the virtuous produce happiness in every situation, the Bodhi·sattva then said to Shakra:

"May I see and hear a wise man. 7.55
May I stay with him, Shakra,
and also speak with him.
Give me this boon, best of gods."

"You certainly seem to support the side of the wise," Shakra replied. "So tell me this:

What has a wise person done for you?
Tell me, Káshyapa,
why you have this almost
unruly desire to see the wise."

Revealing to Shakra the illustrious nature of the virtuous, the Bodhi·sattva said:

"Listen, sir, to why my heart desires to see a wise man.

He travels the path of virtue by himself 7.60
and leads others along the same road too.
He is never intolerant of good advice,
however harsh the words.

Adorned by sincerity and humility,
he is able to accept beneficial advice.
And thus my heart, falling on the side of virtue,
inclines toward those that fall on virtue's side too."

"Excellent! How right!" Shakra applauded. Feeling even greater favor toward the Bodhi·sattva, he then offered him a further boon.

«kāmaṃ saṃtoṣa|s'|ātmatvāt
sarvatra kṛtam eva te.
mad|anugraha|buddhyā tu
grahītuṃ varam arhasi. [32]

upakār'|āśayā bhaktyā
śaktyā c' âiva samastayā
prayuktasy' âti|duḥkho hi
praṇayasy' â|pratigrahaḥ.» [33]

7.65 atha tasya parām upakartu|kāmatām avekṣya Bodhisattvas tat|priya|hita|kāmatayā pradān'|ânutarṣa|prābalyam asmai prakāśayann uvāca:

«tvadīyam annaṃ kṣaya|doṣa|varjitaṃ
manaś ca ditsā|paritoṣa|peśalam
viśuddha|śīl'|ābharaṇāś ca yācakā
mama syur! etāṃ vara|saṃpadaṃ vṛṇe.» [34]

Śakra uvāca, «su|bhāṣita|ratn'|ākaraḥ khalv atra|bhavān. api ca,

yad abhiprārthitaṃ sarvaṃ
tat tath" âiva bhaviṣyati.
dadāmi ca punas tubhyaṃ
varam asmin su|bhāṣite.» [35]

Bodhisattva uvāca:

7.70 «varaṃ mam' ânugraha|saṃpad|ākaraṃ
dadāsi cet, sarva|div'|âukasāṃ vara,
na m" âbhyupeyāḥ punar ity abhijvalann
imaṃ varaṃ daitya|nisūdanaṃ vṛṇe.» [36]

"I realize contentment is so ingrained in you
that all your goals have been fulfilled.
But consider it as a favor to me
and please accept this boon.

For it would cause great pain to refuse
a favor offered with devotion,
given with the hope it is of service
and to the limits of one's capability."

Understanding that Shakra felt an enormous desire to 7.65
serve him, and wishing to benefit the god and to be kind to
him, the Bodhi·sattva revealed how strongly he thirsted to
give by saying:

"May your food, which is free from the fault of decay,
and your mind, which tenderly delights in giving,
and your petitioners, who are adorned by pure virtue,
all be mine! This is the sublime boon I request."

"You are indeed a jewel of wisdom." Shakra replied. "Moreover,

Not only will you receive
everything you have asked for,
I will also give you a further boon
for these fine words."

The Bodhi·sattva answered:

"Most eminent of all gods, 7.70
if you would give me a boon that favors me,
may you never approach me, blazing with splendor.
This is the boon I ask of the destroyer of demons."

atha Śakraḥ s'|âmarṣa|vad enam ati|vismayamāna uvāca: «mā tāvad bhoḥ!

japa|vrat'|êjyā|vidhinā tapaḥ|śramair
jano 'yam anvicchati darśanaṃ mama.
bhavān punar n' êcchati kena hetunā
vara|pradits"|âbhigatasya me sataḥ?» [37]

Bodhisattva uvāca, «alaṃ te manyu|praṇayena. samanuneṣyāmy aham atra|bhavantaṃ deva|rājam. na hy asāv a|dākṣiṇy'|ânuvṛttir n' âpy a|bahu|māna|viceṣṭitam a|samavadhāna|kāmyatā vā bhavataḥ. kiṃ tu,

7.75 nirīkṣya te rūpam a|mānuṣ'|âdbhutaṃ
prasanna|kānti jvalitaṃ ca tejasā
bhavet pramādas tapas', îti me bhayaṃ
prasāda|saumyād api darśanāt tava.» [38]

atha Śakraḥ praṇamya pradakṣiṇī|kṛtya c' âinaṃ tatr' âiv' ântar|dadhe. prabhātāyāṃ ca rajanyāṃ Bodhisattvaḥ Śakra|prabhāv'|ôpahṛtaṃ prabhūtaṃ divyam anna|pānaṃ dadarśa, Śakr'|ôpanimantraṇ'|āhūtāni c' ân|ekāni pratyeka|buddha|śatāni vyāyat'|ābaddha|parikarāṃś ca pariveṣaṇa|sajjān an|ekān deva|kumārān.

ten' ânna|pāna|vidhinā sa munir maha"|rṣīn
saṃtarpayan mudam udāratamām avāpa,
vṛttyā ca tāpasa|jan'|ôcitay" âbhireme
dhyān'|â|pramāṇa|niyamena śamena c' âiva. [39]

Feeling utter amazement, and almost a sense of anger, Shakra replied:

"Do not speak this way, sir!

In their desire to see me, people in the world use
mantras, vows, sacrifices, and strenuous austerities.
Why then do you not wish to see me,
though I've come, eager to give boons?"

"Please don't be angry," the Bodhi·sattva answered. "I entreat you, king of the gods. I am not behaving offensively nor disrespectfully, nor do I wish to show you any lack of reverence. Rather,

When I look at your divine and wondrous form, 7.75
radiantly beautiful and blazing with brightness,
I fear the sight of you, however serene and gentle,
may make me careless of my asceticism."

Bowing before the Bodhi·sattva and circling him reverently, Shakra then disappeared at that very spot. At sunrise, the Bodhi·sattva saw an abundant amount of divine food and drink that had been brought to him through Shakra's power, along with several hundred *pratyéka·buddhas*, who had been summoned at Shakra's request, and numerous gods, who wore tight girdles and were ready to offer their services.

Satisfying the great seers with this food and drink,
the sage acquired supreme joy,
delighting in the subsistence apt for an ascetic
and in the tranquil restraints of the *dhyanas* and
immeasurables.*

tad evaṃ, tapo|vana|sthānām apy alaṃ|kāras tyāga|śauryaṃ, prāg eva gṛha|sthānām iti.

«tyāga|śauryeṇ' âlaṃ|kartavya ev' ātmā sat|puruṣeṇ'» êti dāna|pati|saṃvarṇanāyām† upaneyaṃ lobha|dveṣa|moha|bālya|vigarhāyāṃ kalyāṇa|mitra|saṃparka|guṇe saṃtoṣa|kathāyāṃ* Tathāgata|māhātmye c': «âivaṃ pūrva|janmasv api su|bhāṣita|ratn'|âtiśay'|ākaraḥ sa Bhagavān prāg ev' âbhisaṃbuddha!» iti.

So it is that heroic generosity is an ornament even in forest ascetics, let alone in householders.

One should cite this story when praising generous donors, saying: "A good man should therefore adorn himself with heroic generosity." And one should also cite this story when criticizing greed, hatred, and foolishness, or when discussing the merits of keeping company with good friends, or the topic of contentment. And when discussing the magnanimity of the Tatha·gata, one should cite this story, saying: "In this way, even in his previous births, the Lord was an exceptional jewel of learning; how much more so when he was awakened!"

STORY 8

THE BIRTH-STORY OF MAITRI·BALA

8.1 NA PARA|DUḤKH'|ĀTURĀḤ sva|sukham avekṣante mahā|kāruṇikāḥ.

tad|yath" ânuśrūyate.

Bodhisattvaḥ kila sva|māhātmya|kāruṇy'|âbhiprapanna|jagat|paritrāṇ'|âdhyāśayaḥ, pradāna|dama|saṃyama|sauraty'|ādibhir lok'|ânugrah'|ânukūlair guṇ'|âtiśayair abhivardhamānaḥ, sarva|sattva|maitra|manā Maitrībalo nāma rājā babhūva.

duḥkhaṃ sukhaṃ vā yad abhūt prajānāṃ
tasy' âpi rājñas tad abhūt tath" âiva.
ataḥ prajā|rakṣaṇa|dakṣiṇo 'sau
śastraṃ ca śāstraṃ ca parāmamarśa. [1]

8.5 nar'|êndra|cūḍā|dhṛta|śāsanasya
tasya tv alaṃkāravad āsa śastram.
vispaṣṭa|rūpaṃ dadṛśe ca śāstraṃ
nayeṣu lokasya hit'|ôdayeṣu. [2]

vinigraha|pragrahayoḥ pravṛttir
dharm'|ôparodhaṃ na cakāra tasya.
hit'|āśayatvān naya|naipuṇāc ca
parīkṣakasy' êva pituḥ prajāsu. [3]

tasy' âivaṃ dharmeṇa prajāḥ pālayataḥ satya|tyāg'|ôpaśama|prajñ"|ādibhiś ca para|hita|pariṇāmanāt sa|viśeṣ'|ôdātta|kramair bodhi|saṃbhāra|vidhibhir abhivardhamānasya,

kadā cit kasmiṃś cid aparādhe yakṣāṇām adhipatinā sva|viṣayāt pravrājitā ojo|hārāḥ pañca yakṣāḥ para|vadha|dakṣās tad|viṣayam abhijagmuḥ. vyapagata|sarv'|ôpadravatvāc ca

PAINED BY THE SUFFERING of others, men of great compassion never seek their own pleasure. 8.1

Tradition has handed down the following story.

The Bodhi·sattva is said to have once been a king called Maitri·bala.* Kindhearted toward all creatures, his magnanimity and compassion made him determined to save the world and he swelled with exceptional virtues that were suited to favoring his people, including generosity, self-control, self-restraint, and tenderness.

Whatever the pain or pleasure of his people
the king experienced them as his own.
Through his skill in protecting his subjects,
he managed both sword and government.

His sword was no more than an ornament 8.5
in his rule over the bowed heads of kings.*
But his government was patently evident
in the policies he used to benefit his people.

When issuing punishments and rewards,
he never violated morality.
Through his goodness and political acumen,
he was like a concerned father to his people.

In this way, the king protected his people justly, and by benefiting others through virtues such as truth, generosity, serenity, and wisdom, he developed the superior and elevated qualities that are essential for awakening.

One day five life-sapping *yaksha* demons arrived in the Bodhi·sattva's kingdom. Experts in murder, they had been expelled from their realm by the king of *yaksha*s for some crime. Because there were no calamities in the Bodhi·sattva's

nitya|pravṛtta|vividh'|ôtsavaṃ parayā saṃpadā samupeta|rūpaṃ pramudita|tuṣṭa|puṣṭa|janam abhisamīkṣya taṃ viṣayaṃ tad|viṣaya|nivāsināṃ puruṣāṇām ojāṃsy apahartuṃ eṣām abhilāṣo babhūva.

te pareṇ' âpi yatnena sampravṛttāḥ sva|karmaṇi
n' âiva tad|viṣaya|sthānāṃ hartum ojaḥ prasehire. [4]

8.10 tasya prabhāv'|âtiśayān nṛ|pasya
mam' êti yatr' âiva babhūva buddhiḥ,
s" âiv' âsya rakṣā param" āsa, tasmād
ojāṃsi hartuṃ na viṣehire te. [5]

yadā ca param api prayatnaṃ kurvanto n' âiva śaknuvanti sma kasya cit tad|viṣaya|nivāsina ojo 'pahartum, ath' âiṣāṃ paras|param avekṣy' âitad abhūt:
«kiṃ nu khalv idaṃ, mārṣāḥ?

asmat|prabhāva|pratighāta|yogyā
vidyā|tapaḥ|siddhi|mayā viśeṣāḥ
na santi c' âiṣām. atha c' âdya† sarve
vyarth'|âbhidhānatvam upāgatāḥ smaḥ!» [6]

atha te yakṣā brāhmaṇa|varṇam ātmānam abhinirmāya samanucaranto dadṛśuḥ pratyaraṇya|caram anyatamaṃ go|pālakaṃ sa|śādvale chāyā|druma|mūle s'|ôpānatkaṃ saṃniṣaṇṇaṃ sa|pallavair vana|taru|kusumair viracitāṃ mālām udvahantaṃ dakṣiṇato vinyasta|daṇḍa|paraśum ekākinaṃ rajju|vartana|vyāpṛtaṃ prakṣveḍita|vilāsena gāyantam āsīnam. samupetya c' âinam ūcuḥ:

realm, the people living there enjoyed great prosperity and continuously held various festivals. So when the demons saw the inhabitants of that realm so joyful, content, and prosperous, they yearned to sap them of their strength.

But though they applied
the greatest effort,
they could not sap the strength
of the people in that realm.

The king's power was so exceptional, 8.10
the mere thought of having it
was itself the greatest security
and the demons could not sap their strength.

When, despite their greatest efforts, the demons could not weaken any of the inhabitants in that realm, they looked at each other and said:

"Well, gentlemen, what is this?

They do not possess any special attributes
from spells, austerities, or magical powers
that might thwart our might.
Yet none of us today can live up to our name!"

The demons then transformed themselves into brahmins and, during their wanderings, they spotted a cowherd who lived in the forest. Sitting on some grass at the foot of a shady tree, the cowherd wore sandals and a garland made of blossoms and flowers from forest trees. He had placed his staff and axe on the ground to his right and was sitting all alone, singing and humming playfully, preoccupied with twisting a piece of rope. Approaching this cowherd, the demons said:

8.15 «bho! gavāṃ saṃrakṣaṇ'|âdhikṛta! evaṃ vivikte nir|jana| saṃpāte 'sminn araṇye vicarann evam ekākī kathaṃ na bibheṣ' îti?»

sa tān ulloky' âbravīt, «kuto vā bhetavyam?» iti.

yakṣā ūcuḥ: «kiṃ tvayā na śruta|pūrvā rakṣasāṃ piśācānāṃ vā nisarga|raudrā prakṛtiḥ?

sahāya|madhye 'pi hi vartamāno
vidyā|tapaḥ|svastyayanair upetaḥ
yebhyaḥ kathaṃ cit parimokṣam eti
śauryād avajñāta|bhayo 'pi lokaḥ, [7]

tebhyo nṛ|medaḥ|piśit'|âśanebhyaḥ
kathaṃ bhayaṃ te 'sti na rākṣasebhyaḥ
vivikta|gambhīra|bhayānakeṣu
sahāya|hīnasya van'|ântareṣu?» [8]

8.20 ity ukte sa go|pālakaḥ prahasy' âinān uvāca:

«janaḥ svastyayanen' âyaṃ
mahatā paripālyate.
dev'|êndrair apy a|śakyo 'yaṃ
kiṃ punaḥ piśit'|âśanaiḥ? [9]

tena geha iv' âraṇye rātrāv api yathā divā
jan'|ânta iva c' âiko 'pi nir|bhayo vicarāmy aham.» [10]

ath' âinaṃ te yakṣāḥ kautūhala|prābalyāt s'|ādaram upavatsayanta iv' ōcuḥ:

"Sir! Protector of cows! Why are you not afraid of wandering alone in this isolated forest which is empty of people?" 8.15

"Why should I be afraid?" the cowherd answered, looking up at the demons.

"Have you never heard of the terrifying nature of ogres or goblins?" the demons replied.

"Even when surrounded by friends,
or endowed with spells, ascetic powers, or charms,
it is hard to escape them,
however fearless with courage you are.

They feed off the fat and flesh of men.
How can you not fear ogres, being
in a remote, deep, terrifying forest,
unaccompanied by friends?"

When he heard this, the cowherd laughed and said to them: 8.20

"The people here are protected
by a mighty charm.
Even chief deities have no power over them,
how then could flesh-eating ogres?

Even at night I wander
in the forest as if it were day.
Though alone, I roam fearlessly,
as if among crowds."

Driven by curiosity, the demons then addressed the cowherd respectfully, trying to entice him to speak:

«tat kathaya! kathaya tāvad, bhadra, kīdṛśo 'yaṃ yuṣmākaṃ svastyayana|viśeṣa iti?»

8.25 sa tān prahasann uvāca:

«śrūyatāṃ yādṛśo 'smākam aty|adbhutaḥ svastyayana|viśeṣaḥ.

kanaka|giri|śilā|viśāla|vakṣāḥ
śarad|a|mal'|êndu|manojña|vaktra|śobhaḥ
kanaka|parigha|pīna|lamba|bāhur
vṛṣabha|nibh'|ēkṣaṇa|vikramo nar'|êndraḥ. [11]

īdṛśo 'smākaṃ svastyayana|viśeṣa.»

ity uktvā s'|â|marṣa|vismayas tān yakṣān avekṣamāṇaḥ punar uvāca:

8.30 «āścaryaṃ bat' êdam.

evaṃ prakāśo nṛpati|prabhāvaḥ
kathaṃ nu vaḥ śrotra|pathaṃ na yātaḥ?
aty|adbhutatvād atha vā śruto 'pi
bhavatsu vipratyayato na rūḍhaḥ? [12]

śaṅke guṇ'|ânveṣaṇa|viklavo vā
deśe jano 'sāv a|kutūhalo vā.
vivarjito bhāgya|parikṣayād vā
kīrtyā nar'|êndrasya yato 'bhyupaitha. [13]

tad asti vo bhāgya|śeṣaṃ yat tādṛśād deśa|kāntārād ih' āgatāḥ stha.»

"Tell us! Do tell us, good sir! What is this special charm you possess?"

With a smile, the cowherd replied: 8.25

"Listen then to the miraculous and special charm we own.

His chest is as wide as a rock on Golden Mountain.*
His face shines with the charm of a pure autumn
moon.
His arms are as thick and long as golden bars.
His eyes and gait are like a bull's. Such is our king.

This is the type of special charm we possess."

But after he had spoken these words, he looked at the demons with a mixture of indignation and astonishment and addressed them again, saying:

"But this is amazing. 8.30

When our king's might is so renowned,
how has it not reached your ears?
Or perhaps it was so astonishing to hear
that distrust made you ignore it?

I suppose the people in your country
are loath to pursue virtue or have no curiosity.
Or perhaps it is a lack of good fortune
that deprives them of the king's fame.

But you still have some good fortune remaining: for you have arrived here from your land."

yakṣā ūcuḥ, «bhadra, kiṃ|kṛto 'yam asya rājñaḥ prabhāvo yad asy' â|mānuṣā na prasahante viṣaya|vāsinaṃ janaṃ hiṃsitum?» iti.

8.35 go|pālaka uvāca, «sva|māhātmy'|âdhigataḥ prabhāvo 'yam asmākaṃ mahā|rājasya. paśyata, brāhmaṇāḥ:

maitrī tasya balaṃ dhvaj'|âgra|śabalaṃ
tv ācāra|mātraṃ balaṃ.
n' âsau vetti ruṣaṃ na c' āha paruṣaṃ
samyak ca gāṃ rakṣati.
dharmas tasya nayo na nīti|nikṛtiḥ
pūj"|ârtham arthaḥ satām.
ity āścarya|mayo 'pi dur|jana|dhanaṃ
garvaṃ ca n' ālambate. [14]

evam|ādi|guṇa|śata|samudito 'yam asmākaṃ svāmī. ten' âsya na prasahante viṣaya|nivāsinaṃ janaṃ upadravāḥ.... api ca kiyad ahaṃ vaḥ śakṣyāmi vaktum. nṛpati|guṇa|śravaṇa|kutūhalais tu bhavadbhir nagaram eva yuktaṃ praveṣṭuṃ syāt. tatra hi bhavantaḥ sva|dharm'|ânurāgād vyavasthit'|ārya|maryādaṃ nitya|kṣema|su|bhikṣatvāt pramudita|samṛddham an|uddhat'|ôdātta|veṣam abhyāgat'|âtithi|jana|viśeṣa|vatsalaṃ nṛpati|guṇ'|ākṣipta|hṛdayaṃ tat|kīrty|āśrayāḥ stutīr maṅgalam iva svastyayanam iva ca praharṣād abhyasyantaṃ janaṃ dṛṣṭvā rājño guṇa|vistaram anumāsyante. satyāṃ ca guṇa|bahu|mān'|ôdbhāvanāyāṃ tad|didṛkṣāyām a|vaśyaṃ tad|guṇa|pratyakṣiṇo bhaviṣyath' êti.»

"Good sir," the demons replied. "What kind of power does this king have that demons are unable to harm the people that live in his realm?"

"The power of His Majesty comes from his magnanimity," the cowherd responded. "Look, brahmins: 8.35

Kindness is his true strength. His army,
with its colorful banners, is mere convention.
He knows no anger and never speaks harshly.
He protects the earth rightly.
Justice guides his government, not deceitful politics.
His wealth is used to serve the virtuous.
A wondrous being, he succumbs
to neither pride nor the wealth of the wicked.

Our master is furnished with hundreds of such virtues. That is why the inhabitants of his realm cannot be afflicted by misfortune. But I can only tell you so much. If you are interested in learning the king's virtues, you should go to the city itself. There you will see people maintaining the bounds of decency through their devotion to their particular duties. The permanent security they enjoy, and perpetual good food, brings them happiness and prosperity. Their clothes are humble but elegant and they are exceptionally kind to any guests that arrive. Enthralled by the king's virtues, they joyfully rehearse eulogies dedicated to his glory, as if reciting an auspicious chant or charm. When you see this, you will be able to measure the extent of the king's virtues. And when you develop respect for his virtues, you will desire to see them and certainly witness them yourselves."

atha te yakṣāḥ sva|prabhāva|pratīghātāt tasmin rājani s'|â|marṣa|hṛdayā bhāva|prayuktay" âpi yuktayā tayā tathyayā guṇa|kathayā n' âiva mārdavam upajagmuḥ.

prāyeṇa khalu mandānām a|marṣa|jvalitaṃ manaḥ
yasmin vastuni tat|kīrtyā tad viśeṣeṇa dahyate. [15]

8.40 pradāna|priyatāṃ tu samabhivīkṣya rājñas te yakṣās tad|apakāra|cikīrṣavaḥ samabhigamya rājānaṃ saṃdarśana|kāle bhojanam ayācanta. atha sa rājā pramudita|manās tad|adhikṛtān puruṣān samādideśa, «kṣipram abhirucitaṃ bhojanaṃ brāhmaṇebhyo dīyatām» iti. atha te yakṣāḥ samupahṛtaṃ rāj'|ârham api bhojanaṃ harita|tṛṇam iva vyāghrā n' âiva pratyagṛhṇan, «n' âivaṃ|vidhaṃ bhojanaṃ vayam aśnīma» iti. tac chrutvā sa rājā samabhigamy' âinān abravīt, «atha kīdṛśaṃ bhojanaṃ yuṣmākam upaśete, yāvat tādṛśam anviṣyatām?» iti.

yakṣā ūcuḥ:

«a|tyakt'|ôṣmāṇi māṃsāni
  narāṇāṃ rudhirāṇi ca
ity anna|pānaṃ, padm'|âkṣa,
  yakṣāṇām, a|kṣata|vrata.» [16]

ity uktvā daṃṣṭrā|karāla|vadanāni dīpta|piṅgala|kekara|raudra|nayanāni cipiṭa|virūpa|ghoṇāni jvalad|anala|kapila|keśa|śmaśrūṇi sa|jala|jaladhar'|ândhakār'|ākārāṇi† vikṛta|bhīṣaṇāni svāny eva vapūṃṣi pratyapadyanta.

The demons were furious at the king for obstructing their power and were not at all mollified by the cowherd's praise, true and apt though it was.

For the minds of fools
burn particularly fiercely
when the object of their
blazing anger is praised.

Observing that the king was fond of giving and eager to do him harm, the demons went to the king when it was time for his audience and asked him for food. The king was overjoyed and directed the men in charge of this duty to give the brahmins some delicious food quickly. But though the food was fit for a king, when it was brought to them, the demons rejected it like tigers spurning green grass and said: "We do not eat this kind of food!" Hearing this, the king approached them, saying: "Then what kind of food would suit you so that we can seek it out?" 8.40

The demons replied:

"Chunks of human flesh,
bloody and still warm.
This, vow-keeping lotus-eyed king,
is the food and drink of demons."

Saying this, the demons assumed their true forms. Deformed and horrifying, they were as black as rain-filled thunderclouds. Their mouths gaped open with fangs and their yellow-red squinting eyes blazed terrifyingly. Their noses were flat and misshapen and their hair and beards were as red as blazing fires.

samavekṣya c' âinān sa rājā «piśācāḥ khalv ime na mānuṣās, ten' âsmadīyam anna|pānaṃ n' âbhilaṣant'» îti niścayam upajagāma.

8.45 atha tasya nar'|êndrasya prakṛtyā karuṇ"|ātmanaḥ
bhūyasī karuṇā teṣu samabhūc chuddha|cetasaḥ. [17]

karuṇ"|âikatāna|hṛdayaś ca tān yakṣān anuśocan niyatam īdṛśam arthaṃ cintayām āsa:

«dayāvatas tāvad idam
anna|pānaṃ su|dur|labham.
pratyahaṃ ca tad anveṣyaṃ.
kiṃ nu duḥkham ataḥ param? [18]

nir|dayasy' âpy a|śaktasya
vighāt'|âika|rasaḥ śramaḥ.
śaktasy' âpy a|hit'|âbhyāsāt
kiṃ svit kaṣṭataraṃ tataḥ? [19]

evaṃ|vidh'|āhāra|parāyaṇānāṃ
kāruṇya|śūny'|â|śiva|mānasānām
prety' êha c' âiṣāṃ dahatāṃ svam arthaṃ
duḥkhāni yāsyanti kadā nu nāśam? [20]

8.50 tat katham idānīm aham eṣām āhāra|saṃpādanād ek'|âham api tāvat para|hiṃsā|praṇaya|vighātaṃ kuryām?

na hi smarāmy arthitay" āgatānām
āśā|viparyāsa|hata|prabhāṇi
him'|ânila|mlāpita|paṅkajānāṃ
samāna|dainyāni mukhāni kartum. [21]

On seeing them, the king became convinced that they must be demons and not humans, and that this was the reason they did not like his food.

Compassionate by nature 8.45
and pure in heart,
the lord of men felt even greater
compassion for the demons.

His heart solely absorbed in compassion, the king grieved for the demons and firmly pondered the matter the following way:

"For a person with considerate feelings,
such food would be very hard to obtain.
And it would have to be sought daily.
What greater sorrow can there be than this?

If a callous person were unable to get such food,
their efforts would merely be struck a blow.
But if they succeeded, what could be more grievous
than habitually committing this evil?

By living off this type of food,
these pitiless, evil-hearted demons incinerate
their welfare in this world and the next.
When will their sufferings end?

How, then, can I acquire food for these demons and ob- 8.50
struct their desire to harm others, even for just one day?

I do not recall ever disappointing petitioners,
removing the glow of hope from their faces
and making them look as sad
as lotuses withered by the winter wind.

bhavatu! dṛṣṭam!

svataḥ śarīrāt sthira|pīvarāṇi
dāsyāmi māṃsāni sa|śoṇitāni.
ato 'nyathā ko hi mama kramaḥ syād
ity āgateṣv arthiṣu yukta|rūpaḥ? [22]

svayaṃ|mṛtānāṃ hi nir|uṣmakāṇi
bhavanti māṃsāni vi|śoṇitāni.
priyāṇi c' âiṣāṃ na hi tāni samyag
bubhukṣayā pīḍita|vigrahāṇām. [23]

8.55 jīvato 'pi ca kuto 'ham anyasmān māṃsam ādāsye? mām abhigamya c' âite tath" âiva kṣut|tarṣa|parikṣāma|nayana|vadanā niṣ|phal'|āśā|praṇayatvād adhikatara|vighāt'|ātura|manasaḥ kathaṃ nāma pratiyāsyanti? tad idam atra prāpta|kālam.

duṣṭa|vraṇasy' êva sad" āturasya
kaḍevarasy' âsya rujā|karasya
karomi kāry'|âtiśay'|ôpayogād
atyartha|ramyaṃ pratikāra|khedam.» [24]

iti viniścitya sa rājā praharṣ'|ôdgamāt sphītī|kṛta|nayana|vadana|śobhaḥ sva|śarīram upadarśayaṃs tān yakṣān uvāca:

«amūni māṃsāni sa|śoṇitāni
dhṛtāni lokasya hit'|ârtham eva.
yady ātitheyatvam upeyur adya
mah"|ôdayaḥ so 'bhyudayo mama syāt.» [25]

But wait! I see a solution!

From my own body I will give them
firm and thick bleeding pieces of flesh.
What could be a more suitable act
for these petitioners that approach me?

Moreover, creatures that die a natural death
have cold and bloodless flesh.
This will certainly not please these demons,
whose bodies are pained by hunger.

Besides, how can I take the flesh of another being, es- 8.55
pecially one that is living? And when these demons have approached me this way, their eyes and faces withered by hunger and thirst, how can they return home, their hearts injured even more by disappointed hopes? It is therefore appropriate to act this way.

This body is like a festering wound.
Constantly diseased, it brings suffering.
It will delight me greatly to pay back that pain
by performing an exceptional deed."

On making this resolution, the king's face and eyes gleamed brightly with an eruption of joy. Displaying his body to the demons, he addressed them with the following words:

"This flesh and blood is sustained
solely for the benefit of the world.
If today it provides food for guests,
that would be a great gain for me."

atha te yakṣā jānanto 'pi rājñas tasy' âdhyāśayam aty|adbhutatvād a|śraddadhānā rājānam ūcuḥ:

8.60 «arthin" ātma|gate duḥkhe yācñā|dainyena darśite
jñātum arhati dāt" âiva prāpta|kālam ataḥ param.» [26]

atha sa rāj" «ânumatam idam eṣām» iti pramudita|manāḥ «sirā|mokṣaṇ'|ârthaṃ vaidyā ājñāpyantām» iti samādideśa.... atha tasya rājño 'mātyāḥ sva|māṃsa|śoṇita|pradāna|vyavasāyam avetya sa|sambhram'|â|marṣa|vyākula|hṛdayā vyaktam īdṛśaṃ kaṃ cid arthaṃ sneha|vaśād ūcuḥ:

«n' ârhati devaḥ pradāna|harṣ'|âtirabhasād anuraktānāṃ prajānāṃ hit'|â|hita|kramam an|avekṣitum. na c' âitad a|viditaṃ devasya yathā

yad yat prajānām a|hit'|ôdayāya
tat tat priyaṃ, māna|da, rākṣasānām.
par'|ôparodh'|ârjita|vṛtti|tuṣṭir
evaṃ|svabhāv", ân|agha, jātir eṣām. [27]

sukheṣv a|saktaś ca bibharṣi, deva,
rājya|śriyaṃ loka|hit'|ârtham eva.
sva|māṃsa|dāna|vyavasāyam asmāt
sva|niścay'|ônmārgam imaṃ vimuñca. [28]

Although the demons understood the king's intention, it was so wondrous that they could not believe it and so they addressed the monarch, saying:

"When a supplicant reveals his suffering 8.60
through the wretched act of begging,
it is the donor who should know
the most appropriate course to take."

Understanding from their words that the demons consented, the king became filled with delight and ordered doctors to be summoned so as to open up his veins. But when the king's ministers saw that he intended to give away his flesh and blood, they felt a turmoil of alarm and anger. Moved by affection, they addressed him frankly with words somewhat as follows:

"Your Majesty should not let his impetuous delight in giving make him overlook the good and bad effects of his actions on his doting subjects. Nor can Your Majesty be ignorant of the fact that

demons are fond of anything that brings
ill to your people, generous monarch.
They delight in a life that harms other beings.
Such is the nature of their kind, faultless king.

Unattached to pleasures, you bear your royal splendor
solely to benefit the world, Your Majesty.
Give up then this decision to offer your flesh,
as it deviates from your normal conviction.

8.65 a|saṃśayaṃ na prasahanta ete
tvad|vīrya|guptaṃ, nara|vīra, lokam
an|artha|pāṇḍitya|hatās tathā hi
nayena vāñchanty a|nayaṃ prajānām. [29]

medo|vas"|ādyais tri|daśā makheṣu
prītiṃ hut'|âś'|âbhihutair vrajanti.
sat|kāra|pūtaṃ bhavadīyam annaṃ
saṃpannam eṣāṃ kila n' âiva rucyam. [30]

kāmaṃ n' âsmad | vidha | jan' | ādheya | buddhayo deva | pādāḥ sva | kāry' | ânurāgas tv ayam asmān evam upacāra | pathād bhraṃśayati. pañcānām amīṣām arthe sakalaṃ jagad a|nāthī|kartavyam, iti ko 'yaṃ dharma|mārgo devasya? api ca, kiṃ|kṛt" êyam asmāsv evaṃ niṣpraṇayatā? kena v" âsmākaṃ svāmy|arthe viniyojyamānāni vinigūḍha|pūrvāṇi māṃsa|śoṇitāni yad a|parikṣīṇeṣv ev' âmīṣu svāni devo dātum icchat' îti?»

atha sa rājā tān amātyān uvāca:

«saṃvidyamānaṃ ‹n' âst' îti›
brūyād asmad|vidhaḥ katham,
‹na dadām' îty› a|sabhyaṃ vā
vispaṣṭam api yācitaḥ? [31]

8.70 dharma|vyavasthāsu puraḥ|saraḥ san
svayaṃ vrajeyaṃ yadi kāpathena,
asmad|gat'|ācāra|path'|ânugānāṃ
bhaved avasthā mama kā prajānām? [32]

These demons will certainly never affect the world 8.65
while it is protected by your power, hero among men.
Their cleverness has been rendered worthless.
They are using a ploy to seek your people's ill.

Oblations of fat, marrow, and other offerings
delight the gods when poured into fire at sacrifices.
But your exquisite, refined, carefully prepared food
apparently does not satisfy these demons.

We accept that Your Majesty has thoughts that men of our status cannot conceive. However, concern for our own interests impels us to deviate from courtesy. Is Your Majesty really following the path of virtue by divesting the entire world of its protector just for the sake of these five creatures? Moreover, why does Your Majesty have so little confidence in us? Why are you willing to give up your own flesh and blood, even though ours could be entrusted to our master's cause, as it is still intact and unused?"

The king then answered his ministers with the following words:

"When clearly asked for something,
how can a man such as I say
'I do not have it,' even though I have,
or vilely reply 'I cannot give'?

As their leader in moral issues, 8.70
if I myself tread the wrong path,
what would be my status among my people
if they practice the same conduct as I?

yataḥ prajā eva samīkṣamāṇaḥ
sāraṃ śarīrād aham uddhariṣye,
kaś ca prabhāvo jagad|artha|sādhur
mātsarya|hāry'|âlpa|hṛdo mama syāt. [33]

yad api c' âsmat|prema|bahu|mān'|āvarjitaṃ praṇaya|viśrambha|garbham abhidhīyate bhavadbhiḥ, ‹kiṃ|kṛt" êyam asmāsv evaṃ niṣpraṇayatā yad a|parikṣīṇeṣv eva no māṃsa|śoṇiteṣu svāni devo dātum icchat'› îty atra vo 'nuneṣyāmi.

na khalu me yuṣmāsu pratihata|viṣayaḥ praṇaya|mārgo viśrambha|virahāt pariśaṅkā|gahana|dur|avagāho vā. kiṃ tu,

dhane tanutvaṃ kramaśo gate vā
bhāgy'|ânuvṛttyā kṣayam āgate vā
vijṛmbhamāṇa|praṇayaḥ suhṛtsu
śobheta na sphīta|dhanaḥ kṛśeṣu. [34]

8.75 vivardhiteṣv arthi|jan'|ârtham eva
saṃvidyamāneṣu ca me bṛhatsu
gātreṣu māṃs'|ôpacay'|ônnateṣu
yuṣmāsv api syāt praṇayo virūpaḥ. [35]

a|saṃstutānām api ca kṣameya
pīḍāṃ kathaṃ, k" âiva kathā bhavatsu?
svāny eva māṃsāni yato 'smi ditsur.
māṃ c' âiva yācanta ime, na yuṣmān. [36]

It is because I do consider my people
that I will extract the essence from my body.
What power would I have to help the world
if I had a mean heart overtaken by selfishness?

You have spoken words that are full of love and respect for me. And you showed profound devotion and affection when you asked how I could have so little confidence in you that I would be willing to give up my own flesh and blood while yours still remained intact. But let me persuade you of my opinion on this matter.

My confidence in you has not at all been dealt a blow. Nor has mistrust made me close myself off behind a thicket of suspicion. Rather,

Though one might extend requests to friends
if one's wealth has gradually diminished,
or if, through misfortune, it has disappeared
altogether,
it would look bad for an affluent man to entreat
the poor.

My robust and large limbs 8.75
swell with plenty of flesh
and exist solely to benefit the needy.
It would be grotesque of me to petition you.

How can I tolerate the suffering
even of strangers, let alone you?
I therefore wish to give away only my flesh.
It is me the demons are entreating, not you.

tad alam asmad|atisnehād dharma|vighna|niḥsādhvasatayā. an|ucitaḥ khalv ayam atra|bhavatām asmad|artheṣu† samudācāraḥ. mīmāṃsitavyam api ca tāvad etat syāt:

sv'|ârtham ann'|ādi ditsantaṃ
katham syāt pratiṣedhayan
sādhu|vṛttir a|sādhur vā
prāg ev' âivaṃ|vidhaṃ vidhim? [37]

tad alam anen' âtra vo nirbandhena. nyāy'|ôpaparīkṣayā kriyatām asmat|sācivya|sadṛśam unmārg'|āvaraṇaṃ manasaḥ. anumodan'|ânuguṇa|vacasaḥ khalv atra|bhavantaḥ śobheran, n' âivam a|dhīra|nayanāḥ.

8.80 kutaḥ?

n'|âik'|ôpayogasya dhanasya tāvan
na pratyahaṃ yācanakā bhavanti?
evaṃ|vidhas tv arthi|jano 'dhigantuṃ
na daivat'|ārādhanay" âpi śakyaḥ. [38]

evaṃ|vidhe c' ârthi|jane 'bhyupete
dehe vināśiny a|sukh'|āspade ca
vimarśa|mārgo 'py an|udāttatā syān.
mātsarya|dainyaṃ tu parā tamisrā. [39]

tan na māṃ vārayitum arhanty atra|bhavanta»
ity anunīya sa rājā svāṃ parṣadam āhūya vaidyān pañca sirāḥ sva|śarīre mokṣayitvā tān yakṣān uvāca:

8.85 «dharma|karmaṇi sācivyaṃ
prītiṃ ca paramāṃ mama
bhavantaḥ kartum arhanti
dehasy' âsya pratigrahāt.» [40]

Cease then your excessive affection toward me and your bold obstruction of my moral path. Your conduct is not at all suited to my purposes. You should also consider this:

If it is for their own good that someone
wishes to give food or another gift,
would it be right or wrong to prevent them,
particularly in a situation such as this?

Stop being so stubborn. Consider the matter logically and restrain your mind from deviant thoughts, as suits your ministry to me. It would be splendid to have some words of approval from you instead of these alarmed eyes.

Why do I say this? 8.80

Do beggars not come every day
to request wealth for various uses?
But beggars of this caliber cannot
be acquired even by propitiating deities.

Given the caliber of beggar that has arrived here,
and given the body is perishable, an abode of sorrow,
it would be base even to reflect on the matter.
For the misery of selfishness is the greatest darkness.

Please, then, do not try to obstruct me."

Persuading the assembly this way, the king summoned five doctors, who opened up his veins. He then addressed the demons, saying:

"Good sirs, please assist me 8.85
in my virtuous deed
and give me the greatest joy
by accepting this body."

te tath" êty uktv" âñjali|puṭair eva rājño rakta|candana|ras'|âbhitāmraṃ rudhiraṃ pātum upacakramire.

sa pīyamāna|kṣata|jaḥ kṣit'|īśaḥ
kṣapā|carair hema|vapuś cakāśe
saṃdhy"|ânuraktair jala|bhāra|namraiḥ
payo|dharair Merur iv' ôpagūḍhaḥ. [41]

prīti|prakarṣād dhṛti|saṃpadā ca
vapur|guṇād eva ca tasya rājñaḥ
mamlau na gātraṃ na mumūrcha cetaḥ
saṃcikṣiye na kṣata|jaṃ kṣarad vā. [42]

vinīta|tarṣa|klamās tu te yakṣāḥ «paryāptam anen'» êti rājānam ūcuḥ.

8.90 an|eka|duḥkh'|āyatane śarīre
sadā kṛta|ghne 'pi nar'|âdhipasya
gate 'rthi|saṃmānana|sādhanatvaṃ
harṣ'|ânukūlaṃ grahaṇaṃ babhūva. [43]

atha sa rājā praharṣa|prabodhād adhikatara|nayana|vadana|prasādo nīl'|ôtpala|dala|nīla|vimala|pattraṃ ratna|prabh"|ôdbhāsura|rucira|tsaruṃ niśitaṃ nistriṃśam ādāya sva|māṃsāni cchittvā cchittvā tebhyaḥ prāyacchat.

hriyamāṇ'|âvakāśaṃ tu
dāna|prītyā punaḥ punaḥ
na prasehe manas tasya
ccheda|duḥkhaṃ vigāhitum. [44]

Agreeing, the demons moved forward with cupped hands to drink the king's blood, which was as crimson as the juice of red sandalwood.

As the night-walking demons drank his blood,
the king's body gleamed as if it were gold,
resembling Mount Meru when covered by clouds
tinged by twilight and bulging with rain.

The intense joy, supreme resilience,
and bodily strength of the king meant
his limbs did not languish and he did not faint.
Nor did his blood stop flowing.

After assuaging their thirst and fatigue, the demons informed the king that they had had enough.

Since his body was an ever ungrateful 8.90
source of numerous sorrows
that had been used to honor the needy,
its consumption filled the king with delight.

Roused by joy, the king's eyes and face shone even more brightly. He then took up a sharp sword, the blade of which was as blue and spotless as a lotus petal, its hilt gleaming splendidly with glittering jewels, and repeatedly cut out chunks of his flesh, which he offered to the demons.

The joy of giving repeatedly
denied his mind scope
for wallowing in the pain
caused by the cuts of the sword.

ākṛṣyamāṇaṃ śita|śastra|pātaiḥ
prītyā punar dūraṃ apāsyamānam
khed'|âlasatvād iva tasya duḥkhaṃ
manaḥ|samutsarpaṇa|mandam āsīt. [45]

sa prītimān eva niśā|carāṃs tān
saṃtarpayan svaiḥ piśitais tath" āsa
krūrāṇi teṣām api mānasāni
yen' āsur āviṣ|kṛta|mārdavāni. [46]

8.95 dharma|priyatvāt karuṇā|vaśād vā
tyajan par'|ârthe priyam ātma|deham
dveṣ'|âgni|dagdhāny api mānasāni
prasāda|sāvarṇya|navāni kuryāt. [47]

atha te yakṣās taṃ rājānaṃ sva|māṃs'|ôtkartana|paraṃ tath" âiv' â|skhalita|vadana|prasādam a|vikampyamānaṃ māṃsa|ccheda|vedanābhir abhivīkṣya prasādaṃ vismayaṃ c' ôpajagmuḥ.

«āścaryam adbhutam aho bata kiṃ svid etat
satyaṃ na v"?» êti samudīrṇa|vicāra|harṣāḥ
rājany a|marṣam upamṛdya manaḥ|prasādaṃ
tat|saṃstuti|praṇatibhiḥ prathayām babhūvuḥ. [48]

«alam! alaṃ, deva! viramyatāṃ sva|śarīra|pīḍā|prasaṅgāt! saṃtarpitāḥ smas tav' ânay" âdbhutayā yācanaka|jana|mano|harayā pratipatty"» êti sa|saṃbhramāḥ sa|praṇāmaṃ vinivārya rājānaṃ prasād'|âśru|pariṣikta|vadanāḥ sa|bahu|mānam udīkṣamāṇāḥ punar ūcuḥ:

When pain drew near from the sword's sharp blows,
his joy made it retreat far away again.
Slow to emerge in his mind,
the pain seemed almost idle from exhaustion.

As he satisfied the night-stalkers with his flesh,
the sole emotion he felt was joy,
making even the cruel hearts
of the demons noticeably soften.

Those who give up their dear body for others 8.95
out of compassion or love of virtue
are able to renew tender purity
even in hearts scorched by hatred's fire.

When the demons saw the king so focused on cutting out his flesh and so untroubled by the pain of carving up his body, his face unflinchingly calm, they became filled with devotion and wonder.

"What an astonishing miracle! Can it be real?"
the demons wondered with joy.
Eradicating their anger toward the king,
they declared their devotion with praises and bows.

"Enough! Enough, Your Majesty! Stop this willful torture of your body! We are satisfied by your wondrous gift, a delight for any beggar." Bowing before the king, they then hastily restrained him and, with faces wet with tears of devotion, they looked up at him reverently and said:

sthāne bhakti|vaśena gacchati janas
tvat|kīrti|vācālatāṃ!
sthāne Śrīḥ paribhūya paṅkaja|vanaṃ
tvat|saṃśraya|ślāghinī!
vyaktaṃ Śakra|sanāthatām api gatā
tvad|vīrya|guptām imāṃ
dyauḥ paśyaty udita|spṛhā vasumatīṃ.
no ced aho vañcyate. [49]

8.100 kiṃ bahunā? evaṃ|vidha|jan'|âbhyupapannaḥ sa|bhāgyaḥ khalu manuṣya|lokaḥ. yuṣmad|āyās'|âbhyanumodanāt tu vayam atra dagdhāḥ. bhavad|vidha|jan'|âpaśrayāc chakya ittham|gatair apy ātmā samuddhartum iti sva|duṣ|kṛta|pratīkār'|āśayā pṛcchāmaḥ:

an|ādṛtya sukha|prāptām
anuraktāṃ nṛpa|śriyam
kiṃ tad aty|adbhutaṃ sthānaṃ
path" ânena yad icchasi? [50]

sarva|kṣiti|patitvaṃ nu
Dhaneśatvam ath' Êndratām
Brahma|bhūyaṃ vimokṣaṃ vā
tapas" ânena kāṅkṣasi? [51]

asya hi vyavasāyasya
na dūrataram īpsitam.
śrotavyaṃ cet tad asmābhir,
vaktum arhati no bhavān.» [52]

"How apt that devotion inspires people
to chatter about your glory!
How apt that Fortune snubs her cluster
of lotuses to dwell proudly with you!
Though ruled by Shakra,
heaven must look at the earth with envy
when she sees you protecting it.
If not, she lives a lie.

But why these longwinded words? The human world is 8.100
lucky to be protected by a man of such virtue. However, we ourselves burn with sorrow at having endorsed your suffering. We wish to redeem our wicked deeds, with the hope that by taking refuge in a man such as you, even creatures like us can still be saved. And so we ask you this:

You have no regard for the delights of royal glory,
even though you have easily acquired them.
What extraordinary state do you desire
by following this course of action?

What do you seek through this asceticism?
To rule the entire earth or become the Lord of Wealth?*
To attain Indra's status or become Brahma?*
Or is it liberation?

Your resolve is so strong
that your goal cannot be far.
If we are worthy of hearing it,
please tell us, good sir."

rāj" ôvāca, «śrūyatāṃ yad|artho 'yaṃ mam' âbhyudyamaḥ.

8.105 «prayatna|labhyā yad a|yatna|nāśinī,
na tṛpti|saukhyāya kutaḥ praśāntaye,
bhav'|āśrayā saṃpad, ato na kāmaye
sur'|êndra|lakṣmīm api kiṃ bat' êtarām. [53]

na c' ātma|duḥkha|kṣaya|mātrakeṇa me
prayāti saṃtoṣa|pathena mānasam
amūn a|nāthān abhivīkṣya dehinaḥ
prasakta|tīvra|vyasana|śram'|āturān. [54]

anena puṇyena tu sarva|darśitām
avāpya nirjitya ca doṣa|vidviṣaḥ
jarā|rujā|mṛtyu|mah"|ōrmi|saṃkulāt
samuddhareyaṃ bhava|sāgarāj jagat.» [55]

atha te yakṣāḥ prasāda|saṃhṛṣita|tanū|ruhāḥ praṇamya rājānam ūcuḥ:

«upapanna|rūpam evaṃ|vidhasya vyavasāy'|âtiśayasy' êdaṃ karma! tan na dūre bhavad|vidhānām abhiprāya|saṃpad iti!»

8.110 niścita|manaso vijñāpayām āsuḥ:

«kāmaṃ loka|hitāy' âiva tava sarvo 'yam udyamaḥ.
sva|hit'|âtyādaras tv eṣa smartum arhasi nas tadā. [56]

a|jñānāc ca yad asmābhir
evam āyāsito bhavān
svam apy artham a|paśyadbhir,
mṛṣyatām eva tac ca naḥ. [57]

"Hear then the reason for my endeavor," the king replied.

"Status is attained with effort but easily lost. 8.105
It brings no contentment or happiness, let alone
serenity.
It relies on situation and so I do not desire it,
not even in heaven let alone elsewhere.

When I look at the helpless creatures
incessantly suffering bitter toils and woes,
my mind cannot be satisfied
merely by dispelling my own sorrows.

Through this pure deed, may I attain Omniscience.
By conquering the vices that are my enemies,
may I raise the world out of the ocean of existence,
with its huge surging waves of old age, sickness,
and death."

Their hair bristling with devotion, the demons bowed before the king and said:

"Your deed is suited to your exceptional resolution! Men such as you are never far from accomplishing their will!"

With conviction they then declared the following words: 8.110

"We realize all your efforts are directed
solely toward benefiting the world.
But please have a special regard for our welfare
and remember us at the right time.

Please forgive us
for causing you such suffering.
Blind even to our own welfare,
we acted out of ignorance.

ājñām api ca tāvan nas tvam anugraha|paddhatim
sacivānām iva sveṣāṃ viśrabdhaṃ dātum arhasi.» [58]

atha sa rājā prasāda|mṛdū|kṛta|hṛdayān matv" âinān uvāca:

8.115 «upakāraḥ khalv ayaṃ, n' āyāso mam', êty alam atr' â|kṣam"|āśaṅkayā. api ca,

evaṃ|vidhe dharma|pathe sahāyān
  kiṃ vismariṣyāmy adhigamya bodhim?
yuṣmākam eva prathamaṃ kariṣye
  vimokṣa|dharm'|âmṛta|saṃvibhāgam. [59]
asmat|priyaṃ c' âbhisamīkṣamāṇair
  hiṃsā bhavadbhir viṣavad vivarjyā
lobhaḥ para|dravya|parigraheṣu
  vāg garhitā madya|mayaś ca pāpmā.» [60]

atha te yakṣās tath" êty asmai pratiśrutya praṇamya pradakṣiṇī|kṛtya c' âinaṃ tatr' âiv' ântardadhire.

sva|māṃsa|śoṇita|pradāna|niścaya|sama|kālam eva tu tasya Mahā|sattvasya

8.120 vikampamānā bahudhā vasuṃ|dharā
  vighūrṇayām āsa Suvarṇa|Parvatam.
prasasvanur dundubhayaś ca tad|gatā
  drumāś ca puṣpaṃ sasṛjur vikampanāt. [61]

Please place your trust in us,
as you would your own ministers,
and show us the favor
of issuing us with a command."

Seeing that their hearts had been softened by tender devotion, the king replied:

"It was a service that you performed for me. You caused me no suffering. You need not worry about my not forgiving you. Furthermore, 8.115

When I attain awakening, how can I forget
my companions on the path of virtue?
I will make sure you are the first to share
in the ambrosia of the teaching of liberation.
If you are concerned to please me,
then avoid violence as if it were poison,
have no greed for the wives or possessions of others,
and cease reprehensible speech and the evil of
intoxication."*

Bowing with consent, the demons circled the king reverently and then disappeared at that very spot.

Exactly the same time as the Great Being resolved to give away his flesh and blood,

the earth shook violently, 8.120
rocking Golden Mountain,
making kettledrums on the mountain
resound and its trees shed flowers.

tad abhravad vyomani mārut'|ēritaṃ
patatri|sen" êva vitānavat kva cit
visṛtya mālā grathit" êva kutra cit
samaṃ samantān nṛ|pater vyakīryata. [62]

nivārayiṣyann iva medinī|patiṃ
samuddhat'|āvegatayā mah"|ârṇavaḥ
jalaiḥ prakṛty|abhyadhika|krama|svanaiḥ
prayāṇa|s'|âujaska|vapur vyarocata. [63]

«kim etad» ity āgata|saṃbhramas tataḥ
sur'|âdhipas tasya vicintya kāraṇam
nṛp'|âtyay'|āśaṅkita|tūrṇam āyayau
nṛp'|ālayaṃ śoka|bhay'|ākul'|ākulam. [64]

tathā|gatasy' âpi tu tasya bhū|pater
mukha|prasādāt sa|viśeṣa|vismayaḥ
upetya tat|karma mano|jñayā girā
prasāda|saṃharṣa|vaśena tuṣṭuve: [65]

8.125 «aho prakarṣo bata saj|jana|sthiter!
aho guṇ'|âbhyāsa|vidher udāttatā!
aho par'|ânugraha|peśalā matis!
tvad|arpaṇān nāthavatī bata kṣitiḥ!» [66]

ity abhipraśasy' âinaṃ Śakro dev'|êndraḥ sadyaḥ|kṣata|rohaṇa|samarthair divya|mānuṣyakair auṣadha|viśeṣair nir|vedanaṃ yathā|paurāṇaṃ śarīraṃ kṛtvā dākṣiṇya|vinay'|ôpacāra|madhuraṃ pratipūjitas tena rājñā svam āvāsaṃ pratijagāma.

Blown by the wind, the blossoms spread in the sky,
here resembling a cloud, there a troop of birds,
here a canopy, there an intricate garland,
until they scattered evenly all around the king.

As if eager to restrain the lord of the earth,
the ocean looked glorious as it charged
mightily forward with whipped up force,
its waves surging and roaring stronger than normal.

Anxious as to why this event had occurred,
the king of the gods considered the cause.
Concerned the monarch may be in danger,
he swiftly left for the royal palace, that chaos of grief
and fear.

But despite his plight, the king's face was serene,
filling Shakra with intense wonder.
Driven by devotion and joy, Shakra approached
the king,
praising his deed with a delightful voice:

"This is the highest point of moral standing! 8.125
This is the loftiest state of virtuous practice!
How tender your heart is in favoring others!
By attaining you, the earth indeed has a protector!"

Praising him this way, Shakra, the king of the gods, restored the king's body to its former state and stopped his pain by applying special herbs, both divine and human, that had the power to heal wounds instantly. After the king had honored him in return with charming reverence, politeness, and courtesy, Shakra returned to his own abode.

tad evaṃ, para|duḥkh'|āturā n' ātma|sukham avekṣante mahā|kāruṇikā iti.

«ko nāma dhana | mātrake 'py avekṣāṃ n' ôtsraṣṭum arhat'?» îti dāyaka|jana|samuttejanāyāṃ vācyaṃ, karuṇā|varṇe 'pi Tathāgata|māhātmye sat|kṛtya Dharma|śravaṇe ca.

yac c' ôktaṃ Bhagavatā, «bahu|karāḥ khalv ete pañcakā bhikṣava» iti syād etad abhisaṃdhāya. tena hi samayena te pañca yakṣā babhūvuḥ. teṣāṃ Bhagavatā yathā|pratijñātam eva prathamaṃ dharm'|âmṛta|saṃvibhāgaḥ kṛta iti.

So it is that, pained by the suffering of others, men of great compassion never seek their own pleasure.

One should narrate this story when motivating people who are generous, saying: "Who, then, should not cast aside concern for something as meager as wealth?" And one should also narrate this story when praising compassion, or when honoring the magnanimity of the Tatha·gata, or when discussing the topic of listening to the Teaching with respect.

And one should connect this story with the words spoken by the Lord when he said: "The five monks were very helpful."* For at that time the five monks were the five demons. And it was with them that the Lord first shared the ambrosia of the Teaching, just as he had promised.

STORY 9

THE BIRTH-STORY OF VISHVAN·TARA

9.1 NA BODHISATTVA|CARITAṂ sukham anumoditum apy alpa|sattvaiḥ prāg ev' ācaritum.

tad|yath" ânuśrūyate.

s'|ātmī|bhūt'|êndriya|jayaḥ parākrama|naya|vinaya|saṃpadā samadhigata|vijaya|śrīr vṛddh'|ôpāsana|niyamāt trayy|ānvīkṣikyor upalabdh'|ârtha|tattvaḥ sva|dharma|karm'|ânuraktābhir an|udvigna|sukh'|ôcitābhir anuraktābhiḥ prakṛtibhiḥ prakāśyamāna|daṇḍa|nīti|śobhaḥ samyak|pravṛtta|vārttā|vidhiḥ Saṃjayo nāma Śibīnāṃ rājā babhūva.

guṇ'|ôdayair yasya nibaddha|bhāvā
kul'|âṅgan" êv' āsa nar'|âdhipa|śrīḥ
a|tarkaṇīy" ânya|mahī|patīnāṃ
siṃh'|âbhigupt" êva guhā mṛgāṇām. [1]

9.5 tapaḥsu vidyāsu kalāsu c' âiva
kṛta|śramā yasya sad" âbhyupetāḥ
viśeṣa|yuktaṃ bahu|mānam īyuḥ
pūjābhir āviṣ|kriyamāṇa|sārāḥ. [2]

tasya rājño rājya|pratipatty|an|antaraḥ prathita|guṇa|gaṇa|nirantaro Viśvaṃtaro nāma putro yuva|rājo babhūva. ayam eva sa Bhagavāñ Chākyamunis tena samayena.

THOSE OF MEAN SPIRIT find it difficult even to take pleasure in the Bodhi·sattva's deeds, let alone emulate them.* 9.1

Tradition has handed down the following story.

There was once a king called Sánjaya who ruled over the Shibis. It had become Sánjaya's very nature to control his senses, and his accomplishment in bravery, prudence, and decency invested him with victory and prosperity. Through his rigorous service to his elders, he had grasped the essence of the Vedas and Logic, and his fine administration of justice was displayed by the devotion of his people, who were used to lives of untroubled happiness and were content in their hereditary professions. He was a king of perfect conduct and behavior.

Like a noble lady, Royal Fortune was loyal
to him because of his abundant virtues.
To other kings she was beyond conception,
just as a cave guarded by a lion is to other beasts.

Men strenuous in austerities, sciences, 9.5
and arts constantly visited his palace.
They acquired his special esteem
by showing their worth through acts of honor.

This king had a son, an heir apparent, called Vishvan·tara. Although next to his father in royal status, he matched him in possessing a host of celebrated virtues. It was this prince who was the Lord Shakya·muni at that time.*

yuv" âpi vṛddh'|ôpaśam'|âbhirāmas
tejasvy api kṣānti|sukha|svabhāvaḥ
vidvān api jñāna|mad'|ân|abhijñaḥ
śriyā samṛddho 'py avalepa|śūnyaḥ. [3]

dṛṣṭa|prayāmāsu ca dikṣu tasya
vyāpte ca loka|tritaye yaśobhiḥ
babhūva n' âiv' ânya|yaśo|lavānāṃ
prasartum utsāha iv' âvakāśaḥ. [4]

a|mṛṣyamāṇaḥ sa jagad|gatānāṃ
duḥkh'|ôdayānāṃ prabhut"|âvalepam
dān'|êṣu|varṣī karuṇ"|ôru|cāpas
tair yuddha|saṃrambham iv' ājagāma. [5]

9.10 sa pratyaham abhigatam arthi|janam abhilaṣit'|âdhikair a|kliṣṭair artha|visargaiḥ priya|vacan'|ôpacāra|mano|harair atīva prahlādayām āsa.

parva|divaseṣu ca poṣadha|niyama|praśama|vibhūṣaṇaḥ śiraḥ|snātaḥ śukla|kṣauma|vāsā Himagiri|śikhara|saṃnikāśaṃ mada|lekh"|âbhyalaṃkṛta|mukhaṃ lakṣaṇa|vinaya|java|sattva|saṃpannaṃ gandha|hastinaṃ samājñātam aupavāhyaṃ dvi|rada|varam abhiruhya samantato nagarasy'

Although a youth, he had the charming serenity
of the elderly.
Although mighty, he took a natural pleasure
in forbearance.
Although wise, he knew nothing of intellectual pride.
Although rich in fortune, he was devoid of arrogance.

His fame permeated the threefold world
in every direction as far as the eye can see.
Others had no opportunity for their own petty glories,
seeming to have lost the will to pursue them.

Unable to endure the haughtiness
of the surging sufferings that beset the world,
he seemed to wage a furious war against such foes,
spraying arrows of gifts from his broad bow
of compassion.

Every day he greatly gladdened the petitioners who came 9.10
to him by offering them limitless gifts that exceeded their expectations and that delighted them by being given with pleasing words and deference.

On the days that marked the phases of the moon, Vishvan·tara would become adorned by the tranquil discipline of the *póshadha* vow. Bathing his head and wearing white linen garments, he would mount a fine scent-elephant that resembled a peak on snowy Mount Hímavat.* The face of the renowned elephant was decorated with streaks of ichor. Speedy and courageous, it was well-trained

âbhiniviṣṭāny arthi|jana|nipāna|bhūtāni svāni sattr'|âgārāṇi pratyavekṣate sma. tathā ca prīti|viśeṣam abhijagāma.

na hi tāṃ kurute prītiṃ
 vibhūtir bhavan'|āśritā
saṃkrāmyamāṇ'|ârthi|jane
 s" âiva dāna|priyasya yām. [6]

atha kadā cit tasy' âivaṃ|vidhaṃ dāna|prasaṅgaṃ pramudita|hṛdayair arthibhiḥ samantato vikīryamāṇam upalabhy' ânyatamo bhūmy|an|antaras tasya rājā «śakyo 'yam ati|saṃdhātuṃ dān'|ânurāga|vaśagatvād» iti pratarkya dvi|rada|var'|âpaharaṇ'|ârthaṃ brāhmaṇāṃs tatra praṇidadhe.

atha te brāhmaṇā Viśvaṃtarasya svāni sattr'|âgārāṇi pratyavekṣamāṇasya pramodād adhikatara|nayana|vadana|śobhasya jay'|āśīr|vāda|mukharāḥ samucchrit'|âbhiprasārita|dakṣiṇ'|âgra|pāṇayaḥ purastāt samatiṣṭhanta. sa taṃ† vinigṛhya dvi|rada|varam upacāra|puraḥsaram abhigamana|prayojanam enān paryapṛcchad, «ājñāpyatāṃ ken' ârtha» iti.

9.15 brāhmaṇā ūcuḥ:

«amuṣya tava nāgasya gati|līlā|vilambinaḥ
guṇair arthitvam āyātā dāna|śauryāc ca te vayam. [7]

and bore auspicious marks. Mounting this tusker, Vishvan·tara went to inspect his alms houses, which were situated in every part of the city and had become refuges for supplicants. He derived particular joy from this.

For the joy a generous man feels
at wealth stored indoors
cannot compare with the joy felt
at wealth given to a petitioner.

In every direction the gladdened supplicants spread the news of Vishvan·tara's addiction to giving and, one day, a neighboring king came to hear of it. Speculating that he could take advantage of the young king because of his passion for generosity, he sent some brahmins to Vishvan·tara in order to rob him of his fine elephant.

Vishvan·tara was inspecting his alms houses, his eyes and face gleaming greatly with joy, when the brahmins came and stood in front of him. With their right hands raised and stretched out, they greeted him loudly with benedictions of victory. Vishvan·tara stopped his fine elephant and, after politely greeting the brahmins, he asked them why they had come, telling them to instruct him as to their needs.

The brahmins replied: 9.15

"Inspired by your heroic giving
and the virtues of this elephant,
swaying with so graceful a gait,
we have become supplicants.

Kailāsa|śikhar'|ābhasya pradānād asya dantinaḥ
kuruṣva tāval lokānāṃ vismay'|âika|rasaṃ manaḥ!» [8]

ity ukte Bodhisattvaḥ prītyā samāpūryamāṇa | hṛdayaś cintām āpede:

«cirasya khal' ûdāra | praṇaya | su | mukham arthi | janaṃ paśyāmi. kaḥ punar artha evaṃ | vidhena dvi | rada | patin" âiṣāṃ brāhmaṇānām? vyaktam ayaṃ lobh' | ērṣyā | dveṣa | paryākula|manasaḥ kasy' âpi rājñaḥ kārpaṇya|prayogaḥ.

9.20 āśā|vighāta|dīnatvaṃ
tan mā bhūd asya bhū|pateḥ,
an|ādṛtya yaśo|dharmau
yo 'smadd|hita iv' ôdyataḥ.» [9]

iti viniścitya sa Mah" | ātmā tvaritam avatīrya dvi | rada | varāt, «pratigṛhyatām» iti samudyata | kāñcana | bhṛṅgāras teṣāṃ purato 'vatasthe.

tataḥ sa vidvān api rāja|śāstram
arth'|ânuvṛttyā gata|dharma|mārgam
dharm'|ânurāgeṇa dadau gaj'|êndraṃ
nīti|vyalīkena na saṃcakampe. [10]

Fill the worlds
full of wonder
by giving us this tusker
resembling Kailása's peak!"

Addressed this way, the Bodhi·sattva's heart filled with joy and he had this thought:

"It has been a long time since I have seen a supplicant who is willing to make weighty requests. But what do these brahmins want with a lordly elephant of such stature? This is clearly the pitiful ploy of some king whose mind is turbulent with the flaws of greed and envy.

But this king should not suffer 9.20
the misery of having his hopes dashed.
For without heed to reputation or morality,
he seems intent on benefiting me."

Thinking this, the Great One quickly got down from the fine tusker and, standing in front of the brahmins with a raised golden pitcher, he asked them to accept the elephant as a gift.

Though he knew that in the science of kingship
the path of morality involves pursuing benefit,
in his passion for virtue he gave away the king
of elephants,
unswayed by the falsehood of politics.

tam hema|jāla|rucir'|ābharaṇaṃ gaj'|êndraṃ
vidyut|pinaddham iva śāradam abhra|rāśim
dattvā parāṃ mudam avāpa nar'|êndra|sūnuḥ
saṃcukṣubhe tu nagaraṃ naya|pakṣa|pātāt. [11]

atha dvi|rada|pati|pradāna|śravaṇāt samudīrṇa|krodha|saṃrambhāḥ Śibayo brāhmaṇa|vṛddhā mantriṇo yodhāḥ paura|mukhyāś ca kolāhalam samupajanayantaḥ Saṃjayaṃ rājānam abhigamya sa|saṃbhram'|â|marṣa|saṃrambhāt pariśithil'|ôpacāra|yantraṇam ūcuḥ:

9.25 «kim iyaṃ, deva, rājya|śrīr vilupyamān" âivam apy upekṣyate? n' ârhati devaḥ sva|rājy'|ôpaplavam evam abhivardhamānam marṣayitum.»

«kim etad?» iti ca s'|āvegam uktā rājñā punar enam ūcuḥ:

«kasmād devo na jānīte?

niṣevya matta|bhramar'|ôpagītaṃ
yasy' ānanaṃ dāna|su|gandhi vāyuḥ
mad'|âvalepaṃ para|vāraṇānām
āyāsa|duḥkhena vinā pramārṣṭi; [12]

yat|tejas" ākrānta|bala|prabhāvāḥ
saṃsupta|darpā iva vidviṣas te;
Viśvaṃtareṇ' âiṣa gajaḥ sa datto
rūpī jayas te hriyate 'nya|deśam. [13]

Adorned by a glistening mesh of gold, the lordly elephant
resembled a mass of autumn clouds draped with lightning.
The prince felt the highest joy at giving his gift.
But the city shuddered, choosing the side of pragmatics.

The Shibis were furiously angry when they heard the king of elephants had been given away. Making a great stir, brahmin elders, counselors, soldiers, and eminent citizens all approached King Sánjaya. In their fury and intolerant rage, they addressed him with words that stretched the bounds of courtesy:

"Why does Your Majesty ignore the way his royal fortune 9.25
is being plundered? Your Majesty should not tolerate this escalating disaster that afflicts his kingdom."

"What is that you say?" Sánjaya replied in distress.

"How can Your Majesty not know?" they answered.

"This elephant, whose face, fragrant with ichor,
buzzes with the hum of intoxicated bees,
and is served by a breeze that deftly and gently
wipes away the proud rut-scent of other tuskers;

This elephant, whose power destroys the might
of your enemies' armies, as if putting their pride to sleep;
this is the elephant given by Vishvan·tara.
The embodiment of your victory, it's being taken to a foreign land.

9.30 gāvaḥ suvarṇaṃ vasanāni bhojyam
iti dvi|jebhyo, nṛ|pa, deya|rūpam
yasmiñ jaya|śrīr niyatā dvip'|êndre
deyaḥ sa nām' êty ati|dāna|śauryam. [14]

nay'|ôtpathen' âinam iti vrajantaṃ
kathaṃ samanveṣyati rāja|lakṣmīḥ?
n' ôpekṣaṇaṃ, deva, tav' âtra yuktaṃ
pur" âyam ānandayati dviṣas te.» [15]

tac chrutvā sa rājā putra|priyatvāt kiṃ cit tān eva praty a|prīta|manāḥ kāry'|ânurodhāt sāvegavad evam ity uktvā samanuneṣyañ Chibīn uvāca:

«jāne dāna|prasaṅga|vyasanitāṃ nīti|kram'|ân|apekṣāṃ Viśvaṃtarasya. na c' âiṣa kramo rājya|dhuri saṃniyuktasya. dattaṃ tv anena svaṃ hastinaṃ vānta|kalpaṃ kaḥ pratyāhariṣyati? api tu tath" âham enaṃ kariṣye yathā dāne mātrāṃ jñāsyati. tad alam atra vaḥ saṃrambheṇ' êti.»

Śibaya ūcuḥ: «na khalu, mahā|rāja, paribhāṣaṇā|mātra|sādhyo 'sminn arthe Viśvaṃtara iti.»

9.35 Saṃjaya uvāca, «atha kim anyad atra mayā śakyaṃ kartum?

doṣa|pravṛtter vimukhasya yasya
guṇa|prasaṅgā vyasanī|kriyante
bandho vadho v" ātma|sutasya tasya
kiṃ niṣkrayaḥ syād dvi|radasya tasya? [16]

Cows, gold, clothes, and food; 9.30
these are gifts suitable for brahmins, Your Majesty.
But this king of elephants, our source of victory
and prosperity;
surely this is too excessive a gift.

How can royal fortune ever follow this prince
if he treads a path that strays from prudence?
It is not right to ignore this matter, Your Majesty.
For he will soon bring your enemies joy."

When he heard this, the king, who loved his son dearly, felt some displeasure toward these men. But following his sense of duty, he put on an appearance of shock and agreed they were right. He then tried to conciliate the Shibis, saying:

"I know Vishvan·tara has a passionate addiction for giving and disregards the procedures of politics. This is not the right way for someone to behave when they have been assigned the yoke of kingship. But who would take back this elephant after Vishvan·tara has rejected it like vomit? I will make Vishvan·tara understand that there is a limit to giving. Now stop being angry about this."

"A mere scolding will not influence Vishvan·tara on the matter, Your Majesty," the Shibis replied.

"What else can I do about it?" Sánjaya responded. 9.35

"He turns his back on wicked behavior.
His only vice is attachment to virtue.
Would imprisoning or slaughtering my son
really be compensation for this elephant?

tad alam atra vaḥ saṃrambheṇa. nivārayiṣyāmy aham ato Viśvaṃtaram iti.»

atha Śibayaḥ samudīrṇa|manyavo rājānam ūcuḥ:

«ko vā vadhaṃ bandhana|tāḍanaṃ vā
sutasya te rocayate, nar'|êndra?
dharm'|ātmakas tv eṣa na rājya|bhāra|
kṣobhasya soḍhā karuṇ"|ātmakatvāt. [17]

9.40 siṃh'|āsanaṃ tejasi labdha|śabdās
tri|varga|sevā|nipuṇā bhajante.
dharm'|âti|rāgān naya|nir|vyapekṣas
tapo|van'|âdhyāsana|yogya eṣaḥ. [18]

phalanti kāmaṃ vasudh"|âdhipānāṃ
dur|nīti|doṣās tad|apāśriteṣu.
sahyās ta eṣāṃ tu tath" âpi dṛṣṭā
mūl'|ôparodhān na tu pārthivānām. [19]

kim atra vā bahv abhidhāya? niścayas
tv ayaṃ Śibīnāṃ tvad|a|bhūty|a|marṣiṇām:
prayātu Vaṅkaṃ tapaso 'bhivṛddhaye
nṛp'|ātmajaḥ siddha|niṣevitaṃ girim.» [20]

atha sa rājā sneha|praṇaya|viśrambha|vaśād a|nay'|âpāya|darśinā hit'|ôdyatena tena janena pariniṣṭhuram ity abhidhīyamānaḥ prakṛti|kopād vrīḍ"|âvanata|vadanaḥ putra|

Enough then of your anger. I will restrain Vishvan·tara from now on."

Whipped into a fury, the Shibis, however, replied to the king:

"Who could wish to kill your son,
or imprison or flog him, Your Majesty?
But compassion is so ingrained in his righteous nature
that he is unfit to bear the troubling burden
of kingship.

The lion-throne is for those renowned 9.40
for their strength,
expert in following the three pursuits.*
In his love of virtue the prince disregards politics:
he is suited to a life in an ascetic grove.

When kings are flawed with bad policies,
their subjects are the ones who experience the result.
But whereas subjects can endure the flaws,
kings cannot, their very foundation harmed.

But why these longwinded words?
Unable to endure your ruin, the Shibis have
decided this:
let the prince go to Mount Vanka, the abode
of *siddhas*,*
and let him foster his austerities there."

When he considered that it was out of affection, intimacy, and friendliness that his people spoke such harsh but well-meaning words since they foresaw Vishvan·tara's lack of prudence would bring disaster, the king bowed his head with shame at his subjects' anger. Filled with anxiety at

viyoga|cintā|parigata|hṛdayaḥ s'|āyāsam abhiniśvasya Śibīn uvāca:

«yady eṣa bhavatāṃ nirbandhas tad ekam api tāvad aho| rātram asya mṛṣyatām. prabhātāyāṃ rajanyām abhipretaṃ vo 'nuṣṭhātā Viśvaṃtara iti.»

9.45 «evam astv» iti ca pratigṛhīt'|ânunayaḥ Śibibhiḥ sa rājā kṣattāram uvāca, «gacch' êmaṃ vṛttāntaṃ Viśvaṃtarāya niveday'» êti. sa tath" êti pratiśrutya śok'|âśru|pariṣikta|vadano Viśvaṃtaraṃ sva|bhavana|gatam upetya śoka|duḥkh'|āvegāt sa|svaraṃ rudan pādayor asya nyapatat.

«api kuśalaṃ rāja|kulāy'?» êti ca sa|saṃbhramaṃ Viśvaṃtareṇ' ânuyuktaḥ samavasīdann a|viśada|pad'|âkṣaram enam uvāca:

«kuśalaṃ rāja|kulāy' êti.»

«atha kasmād evam a|dhīro 's' îti?» ca punar anuyukto Viśvaṃtareṇa

kṣattā bāṣpa | veg' | ôparudhyamāna | gadgada | kaṇṭhaḥ śvāsa|viskhalita|lulit'|âkṣaraṃ śanair ity uvāca:

9.50 «sāntva|garbhām an|ādṛtya nṛp'|ājñām apy a|dakṣiṇāḥ
rāṣṭrāt pravrājayanti tvāṃ kupitāḥ Śibayo, nṛ|pa.» [21]

Viśvaṃtara uvāca, «māṃ Śibayaḥ pravrājayanti kupitā, iti kaḥ saṃbandhaḥ?

being separated from his son, he sighed painfully and addressed the Shibis, saying:

"If this is your conviction, then at least show him some mercy for just one day and night. When night turns to dawn, Vishvan·tara will abide by your wishes."

The Shibis consented to Sánjaya's request, whereupon 9.45
the king told his usher to inform Vishvan·tara of what had happened. The usher followed the king's orders and went to see Vishvan·tara in his palace, his face drenched with tears of grief. Weeping loudly with sorrow and anguish, he fell at Vishvan·tara's feet.

"Is all well in the royal household?" Vishvan·tara asked anxiously.

"All is well in the royal household," the usher replied, his words hardly audible from despair.

"Then why are you so distraught?" Vishvan·tara again asked.

With a stuttering, tear-choked throat, the usher then slowly addressed Vishvan·tara with words that faltered as they were punctuated by sighs:

"Disregarding the very orders of the king, 9.50
despite the mild way he tried to appease them,
the uncouth Shibis are exiling you
from the realm out of fury, Your Majesty."

"What do you mean the Shibis are exiling me out of fury?" Vishvan·tara replied.

rame na vinay'|ônmārge
  dveṣmi c' âhaṃ pramāditām.
kutra me Śibayaḥ kruddhā
  yan na paśyāmi duṣ|kṛtam?» [22]

kṣatt" ôvāca, «aty|udāratāyām.

a|lobha|śubhrā tvayi tuṣṭir āsīl
  lobh'|ākulā yācaka|mānaseṣu.
datte tvayā, māna|da, vāraṇ'|êndre
  dhairyāṇi kopas tv aharac Chibīnām. [23]

9.55 ity atītāḥ sva|maryādāṃ rabhasāḥ Śibayas tvayi.
yena pravrājitā yānti pathā tena kila vraja.» [24]

atha Bodhisattvaḥ kṛp"|âbhyāsa|rūḍhāṃ yācanaka|jana| vatsalatāṃ dhairy'|âtiśaya|saṃpadaṃ ca svām udbhāvayann uvāca:
«capala|svabhāvāḥ khalu Śibayo 'n|abhijñā iva c' âsmat| svabhāvasya.

dravyeṣu bāhyeṣu ka eva vādo?
  dadyām ahaṃ sve nayane śiro vā!
imaṃ hi lok'|ârtham ahaṃ bibharmi
  samucchrayaṃ. kiṃ bata vastu bāhyam? [25]

yasya sva|gātrair api yācakānāṃ
  vacāṃsi saṃpūjayituṃ manīṣā,
bhayān na dadyāt sa iti pratarkaḥ
  prakāśanā bāliśa|cāpalasya. [26]

"I never delight in a path straying from decency
and I despise negligent behavior.
Why are the Shibis angry with me?
I do not see that I have done anything wrong."

"They are angry about your extreme magnanimity," the usher replied.

"Your feelings of delight were pure from lack of greed,
but in the supplicants they were turbulent with desire.
Anger robbed the Shibis of their composure
when you gave the lordly elephant, generous prince.

Fury has made the Shibis 9.55
transgress their proper limits.
And now you must travel
the path trodden by exiles."

The Bodhi·sattva then spoke words that revealed his exceptional composure and the affection he felt for petitioners, rooted in his habitual practice of compassion:

"The Shibis are fickle by nature. And they also seem ignorant of my character.

Why talk about external material objects?
I would give away my eyes or my head!
For I bear this body to benefit the world.
What then is a mere external object?

I aim to honor the words of beggars
even if it means offering up my limbs!
The Shibis show their puerile and inane nature
if they believe fear will make me stop giving!

9.60 api ca Śibayas tvay" âivaṃ vācyā mad|vacanena:

n' âiv' âham etad yaśase dadāmi
na bhūtim icchañ, Chibayo, na lobhāt.
nīcair an|āsevita eṣa panthā.
dātavyam ity eva tato dadāmi.* [26]

kāmaṃ māṃ Śibayaḥ sarve
ghnantu pravrājayantu vā!
na tv ev' âhaṃ na dāsyāmi.
gacchāmy eṣa tapo|vanam! [27]

atha Bodhisattvo vipriya|śravaṇa|viklava|mukhīṃ patnīm uvāca:

«śruto 'tra|bhavatyā Śibīnāṃ niścayaḥ?»

9.65 Madry uvāca, «śruto, deva.»

Viśvaṃtara uvāca:

«yad yad asti dhanaṃ kiṃ cid
asmatto 'dhigataṃ tvayā,
nidhehi tad, a|nindy'|âṅgi,
yac ca te paitrikaṃ dhanam.» [28]

Madry uvāca, «kutr' âitad, deva, nidadhām'?» îti.

Viśvaṃtara uvāca:

9.70 «śīlavadbhyaḥ sadā dadyā dānaṃ sat|kāra|śībharam.
tathā hi nihitaṃ dravyam a|hāryam anugāmi ca. [29]

priyaṃ śvaśurayoḥ kuryāḥ,
putrayoḥ paripālanam,
dharma ev' â|pramādaṃ ca,
śokaṃ mad|virahāt tu mā.» [30]

Furthermore, please tell the Shibis this: 9.60

I do not give gifts for glory, Shibis,
nor out of greed nor desire for the earth.
This is a path untrodden by the lowly.
Gifts should be given: that alone is why I give.

Let the Shibis all kill me
or banish me!
I will never stop giving.
I will go to an ascetic grove instead!"

The Bodhi·sattva then addressed his wife, who was distraught from hearing the unhappy news:

"Has my lady heard about the Shibis' decision?"

"'I have, Your Majesty," Madri replied. 9.65

Vishvan·tara answered:

"Make a deposit of all the wealth
you have acquired from me,
as well as your father's wealth,
lady of flawless limbs."

"Where shall I deposit it, Your Majesty?" Madri asked.

Vishvan·tara answered:

"You should give to the virtuous, 9.70
gracing your gift with reverence.
For wealth deposited this way
cannot be lost and follows you after death.*

Be kind to your parents-in-law
and protect your children.
Be conscientious in practicing virtue.
And do not grieve at our separation."

tac chrutvā Madrī saṃtapta|hṛday" âpi bhartur a|dhṛti|parihār'|ârtham an|ādṛtya śoka|dainyam ity uvāca:

«n' âiṣa dharmo, mahā|rāja, yad yāyā vanam ekakaḥ.
ten' âham api yāsyāmi yena, kṣatriya, yāsyasi. [31]

tvad|aṅka|parivartinyā
mṛtyur utsava eva me.
mṛtyor duḥkhataraṃ tat syāj
jīveyaṃ yat tvayā vinā. [32]

9.75 n' âiva ca khalu me, deva, vana|vāso duḥkha iti pratibhāti. tathā hi,

nir|durjanāny an|upabhukta|sarit|tarūṇi
nānā|vihaṃga|virutāni mṛg'|ākulāni
vaiḍūrya|kuṭṭima|manohara|śādvalāni
krīḍā|van'|âdhika|sukhāni tapo|vanāni. [33]

api ca, deva,

alaṃ|kṛtāv imau paśyan kumārau māla|bhāriṇau
krīḍantau vana|gulmeṣu na rājyasya smariṣyasi. [34]

Although Madri's heart burned at hearing these words, to avoid unsettling her husband she disregarded her grief and misery and said:

"It is not right, great king,
for you to go to the forest alone.
Wherever you go
I will go, my prince.

If I am at your side,
even death would be joyful for me.
To live without you would
be more painful than death.

Nor does a life in the forest sound painful to me, Your 9.75
Majesty. For,

Ascetic groves have no wicked people.
Their rivers and trees are pristine.
Abounding with deer, they resound
with the songs of various birds.
The grass there delights the mind,
as if inlaid with lapis lazuli.
Ascetic groves are more enjoyable
even than our pleasure parks.

Moreover, Your Majesty,

When you see your children,
adorned and wearing garlands,
playing in forest thickets,
you will not remember your kingship.

ṛtu|prayatna|racitā vana|śobhā navā navā
vane tvāṃ ramayiṣyanti sarit|kuñjāś ca s'|ôdakāḥ. [35]

9.80 citraṃ viruta|vāditraṃ pakṣiṇāṃ rati|kāṅkṣiṇām;
mad'|ācāry'|ôpadiṣṭāni nṛttāni ca śikhaṇḍinām; [36]

mādhury'|ân|avagītaṃ ca gītaṃ madhupa|yoṣitām
vaneṣu kṛta|saṃgītaṃ harṣayiṣyanti te manaḥ. [37]

āstīryamāṇāni ca śarvarīṣu
  jyotsnā|dukūlena śilā|talāni
saṃbāhamāno vana|mārutaś ca
  labdh'|âdhivāsaḥ kusuma|drumebhyaḥ. [38]

cal'|ôpala|praskhalit'|ôdakānāṃ
  kalā virāvāś ca sarid|vadhūnām
vibhūṣaṇānām iva saṃninādāḥ
  pramodayiṣyanti vane manas te. [39]

ity anunīyamānaḥ sa dayitayā vana|prayāṇa|paryutsuka|matir arthi|jan'|âvekṣayā mahā|pradānaṃ dātum upacakrame.

9.85 ath' êmāṃ Viśvaṃtara|pravrājana|pravṛttim upalabhya rāja|kule tumula ākranda|śabdaḥ prādur|abhūt. śoka|duḥkh'|āvegān mūrcchā|parigata iva c' ârthi|jano matt'|ônmatta iva ca tat tad bahu|vidhaṃ vilalāpa.

The constantly renewed forest splendors,
carefully crafted by the seasons,
and the water-filled river arbors
will delight you in the woods.

The beautiful sounds of birds 9.80
singing with desire to make love;
the dances of peacocks,
learned under the tutelage of Lust;

the buzz of honey bees singing like women,
so sweet it can never be scorned;
all these will captivate your mind
with their collective chorus in the forest.

Slabs of rock draped at night
by a fine shroud of moonlight;
the waft of a forest breeze,
perfumed by blossoming trees;

the soft sounds made by rivers
as their waters jostle through shifting gravel
like the tinkling of women's ornaments:
all this will delight your mind in the forest."

Persuaded this way by his beloved wife, Vishvan·tara felt eager to set out for the forest and, still having a regard for beggars, he prepared to make a huge offering.

A tumultuous lament then arose in the royal household 9.85
when they learned of Vishvan·tara's exile. Overwhelmed by grief and pain, the beggars almost fainted and, like drunks or lunatics, wailed various laments:

«chāyā|taroḥ svādu|phala|pradasya
cched'|ârtham āgūrṇa|paraśvadhānām
dhātrī na lajjāṃ yad upaiti bhūmir,
vyaktaṃ tad asyā hata|cetanatvam. [40]

śīt'|â|mala|svādu|jalaṃ nipānaṃ
bibhitsatām asti na cen niṣeddhā,
vyarth'|âbhidhānā bata loka|pālā
viproṣitā vā śruti|mātrakaṃ vā. [41]

a|dharmo bata jāgarti dharmaḥ supto 'tha vā mṛtaḥ
yatra Viśvaṃtaro rājā svasmād rājyān nirasyate. [42]

ko 'n|artha|paṭu|sāmarthyo
yācñ"|ân|ūrjita|vṛttiṣu
asmāsv an|aparādheṣu
vadh'|âbhyudyama|niṣṭhuraḥ?» [43]

9.90 atha Bodhisattvo n'|âika|śata|sahasra|saṃkhyaṃ maṇi|kanaka|rajata|paripūrṇa|kośaṃ vividha|dhana|dhānya|nicayavanti kośa|koṣṭh'|âgārāṇi dāsī|dāsa|yāna|vāhana|vasana|paricchad'|ādi ca sarvam arthibhyo yath"|ârham atisṛjya,

śoka|duḥkh'|âbhibhūta|dhairyayor mātā|pitroś caraṇān abhipraṇamya sa|putra|dāraḥ syandana|varam abhiruhya puṇy'|âha|ghoṣaṇay" êva mahato jana|kāyasy' ākrandita|śabdena pura|varān niragacchat. anurāga|vaśa|gam anuyāyinaṃ ca janaṃ śok'|âśru|pariklinna|vadanaṃ prayatnād vini-

"The earth, our foster mother,
has clearly lost her mind if she feels no shame
at the axes raised to chop down
this shady tree, this provider of sweet fruits!

If no-one stops those who would destroy
this well, its waters so cool, clear, and sweet,
then the world-protectors bear false names!
Or perhaps they are in exile or merely a rumor.

Evil must be awake,
and Good asleep or dead,
if Prince Vishvan·tara
is banished from his kingdom!

We have committed no crime.
We scrape a meager livelihood from begging.
Who cruelly tries to harm us
with their cunning ability for injury?"

The Bodhi·sattva then dispersed his treasury, which 9.90
abounded with jewels, gold and silver—worth several hundreds and thousands—as well as his coffers and granaries, which contained heaps of various wealth and grain. All his property, including his male and female slaves, carriages and vehicles, clothes and garments, he gave to the beggars according to their deserts.

After reverently bowing to his mother and father, who were beside themselves with grief and anguish, Vishvan·tara climbed onto a fine carriage with his wife and children. As he departed, a huge crowd of people lamented, their wails as loud as the noise of a festive day. Driven by their affection, the crowd followed Vishvan·tara, their faces drenched

vartya svayam eva pragrahān parigṛhya yena Vaṅkaḥ parvatas tena prāyāt.

vyatītya c' â|viklava|matir udyāna|vana|rucira|mālinaṃ pura|var'|ôpacāram anupūrveṇa pravirala|cchāyā|drumaṃ vicchidyamāna|jana|saṃpātaṃ pravicarita|mṛga|gaṇa|saṃbādhaṃ a|saṃbādha|dig|ālokaṃ cīrī|virāv'|ônnāditam araṇyaṃ pratyapadyata.

ath' âinaṃ yad|ṛcchay" âbhigatā brāhmaṇā ratha|vāhāṃs tura|gān ayācanta.

sa vartamāno 'dhvani n'|âika|yojane
sahāya|hīno 'pi kalatravān api
pradāna|harṣād an|apekṣit'|āyatir
dadau dvi|jebhyaś caturas turaṃ|gamān. [44]

9.95 atha Bodhisattvasya svayam eva ratha|dhuryatām upagantu|kāmasya gāḍhataraṃ parikaram abhisaṃyacchamānasya rohita|mṛga|rūpiṇaś catvāro yakṣa|kumārāḥ su|vinītā iva sad|aśvāḥ svayam eva ratha|yugaṃ skandha|pradeśaiḥ pratyapadyanta. tāṃs tu dṛṣṭvā harṣa|vismaya|viśālatar'|âkṣīṃ Madrīṃ Bodhisattva uvāca:

with tears of grief, and it was only after some effort that the prince managed to turn them around. Taking hold of the reins, he then set out for Mount Vanka.

With an untroubled mind, he traveled through the outskirts of the capital, which was wreathed with beautiful gardens and groves, and in due course arrived at the wilderness, where shady trees were scant. Cut off from human contact, the wilderness was crowded only with herds of roaming deer. Resounding with the noise of crickets, it had an unhampered view in every direction.

By chance, some brahmins happened to approach Vishvan·tara and asked him for the horses that pulled his carriage.

Though traveling on the road for a long distance,
without attendants and accompanied by his wife,
he gave the four horses to the twice-born men,*
joyful at giving and unconcerned about the future.

The Bodhi·sattva then fastened the girdle tightly around 9.95
his own body, willing to undertake the task of being a draft animal for the carriage At that moment, however, four young *yakshas*, in the form of red deer, placed the yoke of the carriage on their own shoulders like well-trained thoroughbred horses. When he saw them, the Bodhi·sattva said these words to Madri, whose eyes were wide open with joy and amazement:

«tapo|dhan'|âdhyāsana|sat|kṛtānāṃ
paśya prabhāv'|âtiśayaṃ vanānām,
yatr' âivam abhyāgata|vatsalatvaṃ
saṃrūḍha|mūlaṃ mṛga|puṃgaveṣu!» [45]

Madry uvāca:

«tav' âiv' âham imaṃ manye
prabhāvam ati|mānuṣam
rūḍho 'pi hi guṇ'|âbhyāsaḥ
sarvatra na samaḥ satām. [46]

toyeṣu tārā|pratibimba|śobhā
viśiṣyate yat kumuda|prahāsaiḥ
kautūhal'|âbhiprasṛtā iv' êndor
hetutvam atr' âgra|karāḥ prayānti.» [47]

9.100 iti teṣāṃ anyony'|ânukūlyāt paras|paraṃ priyaṃ vadatām adhvānaṃ gacchatām ath' âparo brāhmaṇaḥ samabhigamya Bodhisattvaṃ ratha|varam ayācata.

tataḥ sva|sukha|niḥ|saṅgo yācaka|priya|bāndhavaḥ
pūrayām āsa viprasya sa rathena mano|ratham. [48]

atha Bodhisattvaḥ prīta|manā rathād avatārya sva|janaṃ† niryātya ratha|varaṃ brāhmaṇāya Jālinaṃ kumāram aṅken' ādāya padbhyām ev' âdhvānaṃ pratyapadyata. a|vimanask" âiva ca Madrī Kṛṣṇājināṃ kumārīm aṅkena parigṛhya pṛṣṭhato 'nvagacchad enam.

"See the immense power of forests
honored by the residence of ascetics:
hospitality has taken root
even in these eminent deer!"

Madri replied:

"It is your power, I believe,
that is beyond human.
For the practice of virtue, however developed,
is not the same everywhere among the good.

When the smiles of night lotuses surpass
the glorious reflection of stars in water,*
the reason for this is the moon,
emitting its rays as if from curiosity."

While they were traveling and having this delightful conversation based on their mutual compatibility, another brahmin came along and asked the Bodhi·sattva for his fine carriage. 9.100

Unattached to his own pleasure,
and a kind kinsman to beggars,
he fulfilled the wish of the brahmin
and gave him his carriage.

Delighted, the Bodhi·sattva had his family descend from the carriage, gave the vehicle to the brahmin, and then continued on the road by foot, carrying his son Jalin on his hip. Feeling no distress at all, Madri took their daughter Krishnájina on her hip and followed behind her husband.

nimantrayām āsur iva drumās taṃ
hṛdyaiḥ phalair ānamit'|âgra|śākhāḥ
puṇy'|ânubhāvād abhivīkṣamāṇāḥ
śiṣyā vinītā iva ca praṇemuḥ. [49]

haṃs'|âṃsa|saṃkṣobhita|paṅkajāni
kiñjalka|reṇu|sphuṭa|piñjarāṇi
prādur|babhūvuś ca sarāṃsi tasya
tatr' âiva yatr' âbhicakāṅkṣa vāri. [50]

9.105 vitāna|śobhāṃ dadhire payo|dāḥ
sukhaḥ su|gandhiḥ pravavau nabhasvān
pariśrama|kleśam a|mṛṣyamāṇā
yakṣāś ca saṃcikṣipur asya mārgam. [51]

iti Bodhisattva udyāna|vana|gata iva pāda|cāra|vinodana|sukham anubhavan mārga|parikheda|rasam an|āsvādya sa|putra|dāraḥ prāpta eva tu Vaṅka|parvatam apaśyat.

tatra ca puṣpa|phala|pallav'|âlaṃkṛta|snigdha|vividha|rucira|taru|vara|nicitaṃ mada|mudita|vihaga|vividha|ruta|ninadaṃ pravṛtta|nṛtta|barhi|gaṇ'|ôpaśobhitaṃ pravicarita|n'|âika|mṛga|kulaṃ kṛta|parikaram iva vimala|nīla|salilayā saritā kusuma|rajo|'ruṇa|sukha|pavanaṃ tapo|vanaṃ vana|carak'|ādeśita|mārgaḥ,

praviśya Viśvakarmaṇā Śakra|saṃdeśāt svayam abhinirmitāṃ manojña|darśanāṃ sarva'|rtu|sukhāṃ tatra praviviktāṃ parṇa|śālām adhyāvasat.

So powerful was his merit that the sight of him
made trees bend the tips of their branches,
bowing before him like well-trained disciples,
as if inviting him to eat their delicious fruits.

Whenever he desired water,
pools would appear before him,
red with a film of pollen
from lotus filaments rubbed by swans' wings.

The clouds spread a radiant canopy over them. 9.105
A soothing and fragrant wind began to blow.
And *yakshas* shortened the path,
unable to endure Vishvan·tara's fatigue and pain.

In this way, the Bodhi·sattva suffered no travel tiredness and instead enjoyed the pleasure of a delightful stroll, as if he had gone on a trip to a park. Arriving at their destination with his wife and children, he then saw Mount Vanka.

Guided by the instructions of a forest-dweller, he entered the ascetic grove, which abounded with different fine charming trees that were smooth-barked and adorned with flowers, fruits, and buds. Resounding with the various songs of birds joyful with lust, it sparkled with troops of dancing peacocks and teemed with numerous wandering deer. A river of pure blue water circled the grove like a girdle and a breeze blew, fragrant with the red pollen of flowers.

Entering this grove, Vishvan·tara took up residence in an isolated leaf-hut that had been built by Vishva·karman himself under Shakra's orders.* A sight to delight the mind, the hut was comfortable in every season.

tasmin vane dayitayā paricaryamāṇaḥ
śṛṇvann a|yatna|madhurāṃś ca suta|pralāpān
udyāna|saṃstha iva vismṛta|rājya|cintaḥ
saṃvatsar'|ârdham adhikaṃ sa tapaś cacāra. [52]

9.110 atha kadā cin mūla|phal'|ârthaṃ gatāyāṃ rāja|putryāṃ putrayoḥ paripālana|nimittam āśrama|padam a|śūnyaṃ kurvāṇe rāja|putre mārga|reṇu|paruṣī|kṛta|caraṇa|prajaṅghaḥ pariśrama|kṣāma|nayana|vadano daṇḍa|kāṣṭh'|âvabaddha|skandh'|âvasakta|kamaṇḍalur brāhmaṇaḥ patnyā paricārak'|ānayan'|ârthaṃ samarpita|dṛḍha|saṃdeśas taṃ deśam abhijagāma.

atha Bodhisattvaś cirasy' ârthi|janaṃ dṛṣṭv" âbhigataṃ manaḥ|praharṣāt saṃjāyamāna|nayana|vadana|prasādaḥ pratyudgamya svāgat'|ādi|priya|vacana|puraḥsaraṃ praveśya c' âinam āśrama|padaṃ kṛt'|âtithi|satkāram āgamana|prayojanam apṛcchat.

atha sa brāhmaṇo bhāry"|ânurāgād utsārita|dhairya|lajjaḥ pratigraha|mātra|sajja īdṛśam artham uvāca:

«āloko bhavati yataḥ samaś ca mārgo
loko 'yaṃ vrajati tato, na dur|gameṇa.
prāyo 'smiñ jagati tu matsar'|ândhakāre
n' ânyena praṇaya|padāni me vahanti. [53]

pradāna|śaury'|ōrjitayā yaśaḥ|śriyā
gataṃ ca gantavyam a|śeṣatas tava.
ato 'smi yācñā|śramam abhyupeyivān:
prayaccha tan me paricārakau sutau!» [54]

Attended by his beloved wife in the forest,
listening to the innocent, sweet prattle of his children,
he practiced austerities for more than half a year,
forgetting the worries of kingship, like an ascetic in a park.

One day, when the princess had gone to collect roots and fruits and the prince had stayed in the hermitage to take care of the children, a brahmin arrived, his feet and calves grubby with dust from the road and his eyes and face emaciated by fatigue. A water-jar hung from his shoulder, tied to a wooden stick, and he had come under his wife's firm orders that he should bring her some servants. 9.110

It had been a long time since the Bodhi·sattva had seen a supplicant and so when the brahmin arrived, his eyes and face beamed with heartfelt joy. Greeting him with friendly words of welcome, he had the brahmin enter his hermitage, where he honored him in the manner appropriate to a guest and asked him why he had come.

Passion for his wife had stripped the brahmin of any self-control or shame. Concerned only to receive a gift, he told the Bodhi·sattva his intent somewhat as follows:

"People walk where there is visibility
and an even road, not along a difficult path.
But in this world, so dark with selfishness,
my requests can proceed along no other route.

Your glorious fame, exalted by your heroic giving,
has traveled everywhere, as it should.
That is why I come to make this arduous request:
please give me your children as servants!"

9.115 ity ukte Bodhisattvo Mahā|sattvaḥ,

dāna|prītau kṛt'|âbhyāsaḥ pratyākhyātum a|śikṣitaḥ
«dadām'» îty avadadd hṛṣṭaṃ dayitau tanayāv api. [55]

«svasty astu! tat kim idānīm āsyata?» iti ca brāhmaṇen' âbhihitaḥ sa Mahā|sattvaḥ pradāna|kathā|śravaṇ'|ôtpatita| viṣāda|viplut'|âkṣayoḥ sutayoḥ sneha|vegen' âvalambyamāna|hṛdayo Bodhisattva uvāca:

«dattāv etau mayā tubhyaṃ. kiṃ tu māt" ânayor gatā
vanaṃ mūla|phalasy' ârthe sāyam ady' āgamiṣyati. [56]

tayā dṛṣṭāv upāghrātau mālināv abhyalaṃkṛtau
ih' âika|rātraṃ viśramya śvo net" âsi sutau mama.» [57]

9.120 brāhmaṇa uvāca: «alam anen' âtra|bhavato nirbandhena.

gauṇam etadd hi nārīṇāṃ
 nāma vāmā iti sthitam.
syāc c' âivaṃ dāna|vighnas te.
 tena vāsaṃ na rocaye.» [58]

Bodhisattva uvāca, «alaṃ dāna|vighn'|āśaṅkayā. saha| dharma|cāriṇī mama sā. yathā v" âtra|bhavate rocate. api ca, mahā|brāhmaṇa,

Addressed this way, the Bodhi·sattva, that Great Being, 9.115

practiced in the joy of giving
and untrained in refusing requests,
joyfully agreed to give the gift,
even though they were his beloved children.

"Bless you!" the brahmin said to the Great Being. "But what are you sitting around for?" The children, however, were distraught when they heard they would be given away and their eyes flooded with tears, making the Bodhi·sattva's heart sway with affection. He therefore said to the brahmin:

"I have given you these children.
But their mother has gone to the forest
to collect roots and fruits
and will return in the evening.

Let her see and kiss her children,
decorated and wreathed in garlands.
Stay here for one night.
You can take my children tomorrow."

"Enough of your stubbornness," the brahmin replied. 9.120

"Women are often
described as contrary.
She might try to stop your gift.
I do not therefore wish to stay."

"Do not worry about your gift being obstructed," the Bodhi·sattva answered. "Madri is my companion in virtue. But do as you please, sir. And yet, eminent brahmin,

su|kumāratayā bālyāt paricaryāsv a|kauśalāt
kīdṛśīṃ nāma kuryātāṃ dāsa|prītim imau tava? [59]

dṛṣṭvā tv itthaṃ|gatāv etau
 Śibi|rājaḥ pitā|mahaḥ
addhā dadyād yad iṣṭaṃ te
 dhanaṃ niṣkrayam etayoḥ. [60]

9.125 yatas tad|viṣayaṃ sādhu tvam imau netum arhasi.
evaṃ hy arthena mahatā dharmeṇa ca sameṣyasi.» [61]

brāhmaṇa uvāca, «na śakṣyāmy aham āśī|viṣa|dur|āsadaṃ vipriy'|ôpāyanena rājānam abhigantum.

ācchindyān mad imau rājā
 daṇḍaṃ vā praṇayen mayi,
yato neṣyāmy aham imau
 brāhmaṇyāḥ paricārakau.» [62]

atha Bodhisattvo «yath"|êṣṭam idānīm» ity a|parisamāpt'|ârtham uktvā s'|ânunayam anuśiṣya tanayau paricary"|ânukūlye pratigrah'|ârtham abhiprasārite brāhmaṇasya pāṇau kamaṇḍalum āvarjayām āsa.

tasya yatn'|ânurodhena
 papāt' âmbu kamaṇḍaloḥ,
padma|patr'|âbhitāmrābhyāṃ
 netrābhyāṃ svayam eva tu. [63]

How can these children
please you as slaves?
They are tender and young,
unskilled in serving others.

If their grandfather, the king of the Shibis,
were to see them in this plight,
he would certainly pay you
whatever price you desired.

It would therefore be best 9.125
if you took them to his realm.
You will then acquire great wealth
and also perform a good deed."

"I cannot approach the king with such a repellent offer," the brahmin said. "He would be as intimidating as a poisonous snake.

The king might tear the children
away from me or punish me.
I will take them instead
to my brahmin wife as servants."

"As you wish," the Bodhi·sattva replied, his goal unaccomplished, and gently instructed his children how to become servants. He then tipped a waterpot over the brahmin's hand, which was stretched out to receive the gift.*

Water fell from the pot,
compelled by physical force.
But water also fell spontaneously
from his eyes that were as red as lotus petals.

9.130 atha sa brāhmaṇo lābh'|âti|harṣāt sa|saṃbhram'|ākulita|matir Bodhisattva|tanay'|âpaharaṇa|tvarayā saṃkṣipta|padam āśīr|vacanam uktvā nirgamyatām ity ājñā|karkaśena vacasā kumārāv āśrama|padān niṣkrāmayitum ārebhe. atha kumārau viyoga|duḥkh'|âtibhāra|vyathita|hṛdayau pitaram abhipraṇamya bāṣp'|ôparudhyamāna|nayanāv ūcatuḥ:

«ambā ca, tāta, niṣkrāntā tvaṃ ca nau dātum icchasi?
yāvat tām api paśyeva, tato dāsyati nau bhavān!» [64]

atha sa brāhmaṇaḥ purā māt" ânayor āgacchaty asya vā putra|snehāt paścāt|tāpaḥ saṃbhavat' îti vicintya padma|kalāpam iv' ânayor hastān ābadhya latayā saṃtarjayan viceṣṭamānau pitaraṃ prati vyāvartita|vadanau prakṛti|su|kumārau kumārau pracakarṣa. atha Kṛṣṇājinā kumārī tat|pūrva|duḥkh'|ôpanipātāt sa|svaraṃ rudatī pitaram uvāca:

«ayaṃ māṃ brāhmaṇas tāta
  latayā hanti nir|dayaḥ!
na c' âyaṃ brāhmaṇo vyaktaṃ,
  dhārmikā brāhmaṇāḥ kila. [65]

yakṣo 'yaṃ brāhmaṇa|cchadmā
  nūnaṃ harati khāditum.
nīyamānau piśācena,
  tāta, kiṃ nāv upekṣase?» [66]

Overjoyed at his gain and agitated by feelings of haste, the brahmin uttered only a brief blessing in his rush to take away the Bodhi·sattva's children. With a harsh voice, he ordered the children to leave and started to exit the hermitage. The children's hearts, however, reeled at the heavy anguish of being separated from their parents and, with tear-filled eyes, they prostrated themselves before their father, saying: 9.130

"Would you give us away, father,
while mother is not here?
Let us just see her first
and then you can give us away!"

The brahmin was worried that their mother might arrive soon or that paternal affection might make Vishvan·tara regret his gift. So he tied up their hands with a creeper, as if they were a bundle of lotuses, and dragged the tender children away, scolding them as they struggled and turned their faces toward their father. This was the first time the young girl Krishnájina had experienced any suffering and she called after her father, wailing loudly:

"This cruel brahmin is hurting me
with this creeper, father!
Clearly this is no brahmin.
For brahmins, I've heard, are good.

Surely this is a demon disguised as a brahmin,
kidnapping us to devour us.
Why do you ignore us, father,
when we're being led away by a demon?"

9.135 atha Jālī kumāro mātaram anuśocayann uvāca:

«n' âiv' êdaṃ me tathā duḥkhaṃ
yad ayaṃ hanti māṃ dvi|jaḥ.
n' âpaśyam ambāṃ yat tv adya
tad vidārayat' îva mām. [67]

rodiṣyati ciraṃ nūnam ambā śūnye tapo|vane
putra|śokena kṛpaṇā hata|śāv" êva cātakī. [68]

asmad|arthaṃ samāhṛtya
vanān mūla|phalaṃ bahu
bhaviṣyati kathaṃ nv ambā
dṛṣṭvā śūnyaṃ tapo|vanam? [69]

ime nāv aśvakās, tāta,
hastikā rathakāś ca ye.
ato 'rdhaṃ deyam ambāyai...
śokaṃ tena vineṣyati. [70]

9.140 vandy" âsmad|vacanād ambā
vāryā śokāc ca sarvathā.
dur|labhaṃ hi punas, tāta,
tava tasyāś ca darśanam. [71]

ehi, Kṛṣṇe. mariṣyāvaḥ.
ko nv artho jīvitena nau?
dattāv āvāṃ janitr" âsmai
brāhmaṇāya dhan'|âiṣiṇe.» [72]

ity uktvā jagmatuḥ.

Grieving for his mother, Jalin, the boy, then said: 9.135

"I am not hurt by the pain
this brahmin inflicts on me.
What tears me apart is that
I have not seen my mother today.

Mother will surely cry for a long time
when she sees the empty hermitage.
She'll be sad with grief for her children,
like a *chátaka* bird that has lost her chicks.

How will mother react
when she sees the hermitage empty
after collecting many roots
and fruits for us?

Here are our toy horses,
elephants and chariots, father.
You should give half to mother.
They will make her less sad.

Say goodbye to mother for us. 9.140
Do everything to stop her being sad.
For it will be hard to see
you and her again, father.

Come, Krishná. Let us die.
What reason is there for us to live?
Our father has given us away
to a greedy brahmin."

Saying these words, they left.

atha Bodhisattvas ten' âti | karuṇena tanaya | pralāpen' ākampita|matir api «ka idānīṃ dattv" ânutāpaṃ kariṣyat'?» îti niṣ|pratīkāreṇa śok'|âgninā nirdahyamāna|hṛdayo viṣa| vega|mūrcchā|parigata iva samuparudhyamāna|cetās tatr' âiva niṣasāda.

śīt'|ânila|vyajana|pratilabdha|saṃjñaś ca niṣkūjam iv' āśrama|padaṃ tanaya|śūnyam abhivīkṣya bāṣpa|gadgada| saṃnirudhyamāna|kaṇṭha ity ātma|gatam uvāca:

9.145 «putr'|âbhidhāne hṛdaye samakṣaṃ praharan mama
n' āśaṅkata kathaṃ nāma dhig a|lajjo bata dvi|jaḥ? [73]

pattikāv an|upānatkau
saukumāryāt klam'|â|sahau
yāsyataḥ katham adhvānaṃ
tasya ca preṣyatāṃ gatau? [74]

mārga|śrama|parimlānau
ko 'dya viśrāmayiṣyati?
kṣut|tarṣa|duḥkh'|âbhihatau
yāciṣyete kam etya vā? [75]

mama tāvad idaṃ duḥkhaṃ
dhīratāṃ kartum icchataḥ;
kā tv avasthā mama tayoḥ
sutayoḥ sukha|vṛddhayoḥ? [76]

The Bodhi·sattva's mind was shaken by the children's pitiable lament. Although he told himself that one should feel no regret after giving a gift, his heart burned with an incurable fire of sorrow. His mind seized up, like someone fainting from a powerful poison, and he collapsed there and then.

Fanned by a cool breeze, he then recovered his senses. And when he saw how silent the hermitage had become now that it was empty of the children, he stuttered the following words, his throat choked with tears:

"How could that shameless brahmin 9.145
feel no qualms in hurting
my children, my very heart,
in front of my eyes?

They are so young. They cannot endure fatigue.
Walking on foot, without any shoes,
how can they travel on the road
and become the servants of this man?

When withered by the exhaustion of the road,
who will provide comfort for them today?
Whom will they turn to, afflicted
by the pain of hunger and thirst?

If I feel pain,
despite my desire to be strong,
what will be the plight of my children,
who have been raised up in comfort?

aho putra|viyog'|âgnir
nirdahaty eva me manaḥ!
satāṃ tu dharmaṃ saṃsmṛtya
ko 'nutāpaṃ kariṣyati?» [77]

9.150 atha Madrī vipriy'|ôpanipāt'|āśaṃsibhir an|iṣṭair nimittair upajanita|vaimanasyā mūla|phalāny ādāya kṣiprataram āgantu|kām" âpi vyāḍa|mṛg'|ôparudhyamāna|mārgā cirataren' āśrama | padam upajagāma. ucitāyāṃ ca pratyudgamana|bhūmāv ākrīḍā|sthāneṣu ca tanayāv a|paśyantī bhṛśataram a|rati|vaśam agāt.

an|īpsit'|āśaṅkita|jāta|saṃbhramā
tataḥ sut'|ânveṣaṇa|cañcal'|ēkṣaṇā
prasaktam āhvānam a|saṃpratigrahaṃ
tayor viditvā vyalapac chuc" āturā: [78]

«samājavad yat pratibhāti me purā
suta|pralāpa|pratināditaṃ vanam
a|darśanād adya tayos tad eva me
prayāti kāntāram iv' â|śaraṇyatām. [79]

kiṃ nu khalu tau kumārau

krīḍā|prasaṅga|śrama|jāta|nidrau
suptau nu naṣṭau gahane vane vā?
cirān mad|abhyāgamanād a|tuṣṭau
syātāṃ kva cid bālatayā nilīnau. [80]

How my mind burns with the fire
of separation from my children!
But who would feel regret
if they remember the morality of the good?"

Madri, meanwhile, had become worried by various ill omens that heralded unfavorable events. Taking her roots and fruits, she was keen to return quickly but her path was blocked by dangerous wild beasts and so it was only after a very long time that she reached the hermitage. When she did not see her children in the usual place they met her, nor in their play-areas, she felt even more disturbed. 9.150

Anxiety arose in her as she feared the worst.
Her eyes flickered, searching for her children.
When her repeated calls received no reply,
she lamented, sick with grief:

"The forest appeared so festive to me before
when it resounded with my children's chatter.
But today, when I cannot see them,
it looks as shelterless as a wilderness.

Have the children

fallen asleep? Drowsy from tiring games?
Are they lost in the dense forest?
Are they hiding somewhere, as children do,
annoyed I have returned late?

9.155 ruvanti kasmāc ca na pakṣiṇo 'py amī?
samākulās tad|vadha|sākṣiṇo yadi?
taraṃga|bhaṅgair a|vinīta|kopayā
hṛtau nu kiṃ nimna|gay" âti|vegayā? [81]

ap' îdānīṃ me vitathā mithyā|vikalpā bhaveyuḥ. api rāja|putrāya sa|putrāya svasti syāt. apy an|iṣṭa|nivedināṃ nimittānāṃ mac|charīra eva vipāko bhavet. kiṃ nu khalv idaṃ nimitt'|âpavṛtta|†praharṣam a|rati|tamisray" âvacchādyamānaṃ vidravat' îva me hṛdayam? visrasyanta iva me gātrāṇi. vyākulā iva dig|vibhāgāḥ. bhramat' îva c' êdaṃ paridhvasta|lakṣmīkaṃ vanam iti.»

ath' ânupraviśy' āśrama|padam ekānte nikṣipya mūla|phalaṃ upacāra|puraḥsaraṃ bhartāram abhigamya «kva dārakāv?» iti papraccha. atha Bodhisattvo jānānaḥ sneha|dur|balatāṃ mātṛ|hṛdayasya dur|nivedyatvāc ca vipriyasya n' âināṃ kiṃ cid vaktuṃ śaśāka.

janasya hi priy'|ârhasya vipriy'|ākhyāna|vahninā
upetya hi manas|tāpaḥ sa|ghṛṇena su|duṣ|karaḥ. [82]

atha Madrī «vyaktam a|kuśalaṃ me putrayor yad ayam evaṃ tūṣṇīṃ|bhūtaḥ śoka|dainy'|ânuvṛtty"» êty avadhārya samantataḥ kṣipta|citt" êva vicinty' āśrama|padaṃ tanayāv a|paśyantī sa|bāṣpa|gadgadaṃ punar uvāca:

Why are the birds not even singing? 9.155
Are they disturbed at seeing the children's death?
Or did the untamed fury of a powerful river
snatch them away with its breaking waves?

I pray my fears prove ill-conceived and false. I pray that the prince and the children are well. I pray that I am the only one to feel the effects of these omens that herald misfortune. Perhaps my heart will tear apart, covered by dark sorrow? For these portents have rid it of all joy. My limbs feel as if they are drooping. The directions seem confused. The forest appears to be spinning. Its charm is destroyed."

Entering the hermitage, Madri placed the roots and fruits to one side and approached her husband. After greeting him politely, she asked him where the children were. But the Bodhi·sattva knew how love makes a woman's heart weak, and because it was difficult to tell her such unpleasant news, he was unable to speak to her.

When someone arrives deserving good news
it is very difficult for a man of compassion
to torment their mind with words
so unpleasant they burn like fire.

Madri judged that something bad must have happened to the children for the Bodhi·sattva to be so silent with grief and sorrow. Almost losing her mind, she scoured every part of the hermitage but was unable to see her children. So again she addressed her husband with a voice that stuttered with tears:

9.160 «dārakau ca na paśyāmi tvaṃ ca māṃ n' âbhibhāṣase.
hatā khalv asmi kṛpaṇā. vipriyaṃ hi na kathyate.» [83]

ity uktvā śok'|âgninā parigata|hṛdayā chinna|mūl" êva latā nipapāta.

patantīm eva c' âināṃ parigṛhya Bodhisattvas tṛṇa|śayanam ānīya śītābhir adbhiḥ pariṣicya pratyāgata|prāṇāṃ samāśvāsayann uvāca:

«sahas" âiva na te, Madri,
duḥkham ākhyātavān aham.
na hi saṃbhāvyate dhairyaṃ
manasi sneha|dur|bale. [84]

jarā|dāridrya|duḥkh'|ārto
brāhmaṇo mām upāgamat.
tasmai dattau mayā putrau.
samāśvasihi. mā śucaḥ. [85]

9.165 māṃ paśya, Madri, mā putrau. paridevīś ca, devi, mā.
putra|śoka|sa|śalye me prahārṣīr iva mā hṛdi. [86]

yācitena kathaṃ śakyaṃ
na dātum api jīvitam?
anumodasva tad, bhadre,
putra|dānam idaṃ mama.» [87]

“I do not see our children. 9.160
And you are not speaking to me.
I am wretched and destroyed.
For this silence cannot be good.”

Saying these words, her heart overwhelmed by burning sorrow, she fell to the ground like a creeper chopped at the root.

The Bodhi·sattva grabbed her as she fell. Taking her to a bed of grass, he sprinkled her with cool water until she recovered her senses. Trying to console her, he said these words:

“I didn’t immediately tell you
the painful news, Madri.
For strength is not found
in a mind weak from love.

A brahmin came to me,
pained by old age and poverty.
I gave him our children.
Take comfort. Do not grieve.

Look to me, Madri, not to the children. 9.165
Do not grieve, my princess.
Do not strike my heart:
grief for our children already pierces it like a barb.

How could I not give
my very life if asked for it?
Rejoice then in my gift
of the children, good lady.”

tac chrutvā Madrī putra|vināśa|śaṅkā|vyathita|hṛdayā putrayor jīvita|pravṛtti|śravaṇāt pratanū|bhūta|śokā patyur a|dhṛti|parihār'|ârthaṃ pramṛjya nayane sa|vismayam udīkṣamāṇā bhartāram uvāca:

«āścaryaṃ! kiṃ bahunā?

nūnaṃ vismaya|vaktavya|cetaso 'pi div'|âukasaḥ
yad ity a|labdha|prasaras tava cetasi matsaraḥ. [88]

9.170 tathā hi dikṣu prasṛta|pratisvanaiḥ
samantato daivata|dundubhi|svanaiḥ
prasakta|vispaṣṭa|pad'|âkṣaraṃ nabhas
tav' âiva kīrti|prathan'|ādarād abhūt. [89]

prakampi|śail'|êndra|payodharā dharā
madād iv' âbhūd abhivṛddha|vepathuḥ.
divaḥ patadbhiḥ kusumaiś ca kāñcanaiḥ
sa|vidyud|uddyotam iv' âbhavan nabhaḥ. [90]

tad alaṃ śoka|dainyena! dattvā cittaṃ prasādaya.
nipāna|bhūto lokānāṃ dāt" âiva ca punar bhava! [91]

atha Śakro dev'|êndraḥ kṣiti|tala|calanād ākampite Sumerau parvata|rāje «kim idam?» iti samutpanna|vimarśo vismay'|ôtphulla|nayanebhyo loka|pālebhyaḥ pṛthivī|kampa|kāraṇaṃ Viśvaṃtara|putra|dānam upalabhya praharṣa|vismay'|āghūrṇita|manāḥ prabhātāyāṃ tasyāṃ rajanyāṃ

Madri's grief lessened when she heard these words. For she knew now that her children were alive, whereas before her heart had been distraught with the fear that they were dead. Wishing to reassure her husband, she dried her eyes and, gazing up at him with amazement, she said:

"It is a miracle! What need to say more?

Surely the very gods
are filled with wonder
at the lack of selfishness
in your heart!

For divine drums rumble on all sides, 9.170
permeating the directions with their sound,
and clear words continuously fill the sky,
proclaiming your glory.

The earth trembles, as if with joy,
her breast-like mountains shaking.
The sky seems to gleam with lightning,
as golden flowers fall from heaven.

Do not grieve with sorrow!
After giving a gift, one should feel joy.
Be a well for the world!
Become a giver once more!"

When Suméru, the lord of the mountains, trembled during the earthquake, Shakra, the king of the gods, was stirred to examine the cause. Their eyes blooming with wonder, the world-protectors then informed him that the earthquake had been caused by Visvhan·tara's gift of his children, making Shakra joyful and amazed. And so, when night turned to dawn, Shakra approached Vishvan·tara in the guise of a

brāhmaṇa|rūpī Viśvaṃtaram arthivad abhyagacchat. kṛt'|âtithi|satkāraś ca Bodhisattvena «ken' ârtha?» ity upanimantrito bhāryām enam ayācata:

«mahā|hradeṣv ambha iv' ôpaśoṣaṃ
na dāna|dharmaḥ samupaiti satsu.
yāce tatas tvāṃ, sura|saṃnibh', āryāṃ.
bhāryām imām arhasi naḥ pradātum.» [92]

9.175 a|vimanā eva tu Bodhisattvas tath" êty asmai pratiśuśrāva.

tataḥ sa vāmena kareṇa Madrīm
ādāya savyena kamaṇḍaluṃ ca
nyapātayat tasya jalaṃ kar'|âgre
Manobhuvaś cetasi śoka|vahnim. [93]

cukopa Madrī na tu, no ruroda.
viveda sā tasya hi taṃ sva|bhāvam.
a|pūrva|duḥkh'|âti|bhar'|āturā tu
taṃ prekṣamāṇā likhit" êva tasthau. [94]

tad dṛṣṭvā parama|vismay'|ākrānta|hṛdayaḥ Śakro devānām indras taṃ Mahā|sattvam abhiṣṭuvann uvāca:

«aho vikṛṣṭ'|ântaratā
sad|a|sad|dharmayor yathā!
śraddhātum api karm' êdaṃ
kā śaktir a|kṛt'|ātmanām? [95]

9.180 a|vīta|rāgeṇa satā
putra|dāram ati|priyam
niḥ|saṅgam iti dātavyaṃ—
kā nām' êyam udāttatā? [96]

brahmin supplicant. On being shown the honor due to a guest, he was invited by the Bodhi·sattva to state what he wanted, whereupon he asked Vishvan·tara for his wife:

"In good men the virtuous act of giving
never dries up, just like water in large lakes.
So, god-like prince, I request your noble wife.
Please give her to me."

The Bodhi·sattva agreed to the request without even flinching. 9.175

Taking Madri in his left hand
and a waterpot in his right,
he poured water over the brahmin's hands,
igniting a fire of grief in the heart of Desire.

Madri was not angry. Nor did she weep.
For she knew her husband's nature.
Afflicted by the great weight of this new suffering,
she stood still like a painting, staring at him.

When he saw this, Shakra, the king of the gods, was deeply astonished and praised the Great Being with the following words:

"How broad is the gap between
the morals of the good and the bad!
How can those with imperfect souls
even believe in this feat?

How can one even describe the nobility 9.180
of a virtuous man, devoid of passion,
who through non-attachment
gives away his beloved wife and children?

a|saṃśayaṃ tvad|guṇa|rakta|saṃkathaiḥ
prakīryamāṇeṣu yaśaḥsu dikṣu te
tiro|bhaviṣyanty aparā yaśaḥ|śriyaḥ
pataṃga|tejaḥsu yath" ânya|dīptayaḥ. [97]

tasya te 'bhyanumodante karm' êdam ati|mānuṣam
yakṣa|gandharva|bhujagās tri|daśāś ca sa|Vāsavāḥ.» [98]

ity uktvā Śakraḥ svam eva vapur abhijvalad āsthāya, «Śakro 'ham asm'» îti ca nivedy' ātmānaṃ Bodhisattvam uvāca:

«tubhyam eva prayacchāmi
Madrīṃ bhāryām imām aham
vyatītya na hi śīt'|âṃśuṃ
candrikā sthātum arhati.» [99]

9.185 *datt" âpi ca† śṛgālasya
siṃha|bhāryā kim asya sā?
siṃhasy' âiva hi sā bhāryā.
dhīrā yacchanti yācitāḥ. [100]

viśiṣṭa|madhya|hīnānāṃ sama|cittā jin'|âṅkurāḥ
tasmād anumatā loke na tu karmaṇā. [101]

tan mā cintāṃ putrayor viprayogād
rājya|bhraṃśān mā ca saṃtāpam āgāḥ.
sārdhaṃ tābhyām abhyupetaḥ pitā te
kartā rājyaṃ tvat|sa|nāthaṃ sa|nātham.» [102]

When eulogies dedicated to your virtue
proclaim your fame in every direction,
the glorious reputations of others will surely disappear,
just as the splendor of the sun dispels other luminaries.

Yakshas, *gandhárvas* and snakes,
Vásava and the gods,
all rejoice in your deed,
which is beyond human."

Saying these words, Shakra took on his true blazing form and, after he had told the Bodhi·sattva who he was, he said to him:

"I give you back
Madri, your wife.
For moonlight should not
exist apart from the moon.

What can a lion's wife be to a jackal, 9.185
even if she is given to him?
For it is the lion to whom that wife belongs.
But the brave always give when asked.

Seedling Buddhas* are equanimous toward people,
whether noble, middling, or inferior.
They are therefore esteemed
in the world for their actions.*

Do not worry about being separated from
your offspring.
Nor feel anguished at losing your kingdom.
Your father will arrive here with your children
and protect his kingdom by making you its protector."

ity uktvā Śakras tatr' âiv' ântar|dadhe. Śakr'|ânubhāvāc ca sa brāhmaṇo Bodhisattva|tanayau Śibi|viṣayam eva saṃprāpayām āsa. atha Śibayaḥ Saṃjayaś ca Śibi|rājas tad ati|karuṇam ati|duṣ|karaṃ ca Bodhisattvasya karma śrutvā samākledita|hṛdayā brāhmaṇa|hastān niṣkrīya Bodhisattva|tanayau prasādy' ānīya ca Viśvaṃtaraṃ rājya eva pratiṣṭhāpayām āsuḥ.

tad evam aty|adbhutā Bodhisattva|cary" êti tad|unmukheṣu sattva|viśeṣeṣu n' âvajñā pratīghāto vā karaṇīyaḥ.

9.190 Tathāgata|varṇe sat|kṛtya Dharma|śravaṇe c' ôpaneyam.

Saying these words, Shakra disappeared at that very spot. Through Shakra's power, the brahmin brought the Bodhi·sattva's children to the realm of the Shibis. When the Shibis, and Sánjaya their king, learned of the Bodhi·sattva's extremely compassionate and difficult deed, their hearts softened and, after buying back the children from the brahmin, they installed Vishvan·tara as king after acquiring his grace.

The conduct of a Bodhi·sattva is therefore a great marvel. And, because of this, one should not condemn or hamper the exceptional beings who aspire to that state.

This story should also be cited when eulogizing the Tatha·gata or when discussing the topic of listening to the Teaching with respect. 9.190

STORY 10

THE BIRTH-STORY ON THE SACRIFICE

10.1 NA KALYĀṆ'|ĀŚAYĀḤ pāpa|pratāraṇām anuvidhīyanta, ity āśaya|śuddhau yatitavyam.

tad|yath" ânuśrūyate.

Bodhisattvaḥ kila sva|puṇya|prabhāv'|ôpanatām ānata|sarva|sāmantāṃ praśānta|sva|para|cakr'|ādy|upadravatvād a|kaṇṭakām a|sapatnām ek'|ātapatrāṃ dāyādya|kram'|āgatāṃ pṛthivīṃ pālayām āsa.

nāthaḥ pṛthivyāḥ sa jit'|êndriy'|ârir
bhukt'|âvagīteṣu phaleṣv a|saktaḥ
prajā|hiteṣv āhita|sarva|bhāvo
dharm'|âika|kāryo munivad babhūva. [1]

10.5 viveda lokasya hi sa sva|bhāvaṃ
pradhāna|cary"|ânukṛti|pradhānam
śreyaḥ samādhitsur ataḥ prajāsu
viśeṣato dharma|vidhau sasañje. [2]

dadau dhanaṃ, śīla|vidhiṃ samādade,
kṣamāṃ siṣeve, jagad|artham aihata.
prajā|hit'|âdhyāśaya|saumya|darśanaḥ
sa mūrtimān Dharma iva vyarocata. [3]

GOOD-HEARTED PEOPLE do not yield to the seductions of the wicked. One should therefore strive for a pure heart. 10.1

Tradition has handed down the following story.

The Bodhi·sattva is said to have once lived as a king, a protector of the earth. Acquiring his position through hereditary succession and the power of his merit, he had no rivals and all his vassals bowed before him, his parasol alone holding sway. Since he had quelled all grievances, in both his own and other realms, his kingdom suffered no hardships.

Unattached to censurable pleasures,*
the lord of the earth had conquered his enemies,
the senses.
His entire being was dedicated to benefiting
his subjects.
Like a sage, his sole duty was to virtue.

Since he knew it was natural for people 10.5
to place a value on emulating eminent men,
he especially committed himself to virtue,
desiring to bring happiness to his subjects.

His donations of wealth, his practice of
the moral precepts,*
his cultivation of forbearance, his endeavor to benefit
the world,
and his kind face as he determined to help his subjects,
all made him as glorious as Virtue incarnate.

atha kadā cit tad|bhuj'|âbhiguptam api taṃ viṣayaṃ sattvānāṃ karma|vaiguṇyāt pramāda|vaśagatvāc ca varṣa|karm'|âdhikṛtānāṃ deva|putrāṇāṃ dur|vṛṣṭi|paryākulatā kva cit kva cid abhidudrāva. atha sa rājā «vyaktam ayaṃ mama prajānāṃ vā dharm'|âpacārāt samupanato 'n|artha» iti niścita|matiḥ saṃrūḍha|hit'|âdhyāśayatvāt prajāsu tad|duḥkham a|mṛṣyamāṇo dharma|tattva|jña|saṃmatān puro|hita|pramukhān brāhmaṇa|vṛddhān mati|sacivāṃś ca tad|uddharaṇ'|ôpāyaṃ papraccha.

atha te veda|vihitam an|eka|prāṇi|śata|vadh'|ārambha|bhīṣaṇaṃ yajña|vidhiṃ su|vṛṣṭi|hetuṃ manyamānās tam asmai saṃvarṇayām āsuḥ. vidita|vṛttāntas tu sa rājā yajña|vihitānāṃ prāṇi|vaiśasānāṃ karuṇ"|ātmakatvān na teṣāṃ tad vacanaṃ bhāven' âbhyanandat. vinay'|ânuvṛttyā c' âinān pratyākhyāna|rūkṣ'|âkṣaram an|uktvā prastāv'|ântareṇ' âiṣāṃ tāṃ kathāṃ tiraś|cakāra. te punar api taṃ rājānaṃ dharma|saṃkathā|prastāva|labdh'|âvasarā gāmbhīrya|gūḍhaṃ tasya bhāvam a|jānānā yajña|pravṛttaye samanuśaśāsuḥ:

kāryāṇi rājñāṃ niyatāni yāni
   lābhe pṛthivyāḥ paripālane ca,
n' âtyeti kālas tava tāni nityaṃ.
   teṣāṃ kramo dharma|sukhāni yadvat. [4]

A disastrous drought, however, happened to afflict various parts of the king's realm, even though it was protected by his arm. This was due partly to a defect in the karma of his people and partly to the negligence of the gods overseeing the task of the rains. The king was certain that the calamity had been caused either by his own immoral conduct or by that of his people. Deeply concerned for the welfare of his subjects and unable to endure their suffering, he therefore consulted his ministers and asked his brahmin elders—who were headed by the king's chief priest and esteemed for their knowledge of religion—how the disaster might be alleviated.

They recommended that the king should perform a sacrificial ritual prescribed by the Vedas, since they believed it would produce an abundance of rain. It was a gruesome act, involving the killing and massacre of several hundreds of living creatures, and when the king learned of the slaughter required by the sacrifice, his compassionate nature made him unable, in all honesty, to approve of their words. Out of politeness, however, he did not harshly rebuff his counselors but instead avoided the conversation by moving on to another topic. But now that they had found an opportunity to discuss the subject of religion, the counselors again advised the king to perform the sacrifice, ignorant of his deeply hidden feelings:

"When seizing and defending land,
you never neglect the proper time
to fulfill your regular royal duties.
Performing them is like the joys of religion.

10.10 tri|varga|sevā|nipuṇasya tasya
prajā|hit'|ârthaṃ dhṛta|kārmukasya
yajñ'|âbhidhāne sura|loka|setau
pramāda|tantr" êva kathaṃ matis te? [5]

bhṛtyair iv' ājñā bahu manyate te
sākṣād iyaṃ siddhir iti kṣit'|īśaiḥ.
śreyāṃsi kīrti|jvalitāni cetuṃ
yajñair ayaṃ te, ripu|kāla, kālaḥ. [6]

kāmaṃ sadā dīkṣita eva ca tvaṃ
dāna|prasaṅgān niyam'|ādarāc ca
Veda|prasiddhaiḥ kratubhis tath" âpi
yuktaṃ bhaven moktum ṛṇaṃ surāṇām. [7]

sv|iṣṭy" âbhituṣṭāni hi daivatāni
bhūtāni vṛṣṭyā pratimānayanti.
iti prajānāṃ hitam ātmanaś ca
yaśas|karaṃ yajña|vidhiṃ juṣasva. [8]

tasya cintā prādur|abhavat: «ati|dur|nyasto bat' âyaṃ para|pratyaya|hārya|pelava|matir a|mīmāṃsako dharma|priya|śraddadhāno jano yatra hi nāma:

10.15 ya eva lokeṣu śaraṇya|saṃmatās
ta eva hiṃsām api dharmato gatāḥ.
vivartate kaṣṭam apāya|saṃkaṭe
janas tad|ādeśita|kāpath'|ânugaḥ. [9]

Skilled in following the three pursuits, 10.10
you wield your bow for the welfare of your people.
Why then does your mind seem negligent
regarding heaven's causeway called "sacrifice"?

*Kings respect your commands like servants.
For they believe that success is evident in them.
The time has come for you, who bring doom
to your enemies,
to gather the blessings that blaze gloriously
through sacrifice!

We accept you are already ever consecrated*
by your devotion to giving and regard for restraint.
But it would be fitting to remove your debt to the gods
by performing the sacrifices celebrated in the Vedas.

When satisfied by proper sacrifices,
the gods return the honor by delivering rain.
Perform, then, a sacrifice to bring you glory:
it will benefit your people as well as yourself."

"These men are in a terrible state!" the king thought. "Their delicate minds are taken in by the trust they place in others, as they unquestioningly believe in those devoted to religion. For,

The very people considered refuges in the world 10.15
are the same who turn to violence in religion's name.
Those following the wrong path indicated by
such men
whirl miserably in the narrow straits of hell.

ko hi nām' âbhisaṃbandho dharmasya paśu|hiṃsayā
sura|lok'âdhivāsasya daivata|prīṇanasya vā? [10]

viśasyamānaḥ kila mantra|śaktibhiḥ
paśur divaṃ gacchati, tena tad|vadhaḥ
upaiti dharmatvam, it' îdam apy asat.
paraiḥ kṛtaṃ ko hi paratra lapsyate? [11]

a|sat|pravṛtter a|nivṛtta|mānasaḥ
śubheṣu karmasv a|virūḍha|niścayaḥ
paśur divaṃ yāsyati kena hetunā
hato 'pi yajñe sva|kṛt'|āśrayaṃ vinā? [12]

hataś ca yajñe tri|divaṃ yadi vrajen,
nanu vrajeyuḥ paśutāṃ svayaṃ dvi|jāḥ.
yatas tu n' âyaṃ vidhir īkṣyate kva cid,
vacas tad eṣāṃ ka iva grahīṣyati? [13]

10.20 a|tulya|gandha'|rddhi|ras'|âujasaṃ śubhāṃ
sudhāṃ kil' ôtsṛjya var'|âpsaro|dhṛtām
mudaṃ prayāsyanti vap"|ādi|kāraṇād
vadhena śocyasya paśor div'|âukasaḥ?» [14]

tad idam atra prāpta|kālam iti viniścitya sa rājā yajñ'|ārambha|samutsuka iva nāma tat teṣāṃ vacanaṃ pratigṛhy' âvocad enān:

How can violence against animals
be connected with morality
or with dwelling in heaven
or pleasing the gods?

They say an animal goes to heaven
when slaughtered by spear-like mantras
and so its murder is moral. But this is false.
Who can obtain in the next world the fruit of another's
action?

An animal's mind has not renounced vice.
Nor has it committed itself to good deeds.
Why would it go to heaven, if merely killed
in sacrifice,
without having performed its own actions?

If one goes to heaven by being killed in sacrifice,
surely brahmins themselves would become sacrificial
animals.
But since one never sees this practiced,
who would accept the words of such men?

Would the gods reject their pure nectar, served by 10.20
fine nymphs,
incomparable in scent, richness, flavor, and potency,
and take joy in the slaughter of a pitiful animal
to feed off its intestines and other parts?"

After deciding on an appropriate course of action, the king pretended he was eager to undertake the sacrifice and agreed with their counsel, saying:

«sa|nāthaḥ khalv aham anugrahavāṃś ca yad evaṃ me hit'|âvahita|manaso 'tra|bhavantaḥ. tad icchāmi puruṣa|medha|sahasreṇa yaṣṭum. anuśiṣyantāṃ tad|upayogya|saṃbhāra|samudānayan'|ârthaṃ yath"|âdhikāram amātyāḥ. parīkṣyatāṃ sattr'|âgāra|niveśa|yogyo bhūmi|pradeśas tad|anuguṇaś ca tithi|karaṇa|muhūrta|nakṣatra|yoga iti.»

ath' âinaṃ purohita uvāca:

«īpsit'|ârtha|saṃpattaye snātu tāvan mahā|rāja ekasya yajñasy' âvabhṛthe. ath' ôttareṣām ārambhaḥ kariṣyate krameṇa. yugapat puruṣa|paśavaḥ sahasraśo hi parigṛhyamāṇā vyaktam udvega|doṣāya prajānāṃ te syur iti.»

10.25 «asty etad» iti brāhmaṇair uktaḥ

sa rājā tān uvāca, «alam atra|bhavatāṃ prakṛti|kop'|āśaṅkayā. tath" âhaṃ saṃvidhāsye yath" ôdvegaṃ me prajā na prayāsyant' îti.»

atha sa rājā paura|jānapadān saṃnipāty' âbravīt:

«icchāmi puruṣa|medha|sahasreṇa yaṣṭum. na ca mayā śakyaḥ kaś cid a|kāmaḥ paśutve niyoktum a|duṣṭaḥ. tad yaṃ yam aham itaḥ prabhṛti vo drakṣyāmi vyavadhūta|pramāda|nidreṇa vimalena cāra|cakṣuṣā śīla|maryād'|âtivartinam asmad|ājñāṃ paribhavantaṃ, taṃ taṃ sva|kula|pāṃsakaṃ deśa|kaṇṭakam ahaṃ paśu|nimittam ādāsyām' îty etad vo viditam astv iti!»

"How protected and favored I am to have men such as you concerned for my welfare. I wish then to perform a sacrifice of a thousand human victims. Let all the ministers in their various areas of jurisdiction be instructed to acquire the necessary materials for this rite. A suitable area of land must be sought for setting up the edifice of a *sattra* sacrifice.* And an investigation should be made into the lunar days, *káranas*, *muhúrtas*, and planetary conjunctions appropriate for the rite."*

The chief-priest then replied:

"To guarantee the success of your goal, Your Majesty should undertake the *avábhritha* bathing ritual at the close of the first sacrifice.* The other sacrifices can then be performed in due succession. For if you seize all one thousand human victims at the same time, there will certainly be turmoil among the people."

"That is true," the brahmins agreed. 10.25

But the king replied: "Do not worry about the people. I will ensure that my subjects do not become agitated."

Gathering together his people from both the city and the countryside, the king then said:

"I wish to perform a sacrifice of a thousand human victims. But I cannot subject an unwilling person to be a sacrificial victim if they have done nothing wrong. Therefore, from this day forth, if I see any of you transgressing the bounds of virtue or scorning my command, I will take that person, that blemish on their family and thorn in their country's side, and use them a sacrificial victim. Spies will act as my untarnished eyes from which carelessness and sleep have been wiped away. Let this be known to you!"

atha teṣāṃ mukhyatamāḥ prāñjalaya enam ūcuḥ:

10.30 «sarvāḥ kriyās tava hita|pravaṇāḥ prajānāṃ..
tatr' âvamānana|vidher, nara|deva, ko 'rthaḥ?
Brahm" âpi te caritam abhyanumantum arhaḥ.
sādhu|pramāṇa|param atra|bhavān pramāṇam. [15]

priyaṃ yad eva devasya tad asmākam api priyam.
asmat|priya|hitād anyad dṛśyate na hi te priyam.» [16]

iti pratigṛhīta|vacanaḥ paura|jānapadaiḥ sa rājā mahatā jana|prakāśen' âḍambareṇa pratyayitān amātyān pāpa|jan'|ôpagrahaṇ'|ârthaṃ janapadaṃ nagarāṇi ca preṣayām āsa. samantataś ca pratyaham iti ghoṣaṇāṃ kārayām āsa:

«a|bhayam a|bhaya|do dadāti rājā
sthira|śuci|śīla|dhanāya saj|janāya
a|vinaya|nirataiḥ prajā|hit'|ârthaṃ
nara|paśubhis tu sahasraśo yiyakṣuḥ. [17]

tad yaḥ kaś cid ataḥ prabhṛty a|vinaya|ślāgh"|
ânuvṛtty|udbhavāt
sāmanta|kṣitip'|ârcitām api nṛ|pasy'
ājñām avajñāsyati
sa svair eva viṣahya yajña|paśutām
āpāditaḥ karmabhir
yūp'|ābaddha|tanur viṣāda|kṛpaṇaḥ
śuṣyañ janair drakṣyate.» [18]

The leaders of the people then addressed the king, cupping their hands in respect:

"All your actions tend toward your people's welfare. 10.30
Why would we malign you on this matter, god
among men?
Brahma himself would approve of your conduct.
You are our paradigm, our highest standard of good.

What is dear to Your Majesty
is also dear to us.
For nothing is dearer to you
than what benefits and is dear to us."

After the people had thus accepted his words, the king dispatched trusted ministers to the countryside and towns to apprehend any wrongdoers, publicized by loud drums. Every day he had the following announcement made in every direction:

"The king provides safety. He gives this safety
to good people who possess strong and pure virtue.
But those who delight in indecency, the king
will sacrifice in their thousands to benefit the people.

From this day forth,
whoever takes gleeful pride in indecency,
sneering at the royal command
revered even by neighboring kings,
will, by their own actions,
be forced to become sacrificial victims.
Wretched with despair, their body tied to a stake,
they will languish before the people's eyes."

10.35 atha tad | viṣaya | nivāsinaḥ puruṣā yajña | paśu | nimittaṃ duḥ | śīla | puruṣ' | ânveṣaṇ' | ādaraṃ avekṣya rājñas tāṃ ca ghoṣaṇām ati | bhīṣaṇāṃ pratyaham upaśṛṇvantaḥ pāpa | jan' | ôpagrah' | âvahitāṃś ca rāja | puruṣān samantataḥ samāpatato 'bhivīkṣya tyakta | dauḥśīly' | ânurāgāḥ śīla | saṃvara | samādāna | parā vaira | prasaṅga | parāṅ | mukhāḥ paras | para | prema | gaurava | su | mukhāḥ praśānta | vigraha | vivādā guru | jana | vacan' | ânuvartinaḥ saṃvibhāga | viśāradāḥ priy' | âtithayo vinaya | naibhṛtya | ślāghinaḥ Kṛta | yuga iva babhūvuḥ.

bhayena mṛtyoḥ para | loka | cintayā
  kul' | âbhimānena yaśo | 'nurakṣayā
su | śukla | bhāvāc ca virūḍhayā hriyā
  janaḥ sva | śīl' | â | mala | bhūṣaṇo† 'bhavat. [19]

yathā yathā dharma | paro 'bhavaj janas
  tathā tathā rakṣi | jano viśeṣataḥ
cakāra duḥ | śīla | jan' | âbhimārgaṇām
  ataś ca dharmān na cacāla kaś ca na. [20]

sva | deśa | vṛttāntam ath' ôpaśuśruvān
  imaṃ nṛ | paḥ prīti | viśeṣa | bhūṣaṇaḥ.
carān priy' | ākhyānaka | dāna | vistaraiḥ
  sa tarpayitvā sacivān samanvaśāt. [21]

The inhabitants of the realm saw that the king was earnest in his quest to find immoral men as sacrificial victims. So when they heard his terrifying daily proclamation and witnessed the king's servants swooping down on all sides and determined to apprehend the wicked, they abandoned any fondness for immoral behavior and became dedicated to practicing moral restraints. Turning their back on hatred, they inclined toward love and mutual respect. They stopped all quarrels and disputes and they followed the advice of their elders. They became used to sharing and they developed a love of hospitality. Taking pride in humility and modesty, it was as if they lived in the Krita Era. 10.35

Fearful of death, they had a regard for the next life.
Proud of their family, they protected their reputation.
Through their pure nature, they developed a sense
    of shame.
Such was the stainless virtue that adorned the people.

Wherever people became devoted to virtue,
the guardians made special efforts
to seek out wrongdoers.
Thus no-one strayed from morality.

The king became adorned by exceptional joy
when he heard what had happened in his country.
Gratifying his scouts with extensive gifts for their
    good news,
he informed his ministers, saying:

«parā manīṣā mama rakṣitum prajā;
gatāś ca tāḥ samprati dakṣiṇīyatām.
idaṃ ca yajñāya dhanaṃ prakalpitaṃ
yiyakṣur asm' îti yathā|pratarkitam. [22]

10.40 yad īpsitaṃ yasya sukh'|êndhanaṃ dhanaṃ,
prakāmam āpnotu sa tan mad|antikāt.
it' îyam asmad|viṣay'|ôpatāpinī
daridratā nir|viṣayī bhaved yathā. [23]

mayi prajā|rakṣaṇa|niścaya|sthite
sahāya|saṃpat|parivṛddha|sādhane
iyaṃ jan'|ārtir mad|a|marṣa|dīpanī
muhur muhur me jvalat' îva cetasi.» [24]

atha te tasya rājñaḥ sacivāḥ param iti pratigṛhya tad|vacanaṃ sarveṣu grāma|nagara|nigameṣu mārga|viśrāma|pradeśeṣu ca dāna|śālāḥ kārayitvā yathā|saṃdiṣṭaṃ rājñā pratyaham arthi|janam abhilaṣitair arthaiḥ saṃtarpayām āsuḥ.

atha vihāya janaḥ sa daridratāṃ
samam avāpta|vasur vasudh"|âdhipāt
vividha|citra|paricchada|bhūṣaṇaḥ
pravitat'|ôtsava|śobha iv' âbhavat. [25]

pramudit'|ârthi|jana|stuti|vistṛtaṃ
pravitatāna nṛ|pasya diśo yaśaḥ,
tanu|taraṅga|vivardhita|vistaraṃ
sara iv' âmbuja|kesara|jaṃ rajaḥ. [26]

"My greatest desire is to protect my people.
And they are now worthy of sacrificial gifts.*
The wealth I intended to be used for sacrifice
I will now give up in sacrifice as planned.

May those who seek wealth to fuel their happiness 10.40
come and receive it from me with delight.
In this way we'll deny all scope
to the poverty that afflicts my realm.

Assisted greatly by my helpers,
I resolved to protect my subjects.
When my people suffer, it kindles my rage,
like a fire blazing incessantly in my mind."

Obeying the king's words with admiration, the ministers had alms halls built in every village, city, and marketplace, and at every resting-spot on the roads, and satisfied the needy every day with whatever they desired, just as the king had ordered.

Acquiring wealth from the king
and casting aside their poverty,
the people wore various glittering clothes and
ornaments,
resembling the splendor of a huge festival.

The king's fame spread in all directions,
extended by the praise of the joyful petitioners,
just as small ripples on a lake spread
the pollen of lotus filaments more and more widely.

10.45 iti nṛ|pasya su|nīti|guṇ'|āśrayāt
su|carit'|âbhimukhe nikhile jane
samabhibhūta|balāḥ kuśal'|ôcchrayair
vilayam īyur a|saṅgam upadravāḥ. [27]

a|viṣamatva|sukhā ṛtavo 'bhavan
nava|nṛpā iva dharma|parāyaṇāḥ.
vividha|sasya|dharā ca vasuṃ|dharā
sa|kamal'|â|mala|nīla|jal'|āśayā. [28]

na janam abhyarujan prabalā rujaḥ.
paṭutaraṃ guṇam oṣadhayo dadhuḥ.
ṛtu|vaśena vavau niyato 'nilaḥ.
pariyayuś ca śubhena pathā grahāḥ. [29]

na para|cakra|kṛtaṃ samabhūd bhayaṃ,
na ca paras|para|jaṃ na ca daivikam.
niyama|dharma|pare nibhṛte jane
Kṛtam iv' âtra yugaṃ samapadyata. [30]

ath' âivaṃ pravṛttena dharma|yajñena rājñā praśamiteṣv arthi|jana|duḥkheṣu sārdham upadravaiḥ pramudita|jana|saṃbādhāyām abhyudaya|ramya|darśanāyāṃ ca vasuṃ|dharāyāṃ nṛ|pater āśīr|vacan'|âdhyayana|sa|vyāpāre loke vitanyamāne samantato rāja|yaśasi, prasād'|āvarjita|matiḥ kaś cid amātya|mukhyo rājānam ity uvāca:
10.50 «su|ṣṭhu khalv idam ucyate:

uttam'|âdhama|madhyānāṃ
kāryāṇāṃ nitya|darśanāt
upary upari buddhīnāṃ
carant' īśvara|buddhayaḥ. [31]

When the king's good guidance made 10.45
the people all incline toward moral conduct,
the calamities disappeared without obstacle,
their force destroyed by the increased virtue.

The seasons became pleasantly regular,
like newly installed kings performing their duty.
The earth bore various crops,
her waters pure, blue, and lotus-covered.

No violent sufferings afflicted the people.
The herbs became more potent.
The wind blew regularly and in season.
The planets moved in auspicious paths.

There was no danger from any enemy,
nor from one another nor the gods.
The people were calm, intent on restraint and
morality.
It was as if the Krita Era had appeared.

Through his virtuous sacrifice, the king thus quelled the sufferings of the needy and the calamities. The earth bore a look of delightful prosperity and thronged with joyful people. The world became dedicated to reciting benedictions for the king and his glory spread in every direction. All of this made one of the chief ministers address the king as follows, his heart filled with devotion:

"There is a fine proverb that states: 10.50

Through their constant regard
for high, low, and middling tasks,
the minds of kings go far
beyond ordinary intellects.

iti devena hi paśu|vaiśasa|vācya|doṣa|virahitena dharma|yajñena prajānām ubhaya|loka|hitaṃ sampāditam. upadravāś ca praśamitā dāridrya|duḥkhāni ca. kiṃ bahunā? sa|bhāgyās tāḥ prajāḥ.

lakṣm' êva kṣaṇadā|karasya vitataṃ
gātre na kṛṣṇ'|âjinaṃ.
dīkṣā|yantraṇayā nisarga|lalitāś
ceṣṭā na mand'|ôdyamāḥ.
mūrdhnaś chattra|nibhasya keśa|racanā|
śobhā tath" âiv' âtha ca.
tyāgais te śata|yajvano 'py apahṛtaḥ
kīrty|āśrayo vismayaḥ. [32]

hiṃsā|viṣaktaḥ kṛpaṇaḥ phal'|ēpsoḥ
prāyeṇa lokasya, naya|jña, yajñaḥ
yajñas tu kīrty|ābharaṇaḥ samas te
śīlasya nir|doṣa|manoharasya. [33]

10.55 aho prajānāṃ bhāgyāni
yāsāṃ gopāyitā bhavān.
prajānām api hi vyaktaṃ
n' âivaṃ syād gopitā pitā!» [34]

apara uvāca:

For through this virtuous sacrifice, free from any fault of animal-slaughter, Your Majesty has created welfare in both this world and the next for his people. You have quelled all calamities and the anguish of poverty. To be brief: your subjects have gained good fortune.

You wear no antelope skin across
your limbs like a mark on the moon.
The natural grace of your gestures
is not dulled by the constraints of initiation.
Glorious too is your hair-arrangement
on your head round as a parasol.
Your gifts rid even the god of a hundred sacrifices
of his awe, the very basis of his glory.*

When people sacrifice to seek a reward,
it is usually a low and violent act, wise king.
But your sacrifice is just and adorned by glory.
For you are virtuous and delightfully free from vice.

How fortunate the people are 10.55
to have you as their protector!
For certainly even a father
could not protect them the same way!"

And another minister said:

«dānaṃ nāma dhan'|ôdaye sati jano
datte tad|āśā|vaśaḥ.
syāc chīle 'pi ca loka|pakty|abhimukhaḥ
svarge ca jāta|spṛhaḥ.
yā tv eṣā para|kārya|dakṣiṇatayā
tvadvat pravṛttis tayor
n' â|vidvatsu na sattva|yoga|vidhureṣv
eṣā samālakṣyate.» [35]

tad evaṃ, na kalyāṇ'|āśayāḥ pāpa|pratāraṇām anuvidhīyanta ity āśaya|śuddhau yatitavyam.

«iti prajā|hit'|ôdyogaḥ
śreyaḥ|kīrti|sukh'|āvahaḥ
yan nṛ|pāṇām ato n' âlaṃ
tam an|ādṛtya vartitum.» [36]

10.60 evaṃ rāj'|âvavāde 'pi vācyam. «dharm'|âbhyāsaḥ prajānāṃ bhūtim āvahat' îti bhūti|kāmena dharm'|ânuvartinā bhavitavyam» ity evam apy upaneyam. «na paśu|hiṃsā kadā cid abhyudayāya, dāna|dama|saṃyam'|ādayas tv abhyudayāy' êti tad|arthinā dān'|ādi|pareṇa bhavitavyam» ity evam api vācyam.

«lok'|ârtha|caryā|pravaṇa|matir evaṃ pūrva|janmasv api sa Bhagavān» iti Tathāgata|varṇe 'pi vācyam.

"People give when their wealth increases
or when driven by hope for a reward.
Regarding virtue too, people seek fame
in the world or desire rebirth in heaven.
But to perform both of these, like you,
by skillfully acting for others:
this is seen only in the wise
and in men dedicated to goodness."

So it is that good-hearted people do not yield to the seductions of the wicked. One should therefore strive for a pure heart. And one should also narrate this story when advising kings, saying:

"The endeavor to benefit one's subjects
thus brings prosperity, fame, and happiness.
Whatever else the task of the kings,
this should never be disregarded."

And one should also draw the following conclusion: "A 10.60
king who seeks wealth ought to act righteously. For virtuous practice brings wealth to his people." And one should further state that: "Harming animals never leads to prosperity. But giving, discipline, self-restraint and other virtues do. Those who seek prosperity should therefore dedicate themselves to giving and other virtues."

And one should narrate this story when praising the Tatha·gata, saying: "In this way, even in his previous births, the Lord was fond of acting for the welfare of the world."

STORY 11

THE BIRTH-STORY OF SHAKRA

11.1 Āpad api mah"|ātmanām aiśvarya|saṃpad vā sattveṣv anukampāṃ na śithilī|karoti.

tad|yath" ânuśrūyate.

Bodhisattvaḥ kil' ân|alpa|kāla|sv|abhyasta|puṇya|karmā s' | ātmī | bhūta | pradāna | dama | saṃyama | karuṇaḥ para | hita|nirata|kriy"|âtiśayaḥ kadā cic Chakro devānām Indro babhūva.

sur'|êndra|lakṣmīr adhikaṃ rarāja
tat|saṃśrayāt sphītatara|prabhāvā
harmye sudhā|seka|nav'|âṅga|rāge
niṣakta|rūpā śaśinaḥ prabh" êva. [1]

11.5 yasyāḥ kṛte Diti|sutā rabhas" āgatāni
diṅ|nāga|danta|musalāny uras" âbhijagmuḥ
sā bhāgya|vistara|sukh'|ôpanat" âpi tasya
lakṣmīr na darpa|malinaṃ hṛdayaṃ cakāra. [2]

tasya divas|pṛthivyoḥ samyak|paripālan'|ôpārjitāṃ sarva|lok'|ânta|vyāpinīṃ kīrti|saṃpadaṃ tāṃ ca lakṣmīm aty|adbhutām a|mṛṣyamāṇā daitya|gaṇāḥ kalpan'|âṭopa|bhīṣaṇatara|dvirada|ratha|turaga|padātinā kṣubhita|sāgara|ghora|nirghoṣeṇa jājvalyamāna|vimala|praharaṇ'|āvaraṇa|

NEITHER A CALAMITY nor the magnificence of kingship can make great men lessen their compassion toward living beings. 11.1

Tradition has handed down the following story.

When the Bodhi·sattva had practiced many pure deeds over a long period of time and performed exceptional feats that were dedicated to the welfare of others, and when charity, discipline, self-restraint, and compassion had become inherent in his nature, he is said to have become Shakra, the king of the gods.

Through him, the glory of divine kingship
shone brighter and with increased power,
like the radiance of the moon when it clings
to a palace freshly plastered with stucco.

For this glorious state, 11.5
Diti's* sons clashed their chests
against the club-like tusks
of world-elephants charging violently.
Yet his majestic position did not
stain his heart with pride,
though its abundant fortune
was his to enjoy.

Due to his righteous protection of heaven and earth, the Bodhi·sattva acquired a magnificent fame that spread to the ends of the entire world. But the hosts of the *Daityas** were unable to endure his fame and extraordinary majesty, and set out with a huge army to wage war against him. Roaring hideously like a stormy ocean, the army's proud battle-formation made its elephants, chariots, horses, and

dur|nirīkṣyeṇa mahatā bala|kāyena yuddhāy' âinam abhijagmuḥ.

dharm'|ātmano 'pi tu sa tasya par'|âvalepaḥ
krīḍā|vighāta|virasaṃ ca bhayaṃ janasya
tejasvitā|naya|path'|ôpanataḥ kramaś ca
yuddh'|ôddhav'|âbhimukhatāṃ hṛdayasya cakruḥ. [3]

atha sa Mahā|sattvas turaga|vara|sahasra|yuktam abhyucchrit'|ârhad|vasana|cihna|rucira|dhvajaṃ vividha|maṇi|ratna|dīpti|vyavabhāsitam abhijvalad|vapuṣaṃ kalpanā|vibhāg'|ôpaniyata|niśita|jvalita|vividh'|āyudha|virājit'|ôbhaya|pārśvaṃ pāṇḍu|kambalinaṃ haimaṃ ratha|varam abhiruhya mahatā hasty|aśva|ratha|padāti|citreṇa dev'|ânīkena parivṛtas tad asura|sainyaṃ samudra|tīr'|ânta eva pratyujjagāma.

atha pravavṛte tatra bhīrūṇāṃ dhṛti|dāraṇaḥ
anyony'|āyudha|niṣpeṣa|jarjar'|āvaraṇo raṇaḥ. [4]

11.10 «tiṣṭha! n' âivam! itaḥ! paśya!
kv' êdānīṃ? mama mokṣyase!
prahar'! âyaṃ na bhavas'!» îty
evaṃ te 'nyonyam ārdayan. [5]

tataḥ pravṛtte tumule sphūrjat|praharaṇe raṇe
paṭaha|dhvanit'|ôtkruṣṭaiḥ phalat' îva nabhas|tale, [6]

infantry even more terrifying, while the blazing glare of their weapons and armor made them painful to look at.

Though he was virtuous, the arrogance of his enemies,
the fear of his people (rudely disrupting their fun),
and the path prescribed by politics and might,
all made his heart turn to the thrill of war.

The Great Being then mounted a fine golden chariot that was draped with a white blanket. Yoked to a thousand excellent horses, it bore a raised banner that glistened with the mark of an *arhat*'s robe. Gleaming with the splendor of various gems and jewels, it blazed brightly, both its sides glittering with various sharp and sparkling weapons that were placed in different sections, ready to be used. Surrounded by a huge army of deities, with various elephants, horses, chariots and infantry, the Bodhi·sattva went to confront the forces of the demons at the edge of the ocean shore.

A battle then ensued,
destroying courage in the timid,
in which clashing weapons
made armor rip apart.

They tormented each other, shouting: 11.10
"Stop! Not like that! Here! Look!
Where are you now? I'll save you!
Strike! Your life is over!"

In this tumultuous conflict
of clattering weapons,
the sky was almost torn apart
by the clamor of booming drums.

dāna|gandh'|ôddhat'|â|marṣeṣv āpatatsu paras|param
yug'|ânta|vāt'|ākalita|śaila|bhīmeṣu dantiṣu, [7]

vidyul|lola|patākeṣu prasṛteṣu samantataḥ
ratheṣu paṭu|nirghoṣeṣ' ûtpāt'|âmbudhareṣv iva, [8]

pātyamāna|dhvaja|cchattra|śastr'|āvaraṇa|mauliṣu
deva|dānava|vīreṣu śitair anyonya|sāyakaiḥ, [9]

11.15 atha prataptā sura|śatru|sāyakair
bhayāt pradudrāva sur'|êndra|vāhinī.
rathena viṣṭabhya balaṃ tu vidviṣāṃ
sur'|êndra ekaḥ samare vyatiṣṭhata. [10]

aty|udīrṇaṃ tv āsuraṃ balam ati|harṣāt paṭutar'|ôtkruṣṭa|kṣveḍita|siṃha|nādam abhipatad abhivīkṣya Mātalir dev'|êndra|sārathiḥ svaṃ ca balaṃ palāyana|parāyaṇam avety' «âpayānam atra prāpta|kālam» iti dev'|âdhipateḥ syandanam āvartayām āsa. atha Śakro dev'|êndraḥ samutpatato rathasy' ēṣ"|âgr'|âbhimukhāny abhighāta|patha|gatāni śālmali|vṛkṣe garuḍa|nīḍāny apaśyat. dṛṣṭv" âiva ca karuṇayā samālambyamāna|hṛdayo Mātaliṃ saṃgrāhakam ity uvāca:

Tuskers charged one another,
rage swelled by the smell of ichor,
terrifying like mountains shaken
by the wind at an era's end.

Chariots streamed everywhere,
flags quivering like lightning,
thundering loudly
like ominous rainclouds.

Gods and demons, both heroic,
fired sharp arrows at one another,
striking banners, parasols,
weapons, armor, and heads.

Scorched by the demons' arrows, 11.15
the army of the divine lord fled in fear.
The king of the gods alone held position in battle,
restraining the enemy army with his chariot.

When Mátali, the chariot-driver of the king of the gods, observed that their own army was intent on flight, whereas the army of the demons was whipped up and charging toward them jubilantly with shrill screams, shouts, and lion-roars, he judged that it was time to retreat and turned around the chariot of the divine lord around. As they were flying up to heaven, however, Shakra, the king of the gods, noticed that there were some *gáruda* nests in a silk-cotton tree lying directly ahead of the tip of the chariot-pole and in danger of being destroyed.* As soon as he saw this, his heart was seized by compassion and he addressed Mátali, his driver, with the following words:

«a|jāta|pakṣa|dvija|pota|saṃkulā
dvij'|ālayāḥ śālmali|pādap'|āśrayāḥ.
amī pateyur na yathā rath'|ēṣayā
vicūrṇitā, vāhaya me rathaṃ tathā.» [11]

Mātalir uvāca, «amī tāvan, mārṣa, samabhiyānti no daityā» iti.

Śakra uvāca, «tataḥ kim? parihara, parihar' âitāni samyag garuḍa|nīḍān'» îti.

11.20 ath' âinaṃ Mātaliḥ punar uvāca:

«nivartanād asya rathasya kevalaṃ
śivaṃ bhaved, amburuh'|âkṣa, pakṣiṇām.
cirasya labdha|prasarā sureṣv asāv
abhidravaty eva hi no dviṣac|camūḥ.» [12]

atha Śakro dev'|êndraḥ svam adhyāśay'|âtiśayaṃ sattva|viśeṣaṃ ca kāruṇya|vaśāt prakāśayann uvāca:

«tasmān nivartaya rathaṃ. varam eva mṛtyur
daity'|âdhipa|prahita|bhīma|gad"|âbhighātaiḥ,
dhig|vāda|dagdha|yaśaso na tu jīvitaṃ me
sattvāny amūni bhaya|dīna|mukhāni hatvā.» [13]

atha Mātalis tath" êti pratiśrutya turaga|sahasra|yuktaṃ syandanam asya nivartayām āsa.

11.25 dṛṣṭ'|âvadānā ripavas tu tasya
yuddhe samālokya rathaṃ nivṛttam
bhaya|druta|praskhalitāḥ praṇeśur
vāt'|âbhinunnā iva kāla|meghāḥ. [14]

"The bird-nests in the silk-cotton tree
are full of unfledged chicks.
Steer my chariot so the nests do not fall,
pulverized by the chariot-pole."

"But my lord," Mátali answered, "the *Daitya*s are catching us up."

"What then?" Shakra replied. "Just be sure to avoid the *gáruda* nests."

Mátali then again addressed Shakra, saying: 11.20

"The birds can only be saved
if we turn the chariot, lotus-eyed god.
But our enemy's army pursues us closely,
finally gaining initiative over the gods."

Driven by compassion, Shakra, the king of the gods, then displayed his outstanding nature and exceptional goodness by replying:

"Then turn the chariot. Far better to die
from the terrifying mace-blows of the *daitya* king
than to kill these creatures, their faces wretched
with fear,
and live a life where glory is incinerated by blame."

Obeying his command, Mátali turned Shakra's chariot, which was yoked to a thousand horses.

On seeing the chariot turn in battle, 11.25
Shakra's foes, witnesses to his previous exploits,
dispersed raggedly with fear, vanquished,
like monsoon clouds dispelled by the wind.

bhagne sva|sainye 'pi nivartamānaḥ
panthānam āvṛtya ripu|dhvajinyāḥ
saṃkocayaty eva mad'|âvalepam
eko 'pi saṃbhāvya|parākramatvāt. [15]

nirīkṣya bhagnaṃ tu balaṃ tad āsuraṃ
sur'|êndra|sen" âpy atha sā nyavartata.
babhūva n' âiva praṇayaḥ sura|dviṣāṃ
bhaya|drutānāṃ vinivartituṃ yataḥ. [16]

sa|harṣa|lajjais tri|daśaiḥ sur'|âdhipaḥ
sabhājyamāno 'tha raṇ'|âjirāc chanaiḥ
abhijvalac|cāru|vapur jaya|śriyā
samutsuk'|ântaḥpuram āgamat puram. [17]

evaṃ sa eva tasya saṃgrāma|vijayo babhūva. tasmād ucyate:

11.30 pāpaṃ samācarati vīta|ghṛṇo jaghanyaḥ.
prāpy' āpadaṃ sa|ghṛṇa eva vimadhya|buddhiḥ.
prāṇ'|âtyaye 'pi tu na sādhu|janaḥ sva|vṛttaṃ
velāṃ samudra iva laṅghayituṃ samarthaḥ. [18]

tad evaṃ deva|rājyaṃ prāṇān api ca parityajya dīrgha|rātraṃ paripālitāni Bhagavatā sattvāni. teṣv iha prājñasy' āghāto 'pi na pratirūpaḥ prāg eva vipratipattir, iti prāṇiṣu day"|āpannen' āryeṇa bhavitavyam.

Though his troops may be crushed,
a single man can, with admirable bravery,
crush the pride and arrogance of his foes
if he turns and blocks their army's path.

Seeing the destroyed army of the demons,
the forces of the divine lord returned.
But the gods' enemies fled with fear,
feeling no desire to return.

Honored by the gods, who felt both shame and joy,
his body blazing beautifully with the glory of victory,
the divine king quietly left the battefield for his city,
where his harem waited for him longingly.

So it was that Shakra won victory in battle. It is therefore said that:

Base people do wrong 11.30
due to lack of compassion.
People of medium intellect do wrong
in times of distress, despite their compassion.
But the good never transgress due conduct,
even when faced with death,
just as the ocean is incapable
of transgressing the shore.

In this way, a long time ago, the Lord protected living beings by sacrificing both his divine kingship and his very life. A noble man should therefore act with compassion toward living beings, reflecting that it is unsuitable for the wise to harm creatures, let alone wrong them.

tathā hi dharmo ha vai rakṣati dharma|cāriṇam, ity atr' âpy upaneyam. Tathāgata|varṇe sat|kṛtya Dharma|śravaṇe c' êti.

One should also cite this story to teach that virtue protects those who are virtuous. And this story should also be told when praising the Tatha·gata and when discussing the topic of listening to the Teaching with respect.

STORY 12

THE BIRTH-STORY OF THE BRAHMIN

12.1 ĀTMA|LAJJAY” ÂIVA sat|puruṣā n’ ācāra|velāṃ laṅghayanti. tad|yath” ânuśrūyate.

Bodhisattvaḥ kila kasmiṃś cid an|upākruṣṭa|gotra|cāritre sva|dharm’|ânuvṛtti|prakāśa|yaśasi vinay’|ācāra|ślāghini mahati brāhmaṇa|kule janma|parigrahaṃ cakāra. sa yathā|kramaṃ garbhādhāna|puṃsavana|sīmantonnayana|jāta-karm’|ādibhiḥ kṛta|saṃskāro ved’|âdhyayana|nimittaṃ śrut’|âbhijan’|ācāra|saṃpanne gurau prativasati sma.

tasya śruta|grahaṇa|dhāraṇa|pāṭavaṃ ca
  bhakty|anvayaś ca vinayaḥ sva|kula|prasiddhaḥ
pūrve vayasy api śam’|ābharaṇā sthitiś ca
  prema|prasāda|su|mukhaṃ gurum asya cakruḥ. [1]

12.5 vaśī|karaṇa|mantrā hi
  nityam a|vyāhatā guṇāḥ
api dveṣ’|âgni|taptānāṃ,
  kiṃ punaḥ svastha|cetasām. [2]

atha tasy’ âdhyāpakaḥ sarveṣām eva śiṣyāṇāṃ śīla|parīkṣā|nimittaṃ sv’|âdhyāya|viśrāma|kāleṣv ātmano dāridrya|duḥkhāny abhīkṣṇam upavarṇayām āsa:

DUE TO THEIR SENSE of shame, virtuous men never 12.1
transgress the bounds of conduct.

Tradition has handed down the following story.

The Bodhi·sattva is said to have once taken his birth in an eminent brahmin family. Praised for its discipline and good conduct, the family enjoyed a celebrated fame for observing the moral code appropriate to its class and was unimpeachable in its practice of family customs. After he had undergone all the sacred rites of passage, including the rite of conception, the rite for producing a male child, the rite of parting hair, and the birth ceremony,* the Bodhi·sattva went on to live with a guru, who was learned, well-bred and virtuous, in order to study the Vedas.

His acumen in learning
and in grasping knowledge,
his devotion and discipline,
for which his family was famed,
and his composure, adorned by
tranquility, even at a young age,
made his teacher incline to him
favorably with love and kindness.

Unimpeded virtues 12.5
act as spells to win over
even those burning with hatred's fire,
let alone those of good heart.

To test the virtue of all his disciples, the teacher, during study breaks, frequently used to describe the sufferings he experienced from poverty:

«sva|jane 'pi nir|ākrandam
utsave 'pi hat'|ānandam
dhik pradāna|kathā|mandaṃ
dāridryam a|phala|cchandam [3]

paribhava|bhavanaṃ śram'|āspadaṃ
sukha|parivarjitam aty|an|ūrjitam
vyasanam iva sad" âiva śocanaṃ
dhana|vikalatvam atīva dāruṇam.» [4]

atha te śiṣyāḥ pratoda|saṃcoditā iva sad|aśvā guru|snehāt samupajāta|saṃvegāḥ saṃpannataraṃ prabhūtataraṃ ca bhaikṣam upāharanti sma. sa tān uvāca:

12.10 «alam anen' âtra|bhavatāṃ pariśrameṇa. na bhaikṣ'|ôpahārāḥ kasya cid dāridrya|kṣāmatāṃ kṣapayanti. asmat|parikleś'|â|marṣibhis tu bhavadbhir ayam eva yatno dhan'|āharaṇaṃ prati yuktaḥ kartuṃ syāt. kutaḥ?

kṣudham annaṃ, jalaṃ tarṣaṃ,
mantra|vāk s'|âgadā gadān.
hanti dāridrya|duḥkhaṃ tu
saṃtaty|ārādhanaṃ dhanam.» [5]

śiṣyā ūcuḥ: «kiṃ kariṣyāmo manda|bhāgyā yad etāvān naḥ śakti|prayāmaḥ? api ca

bhaikṣavad yadi labhyerann,
upādhyāya, dhanāny api,
n' êdaṃ dāridrya|duḥkhaṃ te
vayam evaṃ sahemahi. [6]

"It has no-one to appeal to even among relatives.
It experiences no joy even during festivals.
Horribly enfeebled by the need to request alms,
poverty never fulfills its desires.

It is an abode of disgrace, a source of toil.
Devoid of joy, it is utterly enfeebling.
Like a disaster, it brings constant grief.
Destitution is extremely cruel."

Like thoroughbred horses spurred on by a goad, the disciples were stirred by affection for their teacher and brought him finer and larger helpings of almsfood. But the teacher said to them:

"Stop tiring yourselves out. Offerings of almsfood can 12.10
never destroy a person's debilitating poverty. If you cannot endure my suffering, it would be better to direct your efforts toward acquiring wealth. Why?

Food destroys hunger, water destroys thirst,
spells and medicine destroy disease.
But wealth destroys poverty
and gratifies one's relatives."

"But what should we do?" the disciples replied. "It is our bad luck that we only have such little power. Furthermore,

If we could obtain wealth
as we do alms, teacher,
we would not allow you
to suffer this poverty.

pratigraha|kṛś'|ôpāyaṃ viprāṇāṃ hi dhan'|ârjanam;
a|pradātā janaś c' âyam, ity a|gatyā hatā vayam.» [7]

12.15 adhyāpaka uvāca:

«santy anye 'pi brāhmaṇānāṃ śāstra|paridṛṣṭā dhan'|ârjan'|ôpāyāḥ. jarā|pīta|sāmarthyās tu vayam a|yogya|rūpās tat|pratipattau.»

śiṣyā ūcuḥ: «vayam, upādhyāya, jaray" ân|upahata|parākramāḥ. tad yadi nas teṣāṃ śāstra|vihitānām upāyānāṃ pratipatti|sahatāṃ manyase, tad ucyatām. yāvad adhyāpana|pariśramasy' ān|ṛṇyaṃ te gacchāma» iti.

adhyāpaka uvāca:

«taruṇair api vyavasāya|śithila|hṛdayair dur|abhisaṃbhavāḥ khalv evaṃ|vidhā dhan'|ârjan'|ôpāyāḥ.... yadi tv ayam atra|bhavatāṃ nirbandhas tac chrūyatāṃ sādhu, katama eko dhan'|ôpārjana|kramaḥ.

12.20 āpad|dharmaḥ steyam iṣṭaṃ dvi|jānām.
āpac c' ântyā niḥ|svatā nāma loke.
ten' ādeyaṃ svaṃ pareṣām a|dṛṣṭaiḥ.
sarvaṃ c' âitad brāhmaṇānāṃ svam eva. [8]

Brahmins acquire wealth
by feebly receiving alms.
But people here are uncharitable
and we are stricken with helplessness."

To this, the teacher replied: 12.15

"There are other ways for brahmins to acquire wealth—and they are prescribed by the Treatises.* But because old age has drained me of my strength, I am incapable of performing them."

"But old age has not destroyed our strength, teacher," the disciples answered. "If you think we are capable of carrying out the methods laid down by the Treatises, please tell us what they are. For we will thus repay the effort you have shown in teaching us."

To this the teacher replied:

"These methods of acquiring wealth are difficult for those of lax resolve, however young they are. But if you insist, then well and good, listen to one of the ways of acquiring wealth.

Stealing is approved for brahmins 12.20
as a practice in times of distress.
Since having no possessions is
an extreme distress in the world,
we can take the wealth of others,
without being detected.*
Everything in the world
belongs to brahmins anyway.

kāmaṃ prasahy' âpi dhanāni hartuṃ
  śaktir bhaved eva bhavad|vidhānām,
na tv eṣa yogaḥ. sva|yaśo hi rakṣyaṃ.
  śūnyeṣu tasmād vyavaseyam evam.» [9]

iti mukta|pragrahās tena te cchāttrāḥ param iti tat tasya vacanam a|yuktam api yuktam iva pratyaśrauṣur anyatra Bodhisattvāt.

sa hi prakṛti|bhadratvāt
  tan n' ôtsehe 'numoditum
kṛtyavat pratipannaṃ tair
  vyāhartuṃ sahas" âiva tu. [10]

vrīḍ"|âvanata|vadanas tu Bodhisattvo mṛdu viniśvasya tūṣṇīm abhūt.

12.25 atha sa teṣām adhyāpako Bodhisattvam avekṣya taṃ vidhim an|abhinandantam a|pratikrośantaṃ, niviṣṭa|guṇa|saṃbhāvanas tasmin Mahā|sattve,

«kiṃ nu khalv ayam a|vyavasitatvān niḥ|snehatayā vā mayi steyaṃ na pratipadyate, uta dharma|saṃjñay"?» êti samutpanna|vimarśas tat|svabhāva|vyaktī|karaṇ'|ârthaṃ Bodhisattvam uvāca:

«bho! mahā|brāhmaṇa!

amī dvi|jā mad|vyasan'|â|sahiṣṇavaḥ
  samāśritā vīra|manuṣya|paddhatim.
bhavān an|utsāha|jaḍas tu lakṣyate.
  na nūnam asmad|vyasanena tapyate? [11]

Though men like you have the ability
to seize wealth through open force,
this is not right. Reputations must be protected.
You should only exert yourselves in deserted places."

The teacher thus gave free rein to his students and, though his words were immoral, the students applauded them as if they were moral, all except the Bodhi·sattva.

Due to his natural goodness,
he was unable to condone
what the others undertook as duty
and was suddenly unable to speak.

His head bowed in shame, the Bodhi·sattva sighed softly and stayed silent.

The teacher of the disciples noticed that the Bodhi·sattva 12.25
neither praised nor censured his method and because he had a deep-seated respect for the Great Being's virtue, he reflected:

"Why will he not practice theft? Is it because he has no determination? Is it out of a lack of affection for me? Or is it because he has an awareness of virtue?" To expose the Bodhi·sattva's character, he therefore said to him:

"You sir! Mighty brahmin!

These twice-borns cannot endure my misfortune
and so undertake a practice followed by brave men.
But you seem passive and lazy.
Are you not pained by my misfortune?

pariprakāśe 'py a|nigūḍha|vistare
may" ātma|duḥkhe vacasā vidarśite
katham nu niḥ|saṃbhrama|dīna|mānaso
bhavān iti svasthavad eva tiṣṭhati?» [12]

12.30 atha Bodhisattvaḥ sa|saṃbhramo 'bhivādy' ôpādhyāyam uvāca:

«śāntaṃ pāpam! na khalv ahaṃ niḥ|sneha|kaṭhina|hṛdayatvād a|paritapyamāno guru|duḥkhair evam avasthitaḥ. kiṃ tv a|saṃbhavād upādhyāya|pradarśitasya kramasya. na hi śakyam a|dṛśyamānena kva cit pāpam ācaritum. kutaḥ? raho|'n|upapatteḥ.

n' âsti loke raho nāma pāpaṃ karma prakurvataḥ.
a|dṛśyāni hi paśyanti nanu bhūtāni mānuṣān, [13]

kṛt'|ātmānaś ca munayo divy'|ônmiṣita|cakṣuṣaḥ?
tān a|paśyan raho|mānī bālaḥ pāpe pravartate. [14]

ahaṃ punar na paśyāmi
śūnyaṃ kva cana kiṃ cana.
yatr' âpy anyaṃ na paśyāmi,
nanv a|śūnyaṃ may" âiva tat. [15]

12.35 pareṇa yac ca dṛśyeta duṣ|kṛtaṃ svayam eva vā.
su|dṛṣṭataram etat syād dṛśyate svayam eva yat. [16]

I have plainly revealed my suffering,
keeping no secrets about its extent.
How can you apparently be so well at ease,
your mind neither worried nor sad?"

Paying his respects to his teacher, the Bodhi·sattva anxiously replied: 12.30

"Evil be appeased! It is not through lack of affection or hardheartedness that I am resistant. Nor do I not feel any sorrow at my guru's sufferings. Rather, I cannot agree with the conduct my teacher prescribes. For it is impossible to commit evil anywhere without being detected. Why? Because nothing is secret.

There is nowhere in the world
a person can commit evil in secret.
For do invisible spirits
not look upon men?

Do perfected sages not look
upon humans with divine open eyes?
Blind to these beings, the fool engages
in evil, thinking he acts secretly.

Nowhere do I see
any place that is deserted.
Even where I see no other person,
that place is not deserted by me.

A wicked deed may be seen 12.35
by another or by oneself.
But it is far easier to see it
if it is seen by oneself.

sva|kārya|paryākula|mānasatvāt
paśyen na v" ânyaś caritaṃ parasya.
rāg'|ârpit'|âik'|âgra|matiḥ svayaṃ tu
pāpaṃ prakurvan niyamena vetti. [17]

tad anena kāraṇen' âham evam avasthita iti.»

atha Bodhisattvaḥ samabhiprasādita|manasam upādhyāyam avetya punar uvāca:

«na c' âtra me niścayam eti mānasaṃ,
dhan'|ârtham evaṃ pratared bhavān iti.
avetya ko nāma guṇ'|â|guṇ'|ântaraṃ
guṇ'|ôpamardaṃ dhana|mūlyatāṃ nayet? [18]

12.40 sv'|âbhiprāyaṃ khalu nivedayāmi:

kapālam ādāya vivarṇa|vāsasā
varaṃ dviṣad|veśma|samṛddhir īkṣitā,
vyatītya lajjāṃ na tu dharma|vaiśase
sur'|êndrat"|ârthe 'py upasaṃhṛtaṃ manaḥ!» [19]

atha sa tasy' ôpādhyāyaḥ praharṣa|vismay'|ākṣipta|hṛdaya utthāy' āsanāt sampariṣvajy' âinam uvāca:

«sādhu! sādhu, putra! sādhu, mahā|brāhmaṇa! pratirūpam etat te praśam'|âlaṃkṛtasy' âsya maidhāvakasya!

nimittam āsādya yad eva kiṃ cana
sva|dharma|mārgaṃ visṛjanti bāliśāḥ.
tapaḥ|śruta|jñāna|dhanās tu sādhavo
na yānti kṛcchre parame 'pi vikriyām. [20]

Caught up in their own actions,
people may or may not see the deeds of others.
But if their minds are so engrossed in their passions,
they must know themselves if they commit evil.

That is why I am resistant."

Observing that his teacher showed favor toward him, the Bodhi·sattva continued:

"Nor do I feel certain that you would
deceive us this way for wealth.
Who, knowing the difference between virtue and vice,
would gather wealth in violation of virtue?

Let me tell you my own viewpoint: 12.40

Better to bear an alms bowl and wear ragged robes
and observe the opulent mansion of an enemy
than disregard shame and ponder destroying virtue,
even for the sake of kingship over the gods!"

At these words the Bodhi·sattva's teacher became filled with joy and astonishment. Rising from his seat, he embraced the Bodhi·sattva, saying:

"Excellent! Excellent, my child! Excellent, great brahmin! Your words befit your intelligence, which is so adorned by serenity!

Fools reject the path of duty
when the slightest pretext arises.
But the good never alter, even in great hardship.
Their wealth is asceticism, learning, and knowledge.

12.45 tvayā kulaṃ svam a|malam abhyalaṃkṛtaṃ
samudyatā nabha iva śārad'|êndunā.
tav' ârthavat su|carita|viśrutaṃ śrutaṃ.
sukh'|ôdayaḥ sa|phalatayā śramaś ca me. [21]

tad evam, ātma|lajjay" âiva sat|puruṣā n' ācāra|velāṃ laṅghayant' îti hrī|balasamanviten' āryeṇa bhavitavyam.

«evaṃ hrī|parikhā|sampanna ārya|śrāvako '|kuśalaṃ prajahāt'» îty evam|ādiṣu sūtra|padeṣ' ûpaneyam. hrī|varṇa|pratisaṃyukteṣu sūtr'|ânteṣu lok'|âdhipateye c' êti.

You adorn your stainless family 12.45
like the rising autumn moon adorns the sky.
Proclaimed by your virtue, your learning bears
its meaning.
And the fulfillment of my efforts brings me joy!"

So it is that, due to their sense of shame, virtuous men never transgress the bounds of conduct. A noble man should therefore be endowed with a strong sense of shame.

This story should be cited when dealing with sutra passages such as those that state: "A noble disciple renounces evil by possessing a trench of shame."* And it should also be cited when dealing with sutras that praise shame, and when discussing suitable conduct in the world.

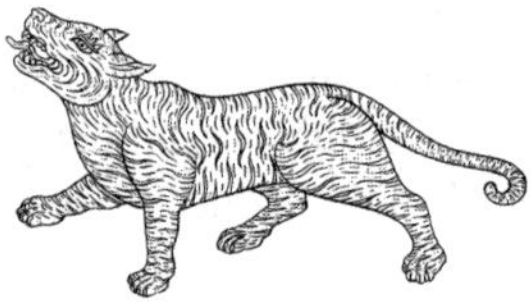

STORY 13
THE BIRTH-STORY OF UNMADAYÁNTI

13.1 TĪVRA|DUḤKH’|ĀTURĀṆĀM api satāṃ nīca|mārga|niṣpraṇayatā bhavati sva|dhairy’|âvaṣṭambhāt.

tad|yath” ânuśrūyate.

satya|tyāg’|ôpaśama|prajñ”|ādibhir guṇ’|âtiśayair loka|hit’|ârtham udyacchamānaḥ kila Bodhisattvaḥ kadā cic Chibīnāṃ rājā babhūva, sākṣād Dharma iva Vinaya iva pit” êva ca prajānām upakāra|pravṛttaḥ.

doṣa|pravṛtter viniyamyamāno
  niveśyamānaś ca guṇ’|âbhijātye
pitr” êva putraḥ kṣiti|pena tena
  nananda loka|dvitaye ’pi lokaḥ. [1]

13.5 sama|svabhāvā sva|jane jane ca
  dharm’|ânugā tasya hi daṇḍa|nītiḥ
a|dharmyam āvṛtya janasya mārgaṃ
  sopāna|māl” êva divo babhūva. [2]

dharm’|ânvayaṃ loka|hitaṃ sa paśyaṃs
  tad|eka|kāryo nara|loka|pālaḥ
sarv’|ātmanā dharma|pathe ’bhireme
  tasy’ ôpamardaṃ ca parair na sehe. [3]

tasya ca rājñaḥ paura|mukhyasya duhitā Śrīr iva vigrahavatī sākṣād Ratir iv’ âpsarasām anyatam” êva ca paramayā rūpa|lāvaṇya|saṃpad” ôpetā parama|darśanīyā strī|ratna|saṃmatā babhūva.

EVEN WHEN THEY SUFFER severe pain, the good are never attracted by the lowly path, so strong is their fortitude. 13.1

Tradition has handed down the following story.

The Bodhi·sattva is said to have once lived as king of the Shibis. Through his truth, generosity, calmness, wisdom, and other exceptional qualities, he strove to benefit the world. Like a personification of Virtue or Decency, he cared for his subjects like a father.

Like a father guiding his son,
the king restrained his people from wrong
and established them in noble virtues,
bringing them joy in this world and the next.

Impartial to both relatives and strangers, 13.5
he administered justice morally,
blocking the path of evil from his people,
like a flowery ladder leading to heaven.

A protector of mankind, he viewed the world's welfare
as central to morality and made this his sole duty.
His entire being delighted in the path of virtue
and he could not bear its violation by others.

In the king's city there was an eminent citizen who had a daughter of such great loveliness she was considered a jewel among women. Blessed by supreme beauty and charm, she was like the embodiment of Shri, or Rati personified, or like one of the *ápsaras*es.*

a|vīta|rāgasya janasya yāvat
sā locana|prāpya|vapur babhūva,
tāvat sa tad|rūpa|guṇ'|âvabaddhāṃ
na dṛṣṭim utkampayituṃ śaśāka. [4]

ataś ca tasyā Unmādayant" îty eva bāndhavā nāma cakruḥ.

13.10 atha tasyāḥ pitā rājñaḥ saṃviditaṃ kārayām āsa: «strī|ratnaṃ te, deva, viṣaye prādur|bhūtam yatas tat|pratigrahaṃ visarjanaṃ vā prati devaḥ pramāṇam iti.» atha sa rājā strī|lakṣaṇa|vido brāhmaṇān samādideśa: «paśyantv enām atra|bhavanto, yady asāv asmad|yogyā na v"» êti. atha tasyāḥ pitā tān brāhmaṇān sva|bhavanam abhinīy' Ônmādayantīm uvāca: «bhadre, svayam eva brāhmaṇān pariveṣay'» êti. sā tath" êti pratiśrutya yathā|kramaṃ brāhmaṇān pariveṣayitum upacakrame. atha te brāhmaṇāḥ

tad|ānan'|ôdvīkṣaṇa|niścal'|âkṣā
Manobhuvā saṃhriyamāṇa|dhairyāḥ
an|īśvarā locana|mānasānām
āsur maden' êva vilupta|saṃjñāḥ. [5]

yadā ca n' âiva śaknuvanti sma pratisaṃkhyāna|dhīra|nibhṛtam avasthātuṃ, kuta eva bhoktum, ath' âiṣāṃ cakṣuṣ|pathād utsārya svāṃ duhitaraṃ sa gṛha|patiḥ svayam eva brāhmaṇān pariveṣya visarjayām āsa. atha teṣāṃ buddhir abhavat:

Anyone not devoid of passion
was transfixed by seeing her body,
unable to tear their eyes
from staring at her fine beauty.

For this reason, her relatives named her Unmadáyanti, "Maddy."

One day, Unmadayánti's father informed the king about his daughter, saying: 13.10

"A jewel among women is present in your realm, Your Majesty. It is up to Your Majesty whether to take or reject her."

The king then instructed some brahmins who were knowledgeable in the characteristics of women to see if she was suitable for him or not. On leading the brahmins to his house, Unmadayánti's father told his daughter to tend to them. Obeying her father, she began to serve the brahmins in the proper manner. The brahmins, however,

gazed at her face with unmoving eyes,
their composure stolen by Desire.
Losing all power over eyes and minds,
their wits seemed robbed by drunkenness.

When the brahmins were unable to control their minds or maintain their composure, let alone eat any food, the head of the house removed his daughter from their sight. After tending to the brahmins himself, he showed them out. The brahmins then pondered the situation thus:

13.15 «kṛtyā|rūpam iva khalv idam ati|manoharam asyā dārikāyā rūpa|cāturyam, yato n' âināṃ rājā draṣṭum apy arhati, kutaḥ punaḥ patnītvaṃ gamayitum. anayā hi rūpa|śobhayā niyatam asy' ônmādita|hṛdayasya dharm'|ârtha|kārya|pravṛtter visrasyamān'|ôtsāhasya rāja|kārya|kāl'|âtikramāḥ prajānāṃ hita|sukh'|ôdaya|patham upapīḍayantaḥ parābhavāya syuḥ.

iyaṃ hi saṃdarśana|mātrakeṇa
  kuryān munīnām api siddhi|vighnam,
prāg eva bhāv'|ârpita|dṛṣṭi|dṛṣṭer
  yūnaḥ kṣit'|īśasya sukhe sthitasya.» [6]

tasmād idam atra prāpta|kālam iti yathā|prastāvam upetya rājñe nivedayām āsuḥ:

«dṛṣṭ" âsmābhir, mahā|rāja, sā kanyakā. asti c' âsyā rūpa|cāturya|mātrakam; apalakṣaṇ'|ôpaghāta|niḥśrīkaṃ tu yato, n' âināṃ draṣṭum apy arhati mahā|rājaḥ, kiṃ punaḥ patnītvaṃ gamayitum.

kula|dvayasy' âpi hi ninditā strī
  yaśo vibhūtiṃ ca tiras|karoti
nimagna|candr" êva niśā sa|meghā
  śobhāṃ vibhāgaṃ ca divas|pṛthivyoḥ.» [7]

13.20 iti śrut'|ârthaḥ sa rāj" âpalakṣaṇā kil' âsau, na ca me kul'|ânurūp" êti tasyāṃ vinivṛtt'|âbhilāṣo babhūva. an|arthitāṃ tu vijñāya rājñaḥ sa gṛha|patis tāṃ dārikāṃ tasy' âiva rājño 'bhipāragāy' âmātyāya prāyacchat.

"This young woman's enchanting beauty captivates the 13.15
mind like a magical spell. The king should not so much as lay eyes on her, let alone make her his wife. For his heart would certainly be intoxicated by her radiant beauty, weakening his zeal for good and beneficial tasks. It would be disastrous if he neglected his royal duties and destroyed his subjects' means of acquiring welfare, happiness and prosperity.

The mere sight of this woman would
obstruct even the perfection of sages,
let alone a young prince immersed in pleasure,
constantly laying his eyes on worldly desires."

After they had decided on the best course of action, the brahmins went and delivered their report to the king when a suitable occasion arose, saying:

"We have seen the young lady, Your Majesty. She only has good looks and her inauspicious marks rid her beauty of any good fortune. Your Majesty should therefore not even look at her, let alone make her your wife.

A bad woman obscures
the fame and riches of two families,
just as a cloudy moon-hidden night conceals
the radiance and design of heaven and earth."

When he heard this, the king concluded that this re- 13.20
portedly inauspicious woman was unsuitable for his family and therefore ceased feeling any desire for her. When the householder saw that the king did not want his daughter, he gave her to the king's minister instead, who was called Abhipáraga.

atha kadā cit sa rājā kram'|āgatāṃ Kaumudīṃ svasmin pura|vare viṣakta|śobhāṃ draṣṭum utsuka|manā ratha|vara|gataḥ sikta|saṃmṛṣṭa|rathy"|ântar|āpaṇam ucchrita|cchattra|†dhvaja|patākaṃ samantataḥ puṣp'|ôpahāra|śabala|bhūmi|talaṃ pravṛtta|nṛtta|gīta|hāsya|lāsya|vāditraṃ puṣpa|dhūpa|cūrṇa|vāsa|māly'|āsava|snān'|ânulepan'|āmoda|prasṛta|surabhi|gandhi prasārita|vividha|rucira|paṇyaṃ tuṣṭa|puṣṭ'|ôjjvalatara|veṣa|paura|jana|saṃbādha|rājamārgaṃ pura|varam anuvicaraṃs tasy' âmātyasya bhavana|samīpam upajagāma. ath' Ônmādayanty «apalakṣaṇā kil' âham ity anena rājñ" âvadhūt"» êti samutpann'|â|marṣā rāja|darśana|kutūhal" êva nāma saṃdṛśyamāna|rūpa|śobhā vidyud iva ghana|śikharaṃ harmya|talam avabhāsayantī vyatiṣṭhata.

«śaktir asy' êdānīm astv apalakṣaṇā|darśana|vicalita|smṛtim ātmānaṃ dhārayitum iti!»

atha tasya rājñaḥ pura|vara|vibhūṣā|darśana|prasṛtā dṛṣṭir abhimukha|sthitāyāṃ sahas" âiva tasyām apatat. atha sa rājā

prakāmam antaḥ|pura|sundarīṇāṃ
vapur|vilāsaiḥ kalit'|ēkṣaṇo 'pi,
an|uddhato dharma|path'|ânurāgād,
udyogavān indriya|nirjaye 'pi, [8]

One day, when the Káumudi festival came around in due course,* the king desired to see the decorations that draped his city. Riding a fine chariot, he took a tour of his capital. The roads and market areas had been swept and sprinkled with water. Parasols, banners, and flags had been raised high. On all sides the ground was dappled with flower offerings and there was dancing, singing, laughter, performances, and music. A sweet fragrance was spread about by flowers, incense, powders, scents, garlands, liquors, bathing-ointments and perfumes, and various splendid wares were displayed for sale. The highways teemed with crowds of joyful and healthy-looking citizens wearing glittering clothes. During his tour, the king arrived at the house of that same minister Abhipáraga. Now Unmadayánti was furious that she had been brushed aside by the king for apparently being inauspicious. So, pretending to be curious to see the king, she stood on the roof of her house and illuminated it by revealing her radiant beauty, just as lightning illuminates the crest of a cloud.

"Let him try to control himself when his composure is shaken by seeing an inauspicious woman!" she thought.

The king was looking at the city's decorations when his gaze suddenly fell on Unmadayánti standing opposite him.

Though his eyes were used to the fine bodies
and flirtations of beautiful women in his palace,
though his love of virtue meant he was never aroused,
though he was strenuous in conquering his senses,

13.25 vipula|dhṛti|guṇo 'py apatrapiṣṇuḥ,
para|yuvat"|īkṣaṇa|viklav'|ēkṣaṇo 'pi,
udita|madana|vismayaḥ striyaṃ tāṃ
ciram a|nimeṣa|vilocano dadarśa. [9]

«Kaumudī kiṃ nv iyaṃ sākṣād?
bhavanasy' âsya devatā?
svarga|strī daitya|yoṣid vā?
na hy etan mānuṣaṃ vapuḥ.» [10]

iti vicārayata eva tasya rājñas tad|darśan'|â|vitṛpta|nayanasya sa rathas taṃ deśam ativartamāno na manorath'|ânukūlo babhūva. atha sa rājā śūnya|hṛdaya iva tad|gat'|âik'|âgra|manāḥ sva|bhavanam upetya Manmath'|ākṣipta|dhṛtiḥ Sunandaṃ sārathiṃ rahasi paryapṛcchat:

«sita|prākāra|saṃvītaṃ vetsi kasya nu tad gṛham?
kā sā tatra vyarociṣṭa vidyut sita iv' âmbu|de?» [11]

sārathir uvāca, «asti devasy' Âbhipārago nām' âmātyas, tasya tad gṛhaṃ, tasy' âiva ca sā bhāryā Kirīṭavatsa|duhit" Ônmādayantī nām'» êti.

13.30 tad upaśrutya sa rājā para|bhāry" êti vitānī|bhūta|hṛdayaś cintā|stimita|nayano dīrgham uṣṇam abhiniśvasya tad|arpita|manāḥ śanair ātma|gatam uvāca:

though greatly composed and sensitive to shame, 13.25
and though he avoided the eyes of other men's wives,
still the king stared at her long, with wide open eyes,
his passion and astonishment stirred.

"Is this Káumudi before my eyes
or the goddess of this house?
Is it a lady from heaven or a female demon?
For it is not a human form."

His eyes were unable to have their fill of her as he pondered these thoughts. But contrary to the monarch's wishes, the chariot continued past the house. The king felt as if his heart was empty. Solely engrossed in Unmadayánti, his composure was destroyed by Desire. As he approached the palace, he therefore secretly asked his chariot-driver, Sunánda, the following question:

"Do you know who owns the house
surrounded by the white wall?
Who was that woman glistening there
like lightning in a white cloud?"

"Your Majesty has a minister called Abhipáraga," the chariot-driver replied. "That is his house and that too is his wife. She is the daughter of Kiríta·vatsa and is called Unmadayánti."

The king was dejected at the news that she was the wife 13.30
of another man. His eyes became rigid with anxiety and he breathed out a long and hot sigh as he quietly spoke the following words to himself, his mind transfixed on Unmadayánti:

«anvartha|ramy'|âkṣara|saukumāryam
aho kṛtaṃ nāma yath" êdam asyāḥ
Unmādayant" îti śuci|smitāyās!
tathā hi s" ônmādam iv' ākaron mām! [12]

vismartum enām icchāmi
paśyām' îva ca cetasā.
sthitaṃ tasyāṃ hi me cetaḥ
sā prabhutvena tatra vā. [13]

parasya nāma bhāryāyāṃ
mam' âpy evam a|dhīratā;
tad unmatto 'smi, saṃtyakto
lajjay" êv' âdya nidrayā. [14]

tasyā vapur|vilasita|smita|vīkṣiteṣu
saṃrāga|niścala|mateḥ sahasā svanantī
kāry'|ântara|krama|nivedana|dhṛṣṭa|śabdā
vidveṣam uttudati cetasi nālikā me.» [15]

13.35 iti sa rājā madana|bala|vicalita|dhṛtir vyavasthāpayann apy ātmānam āpāṇḍu|kṛśa|tanuḥ pradhyāna|niśvasita|vijṛmbhaṇa|paraḥ pravyakta|madan'|ākāro babhūva.

dhṛtyā mahaty" âpi niguhyamānaḥ
sa bhū|pates tasya mano|vikāraḥ
mukhena cintā|stimit'|ēkṣaṇena
kārśyena ca vyaktim upājagāma. [16]

"How aptly she bears the tender,
delightful name of Unmadayánti!
For her bright smile has
almost made me mad!

Though I wish to forget her,
it's as if I see her with my mind.
My mind is fixated on her
or she's fixed herself there through might.

To be so weak over
the wife of another;
I must be mad. Like sleep,
shame seems to abandon me today.

I am so unwaveringly obsessed
with her body, flirtations, smiles, glances,
that the abrupt clang of the gong, boldly
announcing my duties, stirs hatred in my heart."

Such was the extent to which the king's composure was shaken by his passion. Despite his attempts to control himself, his pale and emaciated body, as well as his intense brooding, sighing, and furrowing of his brows, made his infatuation all too clear. 13.35

Though the king tried hard
to conceal his mental agitation,
it was made apparent by his face,
his eyes fixed with anxiety, and his emaciated body.

ath' êṅgit'|ākāra|grahaṇa|nipuṇa|matir Abhipārago 'mātyas taṃ rājño vṛttāntaṃ sa|kāraṇam upalabhya snehāt tad|atyay'|āśaṅkī jānānaś c' âti|balatāṃ madanasya rahasi rājānaṃ viditaḥ samupetya kṛt'|âbhyanujño vijñāpayām āsa:

«ady' ârcayantaṃ, nara|deva, devān
sākṣād upety', âmbu|ruh'|âkṣa, yakṣaḥ
mām āha: ‹n' âvaiṣi nṛ|pasya kasmād
Unmādayantyāṃ hṛdayaṃ niviṣṭam?› [17]

ity evam uktvā sahasā tiro|'bhūd.
vimarśavān ity aham abhyupetaḥ.
tac cet tathā, deva, kim etad evam
asmāsu te niṣpraṇayatva|maunam? [18]

13.40 tat pratigrahītum enām arhati mad|anugrah'|ârthaṃ deva iti.»

atha sa rājā pratyādeśāl lajj"|âvanata|vadano madana|vaśa|go 'pi sv|abhyasta|dharma|saṃjñatvād a|viklavī|bhūta|dhairyaḥ pratyākhyāna|viśad'|âkṣaram enam uvāca:

«n' âitad asti. kutaḥ?

puṇyāc cyutaḥ syām. a|maro na c' âsmi.
vidyāc ca naḥ pāpam idaṃ jano 'pi.
tad|viprayogāc ca mano|jvaras tvāṃ
vahniḥ purā kakṣam iva kṣiṇoti. [19]

Abhipáraga, the king's minister, was skilled in understanding external expressions and signs. And when he observed the king's behavior and realized its cause, his affection for the monarch made him anxious for his lapsed state. Aware of the exceptional power of passion, he approached the king, asking to see him in private, and after gaining permission to speak, addressed him with the following words:

"While I was worshipping the gods today,
a *yaksha* appeared before me, lotus-eyed king.
He told me: 'How can you not notice
the king's heart is fixated on Unmadayánti?'

Saying this, the *yaksha* suddenly disappeared.
And after pondering the matter I came here.
If this is true, Your Majesty,
why do you stay silent and show me mistrust?

Please accept this woman as a favor to me, Your Majesty." 13.40

Abhipáraga's offer made the king lower his head with shame, even though he was gripped by passion. Moral awareness was so entrenched in him that he maintained his mental strength and rejected Abhipáraga with the following clear words:

"That is impossible.

For I would fall from purity. Nor am I immortal.
Even strangers would learn of my wicked deed.
And the mental fever of being separated from her
would consume you like fire consumes dry wood.

yac c' ôbhayor ity a|hit'|āvahaṃ syāl
loke parasminn iha c' âiva karma,
tad yasya hetor a|budhā bhajante,
tasy' âiva hetor na budhā bhajante.» [20]

13.45 Abhipāraga uvāca, «alam atra devasya dharm'|âtikram'|āśaṅkayā.

dāne sāhāyya|dānena
dharma eva bhavet tava.
dāna|vighnāt tv a|dharmaḥ syāt
tāṃ matto '|pratigṛhṇataḥ. [21]

kīrty|uparodh'|âvakāśam api c' âtra devasya na paśyāmi. kutaḥ?

āvābhyām idam anyaś ca ka eva jñātum arhati?
jan'|âpavādād āśaṅkām ato manasi mā kṛthāḥ. [22]

anugrahaś c' âiṣa mama syān, na pīḍā. kutaḥ?

13.50 svāmy|artha|cary"|ârjitayā hi tuṣṭyā
nir|antare cetasi ko vighātaḥ?
yataḥ sa|kāmaṃ kuru, deva, kāmam!
alaṃ mad|utpīḍana|śaṅkayā te.» [23]

rāj" ôvāca, «śāntaṃ pāpam!

vyaktam asmad|ati|snehān
na tvay" âitad avekṣitam
yathā dāne na sarvasmin
sācivyaṃ dharma|sādhanam. [24]

Such a deed would also harm both of us,
in this world and the next.
Only fools would play a part in it,
and for the same reason the wise would not."

"Your Majesty should not worry about violating morality," Abhipáraga replied. 13.45

"By assisting a gift,
you are acting morally.
But if you do not accept her from me,
you obstruct a gift and act immorally.

Nor do I see any potential for Your Majesty's reputation to be harmed.

This matter is between us.
Who else need know?
Do not then worry
about public disgrace.

You would be favoring me, not harming me.

How can a faithful heart be injured 13.50
by the joy of benefiting a master?
Gratify your desire at will, divine lord!
Do not worry about harming me."

"Evil be appeased!" the king replied.

"Your excessive affection for me
obviously blinds you to the fact
that assisting every gift
does not bring about virtue.

yo 'smad|artham ati|snehāt
svān prāṇān api n' ēkṣate,
tasya bandhu|viśiṣṭasya
sakhyur bhāryā sakhī nanu. [25]

tad a|yuktaṃ mām a|tīrthe pratārayitum.

13.55 yad api c' êṣṭaṃ, n' âitad anyaḥ kaś cij jñāsyat', îti kim evam idam a|pāpaṃ syāt?

a|dṛśyamāno 'pi hi pāpam ācaran
viṣaṃ niṣevy' êva kathaṃ śam āpnuyāt?
na taṃ na paśyanti viśuddha|cakṣuṣo
div'|âukasaś c' âiva narāś ca yoginaḥ. [26]

kiṃ ca bhūyaḥ,

śraddadhīta ka etac ca
yath" âsau tava na priyā,
tāṃ parityajya sadyo vā
vighātaṃ na samāpnuyāḥ?» [27]

Abhipāraga uvāca:

13.60 «sa|putra|dāro dāso 'haṃ.
svāmī tvaṃ daivataṃ ca me.
dāsyām asyāṃ yato, deva,
kas te dharma|vyatikramaḥ? [28]

yad api c' êṣṭaṃ, priyā mam' êyam, ity ataḥ kim?

mama priyā, kāma|da, kāmam eṣā.
ten' âiva ditsāmi ca tubhyam enām.
priyaṃ hi dattvā labhate paratra
prakarṣa|ramyāṇi janaḥ priyāṇi. [29]

It is a friend and distinguished kinsman
who, out of exceptional affection,
disregards their very life for me.
Surely then his wife is a friend too.

It is wrong to lure me into acting wickedly.

You contend that no-one else would know of it. Would 13.55
this make it any less evil?

Though undetected, how can a man acquire bliss
if he commits evil, any more than consuming poison?
The gods will not fail to see him with their pure eyes,
nor will the humans who practice Yoga.

Besides,

Who would believe
she is not dear to you
or that you will not suffer pain
the moment you abandon her?"

Abhipáraga answered:

"I am your slave, as are my wife and children. 13.60
You are my master and godhead.
And since she is your slave,
how can Your Majesty be doing wrong?

And so what if she is dear to me?

Of course she is dear to me, desire-granting king.
That's precisely why I want to give her to you.
For those who give what is dear receive
dear objects of great charm in the next life.

yataḥ pratigṛhṇātv ev' âināṃ deva iti.»

rāj" ôvāca, «mā m" âivam! a|krama eṣaḥ. kutaḥ?

13.65 ahaṃ hi śastraṃ niśitaṃ viśeyaṃ
hut'|âśanaṃ visphurad|arciṣaṃ vā
na tv eva dharmād adhigamya lakṣmīṃ
śakṣyāmi tatr' âiva punaḥ prahartum!» [30]

Abhipāraga uvāca:

«yady enāṃ mad | bhāry" êti devo na pratigrahītum icchaty, ayam aham asyāḥ sarva|jana|prārthan'|â|viruddhaṃ veśyā|vratam ādiśāmi. tata enāṃ devaḥ pratigṛhṇīyād iti.»

rāj" ôvāca, «kim unmatto 'si?

a|duṣṭāṃ saṃtyajan bhāryāṃ
matto daṇḍam avāpnuyāḥ
sa dhig|vād'|āspadī|bhūtaḥ
paratr' êha ca dhakṣyase. [31]

13.70 tad alam a|kārya|nirbandhitayā. nyāy'|âbhiniveśī bhav' êti.»

Abhipāraga uvāca:

«dharm'|âtyayo me yadi kaś cid evaṃ
jan'|âpavādaḥ sukha|viplavo vā,
pratyudgamiṣyāmy urasā tu tat tat
tvat|saukhya|labdhena manaḥ|sukhena. [32]

tvattaḥ paraṃ c' āhavanīyam anyaṃ
loke na paśyāmi, mahī|mah"|êndra.
Unmādayantīṃ mama puṇya|vṛddhyai
tvaṃ dakṣiṇāṃ ṛtvig iva pratīccha.» [33]

Please then accept her, Your Majesty."

"Stop!" the king replied. "Stop saying such words! This is not right.

I would rather fall on a sharp sword 13.65
or enter a fire of flickering flames
but I could never violate morality,
the very source of my glory!"

To this Abhipáraga replied:

"If Your Majesty is unwilling to accept her because she is my wife, I'll order her to take up the vow of a harlot, making her open to the solicitation of all. Maybe then Your Majesty would accept her."

"Are you insane?" the king replied.

"If you abandon your innocent wife,
you will suffer my punishment
and will burn in this life and the next,
an object of reproach.

So stop insisting on such wickedness and devote yourself 13.70
to goodness instead."

Abhipáraga replied:

"If by doing this, I violate morality,
incur society's blame, or shipwreck my happiness,
I will bear all this suffering on my chest,
happy at heart I have produced your happiness.

I see no-one else in the world
more worthy of sacrifice than you, great king.
Accept Unmadayánti and increase my merit,
just as a priest accepts his sacrificial fee."

rāj" ôvāca:

13.75 «kāmam asmad|ati|snehād an|avekṣit'|ātma|hit'|â|hita|kramo mad|artha|caryā|samudyogas tav' âyam. ata eva tu tvāṃ viśeṣato n' ôpekṣitum arhāmi.

n' âiva khalu lok'|âpavāda|niḥ|śaṅkena bhavitavyam. paśya:

lokasya yo n' ādriyate 'pavādaṃ
dharm'|ân|apekṣaḥ parataḥ phalaṃ vā,
jano na viśvāsam upaiti tasminn
atīva lakṣmy" âpi vivarjyate saḥ. [34]

yatas tvāṃ bravīmi:

mā te rociṣṭa dharmasya
jīvit'|ârthe 'py atikramaḥ.
niḥ|saṃdigdha|mahā|doṣaḥ
sa|saṃdeha|kṛś'|ôdayaḥ. [35]

13.80 kiṃ ca bhūyaḥ,

nind'|ādi|duḥkheṣu parān nipātya
n' êṣṭā satām ātma|sukha|prasiddhiḥ.
eko 'py an|utpīḍya parān ato 'haṃ
dharme sthitaḥ sv'|ârtha|dhuraṃ prapatsye.» [36]

Abhipāraga uvāca, «svāmy|arthaṃ bhakti|vaśena carato mama tāvad atra ka ev' â|dharm'|âvakāśaḥ syād, devasya vā dīyamānām enāṃ pratigṛhṇataḥ syād, yataḥ sa|naigama|jānapadāḥ Śibayaḥ ‹kim atr' â|dharma?› iti brūyuḥ. tat pratigṛhṇātv ev' âināṃ deva iti.»

The king said:

"I grant that your exceptional affection toward me drives you to endeavor to benefit me, without regard for your own welfare or loss. But this is the very reason why I especially should not neglect you. 13.75

One should never ignore the censure of the world. Consider this:

Those who do not respect the world's censure
or disregard morality and its fruit in the next life,
never gain the trust of people
and lose all prosperity.

That is why I am telling you:

Never delight in wrongdoing,
even for the sake of life.
The fault would be great and certain,
the benefit doubtful and slight.

Furthermore, 13.80

The good do not seek their own pleasure
if it inflicts disgrace and suffering on others.
Established in virtue and never harming others,
I alone will take up the yoke of my welfare."

"But how," Abhipáraga replied, "can I be violating morality if I am acting out of devotion for my master? And how can Your Majesty be doing wrong if you accept her as a gift? All the Shibis, in both the towns and the countryside, would declare that there is nothing wrong in this. Please therefore accept her, Your Majesty."

rāj" ôvāca, «addhā mad|artha|caryā|pravaṇa|matir bhavān. idaṃ tv atra cintayitavyam: sa|naigama|jānapadānāṃ vā Śibīnāṃ tava mama vā ko 'smākaṃ dharma|vittama?» iti.

ath' Âbhipāragaḥ sa|saṃbhramo rājānam uvāca:

13.85 «vṛddh'|ôpasevāsu kṛta|śramatvāc
chrut'|âdhikārān mati|pāṭavāc ca
tri|varga|vidy"|âtiśay'|ârtha|tattvaṃ
tvayi sthitaṃ, deva, Bṛhaspatau ca.» [37]

rāj" ôvāca, «tena hi na mām atra pratārayitum arhasi. kutaḥ?

nar'|âdhipānāṃ caritesv adhīnaṃ
lokasya yasmād a|hitaṃ hitaṃ ca,
bhaktiṃ prajānām anucintya tasmāt
kīrti|kṣame sat|patha eva raṃsye. [38]

jihmaṃ śubhaṃ vā vṛṣabha|pracāraṃ
gāvo 'nugā yadvad anuprayānti,
utkṣipta|śaṅk"|âṅkuśa|nir|vighaṭṭaṃ
prajās tath" âiva kṣiti|pasya vṛttam. [39]

api ca paśyatu tāvad bhavān:

13.90 ātmānam api cec chaktir
na syāt pālayituṃ mama,
kā nv avasthā janasya syān
matto rakṣ"|âbhikāṅkṣiṇaḥ? [40]

iti prajānāṃ hitam īkṣamāṇaḥ
svaṃ c' âiva dharmaṃ vimalaṃ yaśaś ca,
n' êcchāmi cittasya vaśena gantum;
ahaṃ hi netā vṛṣavat prajānām.» [41]

"You are intent on acting for my welfare," the king answered. "But you should consider this: who of us has the most knowledge of virtue? Is it the Shibis, in either the towns or the countryside? Is it you? Or is it I?"

Abhipáraga hastily replied to the king:

"Your toil in serving your elders, 13.85
your command of learning, your sharp mind,
and your outstanding knowledge of the three pursuits
make truth as established in you as in Brihas·pati."*

"Then stop leading me astray," the king answered.

"For the good and bad of the world
depend on the actions of kings.
Since I value the devotion of my subjects,
I'll delight solely in the moral path, as suits my fame.

Just as cows follow behind a roaming bull,
whether the path is wrong or right,
so people follow the behavior of a king,
neither spurred on by fear nor forced by a goad.

Consider this too:

If I cannot protect 13.90
even my own self,
what will be the plight of the people
when they look to me for security?

Concerned for the welfare of my people,
and for my morality and spotless fame,
I will not let my emotions control me.
For I lead my subjects as a bull leads its herd."

ath' Âbhipārago 'mātyas tena rājño 'vasthānena prasādita|manāḥ praṇamya rājānaṃ prāñjalir ity uvāca:

«aho prajānām ati|bhāgya|saṃpad
yāsāṃ tvam evaṃ, nara|deva, goptā!
dharm'|ânurāgo hi sukh'|ân|apekṣas
tapo|vana|stheṣv api mṛgya eva! [42]

mahac|chabdo, mahā|rāja, tvayy ev' âyaṃ virājate.
viguṇeṣu guṇ'|ôktir hi kṣepa|rūkṣatar'|âkṣarā. [43]

13.95 vismayo '|nibhṛtatvaṃ vā
kiṃ mam' âitāvatā tvayi,
samudra iva ratnānāṃ
guṇānāṃ yas tvam ākaraḥ?» [44]

tad evaṃ, tīvra|duḥkh'|āturāṇām api satāṃ nīca|mārga|niṣ|praṇayatā bhavati sva|dhairy'|âvaṣṭambhāt. sv|abhyasta|dharma|saṃjñatvāc c' êti dhairye dharm'|âbhyāse ca yogaḥ kārya iti.

The minister Abhipáraga was filled with devotion at the king's constancy. Bowing before him, he addressed the monarch with the following words, his hands cupped in respect:

"Your subjects are blessed by great fortune
to have you as their protector, god among men!
Even among forest ascetics one would have to hunt
for a devotion to virtue so unheedful of pleasure!

The word "great" sits
gloriously in you, great king.
For words of virtue sound
offensive and harsh in men of vice.

Why should I be surprised or startled 13.95
that such qualities reside in you?
For you are a mine of virtues,
just as the ocean is a mine of jewels."

So it is that, even when they suffer severe pain, the good are never attracted by the lowly path, so strong is their fortitude. This is also due to their moral awareness, which is ingrained in them from habitual practice. Bearing this in mind, one should apply oneself to fortitude and to a regular practice of virtue.

STORY 14

THE BIRTH-STORY OF SUPÁRAGA

14.1 DHARM'|ĀŚRAYAṂ SATYA|vacanam apy āpadaṃ nudati. prāg eva tat|phalam! iti dharm'|ânuvartinā bhavitavyam.

tad|yath" ânuśrūyate.

Bodhisattvaḥ kila Mahā|sattvaḥ parama|nipuṇa|matir nau|sārathir babhūva. dharmatā hy eṣā Bodhisattvānāṃ prakṛti|medhāvitvād yad uta yaṃ yaṃ śāstr'|âtiśayaṃ jijñāsante kalā|viśeṣaṃ vā, tasmiṃs tasminn adhikā bhavanti medhāvino jagataḥ.

atha sa Mah"|ātmā vidita|jyotir|gatitvād dig|vibhāgeṣv a|saṃmūḍha|matiḥ parividita|niyat'|āgantuk'|āutpātika|nimittaḥ kāl'|â|kāla|krama|kuśalo mīna|toya|varṇa|bhauma|prakāra|śakuni|parvat'|ādibhiś cihnaiḥ s'|ûpalakṣita|samudra|pradeśaḥ smṛtimān vijita|tandrī|nidraḥ śīt'|ôṣṇa|varṣ'|ādi|parikheda|sahiṣṇur a|pramādī dhṛtimān āharaṇ'|âpasaraṇ'|ādi|kuśalatvād īpsitaṃ deśaṃ prāpayitā vaṇijām āsīt.

14.5 tasya parama|siddha|yātratvāt Supāraga ity eva nāma babhūva. tad|adhyuṣitaṃ ca pattanaṃ Supāragam ity eva khyātam āsīt. yad etarhi Śūrpārakam iti jñāyate.

so 'ti|maṅgala|saṃmatatvād vṛddhatve 'pi sāṃyātrikair yātrā|siddhi|kāmair vahanam abhyarthana|satkāra|puraḥsaram āropyate sma.

A MERE STATEMENT OF TRUTH can dispel ruin if based on a virtuous act. Imagine then the fruit of virtue! One should therefore act virtuously. 14.1

Tradition has handed down the following story.

The Bodhi·sattva, that Great Being, is said to have once been an extremely intelligent helmsman. For Bodhi·sattvas are so innately clever that whenever they wish to learn an advanced science or a specialized art, it is natural for them to become the wisest men in the world in that field.

Through knowing the movement of the stars, the Great One was never confused about the position of the directions. Well-versed in normal, incidental, and miraculous omens,* he was skilled in the order of timely and untimely events and proficient in recognizing sections of the sea through clues such as fish, water-color, terrain, birds, and crags. Alert and in control of weariness and sleep, he could endure the exhaustion brought on by cold, heat, rain, and other afflictions. Vigilant and brave, he delivered merchandise to its destination through his skill in drawing into land, steering clear of obstacles, and other talents.*

Due to his fine capacity for navigation, the Bodhi·sattva 14.5
was given the name Supáraga, "He that crosses easily to the other shore." The city where he lived was also known as Supáraga, although nowadays it bears the name Shurpáraka.*

So renowned was he for his great auspice that, even when he was old, sea-traders still placed him in charge of their ships to ensure the success of their voyage, plying him with petitions and acts of respect.

atha kadā cid Bharukacchād abhiprayātāḥ Suvarṇabhūmiṃ vaṇijo yātrā|siddhi|kāmāḥ Supāragaṃ pattanam upetya taṃ Mahā|sattvaṃ vahan'|ārohaṇ'|ârtham abhyarthayām āsuḥ. sa tān uvāca:

«jar"|ājñayā saṃhriyamāṇa|darśane,
 śram'|âbhipātaiḥ pratanū|kṛta|smṛtau,
sva|deha|kṛtye 'py avasanna|vikrame
 sahāyatā kā pariśaṅkyate mayi?» [1]

vaṇija ūcuḥ: «vidit" êyam asmākaṃ yuṣmac|charīr'|âvasthā. saty api ca vaḥ parākrama|sahatve n' âiva vayaṃ karma|viniyogena yuṣmān āyāsayitum icchāmaḥ. kiṃ tarhi?

14.10 «tvat|pāda|paṅkaja|samāśraya|sat|kṛtena
 maṅgalyatām upagatā rajasā tv iyaṃ nauḥ.
dur|ge mahaty api ca toya|nidhāv amuṣmin
 svasti vrajed, iti bhavantam upāgatāḥ smaḥ.» [2]

atha sa Mah"|ātmā teṣām anukampayā jarā|śithila|śarīro 'pi tad|vahanam āruroha. tad|adhirohaṇāc ca pramudita|manasaḥ sarva eva te vaṇijo babhūvur, «niyatam asmākam uttamā yātrā|siddhir» iti.

krameṇa c' âvajagāhire vividha|mīna|kula|vicaritam a|nibhṛta|jala|kalakal'|ārāvam anila|vilāsa|pravicalita|taraṅgaṃ bahu|vidha|ratnair bhūmi|viśeṣair arpita|raṅgaṃ phen'|âvalī|kusuma|dāma|vicitram asura|vara|bhujaga|vara|bhavanaṃ dur|āpa|pātālam a|prameya|toyaṃ mahā|samudram.

One day some merchants who had set out from Bharu·kaccha arrived at the city of Supáraga on their way to Suvárna·bhumi.* Eager to ensure a successful voyage, they entreated the Great Being to board their ship. The Bodhi·sattva replied as follows:

"The demands of old age rob me of my sight.
Hardships have weakened my vigilance.
My strength is low, even in bodily tasks.
What help do you expect of me?"

"We already know about your physical condition," the merchants replied. "But even if you were capable of strength, we would not want to weary you by subjecting you to some task. For,

The dust honored by lying on your lotus-feet 14.10
will bring auspice to our ship, leading it safely
across the sea, however vast and perilous.
That is why we have come to you."

Although his body was weak from old age, the Great One boarded the ship out of compassion for the men. When he came on board, every one of the merchants was filled with joy, as they believed their journey was now certain to enjoy the highest success.

In due course they penetrated the immeasurable waters of the vast ocean. Home to the most eminent of *ásuras** and snakes, the inaccessible and infernal realm swirled with various shoals of fish. Roaring clamorously with surging waters, its waves were thrashed by frolicking winds. Colored by various gems that covered different parts of the seabed, it was dappled by strings of foam resembling flower-chains.

ath' êndra|nīla|prakar'|âbhinīlaṃ
sūry'|âṃśu|tāpād iva khaṃ vilīnam
samantato 'ntar|hita|tīra|lekham
a|gādham ambho|nidhi|madhyam īyuḥ. [3]

teṣāṃ tatr' ânuprāptānāṃ sāy'|âhna|samaye mṛdū|bhūta| kiraṇa|cakra|prabhāve savitari mahad autpātikaṃ parama| bhīṣaṇaṃ prādur|abhūt.

14.15 vibhidyamān'|ōrmi|vikīrṇa|phenaś
caṇḍ'|ânil'|āsphālana|bhīma|nādaḥ
naibhṛtya|nirmukta|samagra|toyaḥ
kṣaṇena raudraḥ samabhūt samudraḥ. [4]

utpāta|vāt'|ākalitair mahadbhis
toya|sthalair bhīma|rayair bhramadbhiḥ
yug'|ânta|kāla|pracal'|âcal" êva
bhūmir babhūv' ôgra|vapuḥ samudraḥ. [5]

vidyul|lat"|ôdbhāsura|lola|jihvā
nīlā bhujaṃ|gā iva n'|âika|śīrṣāḥ
āvavrur āditya|pathaṃ payo|dāḥ
prasakta|bhīma|stanit'|ânunādāḥ. [6]

ghanair ghanair āvṛta|raśmi|jālaḥ
sūryaḥ kramen' āstam upāruroha
din'|ânta|labdha|prasaraṃ samantāt
tamo ghanī|bhāvam iv' ājagāma. [7]

dhārā|śarair ācchurit'|ōrmi|cakre
mah"|ôdadhāv utpatat' îva roṣāt
bhīt" êva naur abhyadhikaṃ cakampe
viṣādayantī hṛdayāni teṣām. [8]

So they reached the center of the bottomless sea,
colored blue by heaps of sapphires,
like a sky melted by the sun's burning rays,
its coastline invisible on all sides.

On reaching this area, a huge and extremely terrifying omen suddenly appeared before them in the evening time, just as the strength of the sun's rays was softening.

In an instant the ocean became horrific. 14.15
Crashing waves scattered foam,
violent, pounding winds boomed fearfully,
and the entire sea was released from stillness.

Huge mounds of water swirled
with dread speed, lashed by the sudden gale.
The ocean became as terrifying as the earth
when its mountains shake at an eon's end.*

Like snakes with multiple heads,
dark-blue clouds blocked the path of the sun,
gleaming lightning forks like flickering tongues,
the noise of their thunder constant and terrifying.

The sun gradually reached setting point,
its mesh of rays blocked by thick dense clouds,*
as darkness too seemed to thicken all around,
grasping the opportunity of the day's close.

The sea seemed to rise up in fury,
arrows of rain pelting its waves.
The ship shook violently as if with fear,
saddening the men's hearts.

14.20 te trāsa|dīnāś ca viṣāda|mūkā
dhīrāḥ pratīkāra|sa|saṃbhramāś ca
sva|devatā|yācana|tat|parāś ca
bhāvān yathā|sattva|guṇaṃ vivavruḥ. [9]

atha te sāṃyātrikāḥ pavana|salila|vega|vaśa|gayā nāvā paribhrāmyamāṇā bahubhir apy ahobhir n' âiva kutaś cit tīraṃ dadṛśur na ca yath"|ēpsitāni samudra|cihnāni. a|pūrvair eva tu samudra|cihnair abhivardhamāna|vaimanasyā bhaya|viṣāda|vyākulatām upajagmuḥ.

ath' âinān Supārago Bodhisattvo vyavasthāpayann uvāca: «an|āścaryaḥ khalu mahā|samudram avagāḍhānām autpātika|kṣobha|parikleśaḥ. tad alam atra|bhavatāṃ viṣād'|ânuvṛttyā.

n' āpat|pratīkāra|vidhir viṣādas.
tasmād alaṃ dainya|parigraheṇa.
dhairyāt tu kārya|pratipatti|dakṣāḥ
kṛcchrāṇy a|kṛcchreṇa samuttaranti. [10]

14.25 viṣāda|dainyaṃ vyavadhūya tasmāt
kāry'|âvakāśaṃ kriyayā bhajadhvam.
prājñasya dhairya|jvalitaṃ hi tejaḥ
sarv'|ârtha|siddhi|grahaṇ'|âgra|hastaḥ.» [11]

Wretched with fear, some were struck dumb 14.20
by despair.
Others were brave and zealously sought a remedy.
Others intently entreated their personal deities.
So each revealed their nature according to
their character.

As the ship wandered about, driven by the force of the wind and waves, the voyagers were unable to spot land in any direction for several days and saw no favorable signs in the sea. This was their very first experience of sea omens and so they became increasingly despondent and troubled by fear and despair.

Supáraga, the Bodhi·sattva, then addressed the merchants to fortify them:

"It is hardly surprising that men who venture into the vast ocean should experience the hardship of a sudden storm. So cease your despair.

Despair is no remedy against disaster.
Stop clinging to melancholy.
Those skilled in dealing with a crisis
easily overcome difficulties through bravery.

So shake off your despair and melancholy. 14.25
Take the opportunity to do what is needed by acting.
For a wise man's splendor blazes with bravery:
this is the hand that grasps success in every matter."

iti te sāṃyātrikās tena Mah"|ātmanā dhīrī|kṛta|manasaḥ kūla|saṃdarśan'|ôtsuka|matayaḥ samudram avalokayanto dadṛśuḥ puruṣa|vigrahān āmukta|rūpya|kavacān iv' ônmajjato nimajjataś ca. samyak c' âiṣām ākṛti|nimittam avadhārya sa|vismayāḥ Supāragāya nyavedayanta:

«a|pūrvaṃ khalv idam iha samudre cihnam upalabhyate. ete khalu

āmukta|rūpya|kavacā iva daitya|yodhā
ghor'|ēkṣaṇāḥ kṣura|nikāśa|virūpa|ghoṇāḥ
unmajjan'|âvataraṇa|sphuraṇa|prasaṅgāt
krīḍām iv' ârṇava|jale 'nubhavanti ke 'pi.» [12]

Supāraga uvāca, «n' âite mānuṣā a|mānuṣā vā. mīnāḥ khalv ete, yato na bhetavyam ebhyaḥ. kiṃ tu,

14.30 su|dūram apakṛṣṭāḥ smaḥ
pattana|dvitayād api.
Kṣuramālī samudro 'yaṃ.
tad yatadhvaṃ nivartitum.» [13]

caṇḍa|vega|vāhinā tu salila|nivahen' âik'|ânta|hareṇa ca pāścātyena vāyunā samākṣiptayā nāvā na te sāṃyātrikāḥ śekur vinivartitum. ath' âvagāhamānāḥ krameṇa rūpya|prabhāva|bhāsita|sita|salilaṃ phena|nicaya|pāṇḍaram aparaṃ samudram ālokya sa|vismayāḥ Supāragam ūcuḥ:

With these words the Great One strengthened the minds of the voyagers and their hearts became eager to see the shore. As they scoured the ocean, however, they spotted some human forms diving in and out of the water, seemingly dressed in silver armor. Taking good note of their shape and characteristics, the astonished men informed Supáraga of the matter:

"We have certainly never seen this sign before in the ocean. Over there,

as if dressed in silver armor, *daitya* warriors perhaps,
their eyes terrifying, noses ugly like hooves,
emerging, plunging, springing,
some creatures seem to enjoy games in the sea."

"They are neither human nor non-human," Supáraga answered. "They are fish. So you need not fear them. However,

We have been dragged 14.30
very far from both ports.
This is the Hoof-Garlanded Sea.
Let us try to turn back."

But the voyagers were unable to turn the ship around as it was hurled forward by the violent force of the colossal waters and by a rear wind driving them in a single direction. Penetrating the ocean further, they spotted another sea, white with piles of foam, its bright waters glistening with a silver light. Filled with amazement, they addressed Supáraga, saying:

«sva|phena|magnair iva ko 'yam ambubhir
mah"|ârṇavaḥ śukla|dukūlavān iva
dravān iv' êndoḥ kiraṇān samudvahan
samantato hāsa iva prasarpati?» [14]

Supāraga uvāca, «kaṣṭam! ati|dūraṃ khalv avagāhyate!

Kṣīrārṇava iti khyāta
uda|dhir dadhi|māly asau.
kṣamaṃ n' âtaḥ paraṃ gantuṃ
śakyate cen nivartitum.» [15]

14.35 vaṇija ūcuḥ: «na khalu śakyate vilambayitum api vahanaṃ, kuta eva nivartayitum, ati|śīghra|vāhitvād vahanasya pratikūlatvāc ca mārutasy' êti.»

atha vyatītya tam api samudraṃ suvarṇa|prabh"|ânurañjita|pracal'|ōrmi|mālam agni|jvālā|kapila|salilam aparaṃ samudram ālokya sa|vismaya|kautūhalās te vaṇijaḥ Supāragaṃ papracchuḥ:

«bāl'|ârka|lakṣmy" êva kṛt'|âṅga|rāgaiḥ
samunnamadbhiḥ salilair a|nīlaiḥ
jvalan mahān agnir iv' âvabhāti
ko nāma kasmāc ca mah"|ârṇavo 'yam? [16]

Supāraga uvāca:

«Agnimāl" îti vikhyātaḥ samudro 'yaṃ prakāśate.
atīva khalu sādhu syān nivartemahi yady ataḥ.» [17]

"What is this great sea, as if draped with bright cloth,
its waters almost bathing in their own foam?
Spreading out like a smile on all sides,
it seems to emanate liquid moonbeams."

"Oh dear!" Supáraga said. "We have certainly advanced too far!

These are the milk-garlanded
waters called Milk Sea.
We should not proceed further
if we can turn around."

"It is impossible to slow the ship down, let alone turn her 14.35
around," the traders replied. "She is moving too fast and the wind is blowing against us."

After crossing that ocean, they spied another sea, its reddy brown waters resembling blazing flames, its surging garlands of waves tinged by a golden radiance. Filled with amazement and curiosity, the merchants questioned Supáraga, saying:

"What is this sea called?
Why does it gleam like a vast blazing fire,
its bright towering waters anointed,
it seems, by the beauty of a rising sun?"

Supáraga replied:

"This is the celebrated
Fire-Garlanded Sea.
It would be best
to turn back from here."

14.40 iti sa Mah"|ātmā nāma|mātram akathayat tasya sarit|pater na toya|vaivarṇya|kāraṇaṃ dīrgha|darśitvāt.

atha te sāṃyātrikās tam api samudram atītya puṣpa|rāg'|êndra|nīla|prabh"|ôddyotita|salilaṃ paripakva|kuśa|parṇa|nikāśa|varṇam aparaṃ† samudram ālokya kautūhala|jātāḥ Supāragaṃ papracchuḥ:

«pariṇata|kuśa|parṇa|varṇa|toyaḥ
salila|nidhiḥ katamo nv ayaṃ vibhāti
sa|kusuma iva phena|bhakti|citrair
anila|jav'|ākalitais taraṅga|bhaṅgaiḥ?» [18]

Supāraga uvāca, «bhoḥ s'|ârtha|vāhā, nivartanaṃ prati yatnaḥ kriyatām. na khalv ataḥ paraṃ kṣamate gantum.

Kuśamālī samudro 'yam aty|aṅkuśa iva dvi|paḥ
prasahy' â|sahya|salilo haran harati no ratim.» [19]

14.45 atha te vāṇijakāḥ pareṇ' âpi yatnena nivartayitum a|śaknuvantas tam api samudram atītya vaṃśa|rāga|vaiḍūrya|prabhā|vyatikara|harita|salilam aparaṃ samudram ālokya Supāragam apṛcchan:

«marakata|harita|prabhair jalair
vahati navām iva śādvala|śriyam
kumuda|rucira|phena|bhūṣaṇaḥ
salila|nidhiḥ katamo 'yam īkṣyate?» [20]

In this way the Great One informed the voyagers only 14.40
of the name of the sea and, in his far-sightedness, did not reveal the reason behind the altered color of its waters.

Passing beyond this ocean, the voyagers then spotted another sea, whose waters glistened with sparkling topaz and sapphire and was the color of fully grown *kusha* leaves.* Filled with curiosity, they asked Supáraga:

"What is this glistening sea,
its color like fully grown *kusha* leaves,
its breaking waves driven by swift winds,
forming streaks of foam resembling blossoms?"

"Endeavor to turn back, honorable merchants," Supáraga answered. "It would be best not to go any further.

This is the *Kusha*-Garlanded Sea.
Like an untamable elephant,
its violent, irresistible waters
will steal away our joy."

But although they tried their hardest, the merchants were 14.45
unable to turn the ship back. So passing beyond that sea too, they spied another sea, whose waters were green with emeralds and beryls, and asked Supáraga:

"What is this ocean we see,
adorned by foam as beautiful as water-lilies
its waters radiant with green emeralds,
as if bearing fresh fine grass?"

atha sa Mah"|ātmā tena tasya vaṇig|janasya vyasan'|ôpanipātena paridahyamāna|hṛdayo dīrgham uṣṇam abhiniśvasya śanakair uvāca:

«ati|dūram upetāḥ smaḥ. duḥkham asmān nivartitum.
paryanta iva lokasya Nalamāly eṣa sāgaraḥ.» [21]

tac chrutvā te vāṇijakā viṣād'|ôparudhyamāna|manaso visrasyamāna|gātr'|ôtsāhā niśvasita|mātra|parāyaṇās tatr' âiva niṣeduḥ. vyatītya tam api samudraṃ,

14.50 sāy'|âhna|samaye vilambamāna|manda|raśmi|maṇḍale salila|nidhim iva praveṣṭu|kāme divasa|kare samudvartamānasy' êva salila|nidher aśanīnām iva ca saṃpatatāṃ veṇu|vanānām iva c' âgni|parigatānāṃ visphuṭatāṃ tumulam ati|bhīṣaṇaṃ śruti|hṛdaya|vidāraṇaṃ samudra|dhvanim aśrauṣuḥ.

śrutvā ca saṃtrāsa|vaśa|gāḥ sphuran|manasaḥ sahas" âiv' ôtthāya samantato 'nuvilokayanto dadṛśuḥ prapāta iva śvabhra iva ca mahāntaṃ† tam udak'|âughaṃ nipatantam. dṛṣṭvā ca parama|bhaya|vihvalāḥ Supāragam upety' ōcuḥ:

«nirbhindann iva naḥ śrutīḥ pratibhayaś
cetāṃsi mathnann iva
kruddhasy' êva sarit|pater dhvanir ayaṃ
dūrād api śrūyate.
bhīme śvabhra iv' âgrataś ca nipataty

The Great One's heart burned at the disaster that was about to afflict the traders. Breathing out long and hot sighs, he quietly said:

"We have gone too far.
To turn back from here is hard.
This is the Reed-Garlanded Sea.
It is almost the end of the world."

When they heard this, the traders collapsed on the spot, their minds besieged by despair. Energy seeped from their limbs and they could do nothing but sigh as they passed beyond that ocean too.

Then, at evening time, just as the sun was sinking its 14.50
weakening rays as though eager to enter the ocean, they heard a terrifying and tumultuous noise rising from the sea, tearing apart both their ears and hearts. It was like the din of a swelling ocean, or clashing thunderbolts, or bamboo forests bursting open with flames.

Overwhelmed by fear, their hearts pounding, the men leapt up suddenly at the sound. Scanning the ocean in every direction, they saw that the vast mass of water was spilling into what appeared to be a precipice or abyss. The sight made them tremble with immense fear. Going up to Supáraga, they said:

"Almost bursting our ears
and churning our minds,
the sea makes a terrifying noise
audible from afar, as if from fury.
This entire body of water seems to fall
into a terrifying abyss before us.

etat samagraṃ jalaṃ.
tat ko 'sāv uda|dhiḥ? kim atra ca paraṃ
kṛtyaṃ bhavān manyate?» [22]

atha sa Mah"|ātmā sa|saṃbhramaḥ «kaṣṭaṃ! kaṣṭam!» ity uktvā samudram ālokayann uvāca:

«yat prāpya na nivartante
mṛtyor mukham iv' āmukham
a|śivaṃ samupetāḥ smas
tad etad Vaḍabāmukham.» [23]

14.55 tad upaśrutya te vāṇijakā «Vaḍabāmukham upetā vayam» iti tyakta|jīvit'|āśā maraṇa|bhaya|viklavī|bhūta|manasaḥ

sa|svaraṃ ruruduḥ ke cid, vilepur atha cukruśuḥ,
na kiṃ cit pratyapadyanta ke cit trāsa|vicetasaḥ. [24]

viśeṣataḥ ke cid abhipraṇemur
dev'|êndram ārti|prahatair manobhiḥ
Āditya|Rudr'|Âśvi|Marud|Vasūṃś ca
prapedire sāgaram eva c' ânye. [25]

jepuś ca mantrān apare vicitrān,
anye tu Devīṃ vidhivat praṇemuḥ.
Supāragaṃ ke cid upetya tat tad
viceṣṭamānāḥ karuṇaṃ vilepuḥ: [26]

«āpad|gata|trāsa|harasya nityaṃ
par'|ânukampā|guṇa|saṃbhṛtasya
ayaṃ prabhāv'|âtiśayasya tasya
tav' âbhyupeto viniyoga|kālaḥ. [27]

What is this ocean?
What more can we do now?"

"What a disaster!" the Great One cried, anxiously scanning the ocean.

"This is the place from which none return.
Like the mouth of death,
we're entering right into its fateful jaws.
This is Mare's Mouth."

When they heard this and realized that they had arrived at Mare's Mouth, the traders gave up all hope for life and were beside themselves with fear of death. 14.55

Some wept loudly,
others lamented and yelled.
Some did nothing at all,
distraught with fear.

Stricken with sorrow, some bowed before deities,
especially Indra, king of the gods,
but also the Adítyas, Rudras, Ashvins, Maruts,
and Vasus.
Others turned to the Ocean himself.

Some recited elaborate mantras,
while others duly prostrated before Devi.
Others approached Supáraga,
writhing and lamenting in piteous ways:

"Now is the time for you
to use your exceptional power.
Full of virtuous compassion for others,
it constantly removes fear from those in peril.

14.60 ārtān a|nāthāñ charaṇ'|āgatān nas
tvaṃ trātum āvarjaya, dhīra, cetaḥ.
ayaṃ hi kopād Vaḍabāmukhena
cikīrṣati grāsam iv' ârṇavo 'smān! [28]

n' ôpekṣituṃ yuktam ayaṃ janas te
vipadyamānaḥ salil'|âugha|madhye.
n' ājñāṃ tav' âtyeti mahā|samudras.
tad vāryatām a|praśamo 'yam asya.» [29]

atha sa Mah"|ātmā mahatyā karuṇayā samāpīḍyamāna|hṛdayas tān vāṇijakān vyavasthāpayann uvāca:

«asty atr' âpi naḥ kaś cit pratikāra|vidhiḥ pratibhāti. taṃ tāvat prayokṣye yato muhūrtaṃ dhīrās tāvad bhavantu bhavanta iti.»

atha te vāṇijakā «asty atr' âpi pratīkāra» ity āśayā samupastambhita|dhairyās tad|avahita|manasas tūṣṇīm|babhūvuḥ.

14.65 atha Supārago Bodhisattva ek'|âṃsam uttar'|āsaṅgaṃ kṛtvā dakṣiṇena jānu|maṇḍalen' âdhiṣṭhāya nāvaṃ samāvarjita|sarva|bhāvaḥ praṇamya Tathāgatebhyas, tān sāṃyātrikān āmantrayate sma:

«śṛṇvantv atra|bhavantaḥ sāṃyātrikāḥ salilanidhi|vyom'|āśrayāś ca devatā|viśeṣāḥ:

smarāmi yata ātmānaṃ,
yataḥ prāpto 'smi vijñatām,
n' âbhijānāmi saṃcintya
prāṇinaṃ hiṃsituṃ kva cit. [30]

Lend your mind toward saving us, brave Supáraga. 14.60
Wretched and helpless, we turn to you for refuge.
For the sea is so furious it wishes to swallow us
like a lump of food with its Mare's Mouth!

It would be wrong to disregard these men
as they perish in the middle of the sea.
The great ocean will not disobey your command.
Please then cease its fury."

Struck by an immense feeling of compassion, the Great One bolstered the traders by saying:

"A possible remedy does occur to me, even for the present situation. I will act on it. But you must remain strong for a moment, gentlemen."

The hope that there was a remedy, even in their present plight, strengthened the courage of the traders. And so, fixing their minds on Supáraga, they stayed silent.

Supáraga, the Bodhi·sattva, meanwhile placed his cloak 14.65
over one shoulder and, resting his right knee on the ship's deck, focused his entire being on venerating the Tatha·gatas. He then addressed the voyagers, saying:

"Hear this, you honorable voyagers and you eminent deities inhabiting the ocean and the sky:

Ever since I was aware of myself
and able to discriminate,
I cannot recall ever purposefully
harming a breathing being.

anena satya|vākyena
mama puṇya|balena ca
Vaḍabāmukham a|prāpya
svasti naur vinivartatām!» [31]

atha tasya Mah"|ātmanaḥ saty'|âdhiṣṭhāna|prabhāvāt puṇya|tejasā ca saha salila|javena sa māruto vyāvartamānas tāṃ nāvaṃ vinivartayām āsa. nivṛttāṃ tu tāṃ nāvam abhisamīkṣya te vāṇijakāḥ parama|vismaya|praharṣ'|ôddhata|mānasā «nivṛttā! nivṛttā naur!» iti praṇāma|sabhājana|puraḥsaraṃ Supāragāya nyavedayanta.

14.70 atha sa Mah"|ātmā tān vāṇijakān uvāca: «sthirī|bhavantu bhavantaḥ. śīghram āropyantāṃ śītāni. iti ca tena samādiṣṭāḥ pramodād udbhūta|bal'|ôtsāhās te tad|adhikṛtās tathā cakruḥ.

atha mudita|jana|prahāsa|nādā
pravitata|pāṇḍara|śīta|cāru|pakṣā
salila|nidhi|gatā rarāja sā naur
gata|jalade nabhas' îva rāja|haṃsī. [32]

nivṛttāyāṃ tu tasyāṃ anukūla|salila|mārutāyāṃ vimāna|līlayā sv'|êcchay" âiv' âbhiprayātāyāṃ nāvi, n'|âti|śyāmī|bhūta|saṃdhy"|âṅga|rāgāsu pravitanyamāna|tamo|vitānāsv ālakṣya|nakṣatra|bhūṣaṇāsu dikṣu kiṃ cid avaśeṣa|prabhe divasa|kara|mārge pravṛtte kṣaṇad"|âdhikāre Supāragas tān vāṇijakān uvāca:

By this statement of truth
and by the power of my merit,
may this ship turn safely around
without entering Mare's Mouth!"

The power of the Great One's affirmation of truth, combined with the strength of his merit, forced the wind and the ocean current to change course, resulting in the ship turning around. When they saw the ship turn back, the traders were elated by intense feelings of astonishment and joy. Bowing respectfully before Supáraga, they informed him of what had happened, shouting: "The ship is turning back! The ship is turning back!"

The Great One then told the men to stay calm and to 14.70
hoist the sails quickly. The men in charge of this task did as they were commanded, their strength and energy intensified by their joy.

Resounding with the laughter of her joyful crew,
the ship looked glorious as it glided along the sea,
the beautiful wings of her white sails spreading
like a royal swan in a cloudless sky.

Helped by a favorable sea and wind, the ship turned back, proceeding at will with the grace of a celestial palace. It was the time of day when the hue of twilight was not too murky, a canopy of darkness was spreading over the sky, jewel-like stars could just be marked out, a glimmer of the sun's path still survived, and the night was coming into ascendance, when Supáraga addressed the traders, saying:

«bhoḥ sārtha|vāhā, Nalamāli|prabhṛtibhyo yathā|dṛṣṭebhyaḥ samudrebhyo vālikā|pāṣāṇā vahanam āropyantāṃ yāvat sahate. evam idaṃ yāna|pātraṃ nirghāta|bhar'|ākrāntaṃ na ca pārśvāni dāsyati. maṅgala|saṃmatāś c' âite vālikā|pāṣāṇā niyataṃ lābha|siddhaye vo bhaviṣyant' îti.»

te Supāraga|prema|bahu|mān'|āvarjita|matibhir devatābhir anupradarśitebhyaḥ sthalebhya ādāya vālikā|pāṣāṇa|buddhyā vaiḍūry'|ādīni ratnāni vahanam āropayām āsuḥ. ten' âiva c' âika|rātreṇa sā naur Bharukaccham upajagāma.

14.75 atha prabhāte rajat'|êndra|nīla|
vaiḍūrya|hema|pratipūrṇa|naukāḥ
sva|deśa|tīr'|ântam upāgatās te
prītyā tam ānarcur udīrṇa|harṣāḥ. [33]

tad evaṃ, dharm'|āśrayaṃ satya|vacanam apy āpadaṃ nudati, prāg eva tat|phalam, iti dharm'|ânuvartinā bhavitavyam.

kalyāṇa|mitr'|āśraya|varṇe 'pi vācyam: «evaṃ kalyāṇa|mitr'|āśritāḥ śreyaḥ prāpnuvant' îti.»

"Honorable merchants, load onto the ship as much sand and gravel as possible from the oceans as we encounter them, starting with the Reed-Garlanded Sea. By doing so, the vessel will not split her sides if she is assailed by the force of a storm. Moreover, this sand and gravel are bound to bring you profit, for they are esteemed as auspicious."

Out of love and respect for Supáraga, deities showed the men where to haul onto the ship what they thought was sand and gravel but were actually beryls and other gems. In a single night, the ship then arrived back at Bharu·kaccha.

Arriving at dawn at their country's shore, 14.75
their ship full of silver, sapphire, beryl, and gold,
the men joyfully praised Supáraga,
exhilarated with delight.

So it is that a mere statement of truth can dispel ruin if based on a virtuous act. Imagine then the fruit of virtue! One should therefore act virtuously.

And one should also narrate this story when praising the value of relying on a Good Friend,* saying: "In this way those who rely on a Good Friend acquire happiness."

STORY 15

THE BIRTH-STORY OF THE FISH

15.1 ŚĪLAVATĀM IH' ÂIV' âbhiprāyāḥ kalyāṇāḥ samṛdhyanti, prāg eva paratr', êti śīla|viśuddhau prayatitavyam. tad|yath" ânuśrūyate.

Bodhisattvaḥ kila kasmiṃś cin n' âti | mahati kahlāra | tāmarasa | kamala | kuvalaya | vibhūṣita | rucira | salile haṃsa | kāraṇḍava | cakravāka | mithun' | ôpaśobhite tīr' | ânta | ruha | taru | kusum' | âvakīrṇe sarasi matsy' | âdhipatir babhūva. sv| abhyasta|bhāvāc ca bahuṣu janm'|ântareṣu par'|ârtha|caryā-yās tatra | stho 'pi para | hita | sukh' | ôpapādana | sa | vyāpāro babhūva.

abhyāsa|yogādd hi śubh'|â|śubhāni
karmāṇi s'|ātmy eva bhavanti puṃsām
tathā|vidhāny eva, yad a|prayatnāj
janm'|ântare svapna iv' ācaranti. [1]

15.5 iṣṭānām iva ca sveṣām apatyānām upari niviṣṭa|hārdo sa Mahā|sattvas teṣāṃ mīnānāṃ dāna|priya|vacan'|ârtha|cary"| ādi|kramaiḥ param anugrahaṃ cakāra.

anyonya|hiṃsā|praṇayaṃ niyacchan
paraspara|prema vivardhayaṃś ca
yogād upāyajñatayā ca teṣāṃ
vismārayām āsa sa matsya|vṛttam. [2]

tat tena samyak paripālyamānaṃ
vṛddhiṃ parāṃ mīna|kulaṃ jagāma,
puraṃ vinirmuktam iv' ôpasargair
nyāya|pravṛttena nar'|âdhipena. [3]

THE GOOD INTENTIONS of the virtuous prosper even in this life, let alone in the next. One should therefore strive for moral purity. 15.1

Tradition has handed down the following story.

The Bodhi·sattva is said to have once been a king of fish who lived in a moderately sized lake. Adorned with swans, ducks, and pairs of *chakra·vaka* birds,* the lake was sprinkled with the blossoms of trees growing on the edge of its banks and its waters were beautifully graced by lotuses and water-lilies of various kinds. In numerous previous births the Bodhi·sattva had habitually acted for the benefit of others and so, even in this existence as a fish, he was devoted to producing the welfare and happiness of other beings.

Good and bad deeds become
so ingrained in men through habit
that, without effort and as if in a dream,
they practice exactly the same in another birth.

The Great Being focused his affections on the fish as if 15.5
they were his own dear offspring, favoring them with charity, kind words, beneficial deeds, and other actions.

Restraining any tendency to harm one another,
he increased their mutual love instead.
Through perseverance and a knowledge of strategy,
he made them forget their fish-like ways.

Carefully protected by the Bodhi·sattva,
the shoal of fish prospered greatly,
just as a city is freed from calamities
by the just behavior of its king.

atha kadā cit sattvānāṃ bhāgya|saṃpad|vaikalyāt pramādāc ca varṣ'|âdhikṛtānāṃ deva|putrāṇāṃ na samyag devo vavarṣa. a|samyag varṣiṇi ca deve tat saraḥ phulla|kadamba|kusuma|gaureṇa nava|salilena na yathā|pūrvam āpupūre.

krameṇa c' ôpagate nidāgha|samaye paṭutara|dīptibhiḥ khed'|âlasa|gatibhir iva ca dina|kara|kiraṇais tad|abhitaptayā ca dharaṇyā jvāl"|ânugaten' êva ca hlād'|âbhilāṣiṇā mārutena tarṣa|vaśād iva pratyaham āpīyamānaṃ tat saraḥ palvalī|babhūva.

15.10 nidāgha|kāla|jvalito vivasvāñ
jvāl"|âvakarṣ" îva paṭuś ca vāyuḥ
jvar'|ātur" êv' â|śiśirā ca bhūmis
toyāni roṣād iva śoṣayanti. [4]

atha Bodhisattvo vāyasa|gaṇair api pratarkyamāṇaṃ prāg eva salila|tīr'|ânta|cāribhiḥ pakṣi|gaṇair viṣāda|dainya|vaśa|gaṃ vispandita|mātra|parāyaṇaṃ mīna|kulam avekṣya karuṇāyamāṇaś cintām āpede:

«kaṣṭā bat' êyam āpad āpatitā mīnānām!

pratyahaṃ kṣīyate toyaṃ spardhamānam iv' āyuṣā,
ady' âpi ca cireṇ' âiva lakṣyate jalad'|āgamaḥ. [5]

At a certain point in time, a defect in the creatures' good fortune, combined with the negligence of the gods, meant that the rain-god did not rain properly. As a result of the inadequate rain provided by the god, the lake did not fill up as it usually did with fresh water yellowed by the blossoms of blooming *kadámba* flowers.*

The hot season arrived in due course. The sun's rays seemed exhausted by the fatigue of burning with increasing ferocity; the earth was scorched by the sun; and the wind longed for refreshment, as though it were hounded by flames. And so, as if driven by thirst, they all drank water from the lake daily, transforming it into a pond.

The sun, blazing with summer heat, 15.10
the wind, fierce as if filled with flames,
and the earth, so hot it seemed sick with fever,
dried up the waters as though enraged.

The shoal of fish became overwhelmed by wretchedness and despair and could do nothing but writhe. Even the crows sized them up, let alone the flocks of birds wandering the lake shores. Seeing them in this plight, the Bodhi·sattva became moved by compassion and thought:

"What a terrible calamity afflicts these fish!

Every day the water diminishes,
as if competing with life,
and it will still be long
before the rain clouds arrive.

apayāna|kramo n' âsti. net" âpy anyatra ko bhavet?
asmad|vyasana|saṃhṛṣṭāḥ samāyānti ca no dviṣaḥ. [6]

15.15 asya niḥ|saṃśayam ime
toya|śeṣasya saṃkṣayāt
sphuranto bhakṣayiṣyante
śatrubhir mama paśyataḥ. [7]

tat kim atra prāpta|kālaṃ syād iti?»
vimṛśan sa Mah"|ātmā saty'|âdhiṣṭhānam ekam ārtāyanaṃ dadarśa. karuṇayā ca samāpīḍyamāna|hṛdayo dīrgham uṣṇam abhiniśvasya nabhaḥ samullokayann uvāca:

«smarāmi na prāṇi|vadhaṃ yath" âhaṃ
saṃcintya kṛcchre parame 'pi kartum.
anena satyena sarāṃsi toyair
āpūrayan varṣatu deva|rājaḥ!» [8]

atha tasya Mah"|ātmanaḥ puṇy'|ôpacaya|guṇāt saty'|âdhiṣṭhāna|balāt tad|abhiprasādita|deva|nāga|yakṣ'|ânubhāvāc ca samantatas toy'|âvalambi|bimbā gambhīra|madhura|nirghoṣā vidyul|lat"|âlaṃ|kṛtā† nīla|vipula|śikharā vijṛmbhamāṇā iva pravisarpibhiḥ śikhara|bhujaiḥ pariṣvajamānā iva c' ânyonyam a|kāla|meghāḥ kāla|meghāḥ prādur|abhavan.

15.20 diśāṃ pramiṇvanta iva prayāmaṃ,
śṛṅgair vitanvanta iv' ândhakāram,
nabhas|tal'|ādarśa|gatā virejuś
chāyā girīṇām iva kāla|meghāḥ. [9]

We have no means of escape.
And who will take us elsewhere?
Our enemies crowd around us,
thrilled by our misfortune.

No doubt, 15.15
when the last of the water dries up,
these quivering fish will be eaten
by enemies before my very eyes.

So how should I act in this situation?"

Reflecting this way, the Great One saw just one remedy for their pain: to make an affirmation of truth. Afflicted by compassion, the Bodhi·sattva breathed out a long and hot sigh as he looked up at the sky and said:

"I do not recall ever purposefully harming
a breathing being even when in a dire plight.
By this truth, may the king of gods
pour rain and fill the lake with water!"

As a result of the Great One's accumulation of merit, as well as the force of his affirmation of truth and the power of the gods, *naga*s, and *yaksha*s who were benign toward him, dark clouds appeared all over the sky, out of season but timely.* Hanging with water and emitting a deep and delightful rumble, they were adorned with flickers of lightning and seemed to swell and embrace each other with huge dark crests that spread out like stretching arms.

As though eradicating the horizon 15.20
and spreading darkness with their crests,
the rain clouds were like mountain shadows
reflected in the mirror of the sky.

saṃsakta|kekaiḥ śikhibhiḥ prahṛṣṭaiḥ
 saṃstūyamānā iva nṛtta|citraiḥ
prasakta|mandra|stanitā virejur
 dhīra|prahāsā iva te ghan'|âughāḥ. [10]

muktā vimuktā iva tair vimuktā
 dhārā nipetuḥ. praśaśāma reṇuḥ.
gandhaś cacār' â|nibhṛto dharaṇyāṃ
 vikīryamāṇo jalad'|ânilena. [11]

nidāgha|saṃparka|vivardhito 'pi
 tiro|babhūv' ârka|kara|prabhāvaḥ.
phen'|âvalī|vyākula|mekhalāni
 toyāni nimn'|âbhimukhāni sasruḥ. [12]

muhur muhuḥ kāñcana|piñjarābhir
 bhābhir dig|antān anurañjayantī
payoda|tūrya|svana|labdha|harṣā
 vidyul|latā nṛttam iv' ācacāra. [13]

15.25 atha Bodhisattvaḥ samantato 'bhiprasṛtair āpāṇḍubhiḥ salila|pravāhair āpūryamāṇe sarasi dhārā|nipāta|sama|kālam eva vidrute vāyas'|ādye pakṣi|gaṇe pratilabdha|jīvit'|āśe pramudite mīna|gaṇe prīty" âbhisāryamāṇa|hṛdayo varṣa|nivṛtti|s'|āśaṅkaḥ punaḥ punaḥ Parjanyam ābabhāṣe:

«udgarja, Parjanya, gabhīra|dhīraṃ!
 pramodam udvāsaya vāyasānām!
ratnāyamānāni payāṃsi varṣan
 saṃsakta|vidyuj|jvalita|dyutīni!» [14]

Rumbling deeply and constantly like a loud laugh,
the cloud masses looked glorious,
as peacocks seemed to sing their praises
with continuous cries and beautiful dances.

Torrents of rain fell from the clouds,
released like pearls freed from their shells.
The dust settled. A strong fragrance roamed the earth,
spread by winds created by the raining clouds.

Though intensified by the hot season,
the sun's rays lost their power.
Waters streamed down from the mountains,
their slopes frothing with streaks of foam.

Joyful at the sound of the clouds' music,
a lightning fork seemed to perform a dance,
illuminating the horizon repeatedly
with gold and yellow lights.

The lake filled up on all sides with streams of pale rush- 15.25
ing water and the flocks of crows and other birds fled as soon as the torrent fell. Full of joy, the shoal of fish regained their hope for life and delight flowed into the Bodhi·sattva's heart. But because he was concerned that the rain might stop, the Bodhi·sattva repeatedly addressed Parjánya,* saying:

"Thunder, Parjánya, deep and strong!
Banish the joy of the crows!
Pour down your jewel-like waters,
glistening with the blaze of constant lightning!"

tad upaśrutya Śakro devānām indraḥ parama|vismita|manāḥ sākṣād abhigamy' âinam abhisaṃrādhayann uvāca:

«tav' âiva khalv eṣa, mah"|ânubhāva
matsy'|êndra, saty'|âtiśaya|prabhāvaḥ
āvarjitā yat kalaśā iv' ême
kṣaranti ramya|stanitāḥ payo|dāḥ. [15]

mahat|pramāda|skhalitaṃ tv idaṃ me
yan nāma kṛtyeṣu bhavad|vidhānām
lok'|ârtham abhyutthita|mānasānāṃ
vyāpāra|yogaṃ na samabhyupaimi. [16]

15.30 cintāṃ kṛthā mā tad ataḥ paraṃ tvaṃ.
satāṃ hi kṛty'|ôdvahane 'smi dhuryaḥ.
deśo 'py ayaṃ tvad|guṇa|saṃśrayeṇa
na bhūya evaṃ bhavit" ārti|vaśyaḥ.» [17]

ity evaṃ priya|vacanair abhisaṃrādhya tatr' âiv' ântar|dadhe. tac ca saraḥ parāṃ toya|samṛddhim avāpa.

tad evaṃ, śīlavatām ih' âiv' âbhiprāyāḥ kalyāṇāḥ samṛdhyanti, prāg eva paratr', êti śīla|viśuddhau prayatitavyam iti.

Shakra, the king of the gods, became filled with utter astonishment when he heard this. Approaching the Bodhi·sattva in person, he praised him with the following words:

"King of fish, it must be the mighty power
produced by your exceptional act of truth
that makes these clouds rumble delightfully,
pouring water like tipped jars.

I have erred with great negligence
in not tending to the actions
of creatures such as you
who strive to benefit the world.

Be anxious no more. 15.30
It is my charge to aid the good in their tasks.
As a result of your virtue,
this area will suffer such disaster no more."

Praising him with such pleasing words, Shakra disappeared there and then and the lake became filled with huge amounts of water.

So it is that the good intentions of the virtuous prosper even in this world, let alone in the next. One should therefore strive for moral purity.

STORY 16

THE BIRTH-STORY OF THE QUAIL CHICK

16.1 SATYA|PARIBHĀVITĀṂ vācam agnir api na prasahate laṅghayitum, iti satya|vacane 'bhiyogaḥ karaṇīyaḥ.

tad|yath" ânuśrūyate.

Bodhi|sattvaḥ kil' ânyatamasminn araṇy'|āyatane vartakā|potako bhavati sma. sa katipaya|rātr'|ôdbhinn'|âṇḍa|kośaḥ praviroksyamāṇa|taruṇa|pakṣaḥ paridurbalatvād ālakṣyamāṇ'|âṅga†|pratyaṅga|pradeśaḥ sva|mātā†|pitṛ|prayatna|racite tṛṇa|gahan'|ôpagūḍha|gulma|saṃniśrite† nīḍe saṃbahulair bhrātṛbhiḥ sārdhaṃ prativasati sma.

tad|avastho 'pi c' â|parilupta|dharma|saṃjñatvān mātā|pitṛbhyām upahṛtān prāṇino n' êcchati sm' âbhyavahartum. yad eva tv asya tṛṇa|bīja|nyagrodha|phal'|ādy upajahratur mātā|pitarau ten' âiva vartayām āsa. tasya tayā rūkṣ'|âlp'|āhāratayā na kāyaḥ puṣṭim upayayau, n' âpi samyak pakṣau praviruruhatuḥ.† itare tu vartakā|potakā yath"|ôpanītam āhāram abhyavaharanto balavantaḥ sañjāta|pakṣāś ca babhūvuḥ.

16.5 dharmatā hy eṣā yad uta:

dharm'|â|dharma|nir|āśaṅkaḥ
sarv'|āśī sukham edhate.
dharmyāṃ tu vṛttim anvicchan
vicit'|āś" îha duḥkhitaḥ. [1]

api c' ôktaṃ Bhagavatā†:

NOT EVEN FIRE can overpower words purified by truth. One should therefore apply oneself to truthful speech. 16.1

Tradition has handed down the following story.

The Bodhi·sattva is said to have once been born as a quail chick in a region of the forest. As he had broken out of his shell only a few nights before, his tender wings were still growing and he was so weak that his limbs, both large and small, stood out conspicuously. He lived with his many brothers in a nest that had been carefully built by his parents and that lay in a thicket hidden by dense grass.

Despite being born into that existence, the Bodhi·sattva had lost none of his moral awareness and so he refused to accept the living creatures that his mother and father brought him. Instead he lived solely off grass, seeds, figs, and other such foods that were offered to him by his parents. This crude and scant fare meant that his body was undernourished and his wings did not develop properly. The other quail chicks, on the other hand, accepted whatever food they were offered and consequently grew strong and developed fully grown wings.

For the law of nature is that: 16.5

Those who eat everything,
without heed for right or wrong, prosper happily.
Whereas those who eat only select food,
seeking a moral way of life, suffer in the world.

*And the Lord has also declared the following couplet:

«su|jīvitam a|hrīkeṇa dhvāṅkṣeṇ' â|śuci|karmaṇā
praskandinā pragalbhena su|saṃkliṣṭaṃ tu jīvitam. [2]

hrīmatā tv iha dur|jīvaṃ nityaṃ śuci|gaveṣiṇā
saṃlīnen' â|pragalbhena śuddh'|ājīvena jīvatā.» [3]

16.10 iti gāthā|dvayam.† teṣām evam|avasthānāṃ n' âti|dūre mahān vana|dāvaḥ pratibhaya|prasakta|ninado vijṛmbhamāṇa|dhūma|rāśir vikīryamāṇa|jvāl"|âvalī|lola|visphuliṅgaḥ saṃtrāsano vana|carāṇām a|nayo vana|gahanānāṃ prādur|abhavat.

sa mārut'|āghūrṇita|viprakīrṇa†|
jvālā|bhujair nṛtta|viśeṣa|citraiḥ
valgann iva vyākula|dhūma|keśaḥ
sasvāna teṣāṃ dhṛtim ādadānaḥ. [4]

caṇḍ'|ânil'|āsphālana|cañcalāni
bhaya|drutān' îva vane tṛṇāni
so 'gniḥ sa|saṃrambha iv' âbhipatya
sphurat|sphuliṅga|prakaro dadāha. [5]

bhaya|drut'|ôdbhrānta|vihaṃga|sārthaṃ
paribhramad|bhīta|mṛgaṃ samantāt
dhūm'|âugha|magnaṃ paṭu|vahni|śabdaṃ
vanaṃ tad ārty" êva bhṛśaṃ rarāsa. [6]

"Life is easy but tarnished
for the shameless crow,
who is daring, bold,
and impure in action.

But life is difficult in this world
for those who feel shame, always seeking purity,
and who, modest and bashful,
live a pure way of life."

While they were living this way, a huge forest fire erupted nearby, bringing terror to the creatures in the forest and destruction to the woods and thickets. Roaring with a fearful and incessant noise, the fire belched out clouds of smoke and scattered sparks from its spreading ring of flames. 16.10

The roaring fire robbed the creatures of their courage,
as it seemed to leap around with elaborate dances,
its smoke billowing like disheveled hair,
its wind-tossed flames flailing about like arms.

Charging forward with its mass of spraying sparks,
the fire, as if enraged, incinerated the forest grasses
as they were shaken by the violent wind,
seeming to flee with terror.

Flocks of birds flew away with alarm and fear
and animals wandered everywhere in terror.
The forest roared violently as if with pain,
immersed in a deluge of smoke, crackling loudly
with flames.

kramena c' ôtpīḍyamāna iva sa vahniḥ paṭunā mārutena tṛṇa|gahan'|ânusārī teṣāṃ nīḍa|samīpam upajagāma. atha te vartakā|potakā bhaya|vi|rasa|vyākula|virāvāḥ paraspara|nir|apekṣāḥ sahasā samutpetuḥ. paridurbalatvād a|saṃjāta|pakṣatvāc ca Bodhisattvas tu n' ôtpatituṃ prayatnaṃ cakāra. vidit'|ātma|prabhāvas tv a|saṃbhrānta eva sa Mahā|sattvaḥ sa|rabhasam iv' ôpasarpantam agniṃ s'|ânunayam ity uvāca:

16.15 «vyarth'|âbhidhāna|caraṇo 'smy, a|virūḍha|pakṣas.
tvat|saṃbhramāc ca pitarāv api me praḍīnau.
tvad|yogyam asti na ca kiñ cid ih' ātitheyam
asmān nivartitum itas† tava yuktam, Agne.» [7]

ity ukte satya|paribhāvita|vacasā tena Mahā|sattvena

udīryamāṇo 'py anilena so 'gnir
viśuṣka|saṃsakta|tṛṇe 'pi kakṣe
nadīm iva prāpya vivṛddha|toyāṃ
tad|vācam āsādya śaśāma sadyaḥ. [8]

ady' âpi taṃ Himavati prathitaṃ pradeśaṃ
dāv'|âgnir uddhata|śikho 'pi samīraṇena
mantr'|âbhiśapta iva n'|âika|śirā bhujaṃ|gaḥ
saṃkoca|manda|lulit'|ârcir upaiti śāntim. [9]

tat kim idam upanītam iti? ucyate:

As if pounded by the violent wind, the fire gradually encroached on the grasses and thickets, approaching the vicinity of the quails' nest. Uttering shrill and confused shrieks of terror, the quail chicks instantly flew up into the sky, without any concern for each other. The Bodhi·sattva, however, made no effort to fly as he was weak and lacked wings. But he was completely untroubled, for he knew where his power lay. Respectfully addressing the fire, which advanced forward as if in a rage, the Great Being said:

"My feet are misnamed* and my wings ungrown. 16.15
Your fury has made even my parents take flight.
I have no guest offering worthy of you here.
You should therefore turn back, Agni."*

As soon as the Great Being said these words that were purified by truth,

the fire, though whipped up by the wind,
and though blazing among thickets of dry dense grass,
instantly abated on encountering the chick's words,
as if it had reached a river brimming with water.

Even today, in this celebrated Hímavat region,
a fire ceases, however high the wind fans its flames,
contracting and stilling its unruly blaze
like a many-headed snake entranced by a spell.

What then has this story demonstrated? There is a proverb that states:

16.20 velām iva pracalit'|ōrmi|phaṇaḥ samudraḥ,
śikṣāṃ mun'|îndra|vihitām iva c' ātma|kāmaḥ,†
saty'|ātmanām iti na laṅghayituṃ yad ājñāṃ
śaktaḥ kṛśānur api. satyam ato na jahyāt. [10]

tad evaṃ, satya|paribhāvitāṃ† vācam agnir api na prasahate laṅghayitum, iti satya|vacane 'bhiyogaḥ karaṇīyaḥ. Tathāgata|varṇe 'pi vācyam iti.

Just as the sea 16.20
cannot surpass the shore,
its waves surging like snake-hoods,
and just as spiritual people cannot neglect
the teachings of the Lord of Sages,
so even fire itself cannot defy
the command of the truthful.
One should thus never abandon truth.

So it is that not even fire can overpower words purified by truth. One should therefore apply oneself to truthful speech.

And this story should also be narrated when praising the Tatha·gata.

STORY 17

THE BIRTH-STORY ON THE JAR

17.1 AN | EKA | DOṢ’ | ÔPASṚṢṬAM ati | kaṣṭaṃ ca† madya | pānam iti sādhavaḥ param apy asmād vārayanti, prāg ev’ ātmānam.†

tad|yath” ânuśrūyate.

Bodhisattvaḥ kila karuṇ”|âtiśaya|paribhāvita|matiḥ para| hita | sukh’ | ôpapādana | paraḥ puṇyāṃ pratipadam udbhāvayan dāna | dama | saṃyam’ | ādibhiḥ kadā cic Chakro devānām indro babhūva. sa prakarṣiṇām api divyānāṃ viṣaya| sukhānāṃ nikāma|lābhī sann api karuṇā|vaśagatvān n’ âiva lok’|ârtha|caryā|samudyoga|śithilaṃ manaś cakāra.

prāyeṇa lakṣmī|madir’| ôpabhogāj†
jāgarti n’ âiv’ ātma|hite ’pi lokaḥ.
sur’|êndra|lakṣmy” âpi tu nir|mado ’sāv
abhūt par’|ártheṣv api jāgarūkaḥ. [1]

17.5 an|eka|tīvra|vyasan’|ātureṣu
sattveṣu bandhuṣv iva baddha|hārdaḥ.†
dhairyāt sva|bhāva|jñatayā śriyaś ca†
n’ âsau visasmāra par’|ârtha|caryām. [2]

atha kadā cit sa Mah”|ātmā manuṣya|lokam avalokayann anukampā | samāvarjitena maitrī | snigdhena† sva | prabhāva | mahatā† cakṣuṣā dadarśa Sarvamitraṃ nāma rājānam a | kalyāṇa | mitra | saṃparka | doṣāt sa | paura | jānapadaṃ madya | pāna | prasaṅg’ | âbhimukham. tatra c’ âsy’ â | doṣa | darśitām avekṣya mahā | doṣatāṃ ca madya | pānasya sa Mah” | ātmā mahatyā karuṇayā samāpīḍyamāna|hṛdayaś cintām āpede:

DRINKING ALCOHOL is detrimental and beset with many faults. That is why virtuous people restrain others from alcohol, let alone themselves. 17.1

Tradition has handed down the following story.

The Bodhi·sattva is said to have once lived as Shakra, the king of the gods. Devoted to producing the welfare and happiness of others, his mind was purified by exceptional compassion and he revealed his virtuous behavior through deeds such as giving, discipline, and restraint. Although he took pleasure in the refined sensual enjoyments of the gods, compassion so ruled his mind he never slackened his endeavor to benefit the world.

When intoxicated by their enjoyment of prosperity,
most are unwatchful even over their own welfare.
But he was watchful even over the welfare of others,
unintoxicated even by the opulence of divine kingship.

Toward creatures sick with severe misfortunes, 17.5
he felt the same heartfelt bond as if they were kinsmen.
Steadfast and aware of his status and glory,
he never forgot to act for the benefit of others.

One day the Great One was surveying the human world with his powerful eye, which was full of compassion and tender friendliness, when he spotted a king called Sarva·mitra, "Friend of All." Flawed by keeping company with bad friends, this king was addicted to alcohol, as were the people in the city and countryside. When he saw that the king perceived no fault in the great vice of drinking alcohol, the Great One was struck by a feeling of great compassion and had this thought:

«kaṣṭā bat' êyam āpad āpatitā lokasya!

pramukha|svādu pānaṃ hi doṣa|darśana|viklavān
śreyaso 'paharaty eva ramaṇīyam iv' â|patham. [3]

tat kim atra prāpta|kālaṃ syāt? bhavatu! dṛṣṭam.

17.10 pradhāna|bhūtasya viceṣṭitāni
jano 'nukartuṃ niyata|svabhāvaḥ.
ity atra rāj" âiva cikitsanīyaḥ.
śubh'|â|śubhaṃ tat|prabhavaṃ hi loke.» [4]

iti viniścitya sa Mahā|sattvas tapta|kāñcana|rucira|varṇam† āparuṣ'|ôdgrathita|jaṭā|viṭapa|dharaṃ valkal'|âjina|saṃvītam ojasvi brāhmaṃ vapur abhinirmāya surā|pūrṇaṃ ca vāma|pārśva|sthaṃ n' âti|bṛhantaṃ kumbham atha† Sarvamitrasya rājñaḥ parṣadi† saṃniṣaṇṇasya prastāv'|ôpanatāsu pravṛttāsu sur"|āsava|śīdhu|maireya|madhu|kathāsu purastād antarikṣe† prādur|abhavat. vismaya|bahu|mān'|āvarjitena ca prāñjalinā tena janen' âbhyutthāya pratyarcyamānaḥ sa|jala iva jala|dharo gambhīram abhinadann uccair uvāca:

"What a terrible disaster afflicts these people!

For drink, though sweet at the outset,
is like a delightful but wicked path
that steals away bliss
from those blind to its faults.

What then is the best way to act in this situation? But wait! I see a solution.

It is the unchanging nature of people 17.10
to follow the actions of their leaders.
Only the king therefore need be cured.
For good and bad in his people springs from him."

Thinking this, the Great Being magically transformed himself into a burly-looking brahmin. Clothed in bark and deer-skin, his body gleamed with the color of refined gold and he wore a mop of coarsely tied-up matted hair. On his left side, he carried a medium-sized jar that was full of liquor. Bearing this form, the Great Being appeared in the air before King Sarva·mitra while he was sat in his assembly engaged in a conversation about spirits, liquor, alcohol, wine, and other intoxicating drinks. Filled with amazement and reverence, the people rose up and greeted the Bodhi·sattva with hands cupped in respect. Like a cloud filled with rain, he then loudly addressed them with a deep, booming voice:

«puṣpa|mālā|hasat|kaṇṭham
 imaṃ bharitam ākaṇṭham
avataṃsa|kṛt'|â|kumbhaṃ
 kretum icchati kaḥ kumbham? [5]

sa|valayam iva puṣpa|mālayā
 pravitatay" ânila|kampa|lolayā†
kisalaya|racanā|samutkaṭaṃ
 ghaṭam imam icchati kaḥ krayeṇa vaḥ?» [6]

ath' âinaṃ sa rājā vismay'|āvarjita|kautūhalaḥ sa|bahu|mānam udīkṣamāṇaḥ† kṛt'|âñjalir uvāca:

17.15 «dīptyā nav'|ârka iva cārutayā śaś" îva
 saṃlakṣyase ca vapuṣ" ânyatamo munīnām.
tad vaktum arhasi yathā vidito 'si loke.
 saṃbhāvanā hi guṇatas tvayi no vicitrā.» [7]

Śakra uvāca:

«paścād api jñāsyasi yo 'ham asmi.
 ghaṭaṃ tv imaṃ† kretum ito ghaṭasva—
na ced bhayaṃ te para|loka|duḥkhād
 ih' âiva tīvra|vyasan'|āgamād vā.» [8]

rāj" ôvāca, «a|pūrvaḥ khalv ayam atra|bhavataḥ paṇya|vikray'|ārambhaḥ.†

guṇa|saṃvarṇanaṃ nāma doṣāṇāṃ ca nigūhanam
prasiddha iti lokasya paṇyānāṃ vikraya|kramaḥ. [9]

"Full to the brim,
a festoon of flowers laughs around its neck!
Finely garlanded, it's more than just a jar.
Who wishes to buy this jar?

Sublimely decorated with buds,
a broad garland of flowers circles it
like a bracelet, trembling in the wind.
Which of you wishes to buy this jar?"

The king's astonishment aroused his curiosity. Staring at the brahmin with veneration, he addressed him with the following words, his hands cupped in respect:

"You look as radiant as the newly risen sun. 17.15
As charming as the moon, you resemble a sage in form.
Please tell me how are you known in the world.
For your qualities suggest various opinions about you."

Shakra answered:

"You will know who I am later.
But for now focus on buying this pot—
unless you fear anguish in the next world
or severe misfortunes in this one."

"I have never seen a sales pitch like yours before, good sir," the king replied.

"The recognized way
of selling wares
is to praise their virtues
and conceal their faults.

17.20 yukto v" ân|ṛta|bhīrūṇāṃ
tvad|vidhānām ayaṃ vidhiḥ
na hi kṛcchre 'pi saṃtyaktuṃ
satyam icchanti sādhavaḥ. [10]

tad ācakṣva, mahā|bhāga:
pūrṇaḥ kasya ghaṭo nv ayam?
kiṃ vā vinimayaṃ† prāpyam
asmattas tvādṛśair api?» [11]

Śakra uvāca, «śrūyatāṃ, mahā|rāja:

n' âyaṃ toyada|vicyutasya
payasaḥ pūrṇo, na tīrth'|âmbhasaḥ,
kaiñjalkasya su|gandhino na madhunaḥ,
sarpir|viśeṣasya vā,
na kṣīrasya vijṛmbhamāṇa|kumuda|
vy|abhr'|êndu|pāda|cchaveḥ.
pūrṇaḥ pāpa|mayasya yasya tu ghaṭas
tasya prabhāvaṃ śṛṇu. [12]

yat pītvā mada|doṣa|vihvalatayā
gaty" â|sva|tantraś† caran,
deśeṣv a|prapateṣv api prapatito
manda|prabhāva|smṛtiḥ,
bhakṣy'|â|bhakṣya|vicāraṇā|virahitas
tat tat samāsvādayet,
tat|saṃpūrṇam imaṃ gataṃ kraya|pathaṃ
krīṇīta kumbh'|âdhamam! [13]

Or perhaps this technique suits men like you, 17.20
who stand in horror of lies.
For the good refuse to abandon truth,
even when in dire situations.

Tell me then, illustrious brahmin:
with what is this jar filled?
And what would a man like you
want in exchange from me?"

"Listen, great king," Shakra replied.

"This jar is not filled with rainfall from clouds,
nor with water from sacred sites,
nor with fragrant honey from flower stamens,
nor with refined butter,
nor with milk the color of moonbeams
that open water-lilies on cloudless nights.
This pot is filled with a liquid that contains evil.
Listen to its power.

Those who drink it roam out of control,
their steps bewildered by the evil of intoxication.
Even over flat ground they stumble,
the powers of their awareness weakened.
Unable to distinguish wrong and right food,
they relish anything at all.
That's what fills this jar and it's up for sale.
So buy this vilest of jars!

17.25 an|īśaḥ sve citte
vicarati yayā saṃhṛta|matir,
dviṣāṃ hās'|āyāsaṃ
samupajanayan gaur iva jaḍaḥ,
sado|madhye nṛtyet
sva|mukha|paṭahen' âpi ca yayā,
kray'|ârhā s" êyaṃ vaḥ
śubha|virahitā kumbha|nihitā. [14]

pītv" ôcitām api jahāti yath" ātma|lajjāṃ
Nirgranthavad vasana|saṃyama|kheda|muktaḥ
dhīraṃ caret pathiṣu paura|jan'|ākuleṣu,
sā paṇyatām† upagatā nihit" âtra kumbhe! [15]

yat pītvā vamathu|samudgat'|ânna|liptā
niḥ|śaṅkaiḥ śvabhir avalihyamāna|vaktrāḥ
niḥ|saṃjñā nṛpati|patheṣv† api svapanti,
prakṣiptaṃ kraya|su|bhagaṃ tad atra kumbhe. [16]

upayujya yan mada|balād a|balā
vinibandhayed api tarau pitarau,
gaṇayec ca sā dhana|patiṃ na patiṃ,
tad idaṃ ghaṭe vinihitaṃ nihitam! [17]

This liquid robs people of their wits. 17.25
Roaming about with no mastery over their minds,
they tire their enemies out with laughter,
becoming senseless as cattle.
It makes people dance in the middle of assemblies,
accompanied by the drumbeats of their mouths.
Please buy the contents of this jar,
a liquid devoid of any good!

Those who drink it
lose all their normal shame.
Like Jain ascetics,* they give up
the annoying constraints of clothes
and boldly walk on streets
teeming with townspeople.
This is the liquid for sale
contained in this jar!

Those who drink it sleep senseless
even on royal highways,
soiled with food from their vomit,
their faces licked by bold dogs.
This is the liquid poured into this jar,
a lucky object to purchase!

When a woman is weak from intoxication,
she can even tie her parents to a tree
and ignore her husband, though he were Kubéra
himself.
Such is the treasure stored in this pot!*

yāṃ pītavanto mada|lupta|saṃjñā
  Vṛṣṇy|Andhakā vismṛta|bandhu|bhāvāḥ†
paras|paraṃ niṣpipiṣur gadābhir,
  unmādanī sā nihit" êha kumbhe! [18]

17.30 yatra prasaktāni kulāni neśur
  lakṣmī|niketāny udit'|ôditāni,
ucchedanī vittavatāṃ kulānāṃ
  s" êyaṃ ghaṭe krayyatay" âdhirūḍhā! [19]

a|niyata|rudita|sthita|vihasita|vāg|
  jaḍa|guru|nayano graha|vaśa|ga iva
paribhava|bhavanaṃ bhavati ca niyataṃ
  yad|upahata|matis, tad idam iha ghaṭe! [20]

pravayaso 'pi yad|ākula|cetanāḥ
  sva|hita|mārga|samāśraya|kātarāḥ
bahu vadanty a|samīkṣita|niścayaṃ,
  kraya|pathena gataṃ tad idaṃ ghaṭe! [21]

yasyā doṣāt pūrva|devāḥ pramattā
  lakṣmī|moṣaṃ deva|rājād avāpya
trāṇ'|âpekṣās toya|rāśau mamajjus,
  tasyāḥ pūrṇaṃ kumbham enaṃ† vṛṇīta! [22]

When the Vrishnis and Ándhakas drank this liquid,*
they so lost their wits to drunkenness
they forgot their kinship and pounded each other
with maces.
This is the intoxicating drink in this jar!

Highly elevated families, abodes of prosperity, 17.30
have been destroyed by their addiction to this drink.
This is the liquid for sale in this jar:
a destroyer of wealthy families!

People inevitably become contemptible
when their minds are besieged by this drink.
As if possessed by a demon,
their eyes become heavy.
Weeping uncontrollably, they laugh constantly,
their speech nonsensical.
This is the liquid
contained in this jar!

Bewildered by this drink, even the elderly
shy from acting in a way that benefits them,
nattering away without scrutiny or purpose.
This is the liquid for sale in this pot!

Intoxicated by this evil drink, the primal deities
were robbed of their prosperity by the king of the gods.
Seeking salvation, they drowned in the ocean seas.
Take this pot filled with that drink!

brūyād a|satyam api satyam iva pratītaḥ,
kuryād a|kāryam api kāryam iva prahṛṣṭaḥ,
yasyā guṇena sad a|sat sad a|sac ca vidyāc,
chāpasya mūrtir iva sā nihit" êha kumbhe! [23]

17.35 unmāda|vidyāṃ vyasana|pratiṣṭhāṃ
sākṣād a|lakṣmīṃ jananīm aghānām
a|dvaidha|siddhāṃ† kali|paddhatiṃ† tāṃ
krīṇīta ghorāṃ manasas tamisrām! [24]

parimuṣita|matir yayā nihanyād
api pitaraṃ jananīm an|āgasaṃ vā
a|vigaṇita|sukh'|āyatir yatiṃ vā,
kraya|vidhinā, nṛ|pa, tām ito gṛhāṇa. [25]

evaṃ|vidhaṃ madyam idaṃ, nar'|êndra,
sur" êti loke prathitaṃ, sur'|ābha.
na pakṣa|pāto 'sti guṇeṣu yasya
sa kretum udyogam idaṃ karotu! [26]

niṣevya yad duś|carita|prasaktāḥ
patanti bhīmān naraka|prapātān
tiryag|gatiṃ preta|daridratāṃ ca,
ko nāma tad draṣṭum api vyavasyet? [27]

This drink makes men confidently
tell lies as if they were truth,
joyfully perform wrongs
as if they were right,
and consider good as bad
and bad as good.
Like the incarnation of a curse,
this is what lies in this jar!

Buy this spell of intoxication, this abode of disaster, 17.35
this personification of misfortune, this mother of sin,
this peerless and perfect path to calamity,
this terrible darkness of mind!

This drink so robs people of their senses
they'd kill their father, innocent mother, or an ascetic,
without regard for their happiness or future.
Buy then this drink, Your Majesty!

*Lord among men as radiant as the divine *sura*s,
this type of intoxicant is known in the world as *surá*.
Let those who are not partisans of virtue
endeavor to buy this drink!

Those who drink it become addicted to misconduct
and fall into the terrifying precipices of hell,
or are reborn as animals or destitute ghosts.
Who then would deign even to look at this object?

laghur api ca vipāko madya|pānasya yaḥ syān,
manuja|gati|gatānāṃ śīla|dṛṣṭīḥ sa hanti.
jvalita|dahana|raudre yena bhūyo 'py Avīcau
nivasati pitṛ|loke hīna|tiryakṣu c' âiva. [28]

17.40 śīlaṃ nimīlayati, hanti yaśaḥ prasahya,
lajjāṃ nirasyati, matiṃ malinī|karoti.
yan nāma pītam upahanti guṇāṃś ca tāṃs tāṃs,
tat pātum arhasi kathaṃ, nṛ|pa, madyam adya?»
[29]

atha sa rājā tais tasya hṛdaya|grāhakair hetumadbhir vacobhir avagamita|madya|pāna|doṣo madya|pāna|prasaṅgād† apavṛtt'|âbhilāṣaḥ Śakram ity uvāca:

«snigdhaḥ pitā vinaya|bhakti|guṇād gurur vā
yad vaktum arhati nay'|â|nayavin munir vā,
tāvat tvayā sv|abhihitaṃ hita|kāmyayā me.
tat karmaṇā vidhivad arcayituṃ yatiṣye. [30]

idaṃ ca tāvat su|bhāṣita|pratipūjanam arhati no 'tra|bhavān pratigrahītum:

dadāmi te grāma|varāṃś ca pañca,
dāsī|śataṃ pañca, gavāṃ śatāni,
sad|aśva|yuktāṃś ca rathān daś' êmān.
hitasya vaktā hi gurur mam' âsi. [31]

However slight the effect of drinking liquor,
it destroys the virtue and wisdom of human beings.
Through it one dwells in Avíchi, that horror of
blazing fire,*
or in the ancestor realm or among lowly animals.

Liquor shuts off morality, violently destroys 17.40
reputation,
expels shame, and tarnishes the mind.
When such a drink crushes every virtue,
how can you consume it this day, Your Majesty?"

The Bodhi·sattva's reasoned words seized hold of the king's heart. Realizing the evil of drinking alcohol, the king ceased to desire any attachment to it and addressed Shakra with these words:

"You have spoken these fine words
in your desire to benefit me.
They are worthy of being spoken
by an affectionate father,
a teacher devoted to decency,
or a sage who knows right and wrong.
I will therefore duly strive
to honor you with a deed.

Good sir, may you please accept this gift of mine as a way of honoring your finely spoken words:

I give you five excellent villages,
five hundred female slaves, a hundred cows,
and these ten chariots yoked to thoroughbred horses.
For you are my guru, a speaker of beneficial words.

17.45 yad vā may" ânyat karaṇīyaṃ tat|saṃdeśād arhaty atra| bhavān bhūyo 'pi mām anugrahītum.»

Śakra uvāca:

«artho 'sti na grāma|var'|ādinā me.
sur'|âdhipaṃ mām avagaccha,† rājan.
saṃpūjanīyas tu hitasya vaktā
vāk|pragraheṇa pratipan|mayena. [32]

ayaṃ hi panthā yaśasaḥ śriyaś ca,
paratra saukhyasya ca tasya tasya.
apāsya tasmān madirā|prasaṅgaṃ
dharm'|āśrayān mad|viṣayaṃ bhajasva.» [33]

ity uktvā Śakras tatr' âiv' ântar|dadhe, sa ca rājā sa|paura| jānapado madya|pānād virarāma.

17.50 tad evam, an|eka|doṣ'|ôpasṛṣṭam ati|kaṣṭaṃ ca† madya| pānam iti sādhavaḥ param apy† asmād vārayanti, prāg ev' ātmānam iti.

«evaṃ loka|hit'|âvahitaḥ† pūrva|janmasv api sa Bhagavān» iti Tathāgata|varṇe 'pi vācyam.

Or if there is anything else I can do, please favor me further, good sir, by giving me your instructions." 17.45

Shakra replied:

"I have no need of objects such as fine villages.
Know me to be the king of the gods, Your Majesty.
A speaker of beneficial words should be honored
by accepting his words and acting on them.

For this is the road to glory and prosperity
and to various felicities in the next world.
Drive away, then, your attachment to alcohol
and acquire my realm by applying yourself to virtue."

Saying these words, Shakra disappeared there and then, while the king, along with the people in the city and countryside, abstained from drinking alcohol.

So it is that drinking alcohol is detrimental and beset 17.50
with many faults. That is why virtuous people restrain others from alcohol, let alone themselves.

One should also narrate this story when eulogizing the Tatha·gata, saying: "In this way, even in his past lives, the Lord was devoted to benefiting the world."

STORY 18
THE BIRTH-STORY OF THE CHILDLESS ASCETIC

18.1 ŚĪLA|PRAŚAMA|PRATIPAKṢA|saṃbādhaṃ gārhasthyam ity evam ātma|kāmā na rocayante.

tad|yath" ânuśrūyate.

Bodhisattvaḥ kila kasmiṃś cid ibhya|kule ślāghanīya|vṛtta|cāritra|saṃpanne prārthanīya|saṃbandhe kul'|ôd-bhava|kāmānāṃ†, nipāna|bhūte śramaṇa|brāhmaṇānāṃ, kośa|koṣṭh'|âgāra|nir|viśeṣe mitra|sva|janānām, abhigamanīye kṛpaṇa|vanīpakānām, upajīvye śilpi|janasy', āspada|bhūte lakṣmyā, datt'|ânugraha|sat|kāre rājñā† lok'|âbhisaṃmate janma pratilebhe.

sa kālānām atyayen' âbhivṛddhaḥ kṛta|śramo lok'|âbhimateṣu vidyā|sthāneṣv, a|parokṣa|buddhir vividha|vikalp'|āśrayāsu kalāsu, jana|nayana|kāntena ca vapuṣā dharm'|â|virodhinyā ca loka|jñatayā sva|jana iva lokasya hṛdayeṣu paryavartata.

18.5 na hi sva|jana ity eva sva|jano bahu manyate.
jano vā jana ity eva sva|janād dṛśyate 'nyathā [1]

guṇa|doṣ'|âbhimarśāt tu
  bahu|mān'|âvamānayoḥ
vrajaty āspadatāṃ lokaḥ
  sva|janasya janasya ca.† [2]

THE HOUSEHOLD LIFE teems with qualities that conflict 18.1
with virtue and serenity. That is why spiritual seekers take no delight in it.

Tradition has handed down the following story.

The Bodhi·sattva is said to have once taken his birth in a wealthy family that was esteemed in the world and lauded for its behavior and conduct. Kinship with them was prized by people eager for good family ties. Like a well of water for brahmins and ascetics, they offered their treasuries and stores to both friends and relatives without discrimination. They welcomed the poor and beggars and they supported artisans. Prosperity had set up home in them and the king himself showed them favor and respect.

After some time the Bodhi·sattva grew up. Applying himself vigorously to the world-respected sciences, he showed himself to be manifestly intelligent in the arts and their various areas of thought. His handsome appearance, delighting the eyes of others, and his knowledge of the world, ever in harmony with virtue, meant he dwelled like a relative in people's hearts.

People do not respect relatives 18.5
simply because they are relatives.
Nor do they treat strangers differently from relatives
simply because they are strangers.

Instead people treat
both relatives and strangers
with respect or contempt
after encountering their virtues and faults.

kṛta|pravrajyā|paricayatvāt tu tasya Mahā|sattvasya

paryeṣṭi|duḥkh'|ânugatāṃ viditvā
gṛhasthatāṃ dharma|virodhinīṃ ca,
sukh'|ôdayatvaṃ ca tapo|vanānāṃ
na geha|saukhyeṣu manaḥ sasañje. [3]

sa mātā|pitroḥ kāla|kriyayā saṃvigna|hṛdayas tam an|eka|śata|sahasra|saṃkhyaṃ gṛha|vibhava|sāraṃ mitra|svajana|kṛpaṇa|vanīpaka|śramaṇa†|brāhmaṇebhyoyath"|ârham atisṛjya parivavrāja.† so 'nupūrveṇa grāma|nagara|nigama|rāṣṭra|rājadhānīṣv anuvicarann anyatamaṃ nagaram† upaniśritya† kasmiṃś cid vana|prasthe nivasati sma.

18.10 sa dhyāna|guṇ'|âbhyāsāt s'|ātmī|bhūten' â|kṛtak'|êndriya†|prasādena śruti|hṛday'|āhlādinā ca vidvattā|sūcaken' ân|utsiktena vigata|lābh'|āśā|kārpaṇya|dainyena vinay'|âujasvinā yath"|ârha|madhur'|ôpacāra|sauṣṭhavena dharm'|â|dharma|pravibhāga|nipuṇena† ca vacasā pravrajit'|ācāra|śībharayā ca saj|jan'|êṣṭayā ceṣṭayā tatr' âbhilakṣito babhūva. kautūhalinā ca janena samupalabdha|kula|pravrajyā|kramaḥ suṣṭhutaraṃ loka|saṃmatas tatr' âbhūt.

The Great Being, however, had become attracted to asceticism.

Realizing the household life hindered virtue
and involved the hardship of seeking wealth,
whereas ascetic groves offered great happiness,
he remained unattached to household pleasures.

When his mother and father died, the Bodhi·sattva was filled with spiritual alarm. Adopting the life of an ascetic, he cast aside the wealth and possessions of his household—amounting to several hundreds and thousands—by giving it to friends, relatives, paupers, beggars, ascetics, and brahmins according to their deserts. After wandering through successive villages, cities, towns, kingdoms, and capitals, he took up residence in a forest hermitage, relying on a city for alms.

His continuous practice of meditation and virtue pro- 18.10
duced in him a natural serenity that became ingrained in his character. His speech gladdened people's ears and hearts. Although his words revealed his knowledge, they were not ostentatious. Free from the pitiful misery of seeking profit, it was their modesty that made them powerful. Attractive in their use of due and gentle courtesy, they skillfully distinguished between right and wrong. His conduct too was the kind cherished by virtuous men, made all the more charming by his ascetic practices. For all these reasons—his serenity, his words, and his conduct—the Bodhi·sattva became well-known in the region. And when curiosity led people to learn that he had renounced a good family background to become an ascetic, he became even more esteemed.

ādeyataratāṃ yānti kula|rūpa|guṇād guṇāḥ
āśray'|âtiśayen' êva candrasya kiraṇ'|âṅkurāḥ. [4]

ath' âsya tatr' âbhigamanam upalabhya pitṛ | vayasyaḥ samabhigamya c' âinaṃ guṇa|bahu|mānāt kuśala|paripraśna|pūrvakaṃ c' âsmai nivedy' ātmānaṃ pitṛ|vayasyatāṃ ca saṃkathā|prastāv'|āgatam enaṃ snehād uvāca:
«cāpalam iva khalv idam anuvartitaṃ bhadanten' ân | avekṣya† kula|vaṃśam asmin vayasi pravrajatā.

ārādhyate sat|pratipatti|madbhir
dharmo yad" âyaṃ bhavane vane vā
śrīmanti hitvā bhavanāny atas tvaṃ
kasmād araṇyeṣu matiṃ karoṣi? [5]

18.15 para|prasād'|ârjita|bhaikṣa|vṛttir
a|gaṇyamānaḥ khalavaj janena
ku|cela|bhṛd bandhu|suhṛd|vihīno
van'|ânta|bhūmāv apaviddha|kāyaḥ. [6]

mūrtaṃ daridratvam iv' ôpaguhya
kathaṃ nu śokasya vaśaṃ prayāsi?
imām avasthāṃ hi tav' ēkṣamāṇā
dviṣo 'pi bāṣp'|āpihit'|ēkṣaṇāḥ syuḥ! [7]

Virtues are more favorably received
when aided by the image of a noble family,
just as the moon's rays are more pleasing
when they illuminate a fine object.

One day a friend of the Bodhi·sattva's father learned of the ascetic's arrival in the area and went to visit him out of respect for his virtue. Asking after the Bodhi·sattva's health, he introduced himself and told him about his friendship with the Bodhi·sattva's father. Taking the opportunity for discussion, he then addressed the Bodhi·sattva with words that were spoken out of affection:

"It was rather irresponsible of you, venerable one, to have become an ascetic at your age without any regard for your lineage.

Why have you abandoned your rich home
and fixed your heart on the wilderness,
when good men can practice virtue
in either a house or the forest?

You live off alms acquired from the grace of others. 18.15
People view you as no better than a rogue.
Wearing rags and parted from relatives and friends,
you've removed yourself to an area of the forest.

How can you subject yourself to woe,
embracing what seems the embodiment of poverty?
The eyes of your very enemies would fill
with tears if they saw you in this state!

tad ehi pitryaṃ bhavanaṃ tav' êdaṃ
śrut'|ârtha|sāraṃ bhavat" âpi nūnam.
saṃpādayethā nivasaṃs tvam atra
dharmaṃ ca sat|putra|mano|rathaṃ ca. [8]

loka|pravādaḥ khalv api c' âiṣaḥ:

para|karma|karasy' âpi
sve nipāna|sukhā gṛhāḥ
kiṃ punaḥ sukha|saṃprāptāḥ
samṛddhi|jvalita|śriyaḥ!» [9]

18.20 atha Bodhisattvaḥ praviveka|sukh'|âmṛta|rasa|paribhāvita|matis tat|pravaṇa|hṛdayaḥ samupalabdha|viśeṣo gṛha|vana|vāsayoḥ kām'|ôpabhoga|nimantraṇāyāṃ tṛpta iva bhojana|kathāyām a|sukhāyamāna uvāca:

«idaṃ sneh'|ôdbhavatvāt† te
kāmam alp'|âtyayaṃ vacaḥ
sukha|saṃjñāṃ tu mā kārṣīḥ
kadā cid gṛha|cārake. [10]

gārhasthyaṃ mahad a|svāsthyaṃ
sa|dhanasy' â|dhanasya ca†
ekasya rakṣaṇ'|āyāsād,
itarasy' ârjana|śramāt [11]

yatra nāma sukhaṃ n' âiva
sa|dhanasy' â|dhanasya ca,†
tatr' âbhirati|saṃmohaḥ
pāpasy' âiva phal'|ôdayaḥ. [12]

Return then to your ancestral home.
For even you must have heard of its wealth.
By living there you will fulfill your moral duty
and your desire for a good son.

For there is a popular saying that states:

Even for a servant, to own a house
brings the happiness of a well of water.
Imagine then if it is easily come by
and blazes with opulent riches!"

The Bodhi·sattva's mind was, however, purified by tasting the immortal ambrosia of joyful solitude. Intent on that path, he had grasped the distinction between the householder life and life in the forest. He took no pleasure in this invitation to enjoy sensual desires, just as a person sated with food takes no pleasure in talking about eating. He therefore replied as follows: 18.20

"Because your words spring from affection,
your transgression is only slight.
But never use the word 'happiness'
about someone who lives in a house.

The household life is a great discomfort,
for both the wealthy and the poor.
The wealthy suffer the toil of guarding money,
the poor suffer the toil of acquiring it.

As there is no happiness in such a life,
both for the wealthy and the poor,
to delight in it is a delusion.
Evil in fact is its source.

yad api c' êṣṭaṃ gṛha|sthen' âpi śakyo 'yam† ārādhayituṃ dharma, iti kāmam evam etat. ati|duṣ|karaṃ tu me pratibhāti dharma|pratipakṣa|saṃbādhatvāc chrama|bāhulyāc ca gṛhasya. paśyatu bhavān:

18.25 gṛhā n' ân|īhamānasya na c' âiv' â|vadato mṛṣā
na ca nikṣipta|daṇḍasya† pareṣām a|nikurvataḥ. [13]

tad ayaṃ gṛha|sukh'|āś"|âvabaddha†|hṛdayas tat|sādhan'|ôdyata|matir janaḥ.

yadi dharmam upaiti, n' âsti geham.
yadi† geh'|âbhimukhaḥ, kuto 'sti dharmaḥ?†
praśam'|âika|raso hi dharma|mārgo,
gṛha|siddhiś ca parākrama|krameṇa. [14]

iti dharma|virodha|dūṣitatvād
gṛha|vāsaṃ ka iv' ātmavān bhajeta?
paribhūya sukh'|āśayā hi dharmaṃ
niyamo n' âsti sukh'|ôdaya|prasiddhau. [15]

niyataṃ ca yaśaḥ|parābhavaḥ syād
anutāpo manasaś ca dur|gatiś ca.
iti dharma|virodhinaṃ bhajante
na sukh'|ôpāyam apāyavan naya|jñāḥ. [16]

18.30 api ca sukho gṛha|vāsa iti śraddh"|āgamyam idaṃ me pratibhāti.

As to your claim that householders too can practice virtue, I grant that this is true. But it seems to me extremely difficult. For a house teems with qualities that conflict with virtue and involves a great deal of toil. Consider this, good sir:

A house is not for one devoid of desire, 18.25
nor for one who never lies,
nor for one who never inflicts violence,
nor for one who never injures others.

When a person's heart is caught up with desire for household pleasures, they strive to bring that pleasure about.

If one practices virtue, one cannot have a house.
And if dedicated to a house, how can one have virtue?
The path of virtue is flavored solely by tranquility.
But the household life is realized through struggle.

What self-possessed person would live
as a householder
when it is contaminated by conflict with morality?
For in their desire for pleasure people suppress virtue,
unrestrained in ensuring those pleasures arise.

Inevitably losing their reputation,
they feel remorse and attain a bad rebirth.
That is why wise people avoid, as if it were hell,
any strategy for pleasure that obstructs virtue.

Moreover, to say that life as a householder is happy appears to derive from mere faith. 18.30

niyat'|ârjana|rakṣaṇ'|ādi|duḥkhe
  vadha|bandha|vyasan'|âika|lakṣya|bhūte
nṛ|pater api yatra n' âsti tṛptir,
  vibhavais toya|nidher iv' âmbu|varṣaiḥ, [17]

sukham atra kutaḥ kathaṃ kadā vā
  parikalpa|praṇayaṃ na ced upaiti
viṣay'|ôpaniṣevane† 'pi mohād
  vraṇa|kaṇḍūyana|vat sukh'|âbhimānaḥ? [18]

bāhulyena ca khalu bravīmi:

prāyaḥ samṛddhyā madam eti gehe,
  mānaṃ kulen' âpi, balena darpam,
duḥkhena roṣaṃ, vyasanena dainyaṃ.
  tasmin kadā syāt praśam'|âvakāśaḥ? [19]

18.35 ataś ca khalv atra|bhavantam† anunayāmi:

mada|māna|moha|bhujag'|ôpalayaṃ
  praśam'|âbhirāma|sukha|vipralayam
ka iv' āśrayed abhimukhaṃ vilayaṃ
  bahu|tīvra|duḥkha|nilayaṃ nilayam? [20]

saṃtuṣṭa|jana|gehe tu pravivikta|sukhe vane
prasīdati yathā c' êtas, tri|dive 'pi tathā kutaḥ? [21]

With its constant toil of acquiring and protecting
wealth,
it is a prime target for murder, captivity,
and misfortune.
Even a king is never satisfied by riches,
just as the ocean is never sated with showers of rain.

Why, how, or when is there any happiness
in this world
for someone who has no desire for wisdom,
ignorantly believing happiness lies in pursuing desire,
like a person scratching a wound to make it heal?

In general I would say the following:

In the household life, people are arrogant if rich,
proud if from a noble family, and insolent if strong.
Suffering brings anger and misfortune brings sorrow.
When is there a chance for tranquility in such a life?

That is why I would persuade you of the following, good sir: 18.35

Inhabited by the snakes of arrogance, pride,
and delusion,
a house destroys the delightful joys of tranquility.
Who then would set up home in this source of ruin,
this abode of numerous bitter sufferings?

But one can acquire serenity
in the joyful solitude of the forest,
where people live content.
Can one find this elsewhere, even in heaven?

para|prasād'|ârjita|vṛttir apy ato
rame van'|ânteṣu ku|cela|saṃvṛtaḥ.
a|dharma|miśraṃ tu sukhaṃ na kāmaye
viṣeṇa saṃpṛktam iv' ânnam ātmavān.» [22]

ity avagamita|matiḥ sa tena pitṛ|vayasyo hṛdaya|grāhakeṇa vacasā bahu|mānam eva tasmin Mahā|sattve sat|kāra|prayoga|viśeṣeṇa pravedayām āsa.

18.40 tad evaṃ, śīla|praśama|pratipakṣa|saṃbādhaṃ gārhasthyam, ity evam ātma|kāmāḥ parityajant' îti.

«labdh'|āsvādāḥ praviveke na kāmeṣv āvartanta» iti praviveka|guṇa|kathāyām apy upaneyam.

Though I live off the grace of others,
I delight in the forests, clothed in rags.
I have no desire for pleasures mixed with vice,
just as a self-possessed man avoids food smeared
with poison."

Convinced by these persuasive words, the friend of the Bodhi·sattva's father expressed his great respect for the Great Being through special acts of honor.

So it is that the household life teems with qualities that conflict with virtue and serenity. That is why spiritual seekers take no delight in it. 18.40

One should also narrate this story when discussing the virtues of solitude, saying: "Those who have tasted solitude never return to sensual desires."

STORY 19

THE BIRTH-STORY ON THE LOTUS-STALKS

19.1 PRAVIVEKA|SUKHA|RASA|jñānāṃ viḍamban" êva vihiṃs" êva ca kāmāḥ pratikūlā bhavanti.

tad|yath" ânuśrūyate.

Bodhisattvaḥ kila kasmiṃś cin mahati guṇa | prakāśa | yaśasi vācya|doṣa|virahite brāhmaṇa|kule janma|parigrahaṃ cakāra. tasya† kanīyāṃsaḥ ṣaḍ apare bhrātaras tad|anurūpa| guṇāḥ sneha|bahu|māna|guṇān nity'|ânuguṇā babhūvuḥ, saptamī ca bhaginī.

sa kṛta|śramaḥ s'|âṅgeṣu s'|Ôpavedeṣu Vedeṣu samadhigata|vidvad|yaśāḥ† saṃmato jagati daivatavan mātā|pitarau parayā bhaktyā paricarann ācārya iva pit" êva ca tān† bhrātṝn vidyāsu vinayan naya|vinaya|kuśalo gṛham āvasati sma.

19.5 sa kāla|kramān mātā|pitroḥ kāla|kriyayā saṃvigna|hṛdayaḥ kṛtvā tayoḥ preta|kṛtyāni vyatīteṣu śoka|mayeṣv iva keṣu cid eva divaseṣu tān bhrātṝn saṃnipāty' ôvāca:

«eṣa lokasya niyataḥ śok'|âdi|vi|rasaḥ† kramaḥ,
saha sthitv" âpi su|ciraṃ mṛtyunā yad viyojyate. [1]

tat pravrajitum icchāmi śreyaḥ ślāghyena vartmanā
purā mṛtyu|ripur hanti gṛha|saṃraktam eva mām. [2]

FOR THOSE WHO HAVE tasted the pleasure of solitude, desires are as much an anathema as forgery or violence. 19.1
Tradition has handed down the following story.

The Bodhi·sattva is said to have once taken his birth in a great brahmin family that was renowned for its virtue and free from reprehensible flaws. He had six younger brothers, whose qualities reflected his own and who always emulated him out of affection and respect. He also had a seventh sibling, a sister.

After he had applied himself to the Vedas, the Vedángas, and the Upavédas,* he became famed among the wise and esteemed in the world. Tending to his parents with the greatest devotion as if they were deities, and training his brothers in the sciences as if he were their teacher or father, he lived as a householder, accomplished in morality and decency.

After a period of time, however, the Bodhi·sattva's parents died. This so shocked his heart that after he had performed the *preta* rites* for his parents and spent several days almost replete with mourning, he gathered his brothers together and said: 19.5

"It is the established order of the world,
distasteful with sorrow and other woes,
that death separates us even from those
with whom we have lived a long time.

Before hostile Death slays me
while still enamored with household life,
I wish to set out as an ascetic
on the glorious path to bliss.

yataḥ sarvān eva bhavataḥ saṃbodhayāmi: asty atra brāhmaṇa|kule dharmeṇa yath" âdhigatā vibhava|mātrā śakyam anayā vartitum. tat sarvair eva bhavadbhiḥ paras | para | sneha† | gaurav' | âbhimukhaiḥ śīla | śauc' | ācāreṣv† a | śithil' | ādarair Ved' | âdhyayana | tat | parair† mitr' | âtithi | svajana | praṇaya|vatsalair dharma|parāyaṇair bhūtvā samyag gṛham adhyāvasitavyam.†

vinaya|ślāghibhir nityaṃ
sv'|âdhyāy'|âdhyayan'|ôdyataiḥ
pradān'|âbhirataiḥ samyak
paripālyo gṛh'|āśramaḥ [3]

19.10 evaṃ hi vaḥ syād yaśasaḥ samṛddhir
dharmasya c' ârthasya sukh'|āspadasya,
sukh'|âvagāhaś ca paro 'pi lokas.
tad a|pramattā gṛham āvaseta.» [4]

ath' âsya bhrātaraḥ pravrajyā|saṃkīrtanād viyoga|śaṅkā†| vyathita | manasaḥ śok' | âśru | dur | dina | mukhāḥ praṇamy' âinam ūcuḥ:

«n' ârhaty atra | bhavān pitṛ | viyoga | śoka | śalya | vraṇam a | saṃrūḍham eva no ghaṭṭayitum apareṇa duḥkh'|âbhinipāta| kṣāreṇa.

ady' âpi tāvat pitṛ|śoka|śalya|
kṣatāni rohanti na no manāṃsi.
tat sādhv imāṃ saṃhara, dhīra, buddhiṃ.
mā naḥ kṣate kṣāram ih' ôpahārṣīḥ. [5]

For this reason let me inform all of you that there is enough wealth in this brahmin family for you to support yourselves, all of it honestly acquired. You should all follow the household life properly, treating each other with affection and respect, never slackening your concern for virtue and purity, assiduous in your study of the Vedas, kind to the wishes of friends, guests, and relatives, and dedicated to righteousness.

Ever proud of your discipline,
intent on reciting and studying the Vedas,
you should take delight in giving
and properly guard the householder state.*

You'll thus gain the riches of fame, virtue, 19.10
and profit, the very basis of happiness,
and the next world will be like plunging into joy.
So practice the household life diligently."

But when they heard him speak of asceticism, the Bodhisattva's brothers were alarmed at the prospect of being parted from him. Prostrating themselves before him, they addressed him with the following words, their faces wretched with tears of sorrow:

"Our parents' departure is a barb of sorrow, creating a wound that has far from healed. Do not add salt to it by afflicting us with further pain.

Our hearts still have not recovered from the wound
caused by the barb-like sorrow of our parents' death.
Please retract your decision, wise brother.
Do not add salt to our wound.

ath' â|kṣamam vetsi gṛh'|ânurāgaṃ
śreyaḥ|pathaṃ vā vana|vāsa|saukhyam,
asmān a|nāthān apahāya gehe
kasmād vanaṃ vāñchasi gantum ekaḥ? [6]

19.15 tad y" âtra bhavato gatiḥ s" âsmākam. vayam api pravrajāma iti.»

Bodhisattva uvāca:

«an|abhyāsād vivekasya kāma|rāg'|ânuvartinaḥ
prapātam iva manyante pravrajyāṃ prāyaśo janāḥ. [7]

iti mayā nigṛhya n' âbhihitāḥ stha pravrajy"|āśrayaṃ prati, jānat" âpi gṛha|vana|vāsa|viśeṣam. tad etac ced abhirucitaṃ bhavatāṃ, sarve† pravrajāma iti.»

te sapt' âpi bhrātaro bhaginy|aṣṭamāḥ sphītaṃ gṛha|vibhava|sāram aśru|mukhaṃ ca mitra|svajana|bandhu|vargaṃ vihāya tāpasa|pravrajyayā pravrajitāḥ. tad|anurakta|hṛdayāś† c' âinān sahāya eko dāsī dāsaś c' ânupravrajitāḥ.

19.20 te 'nyatamasmin† mahaty araṇy'|āyatane jvalitam iva vikasita|kamala|vana|śobhayā vihasad iva ca phulla|kumuda|vanair a|nibhṛta|madhu|kara|gaṇam a|mala|nīla|salilaṃ mahat saraḥ saṃniśritya pravivikta|manojñāsu cchayā|druma|samupagūḍhāsv a|saṃnikṛṣṭa|niviṣṭāsu† pṛthak pṛthak parṇa|śālāsu vrata|niyama|parā dhyān'|ânuyukta|manaso vijahruḥ.

If you feel that attachment to a house is wrong
and that the joy of forest life is the road to bliss,
why do you wish to go to the forest alone,
leaving us in our house without a protector?

We will follow the same path as you. We too will become ascetics." 19.15

To this the Bodhi·sattva replied:

"Unfamiliar with solitude,
led by desire and passion,
people tend to consider
asceticism a precipice.

That is why I stopped myself from suggesting to you the path of asceticism, even though I know the difference between the household and forest life. But if it appeals to you, let us all become ascetics."

The seven brothers, with their sister as an eighth, therefore left behind the affluent wealth and riches of their household, as well as their tearful friends, relatives, and kinsmen, and set out on the ascetic path. Out of affection for the brothers, a friend, a male slave, and a female slave also followed them into the ascetic life.

19.20 In a large tract of the wilderness, there was a huge lake of pure blue water, around which swarms of bees loudly buzzed. During the day the lake seemed to blaze radiantly with clusters of expanding lotuses, while at night it seemed to smile with multitudes of blooming water-lilies.* The brothers took up residence next to this lake, living in separate leaf huts that were positioned not too close to one another. Concealed under shady trees, the huts enjoyed an at-

pañcame pañcame divase Bodhisattva|samīpaṃ dharma|śravaṇ'|ârtham upajagmuḥ. sa c' âiṣāṃ dhyān'|ôpadeśa|pravṛttāṃ kām'|ādīnava|darśanīṃ saṃvejanīyāṃ praviveka|saṃtoṣa|varṇa|bahulāṃ kuhana|lapana|kausīdy'|ādi|doṣa|vigarhaṇīm upaśama|prasāda|paddhatiṃ tāṃ tāṃ dharmyāṃ kathāṃ cakāra.

sā c' âinān dāsī bahu|mān'|ânurāga|vaśa|gā† tath" âiva paricacāra. sā tasmāt saraso bisāny uddhṛtya mahatsu padminī|parṇeṣu śucau tīra|pradeśe samān vinyasya† bhāgān kāṣṭha|saṃghaṭṭana|śabdena kālaṃ nivedy' âpakrāmati sma. tatas teṣām ṛṣīṇāṃ kṛta|japa|homa|vidhīnāṃ yathā|vṛddham ek'|âiko 'bhigamya tato bisa|bhāgam ek'|âikaṃ yathā|kramam ādāya svasyāṃ svasyāṃ parṇa|śālāyāṃ vidhivat paribhujya dhyān'|âbhiyukta|matir vijahāra. ta evaṃ pravṛttā n' âiva paras|paraṃ dadṛśur anyatra dharma|śravaṇa|kālāt.

teṣām evaṃ|vidhena nir|avadyena śīla|vṛtta|samudācāreṇa pravivek'|âbhiratyā dhyāna|pravaṇa|mānasatayā ca sarvatra prasṛtaṃ yaśaḥ† samupaśrutya Śakro devānām indras tat|parīkṣā|nimittaṃ tatr' âbhijagāma. tac c' âiṣāṃ dhyān'|âbhimukhatvaṃ ku|kāryeṣv a|prasaṅgam an|utkaṇṭhaṃ praśam'|âbhirāmaṃ c' âvasthānam avekṣya sthiratara|guṇa|saṃbhāvanas tat|parīkṣ"|âvahita|manā† babhūva.

tractive solitude. Here they dwelled with minds focused on meditation, devoted to their vows and practices of restraint.

Every fifth day the brothers would visit the Bodhi·sattva to listen to his teachings. The Bodhi·sattva would preach various inspiring moral sermons that illustrated the path of calmness and serenity. Instructing them on meditation and revealing the perils of desire, he eulogized greatly on the contentment to be found in solitude and criticized vices such as hypocrisy, gossip, and indolence.

Moved by respect and devotion, the slave woman served the brothers as before. Pulling out lotus stalks from the lake, she would place them in equal portions on large lotus leaves on a clean area by the bank. After announcing that the food was ready by striking a piece of wood, she would then withdraw. On finishing their ritual recitations and oblations, each seer would, one by one and in order of age, successively approach the bank and take their individual portion of lotus stalks to eat in their own leaf hut in the prescribed manner. They then resumed their focus on meditation. The ascetics thus conducted themselves so that they never saw each other except when it was time to hear the Bodhi·sattva's teachings.

Their irreproachable moral conduct, delight in solitude, and commitment to meditation meant that the ascetics' fame spread in every direction. And when Shakra, the king of the gods, came to hear of it, he visited the lake to test them. On seeing their commitment to meditation, their detachment from wicked deeds, their lack of desire, and their delight in tranquility, Shakra's respect for their virtue grew stronger and he set his heart on testing them. For,

an|utsuko van'|ânteṣu vasañ chama|parāyaṇaḥ
āropayati sādhūnāṃ guṇa|saṃbhāvanāṃ hṛdi. [8]

19.25 atha dvipa|kalabha|daśana|pāṇḍu|komalāni samuddhṛtya prakṣālya ca bisāni, marakata|harita|prabheṣu śuciṣu† padminī|patreṣu kamala|dala|keśa|ropa|hār'|âlaṃkṛtān viracayya samān bhāgān, kāṣṭha|saṃghaṭṭana|śabdena ca† nivedya kālaṃ teṣām ṛṣīṇām apasṛtāyāṃ tasyāṃ dāsyāṃ Bodhisattva|parīkṣ"|ârthaṃ Śakro devānām indraḥ prathamam eva bisa|bhāgam antardhāpayām āsa.

pravartane hi duḥkhasya
tiras|kāre sukhasya ca
dhairya|prayāmaḥ sādhūnāṃ
visphurann iva gṛhyate. [9]

atha Bodhisattvo 'bhigataḥ prathame bisa|bhāga|sthāne bisa|virahitaṃ† padminī|patraṃ parivyākulī|kṛt'|ôpahāram abhisamīkṣya «gṛhītaḥ ken' âpi me bisa|pratyaṃśa» ity avadhṛta|matir apeta|cetaḥ|saṃkṣobha|saṃrambhas tata eva pratinivṛtya praviśya parṇa|śālāṃ† yath"|ôcitaṃ dhyāna|vidhim ārebhe. vaimanasya|parihār'|ârthaṃ c' êtareṣām ṛṣīṇāṃ tam arthaṃ na nivedayām āsa. itare tv asya bhrātaro

Those who live in the forest,
free from desire and intent on serenity,
generate respect for their virtue
in the hearts of the good.

One day the slave woman pulled up and washed some lotus stalks that were as white and tender as the teeth of a young elephant. She arranged them in equal portions on clean lotus leaves that glistened like green emeralds, decorating them with a sprinkling of lotus petals and filaments. After announcing to the seers that it was time to eat by striking the piece of wood, she then withdrew. It was at this point that Shakra, the king of the gods, made the first portion of lotus stalks disappear in order to test the Bodhi·sattva. 19.25

When difficulties arise
and comforts disappear,
the extent of a good man's strength
practically bursts open to be grasped.

When the Bodhi·sattva approached the place where the first portion of lotus stalks had been put, he noticed that there were no lotus stalks on the leaf and that its decoration had been disturbed. Although he was aware that someone had taken his portion of food, he felt no mental agitation or anger but instead turned around and entered his leaf hut, resuming his meditation practice as usual. To avoid upset, he also did not inform the other seers of the matter. The Bodhi·sattva's brothers assumed that he must have taken his share and so, in due succession, they collected their portions

«nūnam anena gṛhītaḥ pratyaṃśa» iti manyamānā yath"|ôcitān eva svān svān anukrameṇa bisa|bhāgān ādāya yathā|svaṃ parṇa|śālāsu paribhujya dhyāyanti sma.

evaṃ dvitīye tṛtīye caturthe pañcame 'pi ca† divase Śakras tasya taṃ bisa|pratyaṃśam apanidadhe.† Bodhisattvo 'pi ca Mahā|sattvas tath" âiva niḥ|saṃkṣobha|praśānta|citto babhūva.

manaḥ|saṃkṣobha ev' êṣṭo
  mṛtyur n' āyuḥ|kṣayaḥ satām.
jīvit'|ârthe 'pi n' āyānti
  manaḥ|kṣobhamato budhāḥ. [10]

19.30 ath' âpar'|âhṇa|samaye dharma|śravaṇ'|ârtham ṛṣayas te yath"|ôcitaṃ Bodhisattvasya parṇa|śālām abhigatā† dadṛśur enaṃ† kṛśatara|śarīraṃ parikṣāma|kapola|nayanaṃ pari-mlāna|vadana|śobham a|saṃpūrṇa|svara|gāmbhīryaṃ pari-kṣīṇam apy a|parikṣīṇa|dhairya|praśama|guṇam abhinav'|êndu|priya|darśanam, upety' ôpacāra|puraḥsaraṃ sa|saṃ-bhramāḥ «kim idam?» iti kārśya|nimittam enam apṛcchan. tebhyo Bodhisattvas tam arthaṃ yathā|bhūtaṃ† nivedayām āsa. atha te tāpasāḥ paras|param īdṛśam an|ācāram a|saṃbhāvayamānās† tat|pīḍayā ca samupajāta|saṃvegāḥ «kaṣṭaṃ! kaṣṭam!» ity uktvā vrīḍ"|âvanata|vadanāḥ samati-ṣṭhanta. Śakra|prabhāvāc ca samāvṛta|jñāna|gati|viṣayāḥ «kuta idam?» iti na niścayam upajagmuḥ.

atha Bodhisattvasy' ânujo bhrātā svam āvegam ātma|viśuddhiṃ ca pradarśayañ chapath'|âtiśayam imaṃ cakāra:

in the usual manner and ate them in their separate leaf huts, whereupon they too resumed their meditation.

For a second, third, fourth, and even fifth day Shakra again hid the Bodhi·sattva's portion of lotus stalks. But the Bodhi·sattva remained as calm and unagitated as before.

It is mental agitation, not the end of life,
that the virtuous deem as death.
The wise are thus never agitated
even when it concerns their life.

In the afternoon of the fifth day, when the seers had gathered as usual at the Bodhi·sattva's leaf hut to listen to his teachings, they saw that his body was thinner, that his eyes and cheeks were hollow from emaciation, that the glow of his complexion had faded, and that his voice had lost its deep resonance. But despite being so weak, his fortitude, calmness, and virtue still remained undiminished and he looked as charming as a new moon. Approaching the Bodhi·sattva with courtesy, they anxiously asked him why he had become so frail. When the Bodhi·sattva told them exactly what had happened, the ascetics could not imagine such misconduct of one another and they were so alarmed at the Bodhi·sattva's pain that they stood there, bowing their heads with shame and exclaiming: "Oh dear! Oh dear!" For Shakra had used his power to obstruct the ascetics' means of reasoning, making them unable to conclude how this event had occurred. 19.30

To reveal his sense of alarm, as well as his moral purity, the brother who was immediately junior to the Bodhi·sattva then uttered this extraordinary curse:

«samṛddhi|cihn'|ābharaṇaṃ sa gehaṃ
prāpnotu bhāryāṃ ca mano|'bhirāmām
samagratām etu ca putra|pautrair,
bisāni te, brāhmaṇa, yo hy ahārṣīt! [11]

apara uvāca:

«mālāḥ srajaś candanam aṃśukāni
bibhrad vibhūṣāś ca sut'|âbhimṛṣṭāḥ
kāmeṣu tīvrāṃ sa karotv apekṣāṃ,
bisāny ahārṣīd, dvi|ja|mukhya, yas te!» [12]

19.35 apara uvāca:

«kṛṣy'|āśray'|âvāpta|dhanaḥ kuṭumbī
pramodamānas tanaya|pralāpaiḥ
vayo 'py a|paśyan ramatāṃ sa gehe,
bisāni yas te sakṛd apy ahārṣīt!» [13]

apara uvāca:

«nar'|âdhipair bhṛtya|vinīta|ceṣṭair
abhyarcyamāno nata|lola|cūḍaiḥ
kṛtsnāṃ mahīṃ pātu sa rāja|vṛttyā,
lobhād ahārṣīt tava yo bisāni!» [14]

apara uvāca:

19.40 «purohitaḥ so 'stu nar'|âdhipasya
mantr'|ādinā svasty|ayanena yuktaḥ
sat|kāram āpnotu tathā ca rājñas,
tav' âpi yo nāma bisāny ahārṣīt!» [15]

"May whoever took your lotus stalks, brahmin,
obtain a house adorned by marks of wealth
and a wife who delights the heart.
May sons and grandchildren perfect him!"*

The next brother then said:

"May whoever took your lotus stalks,
eminent brahmin,
wear wreaths, garlands, sandal powder, clothes,
and ornaments caressed by his children,
and may he have an ardent regard for desires!"

The next brother then said: 19.35

"May whoever took your lotus stalks, even if just once,
become a householder earning money from plowing,
who revels in the chatter of his children,
delighting in his house without regard for age!"

The next brother then said:

"May whoever greedily took your lotus stalks
protect the entire earth with his royal sway,
honored by kings bowing their trembling heads
and acting with the humility of servants!"

The next brother then said:

"May whoever took your lotus stalks 19.40
become the high priest of a monarch
and acquire the honor of his king,
furnished with mantras and other charms!"

apara uvāca:

«adhyāpakaṃ samyag|adhīta|vedaṃ
tapasvi|saṃbhāvanayā mahatyā
arcantu taṃ jānapadāḥ sametya,
biseṣu lubdho na guṇeṣu yas te!» [16]

sahāya uvāca:

«catuḥ|śataṃ grāma|varaṃ samṛddhaṃ
labdhvā nar'|êndrād upayātu bhoktum
a|vīta|rāgo maraṇaṃ sa c' âitu,
lobhaṃ biseṣv apy ajayan na yas te!» [17]

19.45 dāsa uvāca:

«sa grāma|ṇīr astu sahāya|madhye
strī|nṛtta|gītair upalāpyamānaḥ,
mā rājataś ca vyasanāni labdhā,†
bis'|ârtham ātm'|ârtham aśīśamad yaḥ!» [18]

bhaginy uvāca:

«vidyotamānāṃ vapuṣā śriyā ca
patnītvam ānīya nar'|âdhipas tām
yoṣit|sahasr'|âgra|carīṃ† karotu,
yā† tvad|vidhasy' âpi bisāny ahārṣīt!» [19]

dāsy uvāca:

19.50 «ekākinī sā samatītya sādhūn
svād'|ûpabhoge praṇayaṃ karotu
sat|kāra|labdhā mudam† udvahantī,
bisāny apaśyat tava yā na dharmam!» [20]

The next brother then said:

"Whoever coveted your stalks and not your virtues,
may they become a teacher expert in the Vedas,
honored by crowds of gathered people
esteeming him greatly for his austerities!"

The friend then said:

"Whoever could not quell their greed for your stalks,
may they obtain from a king
four hundred fine and wealthy villages to enjoy.*
And may they die without destroying their passions!"

The slave then said: 19.45

"May whoever crushed his welfare for these lotus stalks
become the head of a village surrounded by friends,
charmed by the songs and dances of women,
never suffering misfortune from kings!"

The sister then said:

"Whoever took the lotus stalks of one such as you,
may she become wedded to a king,
glistening with beauty and glory,
the first among a thousand other women!"

The slave girl then said:

"Whoever had eyes for your lotus stalks and not virtue, 19.50
may she delight in enjoying sweets by herself,
without concern for the good,
taking joy in the honor she acquires!"

atha tatra dharma|śravaṇ'|ârtham āgatās† tad|van'|âdhyuṣitā yakṣa|dvirada|vānarās tāṃ kathām upaśrutya parāṃ vrīḍāṃ saṃvegaṃ c' ôpajagmuḥ. atha yakṣa ātma|viśuddhi| pradarśan'|ârtham iti śapatham eṣāṃ purataś cakāra:

«āvāsikaḥ so 'stu Mahāvihāre
  Kacaṅgalāyāṃ nava|karmikaś ca;
āloka|saṃdhiṃ divasaiḥ karotu
  yas tvayy api praskhalito bis'|ârtham!» [21]

hasty uvāca:

«ṣaḍbhir dṛḍhaiḥ pāśa|śataiḥ sa bandhaṃ
  prāpnotu ramyāc ca vanāj jan'|ântam
tīkṣṇ'|âṅkuś'|ākarṣaṇa|jā rujaś ca,
  yas te muni|śreṣṭha bisāny ahārṣīt!» [22]

19.55 vānara uvāca:

«sa puṣpa|mālī trapu|ghṛṣṭa|kaṇṭho
  yaṣṭyā hataḥ sarpa|mukhaṃ paraitu
vaikakṣya|baddhaś ca vased gṛheṣu,
  laulyād ahārṣīt tava yo bisāni!» [23]

atha Bodhisattvas tān sarvān ev' ânunaya|vinīt'|âkṣaraṃ kṣānti†|gāmbhīrya|sūcakam ity uvāca:

«yo naṣṭam ity āha na c' âsya naṣṭam,
  iṣṭān sa kāmān adhigamya kāmam
upaitu geh'|āśrita eva mṛtyuṃ,
  bhavatsu yaḥ śaṅkata īdṛśaṃ vā!» [24]

At that time, a *yaksha*, an elephant, and a monkey, who dwelled in the forest and who had gathered to listen to the Bodhi·sattva's teachings, heard the above discussion and were filled with great shame and alarm. To reveal his purity, the *yaksha* then uttered this curse in front of the others:

"Whoever wronged you for lotus stalks,
may they live as a renovator
in the Great Monastery at Kachángala,
constructing a window every day!"*

The elephant then said:

"Whoever took your lotus stalks, eminent sage,
may they leave the forest for the realm of men,
tied up by six hundred tight snares,
pained by the sharp goads of their driver!'

The monkey then said: 19.55

"May whoever greedily took your lotus stalks
dance before the face of a snake, struck by a stick,
garlanded with flowers, a tin collar rubbing his neck!
May he live in a house cloaked in a jacket!'

The Bodhi·sattva then addressed all of them with courteous and polite words that indicated the depth of his forbearance:

"Whoever says he does not have it when he does,
may he obtain whatever desires he wishes
and die in the state of a householder.
And may whoever suspects you obtain the same!"

atha Śakro dev'|êndras tena teṣāṃ kām'|ôpabhoga|prāti-kūlya | sūcakena śapath' | âtiśayena samutpādita | vismaya | bahu | mānaḥ sven' âiva vapuṣ" âbhijvalatā tān ṛṣīn abhigamya sāmarṣavad uvāca:

19.60 «mā tāvad bhoḥ!

yat|prāpti|paryutsuka|mānasānāṃ
sukh'|ârthināṃ n' âiti manāṃsi nidrā,
yān prāptum icchanti tapaḥ|śramaiś ca,
tān kena kāmān iti kutsayadhve?» [25]

Bodhisattva uvāca: «an|ant'|ādīnavā, mārṣa, kāmāḥ. saṃkṣepatas tu śrūyatāṃ yad abhisamīkṣya kāmān na praśaṃsanti munayaḥ:

kāmeṣu bandham upayāti vadhaṃ ca lokaḥ
śokaṃ klamaṃ bhayam an|eka|vidhaṃ ca duḥkham.
kām'|ârtham eva ca mahī|patayaḥ patanti
dharm'|ôpamarda|rabhasā narakaṃ paratra. [26]

yat sauhṛdāni sahasā virasī|bhavanti,
yan nīti|śāṭhya|malinena pathā prayānti,
kīrtyā viyogam a|sukhaiḥ parataś ca yogaṃ
yat prāpnuvanti, nanu kāraṇam atra kāmāḥ. [27]

19.65 iti hīna|vimadhyam'|ôttamānām
iha c' âmutra ca yad vadhāya kāmāḥ,
kupitān bhuja|gān iv' âtma|kāmā
munayas tān iti, Śakra, n' āśrayante.» [28]

Shakra, the king of the gods, was filled with wonder and respect at the ascetics' extraordinary curses that demonstrated how averse they were to sensual enjoyment. Assuming his true form, which blazed with beauty, he addressed the seers with feigned fury:

"Don't say such things! 19.60

Men are so keen to acquire these objects
that they cannot sleep in their longing for pleasure.
People seek these objects through hardship and toil.
Why then do you scorn them as desires?"

"Desires bring endless misery, good sir," the Bodhi·sattva replied. "Let me summarize for you why sages do not praise desires:

It is for desires that people suffer bondage, death,
grief, fatigue, fear, and numerous anguishes.
It is for desire that kings fall into hell in the next life
for their violent abuse of morality.

When friendships suddenly turn unsavory,
and men follow the tainted path of deceitful politics,
and people lose fame but suffer in the next world,
surely desires are the cause.

In this world and the next, desires lead to the ruin 19.65
of all people, whether low, middle, or high.
That is why sages avoid them, seeking the spirit
instead,
just as one avoids furious snakes, Shakra."

atha Śakro devānām indras tasya tad vacanaṃ yuktam ity abhinandya tena c' âiṣām† ṛṣīṇāṃ māhātmyena prasādita|manās† tebhyaḥ svam aparādham āviś|cakāra:

«guṇa|saṃbhāvanā|vyaktir
  yat parīkṣy" ôpalakṣyate,†
may" âpanihitāny† asmāt
  parīkṣ"|ârthaṃ bisāni vaḥ [29]

tat sa|nāthaṃ jagad diṣṭyā munibhis tathya|kīrtibhiḥ!
viśuddha|sthira|cāritra,† tad etāni bisāni te!» [30]

ity uktvā tāni bisāni Bodhisattvasya samupajahāra. atha Bodhisattvas tad asy' â|samudācāra|dhārṣṭyaṃ tejasvi|nibhṛtena vacasā pratyādideśa:

19.70 «na bāndhavā n' âiva vayaṃ sahāyā
  na te naṭā n' âpi viḍambakāḥ smaḥ.
kasminn avaṣṭabhya nu, deva|rāja,
  krīḍā|pathen' âivam ṛṣīn upaiṣi?» [31]

ity ukte Śakro dev'|êndraḥ sa|saṃbhram'|âpāsta|kuṇḍala|kirīṭo† vidyud|bhāsura|vadanaḥ sa|bahu|mānam abhipraṇamy' âinaṃ kṣamayām āsa:

ukta|prayojanam idaṃ cāpalaṃ mama, nir|mama,
pit" êv' ācārya iva ca kṣantum arhati tad bhavān. [32]

Pleased by the nobility of the seers, Shakra, the king of the gods, joyfully praised the propriety of the Bodhi·sattva's words and then revealed his own wrongdoing to the ascetics:

"Opinions on virtue are clarified
when revealed by testing.
I therefore hid your lotus stalks
in order to test you.

How fortunate that the world is protected
by sages of such truthful repute!
Your conduct is pure and constant.
Here then are your lotus stalks!"

Saying this, Shakra gave the Bodhi·sattva the lotus stalks. But the Bodhi·sattva criticized Shakra for his unseemly and audacious behavior with powerful but calm words:

"We are not your kinsmen or friends. 19.70
Nor are we your actors or clowns.
Why do you play this way
with seers, king among gods?"

Addressed this way, Shakra, the king of the gods, took off his crown and earrings, his face gleaming like lightning, and asked the Bodhi·sattva for forgiveness as he bowed respectfully and said:

"Selfless sage,
please act like a father or teacher
and forgive my irresponsible act,
done for the reasons I stated.

nimīlita|jñāna|vilocanānāṃ
sva|bhāva eva† skhalituṃ† same 'pi,
kṣamāṃ ca tatr' ātmavatāṃ prapattum.
ato 'py adaś cetasi mā sma kārṣīḥ.» [33]

iti kṣamayitvā Śakras tatr' âiv' ântar|dadhe.

19.75 tad evaṃ, praviveka|sukha|rasa|jñānāṃ viḍamban" êva vihiṃs" êva ca kāmāḥ pratikūlā bhavanti.

tad evaṃ† jātakaṃ Bhagavān vyākārṣīt:

«ahaṃ Śāradvatī|putro
Maudgalyāyana|Kāśyapau
Pūrṇ'|Âniruddhāv Ānanda—
ity āsur bhrātaras tadā. [34]

bhaginy Utpalavarṇ" āsīd,† dāsī Kubjottar" âbhavat,
Citro gṛha|patir dāso, yakṣaḥ Sātāgiris tadā. [35]

Pārileyo 'bhavan nāgo, Madhudāyī ca† vānaraḥ,
Kālodāyī ca Śakro 'bhūd. dhāryatām iti jātakam.» [36]

It is natural for those with eyes closed to wisdom
to stumble even when the ground is even,*
and to gain forgiveness for this from the spiritually
accomplished.
Do not then bear it in your heart."

After asking for forgiveness in this way, Shakra disappeared there and then.

So it is that, for those who have tasted the pleasure of solitude, desires are as much an anathema as forgery or violence. 19.75

*The Lord has explained this birth-story the following way:

"Myself, the son of Sharádvati,
Maudgalyáyana, Káshyapa,
Purna, Anirúddha, and Anánda
were the brothers at that time.*

The sister was Útpala·varna,
the slave girl was Kubjóttara,
Chitra the householder was the slave,
and the *yaksha* was Satágiri.*

Pariléya was the elephant,
Madhu·dayin was the monkey,
and Kalodáyin was Shakra.
Thus the birth-story should be remembered."*

STORY 20

THE BIRTH-STORY OF THE FINANCIER

20.1 A|BHŪTA|GUṆA|SAṂBHĀVANĀ pratoda|saṃcodan" êva bhavati sādhūnām, iti guṇa | saṃpādane prayatitavyam.

tad|yath" ânuśrūyate.

Bodhisattvaḥ kila śruta|kula|vinaya|mahān a|kṣudra|nipuṇa|matir a|viṣama|vyavahāra|ratir an|eka|śāstr'|âbhyāsād ālakṣita|vacana|sauṣṭhavaḥ karuṇ"|ânuvṛttyā samantato visyandamāna|dhana|samṛddhir mahā|pradānair mahā|dhanatvād gṛha|pati|ratna|saṃmato 'nyatamasya rājñaḥ śreṣṭhī babhūva.

sa prakṛty" âiva dharm'|ātmā śrut'|ādi|guṇa|bhūṣaṇaḥ
abhūt prāyeṇa lokasya bahu|mān'|âika|bhājanam. [1]

20.5 atha kadā cit tasmin Mahā|sattve rāja|kulam abhigate kena cid eva karaṇīyena tasya śvaśrūr duhitaram avalokayitum tad|gṛham abhijagāma. kṛt'|âbhyāgamana|sat|kārā ca saṃkathā|prastāv'|āgataṃ svāṃ duhitaraṃ Bodhisattva|bhāryāṃ rahasi kuśala|paripraśna|pūrvakaṃ paryapṛcchat:

«kaccit tvāṃ, tāta, bhartā n' âvamanyate? kaccid vā vetti paricaryā|guṇam? na vā duḥkha|śīlatayā prabādhata iti?»

sā vrīḍ"|âvanata|vadanā lajj"|â|pragalbhaṃ vacanaṃ† śanakair uvāca: «tādṛśo 'yaṃ† śīla|guṇa|samudācāreṇa, pravrajito 'pi dur|labha idānīṃ yādṛśa iti.»† atha sā tasyā mātā

When falsely judged to have virtue, the good are spurred on as if by a goad. For this reason one should strive to attain virtue. 20.1

Tradition has handed down the following story.

The Bodhi·sattva is said to have once been the financier of a king. Magnificent in his learning, lineage, and modesty, his mind was noble and clever. Delighting in fair business practices, he spoke with a notable elegance due to his dedicated study of numerous teachings. His compassion led him to pour out huge donations of abundant riches in every direction and his vast wealth made him renowned as a jewel among householders.

Righteous by nature,
adorned by virtues such as learning,
he was for many people
a singular vessel of respect.

One day, when the Great Being had gone to the king's 20.5
palace, his mother-in-law came to his house to see her daughter on some business. After she had been respectfully welcomed, they asked after each other's health and started to chat together, during which time the mother asked her daughter, the wife of the Bodhi·sattva, the following:

"I hope your husband does not treat you badly, my child? Does he know how to care for you? I hope he does not trouble you by being bad-tempered?"

Her face lowered with embarrassment, the daughter replied softly with bashful modesty: "It would be hard to find someone with such virtue and moral conduct, even if they were an ascetic." But the mother's hearing and aware-

jar"|ôpahata|śruti|smṛtitvāl lajjā|saṃkucit'|âkṣaratayā† tad|vacanam abhidhīyamānaṃ na samyag upadhārayām āsa. pravrajita|saṃkīrtanāt tu «pravrajito me jāmāt"» êti niścayam upajagāma. sā sa|svaram abhiruditā duhitaram† anuśocantī duḥkh'|āvega|vaśāt paridevana|parā babhūva:

«kīdṛśas tasya śīla|guṇa|samudācāro ya evam anuraktaṃ sva|janam apahāya pravrajitaḥ? kiṃ vā tasya pravrajyayā?

taruṇasya vapuṣmataḥ sataḥ
su|kumārasya sukh'|ôcit'|ātmanaḥ
kṣiti|p'|âbhimatasya tasya vai
vana|vāse praṇatā matiḥ kutaḥ?† [2]

20.10 sva|janād an|avāpya vipriyaṃ
jarayā c' ôpahṛtāṃ† virūpatām
katham eka|pade rujaṃ vinā
vibhav'|ôdgāri gṛhaṃ sa muktavān? [3]

vinay'|ābharaṇena dhīmatā
priya|dharmeṇa par'|ânukampinā
katham abhyupapannam īdṛśaṃ
sva|jane niṣkaruṇatva|cāpalam? [4]

śramaṇa|dvija|mitra|saṃśritān
sva|janaṃ dīna|janaṃ ca mānayan
śuci|śīla|dhanaḥ kim āpnuyāt
sa na† geheṣu, vane yad īpsati? [5]

ness were so impaired by old age that she did not understand her daughter's words properly because they were spoken so softly out of shyness. Instead, when she heard the word "ascetic," she concluded her son-in-law had become a renouncer. Weeping loudly with grief for her daughter and overwhelmed by a surge of anguish, she became rapt in lamentation:

"What kind of virtue and moral conduct does he have if he abandons his loving family and becomes an ascetic? What does he see in renunciation?

Young, handsome, and delicate,
he is accustomed to comfort,
a favorite of the king.
Why is he attracted to forest life?

He never suffered any wrong from his family, 20.10
nor the deformities inflicted by old age.
How could he leave his home in one stride,
painlessly vomiting away his wealth?

Adorned by courtesy, he was fond of virtue.
He was wise and compassionate to others.
How could he have committed
this cruel and reckless act against his family?

Rich in purity and virtue, why couldn't he attain
in his house what he seeks in the forest
by honoring ascetics, brahmins, friends,
dependents, relatives, and people in distress?

aparādha|vivarjitāṃ tyajann
  anukūlāṃ saha|dharma|cāriṇīm,
ati|dharma|paraḥ sa n' ēkṣate
  kim imaṃ dharma|patha|vyatikramam? [6]

dhig aho bata daiva|dur|nayād
  yadi bhaktaṃ janam evam ujjhatām
na ghṛṇā|patham eti mānasaṃ,
  yadi vā dharma|lavo 'pi sidhyati!» [7]

20.15 atha sā Bodhisattvasya patnī tena mātuḥ karuṇen' â|kṛtakena paridevitena pati|pravrajy"|âbhisaṃbaddhena† strī|svabhāvād vyathita|hṛdayā sa|saṃbhramā viṣāda|viklava|mukhī śoka|duḥkh'|âbhinipāta|saṃkṣobhād vismṛta|kathā|prastāva|saṃbandhā «pravrajito me bhart", êti mad|vyavasthāpan'|ârtham ambā gṛham idam abhigatā vipriya|śravaṇād» iti niścayam upetya sa|paridevitaṃ sa|svaraṃ rudatī moham upajagāma bālā.

tad upaśrutya gṛha|janaḥ parijana|vargaś ca śoka|duḥkh'|āvegād ākrandanaṃ cakāra. tac chrutvā prātiveśya|mitra|sva|jana|bandhu|vargaḥ saṃśrita|jano brāhmaṇa|gṛha|patayaś ca tasya gṛha|pater anurāga|vaśa|gāḥ† prāyaśaś ca paurās tad gṛham abhijagmuḥ.

prāyeṇa lokasya babhūva yasmāt
  tulya|kramo 'sau sukha|duḥkha|yoge,
ato 'sya loko 'py anuśikṣay" êva
  tulya|kramo 'bhūt sukha|duḥkha|yoge. [8]

He has abandoned his companion in virtue,
a devoted wife who is devoid of sin.
Can't he see that his extreme obsession with morality
violates the path of righteousness?

Alas! How terrible is the rule of fate
when men can attain even a snippet of merit
by abandoning their devoted family
without a thought for compassion!"

Her mother's pitiful and earnest lament at her son-in-law's renunciation made the heart of the Bodhi·sattva's wife tremble, as women are wont to do. Filled with anxiety, her face distraught with despair, she was so shaken by the impact of her grief and anguish that she forgot the context of their conversation and became convinced that her husband had become a renouncer and that her mother had come to her house to provide support after hearing the sad news. Weeping loudly with lamentation, the foolish young woman then fainted. 20.15

When they heard this, the family members and servants howled with grief and sorrow. And when this was heard, neighbors, friends, relatives, kinsmen, dependents, brahmins, householders, and the majority of the citizens all came to the house, driven by affection for the householder.

It was the financier's habit to take equal share
in the happiness and suffering of the people.
And so the people, as though under his tutelage,
took equal share in his happiness and suffering too.

atha Bodhisattvo rāja|kulāt sva|bhavana|samīpam upagataḥ s'|ākranda|śabdaṃ sva|bhavanam avetya mahataś ca jana|kāyasya saṃnipātaṃ svaṃ puruṣam anvādideśa, «jñāyatāṃ kim etad» iti. sa taṃ vṛttāntam upalabhya samupety' âsmai nivedayām āsa:

«utsṛjya bhavanaṃ sphītam āryaḥ pravrajitaḥ kila.
iti śrutvā kuto 'py eṣa snehād evaṃ|gato janaḥ.» [9]

20.20 atha sa Mahā|sattvaḥ prakṛtyā śuddh'|āśayaḥ pratyādiṣṭa iva tena vacasā samupajāta|vrīḍā|saṃvegaś cintām āpede:
«bhadrā bata mayi janasya saṃbhāvanā!

ślāghanīyām avāpy' âitāṃ
guṇa|saṃbhāvanāṃ janāt
gṛh'|âbhimukha eva syāṃ
yadi, kiṃ mama pauruṣam? [10]

syād doṣa|bhaktiḥ prathitā may" âivaṃ
guṇeṣv avajñā vi|rasā ca vṛttiḥ.
yāyām ataḥ sādhu|jane laghutvaṃ.
kiṃ jīvitaṃ syāc ca tathā|vidhasya? [11]

saṃbhāvanām asya janasya tasmāt
kriyā|guṇena pratipūjayāmi
a|sat|parikleśa|mayaṃ vimuñcaṃs
tapo|vana|prema|guṇena geham.» [12]

The Bodhi·sattva then arrived back home from the royal palace. When he noticed that his house was full of lamentation and saw the crowd of gathered people, he told his servant to find out what had happened. The servant learned the news and came back and informed him, saying:

“Rumor has it, noble sir, that you’ve left
your rich house to become an ascetic.
Their affection for you reduced the people
to this state when they heard the news.”

The Great Being was pure by nature and he felt almost rebuked by these words. Filled with shame and alarm, he had this thought: 20.20

“The people have such a fine opinion of me!

Would I not be a coward
to be attached to the household life
when the people have such
a high opinion of my virtue?

I would make myself renowned for devotion to evil,
for my disdain of virtue, and my distasteful behavior.
And good men would treat me with contempt.
What would life be for a man such as me?

Out of love for the ascetic groves,
I will give up my house and its evil hardships.
And by acting on the people’s opinion of me,
I will show them honor in return.”

20.25 iti viniścitya† sa Mah"|ātmā tata eva pratinivṛttya† rājñaḥ pratihārayām āsa: «śreṣṭhī punar draṣṭum icchati devam» iti. kṛt'|âbhyanujñaś ca praviśya yath"|ôpacāraṃ rāja|samīpam upajagāma. «kim idam?» iti ca rājñā paryanuyukto 'bravīt, «icchāmi pravrajitum, tad abhyanujñātum arhati māṃ deva» iti.

ath' âinaṃ sa rājā sa|saṃbhram'|āvegaḥ snehād ity uvāca:

«mayi sthite bandhu|suhṛd|viśiṣṭe
  tvaṃ kena duḥkhena vanaṃ prayāsi,
yan n' âpahartuṃ prabhutā mama syād
  dhanena nītyā bala|saṃpadā vā? [13]

artho dhanair yadi, gṛhāṇa dhanāni mattaḥ.
  pīḍā kutaś cid atha, tāṃ pratiṣedhayāmi.
māṃ yācamānam iti bandhu|janaṃ ca hitvā
  kiṃ vā tvam anyad abhivīkṣya vanaṃ prayāsi?» [14]

iti sa Mah"|ātmā sa|sneha|bahu|mānam abhihito rājñā s'|ânunayam enam uvāca:

20.30 «pīḍā kutas tvad|bhuja|saṃśritānāṃ,
  dhan'|ôday'|âvekṣaṇa|dīnatā vā?
ato na duḥkhena vanaṃ prayāmi.
  yam artham uddiśya tu, taṃ nibodha. [15]

dīkṣām upāśrita iti prathito 'smi, deva
  śok'|âśru|dur|dina|mukhena mahā|janena.
icchāmi tena vijaneṣu vaneṣu vastuṃ
  śraddheyatām upagato 'smi guṇ'|âbhipattau.» [16]

Making this resolution, the Great One turned back and had himself announced to the king, saying: "The financier wishes to see the king once more." When permission had been granted, he entered the palace and approached the king courteously. On being asked why he had returned, he said: "I wish to become a renouncer. Please give me your consent, Your Majesty." 20.25

Anxious and emotional, the king then replied with affection:

"What misfortune makes you leave for the forest,
when I, more special than a relative or friend, still live?
For there is nothing I cannot dispel,
whether by wealth, politics, or force.

If you need money, then take it from me.
If something is making you suffer, I will fend it off.
Or does another concern make you leave for the forest,
abandoning me and your relatives, despite my pleas?"

Addressed this way by the king with affection and respect, the Great One politely replied:

"How can people suffer if they lean on your arm? 20.30
How can they be distressed by fears about wealth?
No misfortune makes me leave for the forest.
Let me tell you the reason.

Distraught with tears of grief, the people have spread
the rumor I am initiated as an ascetic, divine king.
Since I am believed capable of such virtue,
I wish to live in the desolate forests."

rāj" ôvāca, «n' ârhati bhavāñ jana|pravāda|mātrakeṇ' âsmān parityaktum. na hi bhavad|vidhānāṃ jana|pravāda|saṃpādan'|âbhirādhyā guṇa|vibhūtis, tad|a|saṃpādana|virādhyā vā.

svecchā|vikalpa|grathitāś ca tās tā
nir|aṅkuśā loka|kathā bhramanti.
kurvīta yas tā hṛdaye 'pi tāvat, syāt
so 'pahāsyaḥ, kim uta prapattā.» [17]

Bodhisattva uvāca, «mā m" âivaṃ, mahā|rāja! na hi kalyāṇo jana|pravādo n' ânuvidheyaḥ. paśyatu devaḥ:

20.35 kalyāṇa|dharm" êti yadā, nar'|êndra,
saṃbhāvanām eti manuṣya|dharmā,
tasyā na hīyeta naraḥ sa|dharmā;
hriy" âpi tāvad dhuram udvahet tām. [18]

saṃbhāvanāyāṃ guṇa|bhāvanāyāṃ
saṃdṛśyamāno hi yathā tathā vā
viśeṣato bhāti yaśaḥ|prasiddhyā.
syāt tv anyathā śuṣka iv' ôda|pānaḥ. [19]

guṇa|pravādair a|yath"|ârtha|vṛddhair
vimarśa|pāt'|ākulitaiḥ patadbhiḥ
vicūrṇitā kīrti|tanur narāṇāṃ
duḥkhena śaknoti punaḥ prasartum. [20]

tad varjanīyān parivarjayantaṃ
parigrahān vigraha|hetu|bhūtān
krodh'|ôcchiraskān iva kṛṣṇa|sarpān
arho 'si† māṃ, deva, na saṃniṣeddhum. [21]

"But you do not have to abandon us merely because of some popular rumor," the king replied. "The rich virtues of men such as you are neither determined by acquiring popular opinion nor thwarted by not acquiring it.

Various rumors wander about unchecked,
cobbled together by willful fancy.
Those who take them to heart should be ridiculed,
let alone those who act upon them!"

"No, no, Your Majesty!" the Bodhi·sattva replied. "Popular opinion, when noble, should not be ignored. Let Your Majesty consider this.

When a person is believed 20.35
to be moral, Your Majesty,
they cannot, if virtuous, disappoint this opinion
but must bear it as a yoke, out of shame at least.

For if they are seen to cultivate
the same virtue they are esteemed to own,
they shine brightly with glorious fame.
If not, they resemble a dried up well.

Human reputation is like a body:
when crushed and pummeled by rumors of virtue
that are exaggerated by lies and confused by doubt,
it is difficult for it to move forward again.

You should therefore not stop me
from shunning my possessions, Your Majesty.
Like black snakes with heads raised in fury,
they are a cause of strife and need to be shunned.

snehena bhakti|jñatayā ca kāmaṃ
yukto vidhir bhṛtya|jane tav' âyam.
vittena tu pravrajitasya kiṃ me
parigraha|kleśa|parigraheṇa?» [22]

20.40 ity anunīya sa mah"|ātmā taṃ rājānaṃ kṛt'|âbhyanujñas tena tata eva tapo|vanāya† pratasthe. ath' âinaṃ suhṛdo jñātayaḥ saṃśritāś c' âbhigamya śok'|âśru|paripluta|nayanāḥ pādayoḥ saṃpariṣvajya nivārayitum īṣuḥ.† ke cid añjali|pragraha|puraḥsaraṃ mārgam asy' āvṛtya vyatiṣṭhanta.† sa|pariṣvaṅga|saṃgat'|ânunayam apare gṛh'|âbhimukham enaṃ netum īṣuḥ.† yat|kiñ|cana kārit'|ākṣepa|karkaś'|âkṣaram anye praṇayād enam ūcuḥ. mitra|sva|jan'|âpekṣā|kāruṇya|pradarśanam apare 'sya pracakruḥ. gṛh'|āśrama eva puṇyatama ity enam† anye śruti|yukti|saṃgrathitaṃ grāhayitum īhāṃ cakrire. tapo|vana|vāsa|duḥkhatā|saṃkīrtanaiḥ kārya|śeṣa|parisamāpti|yācñayā† para|loka|puṇya|phala†|saṃdeha|kathābhis tais taiś ca śruti|viśeṣair† nivartayitum enaṃ prāyatanta.†*

tasya tān pravrajy"|āśraya|vimukhān vana|gamana|nivāraṇa|dhīra|mukhān nayana|jal'|ārdra|mukhān unmukhān† suhṛdo 'bhivīkṣya «vyaktam!» iti cintā babhūva:

Though you would be right to show your servants
such affection and gratitude for their devotion,
what need do I, a renouncer, have for wealth,
when it involves the evil of owning possessions?"

Winning him over with these words, the financier received the king's permission and set out for the ascetic groves. His friends, relatives, and dependents, however, tried to turn him back by going up to him and embracing him, their eyes wet with tears. Some stood in front of him, blocking his path, their hands folded in respect. Some tried to lead him back to his home, using persuasion mixed with physical constraint. Driven by affection, some addressed him with harsh and abusive words. Some pointed out to him the importance of compassion and regard for friends and relatives. Some attempted to convince him that the householder state was the purest by stringing together arguments based on the Vedas and inference. Some strove to turn him around by referring to the hardships of ascetic life in the forest, or by requesting him to fulfill the rest of his social duties, or by raising doubts about rewards for merit in the next life, or through various other sophisticated arguments. 20.40

When the Bodhi·sattva saw how intently hostile his friends were against the renunciant life and how determined they were to stop him from entering the forest, their faces wet with tears, he had the following thought: "Of course!

«suhṛt|pratijñaiḥ suhṛdi pramatte
 nyāyyaṃ hitaṃ rūkṣam api prayoktum.
rūḍhaḥ satām eṣa hi dharma|mārgaḥ,
 prāg eva rucyaṃ ca hitaṃ ca yat syāt. [23]

vanād gṛhaṃ śreya, idaṃ tv amīṣāṃ
 sva|stheṣu citteṣu kathaṃ nu rūḍham,
yan nir|viśaṅkā vana|saṃśrāyān māṃ
 pāpa|prasaṅgād iva vārayanti? [24]

mṛto mariṣyann api vā manuṣyaś
 cyutaś ca dharmād iti roditavyaḥ.†
kayā nu buddhyā vana|vāsa|kāmaṃ
 mām eva jīvantam amī rudanti? [25]

20.45 mad|viprayogas tv atha śoka|hetur,
 mayā samaṃ kiṃ na vane vasanti?
gehāni cet kāntatarāṇi mattaḥ,
 ko nv ādaro bāṣpa|parivyayena? [26]

atha tv idānīṃ sva|jan'|ânurāgaḥ
 karoti n' âiṣāṃ tapase 'bhyanujñām,
sāmarthyam āsīt katham asya n' âivaṃ†
 vyūḍheṣv anīkeṣv api tatra tatra? [27]

dṛṣṭ'|âvadāno vyasan'|ôdayeṣu,
 bāṣp'|ôdgamān mūrta iv' ôpalabdhaḥ,
saṃrūḍha|mūlo 'pi suhṛt|svabhāvaḥ
 śāṭhyaṃ prayāty atra vin" ânuvṛttyā. [28]

When a friend is remiss, those sworn to be his friends
use fitting and beneficial words, however harsh.
This is the established path of virtue for the good,
how much more if the words are pleasant
and beneficial!

But they boldly restrain me from living in the forest,
as if stopping me from an attachment to evil.
They believe the house is better than the forest;
how can this opinion spring from sound minds?

A man should be mourned if he is dead,
or about to die, or has fallen from morality.
What manner of thinking makes these people weep
when I am alive, desiring simply to live in the forest?

If separation from me causes their sorrow, 20.45
why do they not live with me in the forest?
And if their houses delight them more than I,
why this concern with expending tears?

If family attachment
makes them scorn asceticism,
why are they incapable of this
when armies are drawn up on all sides for war?

I have witnessed their friendship during surges
of misfortune,
taking almost physical form in the welling
of their tears.
But though deeply rooted, their friendship is false
if they do not follow me into the forest.

nivāraṇ'|ârthāni sa|gadgadāni
vākyāni s'|âśrūṇi ca locanāni
praṇāma|lolāni śirāṃsi c' âiṣāṃ
mānaṃ sa|mānasya yathā karoti, [29]

snehas tath" âiv' ârhati kartum eṣāṃ
ślāghyām anupravrajane 'pi buddhim,
mā bhūn naṭānām iva vṛttam etad
vrīḍā|karaṃ saj|jana|mānasānām. [30]

20.50 dvi|trāṇi mitrāṇi bhavanty a|vaśyam
āpad|gatasy' âpi su|nir|guṇasya.
sahāya eko 'py ati|dur|labhas tu
guṇ'|ôditasy' âpi vana|prayāṇe. [31]

ye me haranti sma puraḥsaratvaṃ
raṇeṣu matta|dvipa|saṃkaṭeṣu,
n' ânuvrajanty adya vanāya te mām.
kiṃ svit sa ev' âsmi? ta eva c' ême? [32]

smarāmi n' âiṣāṃ viguṇaṃ prayātuṃ
snehasya yat saṃkṣaya|kāraṇaṃ syāt.
suhṛj|janaś c' âivam† ayaṃ sthito me†
kaccid bhavet svasti|nimittato 'smāt? [33]

mam' âiva vā nir|guṇa|bhāva eṣa,
n' ânuvrajanty adya vanāya yan mām?
guṇ'|âvabaddhāni hi mānasāni
kasy' âsti viśleṣayituṃ prabhutvam? [34]

If honor for an esteemed friend
drives them to try to stop me
with stuttering words, tear-filled eyes,
and heads bowed with respect,

then affection ought to produce in them
the noble decision to follow me into asceticism,
lest their behavior resembles actors,
embarrassing the minds of virtuous men.

Even a villain can certainly find 20.50
two or three friends when calamity strikes.
But for a man of great virtue, it is hard to find
even one companion to join him to leave for the forest.

The very men who seized the occasion to charge
    before me
on battlefields crowded with frenzied elephants,
do not follow me now into the forest.
Am I the same person? Are they the same people?

I do not recall committing a crime
that would destroy their affection.
Perhaps my friends are behaving this way
out of concern for my welfare?

Or does some fault of my own make them
unwilling to follow me today to the forest?
For who has the power to loosen
hearts bound by virtue?

ye vā prakāśān api geha|doṣān
  guṇān na paśyanti tapo|vane vā,
nimīlita|jñāna|vilocanāṃs tān
  kim anyath" âhaṃ pariśaṅkayāmi?† [35]

20.55 paratra c' âiv' êha ca duḥkha|hetūn
  kāmān vihātuṃ na samutsahante.
tapo|vanaṃ tad|viparītam ete
  tyajanti māṃ c' âdya! dhig astu moham! [36]

yair vipralabdhāḥ suhṛdo mam' âite
  na yānti śāntiṃ nikhilāś ca lokāḥ,
tapo|van'|ôpārjita|sat|prabhāvas
  tān eva doṣān prasabhaṃ nihanmi!» [37]

iti sa pariganayya niścit'|ātmā
  praṇaya|mayāni suhṛd|viceṣṭitāni
anunaya|madhur'|âkṣarair vacobhir
  viśadam apāsya tapo|vanaṃ jagāma. [38]

tad evam, a|bhūta|guṇa|saṃbhāvanā pratoda|saṃcodan" êva bhavati sādhūnām, iti guṇa|saṃpādane prayatitavyam. yato bhikṣur ity upāsaka iti vā guṇataḥ† saṃbhāvyamānena sādhunā tad|bhāva|sādhubhir guṇair abhyalaṃkartavya ev' ātmā. «evaṃ dur|labhā dharma|pratipatti|sahāyā» ity evam apy upaneyam.†

But why should I worry about these people?
Unable to see the blatant flaws of the household life
or the virtues of an ascetic life in the forest,
their eyes of wisdom remain closed.

Incapable of abandoning their desires, 20.55
the very cause of suffering in this world and the next,
they today discard the ascetic groves, the cure
for suffering,
and me as well! How terrible is delusion!

By attaining virtuous powers in the ascetic forests,
I will violently destroy the evils
that seduce my friends and the entire world
and that make them unable to acquire peace."

Considering the matter this way,
he plainly rejected his friends' pleading gestures
with polite and gentle words
and resolutely entered the ascetic forests.

So it is that, when falsely judged to have virtue, the good are spurred on as if by a goad. For this reason one should strive to attain virtue.

A good man who is deemed to possess the virtue of being a monk or a lay-disciple should therefore adorn himself with virtuous qualities suited to that role. One should also draw the following conclusion from this story: "In this way it is difficult to acquire friends for virtuous practice."

NOTES

Bold *references are to the English text;* ***bold italic*** *references are to the Sanskrit text. An asterisk (*) in the body of the text marks the word or passage being annotated.*

3 [2] The term used for **Buddha** is here Sugata, which literally means "in a good state."

4 [3] **Sacred tradition**: this refers to the *āgama*s, or *sūtra*s (discourses), of the Buddhist canon. **Buddha's words**: this refers to the Buddhist canon (*tri/piṭaka*), traditionally considered to be the original word of the Buddha (*Buddha/vacana*). I am grateful to MICHAEL HAHN for his comments on this verse.

5 [4] **This matchless being, the Teaching, and the Community**: the Buddha, the Dharma, and the Sangha are the Three Jewels (*tri/ratna*), in which all Buddhists take refuge. The Dharma represents the teachings of the Buddha and is often translated in this volume as Teaching. In various contexts, the word also signifies morality and the true nature of things. The Sangha is the community of monks and nuns.

1.6 **Lord**: a standard name for the Buddha, *Bhagavat* is notoriously difficult to translate. Literally meaning "he who has a share," the word is variously analyzed by Buddhist traditions but essentially refers to the sublime spiritual state that the Buddha has attained (or acquired a "share" of). The word *bhagavat* is also frequently found in non-Buddhist contexts to refer to God, as is illustrated by the famous Hindu text the *Bhagavadgītā* ("The Song of the Lord"). Due to its pan-Indic usage, I translate *Bhagavat* as "Lord" as a way of expressing the devotional connotations of the word, while at the same time avoiding doctrinally awkward translations such as "Blessed One."

1.7 **The Three Jewels**: the Buddha, the Dharma, and the Sangha.

1.7 It is impossible to convey in English how Arya·shura plays on different connotations of the word **guru** in this sentence. Literally meaning "heavy," *guru* also refers to something "serious" or "profound," and by extension commonly means "teacher."

1.8 **Bodhi·sattva**: ("Awakening Being") a person who has made a vow to practice the perfections (*pāramitā*) and become a fully awakened Buddha (*samyak/saṃbuddha*). See the introduction for more details.

1.8 **The extraordinary vow he had made**: the vow in question is the Bodhi·sattva's resolution to become a fully awakened Buddha and thereby save the world from samsara.

1.9 **The eighteen sciences**: the four Vedas, the six Vedángas, the Puránas, Mimánsa, Nyaya, Dharma, and the four Upavédas (see MONIER-WILLIAMS s.v.).

1.10 [5] **Brahman**: the absolute principle governing the universe in Brahmanical thought. To be distinguished from the deity Brahma.

1.10 [5] Said to have one thousand eyes, **Shakra** (*Śakra*) is the king of the gods in Trayas·trinsha, one of six heavens in the Sphere of Desire (*kāma/dhātu*). In Brahmanical and Hindu texts, he is usually given the name Indra, but whereas Indra's role diminished greatly in Hinduism after the period of the Vedas and the *Mahābhārata*, Shakra continued to remain important in Buddhism.

1.11 [5] This verse offers an example of Arya·shura's fondness for word-play: for example, the play on sounds in *Brahmavad Brahma/vidāṃ* and the play on the word *akṣa* ("eye") in *s'/âkṣāt sahasr'/âkṣa*.

1.19 **Great One**: Literally meaning "great-spirited" or "he whose self is great," *mah"/ātmā* (Mahatma) is a pan-Indic term of respect, frequently found in both Buddhist and non-Buddhist literature. In Hindu epic, it often simply means "hero" and the example of Mahatma Gandhi illustrates how the term is still used in the modern day to refer to a person of high spiritual status. In the "Garland of the Buddha's Past Lives," *Mah"/ātmā* is used interchangeably with *mahā/sattva* ("Great Being"). I follow KHOROCHE's translation of "Great One" for *Mah"/ātmā*.

1.27 [18] **Samsara**: the cycle of continuous rebirth and death.

1.36 [24] **Murderer**: an *ātatāyin* is literally an archer, "one who draws (a bow)."

1.40 [27] The personification of Death, **Mara** (*Māra*) is a demonic figure who strives to defeat the Buddha in order to preserve the desire-based world of samsara.

1.41 [28] **Supreme vehicle**: the path (literally "vehicle") to perfect Buddhahood practiced by Bodhi·sattvas, as opposed to the path to becoming an *arhat* or a *pratyéka·buddha*. A defining characteristic of Mahayana (*mahā/yāna*) Buddhism is its insistence on exclusively following the Bodhi·sattva path and rejecting the other two paths. It is, however, not necessary to conclude that such a sentiment is being expressed by the above verse. Rather, the verse may simply express the viewpoint, universally accepted in both non-Mahayana and Mahayana traditions, that the Bodhi·sattva path is superior to other paths, without implying that it is the sole path to be followed. See the introduction for a more detailed discussion of Arya·shura's doctrinal affiliations.

1.51 [35] The verse plays on two meanings of *tanu*: the one "body" and the other "slender."

1.56 [38] **Gandhárvas** are celestial musicians. **Yakshas** are a class of demon or semi-divine being.

1.56 [38] The verse plays on the literal meaning of *vasu/dhā*: "wealth-producer," a common phrase used for the earth.

1.58 **Teaching**: the Dharma of the Buddha.

2.3 The **king of the Shibis** is the protagonist in several Buddhist narratives (see also stories 9 and 13 in this collection). Such stories are often concerned with the virtue of giving.

2.5 [1] **Three pursuits**: Brahmanical thought extols three different pursuits in life: *kāma* (desire or pleasure), *artha* (benefit or profit), and *dharma* (morality or righteousness). A fourth pursuit of "liberation" (*mokṣa*) is sometimes added to the list.

2.8 **Krita Era**: the first of the four eras, described as a golden age.

2.13 [6] The verse plays on the double meaning of *mada* as "pride" and "ichor." A *gandha/dvipa* is a "scent-elephant," i.e. an elephant that produces strong-smelling ichor from being in rut.

2.18 **Suméru**, or Meru, is a mountain at the center of the cosmos.

2.32 [15] **Wrong and damaging**: The word *a/naya* often refers to actions that are imprudent or wrong in a practical as well as moral sense. Its positive form is *naya*, which often simply means "prudence" or "policy." Likewise, the word *a/hita* (translated above as "damaging") can refer to an action that is both immoral and unbeneficial. Its positive form is *hita* ("benefit").

2.61 **Courage**: the word *sattva* has various connotations, including "character," "goodness," and "courage." It can also mean "being." The compound *āścarya/sattvaś* can therefore mean someone who has astounding courage or integrity (taken as a *bahuvrīhi* compound), or simply "an astonishing being" (taken as a *karmadhāraya* compound). This ambiguity is also played on in 2.60 [31]: "What courage [*sattva*]! What desire to benefit living beings [*sattva*]!"

2.93 **Tatha·gata** is a common epithet of the Buddha. Buddhist traditions analyze the compound in various ways, depending on whether it is construed as *tathā/gata* ("thus-gone") or *tath"/āgata* ("thus-come"). At the end of a compound, *-gata* often simply means "is," resulting in the literal rendition of "is thus" for *tathā/gata*. The abstract nature of the phrase can be seen as an effective way of conveying the Buddha's transcendent state. I am grateful to Richard Gombrich for his comments on this word.

3.7 **Alarmed**: the experience of *saṃvega* involves a type of spiritual shock whereby one's ordinary conceptions are "shaken up" through gaining an insight into impermanence. In Buddhist narratives, *saṃvega* often provides the trigger for the protagonist to embark on a path of renunciation.

3.7 **Noble moral restraints**: the five precepts (*pañca/śīla*). These are: no killing, no stealing, no immoral sexual conduct, no lying, and no intoxication by alcohol. The *póshadha* vow is taken by Buddhist laymen on sacred days marked by the lunar calendar. It involves undertaking three further precepts in addition to the five listed above (with precept no. 3 also changing from no immoral sexual conduct to chastity): no eating after noon, no wearing of ornaments or perfumes or enjoyment of entertainment, and no lying on high or large beds.

3.19 [13] **Arhat**: a person who has overcome rebirth and become awakened by following the *śrāvaka* path.

3.28 [17] **Corruptions** (*āsrava*): a set of four vices—desire (*kāma*), becoming (*bhava*), ignorance (*a/vidyā*) and view (*dṛṣṭi*)—which *arhats* destroy to become awakened. See Edgerton (1953) s.v.

3.38 **Community of Nobles**: the Sangha, or community of monks and nuns.

4.7 **Great Being**: a translation of *mahā/sattva*. This important Buddhist term may originally have been appropriated from non-Buddhist sources such as Brahmanical epic literature, where it often means someone who has great purity, character, or courage, or simply a "hero." In the Brahmanical epics the compound is treated as a *bahuvrīhi* ("whose *sattva* is great"), whereas in Buddhist texts such as the "Garland of the Buddha's Past Lives" it tends to be treated as a *karmadhāraya* compound ("great being"), using the meaning of *sattva* as "being." I am grateful to RICHARD GOMBRICH for his insights on this matter.

4.7 **Pratyéka·buddha**: a person who has become awakened without access to the Buddha's teachings. See introduction.

4.7 **Defilements**: *kleśa*s are variously defined in Buddhism and are often linked with passion or desire.

4.12 **Maha·ráurava**: in *Mahāvastu* 1.23f., this hell is described as a place of burning iron. The same passage states that the name *raurava* derives from the fact that tortured hell-beings call after their parents in distress (from the verb *ru*, meaning "yell").

4.18 See HANISCH for the inclusion of the word *akṣara* in this compound.

5.3 **Kubéra**: the king of the *yaksha*s, known for his riches.

5.6 [3] **Goods**: the verse plays on the word *artha*, which, depending on the context, can have various connotations, including wealth, profit, benefit, success, or goal. I use SPEYER's opportune translation of "goods" to convey the notion that *artha* ("goods" in the sense of material benefit) is not *artha* ("goods" in the sense of moral benefit). The word-play is further heightened by the fact that the Sanskrit word for "beggar" is here *arthin*: a person who seeks *artha*.

5.7 [4] **There are three types of bad rebirth in Buddhism**: rebirth as a hell-being, as a ghost, or as an animal. The Sanskrit *dur|gati* literally means "a bad place to go," or "a bad destination," and therefore neatly fits the metaphor of traveling caravans.

6.37 **Virtuous heroes**: this is a startling example of *mahā|sattva* being used for characters other than the Bodhi·sattva. While it would be intriguing to consider whether the other three animals are also being viewed as Great Beings, it is more likely that the word is being used as a generic term for anyone that is virtuous or heroic, rather than specifically referring to a

Bodhi·sattva. As mentioned previously, *mahā/sattva* can be taken either as a *karmadhāraya* compound meaning "Great Being" or as a *bahuvrīhi* compound meaning "having great goodness" or "having great courage." The latter interpretation suits the general meaning that appears to be implied here.

6.58 ***tad***: this is a conjectural reading proposed by Kern and accepted by Hanisch. All Sanskrit manuscripts read *taṃ*. If one kept the reading *taṃ* ("him"), while the syntax would be slightly awkward, it would emphasize that Shakra's eyes are focused on the Bodhi·sattva's person.

6.59 **Rejoice**: *anumodana* ("rejoicing") is an important moral attitude in Buddhism, whereby one feels empathetic joy for the moral act of another person and for the merit they derive from that act.

6.65 [38] **Night lotuses**: *kumuda* lotuses are known for opening at night and closing during the day. The word *hāsana*, translated here as "opener," literally means "causing a smile." Indian poets often compare beautiful faces to lotuses. Here the metaphor is reversed so that the expanding lotus is compared to a face that smiles. **Ornament on the forehead**: a *tilaka* is an ornament used in the center of the forehead. It can sometimes signify a religious affiliation.

7.4 The **Vedas** are the most authoritative texts in Brahmanical thought, said to be direct hearings (*śruti*) of sacred truth. The four Vedas are: the *Ṛg Veda*, *Sāma Veda*, *Yajur Veda*, and *Atharva Veda*. Auxiliary subjects: the six Vedángas (*ved'/âṅgas*, literally "limbs of the Veda"). They are: phonetics (*śikṣā*), meter (*chandas*), grammar (*vyākaraṇa*), etymology (*nirukta*), astrology (*jyotiṣa*), and ritual (*kalpa*). See Monier-Williams s.v.

7.30 [13] **Káshyapa**: descended from, or connected to, the ascetic Kashyapa (Kaśyapa), one of the famous seven seers.

7.34 The Tibetan translation marks only one *sādhu*.

7.37 [17] **Vásava**: a name for Shakra, meaning "chief of the Vasus."

7.77 [39] **Dhyanas**: four levels of meditation, each increasing in subtlety and concentration. The immeasurables refer to the cultivation of four mental attitudes: loving kindness, compassion, joy, and equanimity (the *brahma/vihāras*).

7.79 ***lobha ... kathāyāṃ*** is omitted in the Tibetan translation.

8.3 **Maitri·bala**: the name means "powerful in friendliness."

8.5 [2] **Bowed heads**: literally the "top-knots of kings."

8.27 [11] **Golden Mountain**: Mount Meru.

8.102 [51] **Lord of Wealth**: Kubéra.

8.102 [51] **Indra**: another name for Shakra. **Brahma**: a deity living in a heavenly realm above Shakra in the Sphere of Pure Form (*rūpa/dhātu*).

8.117 [60] **Violence, etc**: these are the five precepts (*pañca/śīla*). See note to 3.7.

8.129 **The five monks were very helpful**: Pali *bahukārā kho me pañcavaggiyā bhikkhū ye maṃ padhānapahitattaṃ upaṭṭhahiṃsu*; *Vinaya* 1.8, *Majjhima Nikāya* 1.170. This refers to the Buddha's first teaching of the Dharma in the deer park in Varánasi. The Buddha recalls the five monks that helped him when he was an ascetic practicing severe austerities and high states of meditation prior to his awakening.

9.1 The Vishvan·tara story does not follow the normal convention of repeating the opening statement at the end of the tale. See also story 11 for a similar anomaly.

9.6 In other stories, we are immediately informed of the identity of the Bodhi·sattva. In this tale, however, the introductory passage on Sánjaya delays the identification of the Bodhi·sattva, thereby also postponing the mention of the "Lord," which usually occurs in the first sentence of the narrative (after *tad/yath" ânuśrūyate*) and before any verses have occurred.

The mention of the name Shakya·muni (Śākyamuni) is also unique; it is omitted in the Tibetan translation. See HANISCH.

9.11 **Hímavat**: the Himálaya mountains.

9.40 [18] **Three pursuits**: see note to 2.5.

9.42 [20] **Siddha**: a semi-divine being.

9.61 [26] The section from ***api ca Śibayas*** to the end of verse 26 is found only in some sources. See HANISCH for details.

9.70 [29] The wealth that follows a person after death is their merit, seen here as a reward for "depositing" material wealth by giving it to virtuous people.

9.94 [44] **Twice-born**: a person who has had a second birth by being invested with the sacred thread at the *upanayana* ceremony. Although all of the first three of the four classes in Brahmanism undergo this ceremony (brahmins, kshatriyas, and vaishyas), the term "twice-born" often refers specifically to brahmins.

9.99 [47] **Night lotuses**: see note to 6.65.

9.108 **Vishva·karman**: a divine craftsman.

9.128 **Tipped a waterpot over the brahmin's hand**: a conventional ritual when offering a gift.

9.185 [100] Verses 100 and 101 are found in only one manuscript (N) and in the Tibetan translation.

9.186 [101] **Seedling Buddhas** are Bodhi·sattvas. The word used for Buddha is here *jina*, which means "conqueror."

9.186 [101] **For their actions**: I offer only a tentative translation for the last quarter since there are three syllables missing. The word *tu* might imply some sort of contrast but it is not possible in the present circumstances to expand on what this contrast might be.

10.4 [1] **Unattached to censurable pleasures**: literally, "Unattached to fruits that are reprehensible to enjoy."

10.6 [3] **Moral precepts**: the five moral precepts (*pañca/śīla*). See note to 3.7.

10.11 [6] The verse plays on the notion of Time (*kāla*) as signifying fate or death.

10.12 [7] **Consecrated**: the reference is to the rite of *dīkṣā* ("initiation"), which occurs before the performance of a sacrifice and serves to purify the patron holding the ritual. The train of thought is that moral behavior such as giving and self-discipline is itself a purifying activity and therefore exempts the king from having to undergo normal *dīkṣā*.

10.22 **Sattra**: a sacrificial session of varying periods of time, ranging from twelve days to several years.

10.22 **Káranas**: a division of the lunar month (with eleven divisions in total). **Muhúrta**: a thirtieth part of a day (48 minutes). See Monier-Williams s.v.

10.24 **Avábhritha bathing ritual**: an act of purification performed after a sacrifice by the patron.

10.39 [22] **Sacrificial gifts**: the people are being compared to priests who receive gifts for performing a sacrifice. In this case, the "sacrifice" performed by the people is their practice of virtue.

10.53 [32] **The god of one hundred sacrifices**: Shakra.

11.5 [2] **Diti**: the deity who gave birth to the *daitya* demons.

11.6 **Daitya**: a category of demon.

11.16 **Gáruda**: a divine bird.

12.3 **The rite of conception, the rite for producing a male child, the rite of parting hair, and the birth ceremony**: these are four of the rites of passage (*saṃskāra*) in Brahmanical thought. The rite of conception is performed to enable the conception of a child. The rite for producing a male child is performed in the third month of pregnancy. The rite of parting hair involves parting the hair of the pregnant woman and takes place in the fourth, sixth, or eighth month of pregnancy. The birth ceremony occurs, as one would expect, at the birth of a child.

12.16 **Treatises**: the Brahmanical texts called shastra (*śāstra*).

12.20 [8] **Undetected**: the force of the idea of being "undetected" is brought out later in the story. See 12.32 [13]–37.

12.47 See *Aṅguttara Nikāya* 4.109.

13.7 An **ápsaras** is a type of celestial nymph.

13.21 The **Káumudi** (Kaumudī) festival is held on the full-moon day of the month of Kārttika (October to November) in honor of Kārttikeya. The word *kaumudī* itself means "moonlight" and is personified as a goddess.

13.85 [37] **Brihas·pati**: the chief priest of the gods in Brahmanism, known for his wisdom.

14.4 **Incidental and miraculous omens**: the *ṭīkā* explains that "incidental" signs arise from factors such as wind, sun, and drought, whereas "miraculous" signs are caused by gods.

14.4 **Drawing into land, steering clear**: The precise meaning of *āharaṇ'|âpasaraṇ'|ādi* is not clear, although the context strongly suggests that they are nautical terms. The *ṭīkā* glosses *āharaṇa* as *ākarṣaṇa*, which simply means "attracting" or "pulling." The word *apasaraṇa* is glossed as *viṣama|parivarjana*, "avoiding danger." See Hanisch for more details.

14.5 **Shurpáraka**: modern-day Sopara, just north of Bombay.

14.7 **Bharu·kaccha**: modern-day Broach in Gujarat. **Suvárna·bhumi**: the exact location of this area is unsure, but it is often identified with South Burma and the Malay peninsula.

14.12 **Ásuras** are a type of anti-god or demon.

14.16 [5] The comparison between the earth and the sea is given further force by the phrase *toya|sthala* ("mound of water"). The word *sthala* is often used to refer to dry land.

14.18 [7] **Thick dense clouds**: there is wordplay here on *ghana*, which can mean both "thick" and "cloud."

14.41 **Kusha**: *Poa cynosuroides*. A sacred grass used in rituals.

14.77 A **Good Friend** (*kalyāṇa/mitra*) is a technical term in Buddhist thought and refers to a person who provides spiritual aid.

15.3 **Chakra·vaka birds** (*Anas casarca*) are renowned for their attachment to each other and are often used as symbols of conjugal love in Indian literature.

15.8 The **kadámba tree** (*Nauclea cadamba*) produces orange blossoms.

15.19 **Out of season but timely**: the phrase *a/kāla/meghāḥ kāla/meghāḥ* plays on two different meanings of *kāla* as "time" and "black." Although a straightforward translation would be "black [*kāla*] clouds that are out of season [*a/kāla*]," the wordplay implies that *kāla* in *kāla/megha* bears the sense of both "black" and "timely," hence the above translation.

15.25 **Parjánya**: the god of rain, often identified with Shakra.

16.7–10 The following section contains two verses that are very close to a couplet found in the canonical text the *Dharmapada*. Compare *Gandhari Dharmapada* 221–222, *Pali Dhammapada* 244–245, *Patna Dharmapada* 164–165, and *Udānavarga* 27.3–27.4, none of which fully match the verses found here. See also KHOROCHE (1989: 264), who points out that HEINRICH LÜDERS suggests the verses may be a later interpolation. Some manuscripts also remark that this couplet is recited in the "Sthávira collection of texts;" KHOROCHE (ibid.) states that these comments "are presumably annotations by a scribe who recognized their provenance."

16.15 [7] **My feet are misnamed**: the Sanskrit for foot is *caraṇa*, a word that literally denotes something that moves or travels. The sense is therefore not simply that the quail's feet are undeveloped (and thus misnamed because they cannot yet be called feet) but rather that he has no means of motion to escape the fire.

16.15 [7] **Agni**: the god Fire.

17.26 [15] **Jain ascetics**, particularly those from the Dig·ámbara sect, are well-known for being naked.

17.28 [17] Notice the stylistic technique (*yamaka*) or repeating the last three syllables at the end of every quarter verse.

17.29 [18] The **Vrishnis** and **Ándhakas** are both linked to the Yádava lineage.

17.37 [26] The verse plays on *surā* meaning "liquor" and *sura* meaning "god."

17.39 [28] **Avíchi**: a hell realm.

19.4 **Upavédas**: There are four Upavédas ("sub-Vedas"), each of which is linked to one of the four main Vedas. They are: the *Āyurveda* (medicine), *Dhanurveda* (archery), *Gāndharvaveda* (music), and *Śilpaśāstra* (arts). In some texts the fourth Upavéda is *Śastraśāstra* (weaponry) or *Sthāpatyaveda* (architecture). See MONIER-WILLIAMS s.v.

19.5 **Preta rites**: funeral rites performed to provide merit to deceased relatives who may have been reborn as hungry ghosts (*preta*).

19.9 [3] **Householder state**: one of four áshramas (*āśramas*), or states of life, conceived by the Brahmanical tradition. The four states are: a student following a vow of chastity (*brahma/cārin*), a householder (*gṛha/stha*), an ascetic living in a forest hermitage (*vānaprastha*), and a renouncer (*saṃnyāsin*). The relationship between these four states involves some tensions. PATRICK OLIVELLE (1993) has convincingly shown that while the classical formulation of the four *āśramas* saw them as successive stages, earlier formulations viewed them as separate alternatives.

19.20 The words **day** and **night** are not directly expressed in the Sanskrit but are understood by the context. Kúmuda (***kumuda***) flowers are particularly known for opening their petals at night. See SPEYER (1895: 156, n. 1) and KHOROCHE (1989: 120f.).

19.32 [11] **Sons and grandchildren**: in Brahmanical thought a man is only "made complete" by having male offspring.

19.44 [17] **Four hundred**: KERN (p. 247) points out that *catuḥ/śataṃ* is a wrong Sanskritization of the Pali *catussadaṃ* (Sanskrit: *catur/utsadaṃ*), meaning "four plenties," which is explained in the Pali commentary as people, grain, wood, and water. KERN's analysis is certainly instructive in terms of linguistic evolution. However, a direct translation of *catuḥ/śataṃ* does not pose any significant problems with meaning, and since *catuḥ/śataṃ* is the established reading in Arya·shura's "Garland of the Buddha's Past Lives," I tend to the viewpoint that it needs to be treated as a separate version with its own authority and have therefore decided not to translate based on the Pali. Contrast, however, verse 33 of story 22, where it is necessary to use a Pali parallel and reject the extant Sanskrit readings.

19.52 [21] **Kachángala**: a town in North-East India. The Pali commentary (*Jātaka* 4.311) states that building materials are scarce at Kachángala. It also tells the story that the *yakṣa* (in the Pali story a tree-spirit) used to be a monk at this old monastery in the time of the Buddha Kassapa and that he suffered greatly from doing renovation work there.

19.73 [33] **To stumble even when the ground is even**: a second level of meaning is also present: "to wrong others even though they are just."

19.76–79 [36] The following section identifies characters in the past with characters in the Buddha's lifetime. This narrative technique is common at the end of *jātaka* stories in collections such as the Pali *Jātakaṭṭhavaṇṇanā*, where it is called a "connection" (*samodhāna*). In the "Garland of the Buddha's Past Lives," however, this technique is rare and scholars have suggested that the passage may be an interpolation. One problem with the interpolation argument is that the passage is found in all extant Sanskrit manuscripts. It is also striking that the corresponding section in Pali (*Jātaka* no. 488, vv. 22–24) is almost identical to the one found here. This parallel is all the more noticeable given that the Pali *samodhāna* is also in verse, which is unusual for the *Jātakaṭṭhavaṇṇanā*).

19.77 [34] This verse lists six of the Buddha's most important monks. The **son of Sharádvati** is Shari·putra (*Śāriputra*).

19.78 [35] **Útpala·varna** was a nun in the Buddha's lifetime and **Kubjóttara** was a female lay-disciple (said to be the maidservant of a queen). **Chitra** was a male lay-disciple in the Buddha's lifetime and **Satágiri** a *yakṣa*.

19.79 [36] **Pariléya** and **Madhu·dayin** were an elephant and a monkey who served the Buddha while he was in the forest (see *Dhammapada-aṭṭhakathā* 1.58ff.). Madhu·dayin is both a name and an epithet, as it means "honey-giver," recalling the fact that the monkey gave the Buddha some honey. **Kalodáyin** was a playmate of prince Gótama; when Gótama became awakened as the Buddha, Kalodáyin became a monk.

20.40 Following A (sec. manu) NT.

EMENDATIONS TO THE SANSKRIT TEXT

Manuscripts and Editions Cited

A	Add. MS 1328, University Library, Cambridge. See KHOROCHE (1987: 6).
B	Add. MS 1415, University Library, Cambridge. See KHOROCHE (1987: 6).
H	Edition of HANISCH (2005)
K	Edition of KERN (1891). KERN based his edition on MSS A, B, and P.
Kem	Emendation made by KERN (1891)
N	MS III.359.I, Durbar Library, Nepal. See KHOROCHE (1987: 9) and HANISCH (2005: xlvii)
Nac	MS N before scribal correction (ante corr.)
Npc	MS N after scribal correction (post corr.)
O	MS G 9980, Asiatic Society, Calcutta. Same as MS Ca in KHOROCHE (1987: 8). See HANISCH (2005: xlviii).
P	MSS nos. 45/6, Fonds Sanscrit, Bibliothèque Nationale, Paris. See KHOROCHE (1987: 6).
R	MS 608, Ryukoku University Library, Kyoto. See HANISCH (2005: xlviii).
T	MS 136, University Library, Tokyo. See KHOROCHE (1987: 8) and HANISCH (2005: xlvii–xlviii).
Toyoq	Fragments from Turfan. See edition of WELLER (1955) and comments by KHOROCHE (1987: 5–6).
U	MS 135, Tokyo University Library. See HANISCH (2005: xlviii).

Emendations Made

2.8 *°mālyasuvarṇarajatādi* H : *°mālyarajatasuvarṇādi* T R : *°mālyarajatasuvarṇādikaṃ* K. Following HANISCH's conjectural reading based on the Tibetan translation.

2.86 *°pramukhyasya* T A B P R : *°pramukhasya* Kem.

3.13 *prītyatisnigdhayā* H : *prītyabhisnighdhayā* T R K. Following Hanisch's conjectural reading based on the Tibetan translation and Tibetan *ṭīkā*.

4.11 *antarikṣe* Kem : *antarīkṣe* T A B O P R U.

5.6 [3] *akāraṇakṣipravināśino* H : *akāraṇakṣipravirāgiṇo* T O R U K. Following Hanisch's conjecture based on the Tibetan translation and *ṭīkā*.

5.14 *asahamānena* T O R U K : *asahamānāḥ* H. Keeping the reading of TORU, K. Hanisch reads *a/sahamānāḥ*, following the *ṭīkā*.

6.1 *api mahāsattvānāṃ* H : *api satāṃ mahātmanāṃ* O R U K : *api mahātmānāṃ* T. Following Hanisch's emendation based on the Tibetan translation and on the corresponding sentence found at the end of the story.

7.34 *sādhu sādhv* N T R U K : *sādhv* H.

7.79 *°saṃvarṇanāyām* H : *°saṃharṣanāyām* N T : *°saṃpraharṣanāyām* R K. Following Hanisch's conjectural reading based on the Tibetan.

8.13 [6] *atha cādya* Kem : *atha vādya* N T A B P R.

8.43 *sajalajaladharāndhakārākārāṇi* H : *sajalajaladharāndhākārāṇi* Nac : *sajalajaladharāndhakārāṇi* Npc A P K : *sajalajaladharākārāṇi* B : *sajalajaladharānukārāṇi* R. Following Hanisch's conjectural reading.

8.77 *asmadartheṣu* H : *asmadarthiṣu* N T R K. Following the conjectural reading by Hanisch based on the Tibetan translation.

9.14 *taṃ* H : *tān* N T A B R : *tato* Kem. Following Hanisch's conjecture based on the Tibetan.

9.102 *svajanaṃ* H : *svaṃ janān* Nac A B R : *svaṃ janan* Npc : *svatanayau* T : *svajanān* K.

9.156 *nimittāpavṛtta°* H : *animittāpavṛtta°* N T R K. Following Hanisch's conjecture based on the Tibetan translation. Sanskrit manuscripts read *idam a / nimitt' / âpavṛtta / praharṣam* which can be translated as: "Why has my heart become joyless for no reason?"

9.185 [100] *dattāpi ca* H : om. N. Following HANISCH's conjectural reading based on the Tibetan translation.

10.36 [19] *svaśīlāmalabhūṣaṇo* H : *sa śīlāmalabhūṣaṇo* N T R U K. Following HANISCH's conjecture based on the Tibetan translation.

13.21 *°cchattra°* H : *°vicitra°* N T R U K. Following HANISCH's conjectural reading based on the Tibetan translation.

14.41 *aparaṃ* H : om. N T R U K. Adding the word *aparaṃ*, following HANISCH's conjecture based on the Tibetan translation.

14.51 *mahāntaṃ* H : *mahati* N T R U K. Following HANISCH's conjectural reading based on the Tibetan translation. Sanskrit manuscripts read *mahati*, which would slightly change the meaning as follows: "they saw that the mass of water was spilling into what appeared to be a precipice or a huge abyss."

15.19 *vidyullatālaṃkṛtā* H : *vidyullatālaṃkṛta°* N T U K : *vidyullatālaṃkṛla°* R. Following HANISCH's conjecture based on the Tibetan translation.

16.3 *ālakṣyamāṇāṅga°* B N T : *ālakṣyaṇāṅga°* A : *alakṣyamāṇāṅga°* Kem.

16.3 *svamātā°* Kem : *samātā°* A B N P T.

16.3 *°opagūḍhagulmasaṃniśrite* N T : *°opagūḍhagulmalatāsaṃniśrite* A B P : *°opagūḍhe gulmalatāsaṃniśrite* Kem.

16.4 *samyak pakṣau praviruruhatuḥ* N T : *pakṣau samyak praviruruhituḥ* K.

16.7 *bhagavatā* N T : *bhagavatā sujīvitam ahrīkeṇeti gāthādvayam* K.

16.10 *iti gāthādvayam* N : *iti gāthādvayam etad āryasthāvarīyakanikāye paṭhyate* A B T : *iti gāthādvayam etad āryasthāvirīyakanikāye paṭhyate* K.

16.11 [4] *°viprakīrṇa°* T : *°viprakīrṇair* A N K : *°viprakīrṇe* B.

16.15 [7] *itas* N : *atas* T K.

16.20 [10] *cātmakāmaḥ* A B N P T : *satyakāmaḥ* K.

16.21 *satyaparibhāvitāṃ* N T : *satyavacanaparibhāvitāṃ* K.

17.1 *ca* N : om. T K.

17.1 *ātmānam* T : *ātmānam iti* N K.

17.4 [1] *°opabhogāj* T : *°opayogāj* N K.

17.5 [2] *baddhahārdaḥ* N T : *jātahārdaḥ* K.

17.5 [2] *svabhāvajñatayā śriyaś ca* A B N T : *svabhāvajñatayāśritaś ca* K.

17.6 *maitrīsnigdhena* N T : *maitrasnigdhena* K.

17.6 *svaprabhāvamahatā* N T : *svabhāvamahatā* K.

17.11 *°kāñcanaruciravarṇam* A B N P T : *°kāñcanavarṇam* K.

17.11 *atha* N T : om. K.

17.11 *parṣadi* N T : *pariṣadi* K.

17.11 *antarikṣe* N T K : *antarīkṣe* A B : om. P.

17.13 [6] *°lolayā* A B N P T : *°līlayā* K.

17.14 *udīkṣamāṇaḥ* N T : *īkṣamāṇaḥ* K.

17.17 [8] *imaṃ* N T : *idaṃ* K.

17.18 *paṇyavikrayārambhaḥ* A B N P T : *paśya vikrayārambhaḥ* K.

17.21 [11] *vinimayaṃ* A B N P T : *vinimaye* Kem. Following A B N P T. But usually *vinimaya* is masculine.

17.24 [13] *gatyāsvatantraś* A B N P T : *°svatantraś* K.

17.26 [15] *paṇyatām* A B N P T : *paśya tām* K.

17.27 [16] *nṛpatipatheṣv* A B N P T : *nṛpatipathiṣv* K.

17.29 [18] *vismṛtabandhubhāvāḥ* A B N T : *vismitabandhubhāvāḥ* P K.

17.33 [22] *enaṃ* N T : *imaṃ* A B P : *etaṃ* Kem.

17.35 [24] *advaidhasiddhāṃ* N T : *advaitasiddhāṃ* K.

17.35 [24] *°paddhatiṃ* N : *°paddhatīṃ* A B P T K.

17.41 *madyapānaprasaṅgād* T : *madyaprasaṅgād*, with °*pāna*° added in the margin N : *madyaprasaṅgād* K.

17.47 [32] *avagaccha* N T : *abhigaccha* K.

17.50 *ca* N : om. T K.

17.50 *apy* A B N P T : om. K.

17.51 *lokahitāvahitaḥ* A N P T : *lokahitaḥ* B K.

18.3 *kulodbhavakāmānāṃ* A B N P T : *kulodbhavānāṃ* K.

18.3 *rājñā* A B N P T : *rājño* K.

18.6 [2] *ca* A B N P T : *vā* K.

18.9 °*kṛpaṇavanīpakaśravaṇa*° (=*śramaṇa*) N : °*kṛpaṇaśramaṇa*° T K.

18.9 *parivavrāja* N T : *pravavrāja* K.

18.9 *anyatamaṃ nagaram* N T : *anyatamanagaram* K.

18.9 *upaniśritya* N : *upanisṛtya* T : *upaśritya* K.

18.10 *ākṛtakendriya*° T : *ākṛtakena indriya*° N : *ākṛtakenendriya*° K.

18.10 °*pravibhāganipuṇena* N T : °*vibhāganipuṇena* K.

18.13 *ānavekṣya* N T : *ānapekṣya* K.

18.21 [10] *snehodbhavatvāt* T : *snehodgatatvāt* N K.

18.22 [11] *ca* A B N P T : *vā* K.

18.23 [12] *ca* A B N P T : *vā* K.

18.24 *śakyo 'yam* N : *śakyam ayam* T K.

18.25 [13] *na ca nikṣiptadaṇḍasya* N : *na cānikṣiptadaṇḍasya*, with *-ā-* scratched out B : *na cānikṣiptadaṇḍasya* A P T K.

18.26 °*sukhāśāvabaddha*° A B N P : damaged om. T : °*sukhāvabaddha*° K.

18.27 [14] *yadi* N T : *atha* K.

18.27 [14] *'sti dharmaḥ* T : *'sya dharmaḥ* N K.

18.32 [18] *viṣayopaniṣevane* N T : *viṣayopanivaśane* A : *viṣayopaniveśane* B K.

18.35 *khalv atrabhavantam* A B N P T : *khalv aham atrabhavantam* K.

19.3 *tasya* N T : *tasya yatra* K.

19.4 °*vidvadyaśāḥ* A : °*vidvadyasāḥ* N : °*vidvadyaśā* B : °*vidvadyaśasā* T : °*vidyāyaśāḥ* K.

19.4 *ca tān* N T : *tān* K.

19.6 [1] *śokādivirasaḥ* T : *śokātivirasaḥ* N K.

19.8 *parasparasneha*° N T : *parasparaṃ sneha*° K.

19.8 *śīlaśaucācāreṣv* N T A : *śīlasamudācāreṣv* B K.

19.8 *vedādhyayanatatparair* T : *vedādhyayanaparair* N K.

19.8 *adhyāvasitavyam* A B N P T : *adhyāvastavyam* K.

19.11 *viyogaśaṅkā*° N T : *viyogāśaṅkā*° K.

19.18 *bhavatāṃ sarve* N : *bhavatām eva* T.

19.19 °*hṛdayāś* N T : °*hṛdayaś* K.

19.20 *'nyatamasmin* A B N P T : *'nyatarasmin* K.

19.20 °*niviṣṭāsu* N T : °*viniviṣṭāsu* K.

19.22 °*vaśagā* B N P T : °*vaśagās* A : °*vaśā* K.

19.22 *vinyasya* N T : *vinyasya ca* K.

19.23 *sarvatra prasṛtaṃ yaśaḥ* A B N P : *sarvatra pravisṛtaṃ yaśaḥ* T : *sarvatra yaśaḥ* K.

19.23 *tatparīkṣāvahitamanā* N T : *tatparīkṣānimittam avahitamanā* K.

19.25 *śuciṣu* A B N P T : om. K.

19.25 *ca* N T : om. K.

19.27 *bisavirahitaṃ* N T : *bisabhāgavirahitaṃ* K.

19.27 *parṇaśālāṃ* T : *parṇaśālāyāṃ* N K.

19.28 *pañcame 'pi ca* A P T : *pañcame ca* B N K.

19.28 *apanidadhe* N : *antardadhe* T : *upanidadhe* K.

19.30 *parṇaśālām abhigatā* T : *parṇaśālāyām abhigatā* N : *parṇaśālāṃ samabhigatā* K.

19.30 *dadṛśur enaṃ* N T : *dadṛśuś cainaṃ* A B P K.

19.30 *yathābhūtaṃ* N T : *yathānubhūtaṃ* K.

19.30 *asaṃbhāvayamānās* N T : *asaṃbhāvayantas* K.

19.46 [18] *labdhā* A B N P T : *labdha* Kem.

19.48 [19] *yoṣitsahasrāgracarīṃ* A B N : *yoṣitsahasrāgracarī* P : *yoṣitsahasrāgravarāṃ* T : *yoṣitsahasrāgrasarīṃ* K.

19.48 [19] *yā* A B N P T : *yas* K.

19.50 [20] *satkāralabdhā mudam* A B P : *satkāralabdhaṃ madam* N : damaged om. T : *satkāralabdhāṃ mudam* Kem.

19.51 *°ārtham āgatās* N T : *°ārthaṃ samāgatās* K.

19.57 *kṣānti°* A B N P T : *śānti°* K.

19.66 *tena caiṣām* A B N P : *tena teṣām* T : *tena caiteṣām* K.

19.66 *māhātmyena prasāditamanās* N : damaged om. T : *māhātmyenābhiprasāditamanās* K.

19.67 [29] *opalakṣyate* Toyoq N : *opalabhyate* K.

19.67 [29] *mayāpanihitāny* Toyoq N T : *mayā vinihitāny* K. Following Toyoq fr. ii, N.

19.68 [30] *viśuddhasthiracāritra* N T : *viśuddhisthiracāritra* A B : *viśuddhiḥ sthiracāritre* K.

19.71 *°kirīṭo* N : *°kirīṭa°* K.

19.73 [33] *eva* N T : *eṣa* K.

19.73 [33] *skhalituṃ* N T : *skhalitaṃ* K.

19.76 *tad evaṃ* N : *tac cedaṃ* T K.

19.78 [35] *utpalavarṇāsīd* A B N P T : *utpalāvarṇāsīd* K.

19.79 [36] *madhudāyī ca* N T : *madhudātaiva* K.

20.7 *vacanaṃ* N T : om. K.

20.7 *tādṛśo 'yaṃ* N : damaged om. T : *yādṛśo 'yaṃ* K.

20.7 *durlabha idānīṃ yādṛśa iti* N : *durlabha iti. idānīṃ yādṛśaḥ sa iti* T : *durlabhaḥ ka idānīṃ tādṛśa iti* K.

20.7 *lajjāsaṃkucitākṣaratayā* T : *lajjāsaṃkucitākṣaraṃ tayā* N : *lajjāsaṃkucitākṣaraṃ tanayayā* K.

20.7 *duhitaram* N T : *svāṃ duhitaram* K.

20.9 [2] *kutaḥ* B : *[ku]taḥ* T : illegible om. N : *katham* K.

20.10 [3] *copahṛtāṃ* A B N P T : *vopahṛtāṃ* K.

20.12 [5] *sa na* N T : *na sa* K.

20.15 *patipravrajyābhisaṃbaddhena* T : *patipravrajyāsaṃbaddhena* N : *patipravrajyābhisaṃbandhena* K.

20.16 *anurāgavaśagāḥ* T : *anurāgavaśānugāḥ* N K.

20.25 *viniścitya* N T : *vicintya* K.

20.25 *pratinivṛttya* T : *pratinivṛtya* N K.

20.38 [21] *arho 'si* N T : *arho 'si*, with *yukto* in the margin A : *yukto 'si* B K.

20.40 *tapovanāya* B N P T : *vanāya* A K.

20.40 *īṣuḥ* Kem : *īyuḥ* A B N P T.

20.40 *vyatiṣṭhanta* N T : *samatiṣṭhanta* A B : *samavātiṣṭhanta* K.

20.40 *īṣuḥ* Kem : *īyuḥ* A B N P T.

20.40 *enam* N T : *evam* K.

20.40 *°parisamāptiyācñayā* N Kem : *°parisamāptyāyacñayā* A B P.

20.40 *paralokapuṇyaphala°* A B N P T : *paralokaphala°* K.

20.40 *śrutiviśeṣair* N P T : *vārttāviśesair*, but A has *śruti* written above A B K.

20.40 *prāyatanta* A N T : *prāyacchanta* A B : *prāyacchat* P : *vyāyacchanta* K.

20.41 *unmukhān* A B N P T : om. K.

20.44 [25] *roditavyaḥ* N T : *roditavyam* K.

20.46 [27] *aivaṃ* N T : *aiva* K.

20.52 [33] *suhṛjjanaś caivam* N T : *suhṛjjanasyaivam* K.

20.52 [33] *ayaṃ sthito me* A B N P T : *iyaṃ sthitir me* Kem.

20.54 [35] *pariśaṅkayāmi* N T : *paritarkayāmi* K.

20.59 *iti vā guṇataḥ* A B N P T : *iti guṇataḥ* K.

20.59 *upaneyam* N T : *upenneyam* A B : *unneyam* K.

GLOSSARY OF COMMON NAMES, TERMS, AND EPITHETS

ABHIPÁRAGA the husband of Unmadayánti and a minister of the king of the Shibis (story 13).

AGÁSTYA an ascetic. The Bodhi·sattva in story 7.

AGNI the god Fire.

ÁJITA a disciple of the Bodhi·sattva in story 1.

ANÁNDA a chief disciple of the Buddha, known for his devoted nature.

ÁNDHAKA name of a people.

ANIRÚDDHA one of the Buddha's chief disciples.

ÁPSARAS a divine nymph.

ARHAT a person who becomes awakened through listening to the Buddha's teaching.

ÁSURA a class of demon or anti-god.

AVÍCHI a hell realm.

AVISHÁHYA the Bodhi·sattva in story 5. A merchant noted for his generosity.

BHARU·KACCHA modern-day Broach in Gujarat.

BODHI·SATTVA "Awakening Being." A person who has made a vow to practice the perfections (*pāramitā*) and become a fully awakened Buddha (*samyak/saṃbuddha*). The Buddha in his past lives.

BRAHMA a type of deity living in the Sphere of Pure Form (*rūpa/dhātu*). The Bodhi·sattva is a Brahma deity in story 29.

BRAHMAN the absolute principle of the universe in Brahmanical thought.

BRIHAS·PATI the chief priest of the gods.

CHITRA a lay-disciple of the Buddha.

DAITYA a class of demon.

DITI the god who gave birth to the *daityas*.

EVIL ONE Mara, q.v.

GANDHÁRVA a type of celestial musician.

GANGES (*Gaṅgā*), a river in North India.

GÁRUDA a divine bird. The enemy of snakes.

GOLDEN MOUNTAIN Mount Meru.

GREAT BEING (*mahā/sattva*), an epithet of the Bodhi·sattva.

GREAT ONE (*Mah"/ātmā*), an epithet of the Bodhi·sattva, used synonymously with Great Being (*mahā/sattva*).

HÍMAVAT the Himálaya mountains.

INDRA a name for Shakra.

JALIN the son of Vishvan·tara.

KACHÁNGALA a town in North-East India.

KALODÁYIN a monk of the Buddha. Used to be his playmate when the Buddha was a prince.

KARA an island.

KÁSHYAPA (Kāśyapa) descended from, or connected to, the ascetic Kashyapa (Kaśyapa). A disciple of the Buddha.

KÁUMUDI the goddess of Moonlight. The Káumudi festival is held in October to November.

KIRÍTA·VATSA the father of Unmadayánti.

KÓSHALA an area of North India.

KRISHNÁJINA the daughter of Vishvan·tara.

KRITA ERA the first of four eras. A type of golden age.

KUBJÓTTARA a female lay-disciple of the Buddha.

MADHU·DAYIN a monkey.

MADRI the wife of Vishvan·tara.

MAHA·RÁURAVA name of a hell.

MAITRI·BALA a king. The Bodhi·sattva in story 8.

MARA a demonic figure hostile to the Buddha.

MÁTALI the charioteer of Shakra.

MAUDGALYÁYANA one of the Buddha's chief monks.

MERU a mountain at the center of the cosmos.

naga a semi-divine snake.

PARILÉYA an elephant.

PARJÁNYA the god of rain. Often identified with Shakra.

PRATYÉKA·BUDDHA a being that becomes awakened without access to a Buddha's teaching.

PURNA one of the Buddha's chief monks.

SÁNJAYA the father of Vishvan·tara

SARVA·MITRA a king addicted to alcohol in story 17.

SATÁGIRI a *yakṣa*.

SHAKRA the king of the gods in the Trayas·trinsha heaven in the Sphere of Desire (*kāma/dhātu*).

SON OF SHARÁDVATI Shari·putra. One of the Buddha's chief monks.

SHIBI a king, often noted for generosity. The Bodhi·sattva in stories 2 and 13.

SHIBIS the people of the Shibi kingdom. In stories 2 and 13, the Bodhi·sattva is king of the Shibis. In story 9, he is prince of the Shibis.

SHURPÁRAKA modern-day Sopara, just north of Bombay.

SIDDHA a semi-divine being.

SUDHÁRMA an assembly hall in Shakra's heaven.

SUMÉRU see Meru.

SUNSET MOUNTAIN a mountain in the West, behind which the sun is supposed to set.

SUPÁRAGA a helmsman. The Bodhi·sattva in story 14.

SUTA·SOMA a prince. The Bodhi·sattva in story 31.

SUVÁRNA·BHUMI uncertain location, but often identified with South Burma and the Malay peninsula.

TATHA·GATA an epithet of the Buddha ("Thus-gone").

TEACHING the Dharma, or teaching of the Buddha.

THREE JEWELS the Buddha, the Dharma (the Teaching), and the Sangha (monastic community).

THREE PURSUITS the pursuits of desire (*kāma*), profit (*artha*), and morality (*dharma*).

TREATISES the Brahmanical shastra (*śāstra*) texts.

UNMADAYÁNTI a woman who "intoxicates" men with her beauty (story 13).

UPAVÉDAS four "sub-Vedas," each linked to one of the major Vedas. They are: *Āyurveda* (medicine), *Dhanurveda* (archery), *Gāndharvaveda* (music), and *Śilpaśāstra* (arts).

ÚTPALA·VARNA one of the Buddha's most important nuns.

VAIJAYÁNTA the palace of Shakra.

VARÁNASI a city in North India.

VÁSAVA "chief of the Vasus." An epithet of Shakra.

VEDÁNGAS six auxiliary subjects to the Vedas. Phonetics, meter, grammar, etymology, astrology, and ritual.

VEDAS four collections of texts in Brahmanism, said to be direct hearings (*śruti*) of sacred truth. They are: the *Ṛg Veda*, *Sāma Veda*, *Yajur Veda*, and *Atharva Veda*.

VISHVA·KARMAN a divine craftsman.

VISHVAN·TARA a prince noted for his generosity. The Bodhi·sattva in story 9.

VRISHNI name of a people.

YAKSHA a demon or type of divine spirit.

THE CLAY SANSKRIT LIBRARY

The volumes in the series are listed here in order of publication.
Titles marked with an asterisk* are also available in the
Digital Clay Sanskrit Library (eCSL).
For further information visit www.claysanskritlibrary.org

1. The Emperor of the Sorcerers (*Bṛhatkathāślokasaṃgraha*) (vol. 1 of 2) by *Budhasvāmin*. SIR JAMES MALLINSON
2. Heavenly Exploits (*Divyāvadāna*). JOEL TATELMAN
3. Maha·bhárata III: The Forest (*Vanaparvan*) (vol. 4 of 4)* WILLIAM J. JOHNSON
4. Much Ado about Religion (*Āgamaḍambara*) by *Bhaṭṭa Jayanta*. CSABA DEZSŐ
5. The Birth of Kumára (*Kumārasaṃbhava*) by *Kālidāsa*. DAVID SMITH
6. Ramáyana I: Boyhood (*Bālakāṇḍa*) by *Vālmīki*. ROBERT P. GOLDMAN
7. The Epitome of Queen Lilávati (*Līlāvatīsāra*) (vol. 1 of 2) by *Jinaratna*. R.C.C. FYNES
8. Ramáyana II: Ayódhya (*Ayodhyākāṇḍa*) by *Vālmīki*. SHELDON I. POLLOCK
9. Love Lyrics (*Amaruśataka, Śatakatraya & Caurapañcāśikā*) by *Amaru, Bhartṛhari & Bilhaṇa*. GREG BAILEY & RICHARD GOMBRICH
10. What Ten Young Men Did (*Daśakumāracarita*) by *Daṇḍin*. ISABELLE ONIANS
11. Three Satires (*Kaliviḍambana, Kalāvilāsa & Bhallaṭaśataka*) by *Nīlakaṇṭha, Kṣemendra & Bhallaṭa*. SOMADEVA VASUDEVA
12. Ramáyana IV: Kishkíndha (*Kiṣkindhākāṇḍa*) by *Vālmīki*. ROSALIND LEFEBER
13. The Emperor of the Sorcerers (*Bṛhatkathāślokasaṃgraha*) (vol. 2 of 2) by *Budhasvāmin*. SIR JAMES MALLINSON
14. Maha·bhárata IX: Shalya (*Śalyaparvan*) (vol. 1 of 2)* JUSTIN MEILAND

15. Rákshasa's Ring (*Mudrārākṣasa*)*
by *Viśākhadatta*. Michael Coulson
16. Messenger Poems (*Meghadūta, Pavanadūta & Haṃsadūta*)
by *Kālidāsa, Dhoyī & Rūpa Gosvāmin*. Sir James Mallinson
17. Ramáyana III: The Forest (*Araṇyakāṇḍa*)
by *Vālmīki*. Sheldon I. Pollock
18. The Epitome of Queen Lilávati (*Līlāvatīsāra*) (vol. 2 of 2)
by *Jinaratna*. R.C.C. Fynes
19. Five Discourses on Worldly Wisdom (*Pañcatantra*)*
by *Viṣṇuśarman*. Patrick Olivelle
20. Ramáyana V: Súndara (*Sundarakāṇḍa*) by *Vālmīki*.
Robert P. Goldman & Sally J. Sutherland Goldman
21. Maha·bhárata II: The Great Hall (*Sabhāparvan*)
Paul Wilmot
22. The Recognition of Shakúntala (*Abhijñānaśākuntala*) (Kashmir Recension) by *Kālidāsa*. Somadeva Vasudeva
23. Maha·bhárata VII: Drona (*Droṇaparvan*) (vol. 1 of 4)*
Vaughan Pilikian
24. Rama Beyond Price (*Anargharāghava*)
by *Murāri*. Judit Törzsök
25. Maha·bhárata IV: Viráta (*Virāṭaparvan*)
Kathleen Garbutt
26. Maha·bhárata VIII: Karna (*Karṇaparvan*) (vol. 1 of 2)
Adam Bowles
27. "The Lady of the Jewel Necklace" & "The Lady who Shows her Love" (*Ratnāvalī & Priyadarśikā*) by *Harṣa*.*
Wendy Doniger
28. The Ocean of the Rivers of Story (*Kathāsaritsāgara*) (vol. 1 of 7)
by *Somadeva*. Sir James Mallinson
29. Handsome Nanda (*Saundarananda*)*
by *Aśvaghoṣa*. Linda Covill
30. Maha·bhárata IX: Shalya (*Śalyaparvan*) (vol. 2 of 2)*
Justin Meiland
31. Rama's Last Act (*Uttararāmacarita*) by *Bhavabhūti*.
Sheldon Pollock. Foreword by Girish Karnad

32. "Friendly Advice" (*Hitopadeśa*) by *Nārāyaṇa* &
"King Víkrama's Adventures" (*Vikramacarita*). JUDIT TÖRZSÖK
33. Life of the Buddha (*Buddhacarita*)
by *Aśvaghoṣa*. PATRICK OLIVELLE
34. Maha·bhárata V: Preparations for War (*Udyogaparvan*) (vol. 1 of 2)
KATHLEEN GARBUTT. Foreword by GURCHARAN DAS
35. Maha·bhárata VIII: Karna (*Karṇaparvan*) (vol. 2 of 2)
ADAM BOWLES
36. Maha·bhárata V: Preparations for War (*Udyogaparvan*) (vol. 2 of 2)
KATHLEEN GARBUTT
37. Maha·bhárata VI: Bhishma (*Bhīṣmaparvan*) (vol. 1 of 2)*
Including the "Bhagavad Gita" in Context
ALEX CHERNIAK. Foreword by RANAJIT GUHA
38. The Ocean of the Rivers of Story (*Kathāsaritsāgara*) (vol. 2 of 7)
by *Somadeva*. SIR JAMES MALLINSON
39. "How the Nagas were Pleased" (*Nāgānanda*) by *Harṣa* &
"The Shattered Thighs" (*Ūrubhaṅga*) by *Bhāsa*.*
ANDREW SKILTON
40. Gita·govínda: Love Songs of Radha and Krishna (*Gītagovinda*)*
by *Jayadeva*. LEE SIEGEL. Foreword by SUDIPTA KAVIRAJ
41. "Bouquet of Rasa" & "River of Rasa" (*Rasamañjarī & Rasataraṅgiṇī*) by *Bhānudatta*. SHELDON POLLOCK
42. Garland of the Buddha's Past Lives (*Jātakamālā*) (vol. 1 of 2)*
by *Āryaśūra*. JUSTIN MEILAND
43. Maha·bhárata XII: Peace (*Śāntiparvan*) (vol. 3 of 5)*
"The Book of Liberation" (*Mokṣadharma*). ALEXANDER WYNNE
44. The Little Clay Cart (*Mṛcchakaṭikā*) by *Śūdraka*.
DIWAKAR ACHARYA. Foreword by PARTHA CHATTERJEE
45. Bhatti's Poem: The Death of Rávana (*Bhaṭṭikāvya*)*
by *Bhaṭṭi*. OLIVER FALLON

46. "Self-Surrender," "Peace," "Compassion," and "The Mission of the Goose": Poems and Prayers from South India (*Ātmārpaṇastuti, Śāntivilāsa, Dayāśataka & Haṃsasaṃdeśa*) by *Appayya Dīkṣita, Nīlakaṇṭha Dīkṣita & Vedānta Deśika.* Yigal Bronner & David Shulman
Foreword by Gieve Patel
47. Maha·bhárata VI: Bhishma (*Bhīṣmaparvan*) (vol. 2 of 2)*
Alex Cherniak
48. How Úrvashi Was Won (*Vikramorvaśīya*) by *Kālidāsa*
Velcheru Narayana Rao & David Shulman
49. The Quartet of Causeries (*Caturbhāṇī*)
by *Śūdraka, Śyāmilaka, Vararuci & Īśvaradatta.*
Csaba Dezső & Somadeva Vasudeva
50. Garland of the Buddha's Past Lives (*Jātakamālā*) (vol. 2 of 2)*
by *Āryaśūra.* Justin Meiland
51. Princess Kadámbari (*Kādambarī*) (vol. 1 of 3)
by *Bāṇa.* David Smith
52. The Rise of Wisdom Moon (*Prabodhacandrodaya*)*
by *Kṛṣṇamiśra.* Matthew T. Kapstein
Foreword by J.N. Mohanty
53. Maha·bhárata VII: Drona (*Droṇaparvan*) (vol. 2 of 4)*
Vaughan Pilikian
54. Maha·bhárata X & XI: Dead of Night & The Women (*Sauptikaparvan & Strīparvan*).* Kate Crosby
55. Seven Hundred Elegant Verses (*Āryāsaptaśatī*)*
by *Govardhana.* Friedhelm Hardy
56. Málavika and Agni·mitra (*Mālavikāgnimitram*) by *Kālidāsa.*
Dániel Balogh & Eszter Somogyi